I0726664

Sultana: The Bride Price

By Lisa J. Yarde

Sultana: The Bride Price
Copyright © Lisa J. Yarde 2014

ISBN-10: 1939138159
ISBN-13: 978-1939138156

This is a work of fiction. The names, characters, locations, and incidents portrayed in it are the work of the author's imagination, or have been used fictitiously. Any resemblance to actual persons living or dead, locations or events is entirely coincidental.
All rights reserved.

No portion of this book may be transmitted or reproduced in any form, or by any means, without the prior written permission of the Author.

www.lisajyarde.com

Cover Artwork
In a courtyard, Tunis, Ferdinand Max Brett (1921)

Cover design and Alhambra Press logo by Lance Ganey
www.freelanceganey.com

Also by Lisa J. Yarde

The *Sultana* series

Sultana (2011)

Sultana's Legacy (2011)

Sultana: Two Sisters (2013)

Sultana: The Bride Price (2014)

Sultana: The Pomegranate Tree (2015)

Sultana: The White Mountains (2017)

Other Historical Fiction titles

On Falcon's Wings (2010)

The Burning Candle (2012)

Novellas

Long Way Home (2011)

Short Stories

The Legend Rises - HerStory anthology (2013)

To Pat, Yvonne, and Juanita

Acknowledgments

The final version of this novel would not have been possible without the suggestions and support of Patricia Rich, Yvonne Conde, and Juanita Bobbitt, members of the Historical Novel Society – New York City chapter. Thank you, dear ladies, for your commitment and generosity.

To my editor Jessica Lux, who is always thorough with her edits and comments, and remains incredibly patient and kind. Jess, thank you for shaping the rough draft into a readable story. I look forward to our continued partnership.

Foreword

Sultana: The Bride Price takes place in fourteenth-century Moorish Spain, during the turbulent, but glorious reign of Sultan Muhammad V of Granada. Muhammad was the only son of Sultan Abdul Hajjaj Yusuf I and his first wife, a former Christian captive who bore the name Butayna. This novel is a fictional account of Muhammad's rule, and the difficult relationships he encountered with his spouse and his half-siblings, the children of Yusuf's second wife Maryam.

This work would have been impossible to complete without the following sources.

The Alhambra by Robert Irwin (Harvard University Press – 2004)

Arab Women in the Middle Ages: Private Lives and Public Roles by Shirley Guthrie (Saqi Books – 2001)

A history of the Maghrib in the Islamic period, by Jamil M. Abun-Nasr (Cambridge University Press – 1987)

A History of Medieval Spain by Joseph F. O'Callaghan (Cornell University – 1975)

Daily Life in the Medieval Islamic World, by James E. Lindsay (Hackett Publishing Company, Inc. – 2005)

Ibn Khaldun: Life and Times, by Allen Fromherz (Edinburgh University Press - 2011)

Las Sultanas de la Alhambra: Las grandes desconocidas del Reino Nazari de Granada (siglos XIII-XV), by Barbara Boloix Gallardo (Patronato de la Alhambra y del Generalife Editorial Comares – 2013)

Marriage, Money and Divorce in Medieval Islamic Society (Cambridge Studies in Islamic Civilization), by Yossef Rapoport (Cambridge University Press – 2005)

Medieval Cuisine of the Islamic World – A Concise History with 174 Recipes, by Lilia Zaouali (University of California Press – 2007)

Reading the Alhambra – A visual guide to the Alhambra through its inscriptions, by Jose Miguel Puerta Vilchez (The Alhambra and

Generalife Trust and EDILUX s.l., in collaboration with The Ibn Tufayl Foundation for Arabic Studies – 2011)

The History of Pedro the Cruel, King of Castile and León, by Prosper Merimee (BiblioBaazar edition – 2009)

The New Islamic Dynasties: A chronological and genealogical manual, by Clifford Edmund Bosworth (Columbia University Press – 1996)

"The Three Great Sultans of al-Dawla al-Ismailiyya al-Nasriyya who Built the Fourteenth-Century Alhambra: Ismail I, Yusuf I, Muhammad V (713-793 or 1314-1391)" by Alfonso Fernandez-Puertas, Journal of the Royal Asiatic Society, Third Series, Vol. 7, No. 1 (Apr. 1997), http://www.jstor.org/stable/25183293

Characters

The Nasrids

Abu Abdallah Muhammad V ibn Yusuf, the eighth Sultan of Gharnatah (r. from A.D. 1354-1359 and A.D. 1362-1393 or 755-759 AH and 762-792 AH), son of Abdul Hajjaj Yusuf I ibn Ismail of Gharnatah and Butayna

Butayna, first widow of Abdul Hajjaj Yusuf I ibn Ismail of Gharnatah, mother of Abu Abdallah Muhammad V ibn Yusuf and Aisha bint Yusuf

Aisha bint Yusuf, daughter of Abdul Hajjaj Yusuf I ibn Ismail of Gharnatah and Butayna

Abu'l-Walid Ismail II ibn Yusuf, the ninth Sultan of Gharnatah (r. from A.D. 1359-1360 or 759-760 AH), eldest son of Abdul Hajjaj Yusuf I ibn Ismail of Gharnatah and Maryam

Maryam, second widow of Abdul Hajjaj Yusuf I ibn Ismail of Gharnatah, Butayna's former friend

Qays ibn Yusuf, second son of Abdul Hajjaj Yusuf I ibn Ismail of Gharnatah and Maryam

Khadija bint Yusuf, second daughter of Abdul Hajjaj Yusuf I ibn Ismail of Gharnatah and Maryam

Shams bint Yusuf, third daughter of Abdul Hajjaj Yusuf I ibn Ismail of Gharnatah and Maryam

Mumina bint Yusuf, fourth daughter of Abdul Hajjaj Yusuf I ibn Ismail of Gharnatah and Maryam

Zoraya bint Yusuf, fifth daughter of Abdul Hajjaj Yusuf I ibn Ismail of Gharnatah and Maryam

Abu Abdallah Muhammad VI the Red, the tenth Sultan of Gharnatah (r. from A.D. 1360-1362 or 760-762 AH), son of Ismail ibn Muhammad, cousin to Abu Abdallah Muhammad V ibn Yusuf and Abu'l-Walid Ismail II ibn Yusuf, husband of Fatima bint Yusuf

Fatima bint Yusuf, eldest daughter of Abdul Hajjaj Yusuf I ibn Ismail of Gharnatah and Maryam, wife of Abu Abdallah Muhammad VI the Red

Ismail ibn Ismail, second son of Abu'l-Walid Ismail I ibn Faraj and Arub bint Muhammad, brother of Abdul Hajjaj Yusuf I ibn Ismail of Gharnatah and uncle to Abu Abdallah Muhammad V ibn Yusuf

Jazirah bint Ismail, daughter of Ismail ibn Ismail and wife to her cousin, Abu Abdallah Muhammad V ibn Yusuf

Abdul Hajjaj Yusuf ibn Muhammad, eldest son of Abu Abdallah Muhammad V ibn Yusuf and Jazirah bint Ismail

Nasr ibn Muhammad, second son of Abu Abdallah Muhammad V ibn Yusuf and Jazirah bint Ismail

Muhammad ibn Muhammad, third son of Abu Abdallah Muhammad V ibn Yusuf and Jazirah bint Ismail

Leila bint Muhammad, daughter of Abu Abdallah Muhammad V ibn Yusuf and Haziyya al-Riyad

Saad ibn Muhammad, son of Abu Abdallah Muhammad V ibn Yusuf and Haziyya al-Riyad

Courtiers, Ministers, and Aides

Abu'l-Nu'aym Ridwan, the chief minister to Abu Abdallah Muhammad V ibn Yusuf and head of the Sultan's chancery (A.D. 1354-1359 or 755-760 AH), the chief royal tutor

Faraj ibn Ridwan, commander of Abu Abdallah Muhammad V ibn Yusuf's forces at Tereul, son of Abu'l-Nu'aym Ridwan

Abdullah Hisham, chief eunuch in the harem of Abu Abdallah Muhammad V ibn Yusuf, brother to Abu'l-Nu'aym Ridwan

Abu'l-Hasan Ali ibn Yusuf ibn Kumasha, the chief minister to Abu Abdallah Muhammad V ibn Yusuf at Runda and head of the Sultan's chancery (after A.D. 1362 or 763 AH)

Lisan ad-Din ibn al-Khatib, chief secretary to Abu Abdallah Muhammad V ibn Yusuf

Abu'l-Qasim Sharif al-Sabti, chief qadi and head of the judiciary

Abu'l-Hasan al-Nubahi, chief qadi and head of the judiciary (after A.D. 1362 or 763 AH)

Muhammad al-Shaquri, chief personal physician to Abu Abdallah Muhammad V ibn Yusuf

Ibn Zamrak, a minister of the Diwan al-Insha

Ibn Khatima al-Ansari, a doctor and poet

Pharez ben Abraham ben Zarzar, a Jewish doctor

Abraham ben Pharez ben Zarzar, a Jewish doctor and son to Pharez ben Abraham ben Zarzar

The Marinids

Abu Salim Ibrahim ibn Abu'l-Hasan Ali, the Sultan of Al-Maghrib al-Aksa (r. from A.D. 1359-1361 or 760-762 AH), a son of Abu'l-Hasan Ali ibn Uthman

Shams ed-Duna, favorite of Abu'l-Hasan Ali ibn Uthman

Yahya ibn Umar ibn Rahhu, the Shaykh al-Ghuzat, the commander of the Marinid Volunteers of the Faith at Wadi-Ash
Uthman ibn Yahya ibn Rahhu, son of Yahya ibn Umar ibn Rahhu, the commander of the Marinid Volunteers of the Faith at Runda

Ali ibn Musa Rahhu Badruddin, the Shaykh al-Ghuzat, the commander of the Marinid Volunteers of the Faith at Wadi-Ash

Ibn Battuta, an Andalusi judge living in Al-Maghrib al-Aksa

Umar ibn Abdullah al-Yabani, wazir of the Marinid Sultans

Ibn Khaldun al-Hadhrami, a Tunisian scholar living in Al-Maghrib al-Aksa

The Castillans

Pedro of Castilla-León, the King of Castilla-León (r. from A.D. 1350-1369), son of King Alfonso XI of Castilla-León and Maria of Portugal, Queen Consort of Castilla-León

Don Pero López de Ayala, councilor to Pedro of Castilla-León

Don Diego Garcia Padilla, Grand Master of the Order of Calatrava

Fray Antonio Navas y Montilla, a Trinitarian friar

Retainers, Slaves, and Others

Juan Manuel Gomero, a Jewish slave merchant
Binta, a Nubian slave in the service of Juan Manuel Gomero

Pero Ruiz, a former Christian captive, the captain of Abu Abdallah Muhammad V ibn Yusuf's eunuch guards
Alfonso Ruiz, a former Christian captive and brother of Pero Ruiz, the captain of Butayna's eunuch guards

Pello Zabala, a former Christian captive, the captain of Jazirah bint Ismail's eunuch guards

Garcia, the captain of Butayna's eunuch guards in Al-Maghrib al-Aksa

Mufawwiz, the chief steward of Abu Abdallah Muhammad V ibn Yusuf

Haziyya al-Riyad, the favorite concubine of Abu Abdallah Muhammad V ibn Yusuf, a free Tuareg woman

Bahar, Qamar, and Suna, the Nubian body slaves of Abu Abdallah Muhammad V ibn Yusuf

Jawla and Hafsa, servants of Butayna

Nazhun, a body slave of Maryam

Lubna, Jazirah's former nurse and the stewardess of her household

Gonzalo, a Castillan Christian eunuch in Ismail ibn Ismail's household
Beatriz, a Castillan Christian maid in Jazirah bint Ismail's household, Gonzalo's wife

Jyoti, a cook from the Deccan Peninsula in Ismail ibn Ismail's household
Dhanu, a eunuch from the Deccan Peninsula in Ismail ibn Ismail's household, Jyoti's only child

Kissenga, a Nubian Christian eunuch in Jazirah bint Ismail's household

Harun, the jailor at Shalabuniya

Samir, the former jailor at Shalabuniya
Asiya, his wife, a former maidservant to the Nasrids
Faraj, the son of Samir and Asiya
Fatima, the daughter of Samir and Asiya

Thalj, a cat in the harem, and **Nawar**, **Hamza** and **Usaamah**, her offspring

Chapter 1
The Offer

Princess Jazirah

Shalabuniya, Al-Andalus or Salobrena, Andalusia
Dhu al-Qa`da 756 AH or December A.D. 1355 or Kislev 5116

The first warning came like thunder and shattered the relative quiet. Jazirah bint Ismail gripped the edge of the battlement and scanned the wide vista. No portent of rain darkened the horizon. The same turquoise sky dotted with tufts of white clouds as had greeted her for ten years still shone overhead. South of Shalabuniya's fortress atop an escarpment, ships crowded the gravel outcrop, which the town's denizens dared call a harbor.

Jazirah cocked her head as the wind carried the snorts of horses. Before this morning, she could count on one hand the number of visitors who had borne witness to her family's wretched state, but her father's chief persecutors never numbered among them. Prior to the murder of Jazirah's paternal uncle the Sultan of Gharnatah Yusuf I, he had consigned her father to exile for a supposed act of treason. In the fourteen months encompassing the reign of Yusuf's merciless successor, his eldest son Abu Abdallah Muhammad V had never inquired about his uncle's fate.

Once, before Jazirah's eighth birthday, an old woman with speckled hands and silvery hair had come to Shalabuniya. Jazirah's father called her 'Grandmother' while he urged his daughter to join their embrace. Instead, Jazirah had shied away. She also recalled a small-framed woman with black hair coiled like snakes on her head who had brought gifts for Ramadan and begged for a smile, as if a frightened girl knew cause for joy. Neither woman ever returned after the great pestilence had descended on Shalabuniya six years ago.

When Lubna appeared on the parapet, Jazirah straightened rather than endure reminders about proper posture. In their lowly prison, who cared about etiquette?

Sunlight cast its glare upon Lubna's features and she closed her eyes. Rat-brown hair streaked past her narrow shoulders. She finally looked at Jazirah, who offered the usual smile her former nurse expected. Not once in sixteen years had Lubna failed to return an affectionate gesture, until now.

The freckle-faced woman regarded Jazirah with a murky stare, the color of a muddied pond. Lubna's downturned mouth trembled, skin stretched taut over her prominent bones. Tears glided across a livid blotch on her left cheek, riper than a pomegranate.

Jazirah swallowed. "They are coming for him at last."

Lubna turned away, providing confirmation of the guess. Quiet sobs wracked her body.

Jazirah held her sorrow at bay. Since her father's undeserved banishment from the capital, she had oft shed tears of dismay over the cruelty of brother against brother. Ismail ibn Ismail's troubles would soon be over. What of Jazirah's worries?

She clutched the dappled wall, braced her belly against the masonry, and gazed across the White Sea. Sailors aboard two small ships competed for a berth and heckled each other. The oars of a sleek galley skimmed the surface. The crew guided their vessel toward the skyline, aided by the morning breeze. A flock of gulls screeched and wheeled, tracking the boat's course.

Jazirah eyed the progress of men, ships, and birds. "The Sultan of Gharnatah sends his henchmen to kill my father after ten long years."

"Pray Sultan Muhammad is merciful and grants your father a quick death." Although scant space separated them, Lubna's voice echoed as if from afar.

A snort of laughter from Jazirah disturbed seabirds nesting below the bluff. Their shrieks vied with the cries of fishermen returning with the morning's bounty.

"Dare I hope for mercy from one who shed no tears when his father died, Lubna?"

"Do not heed gossip. The Sultan could not have killed his father to gain the throne."

"I need no far-flung tales of Muhammad's cruelty. I have lived with proof of his father's callousness for far too long to expect better from the son. What does my father intend to do when his executioner arrives? Will Father submit?"

"Prince Ismail faces his death as any proud man should do. He maintains his dignity. What else is there for him, my princess?"

Jazirah's hold on the stonework tightened. "Don't call me by a title!" Rock, cool to the touch despite the morning sun, scraped her fingertips callused by years of mucking out her cell and hauling buckets of water to her father's adjoining room. "My father has not been a prince of Gharnatah for ten years. I am not a princess. My mother was Father's slave, naught more."

"He shall always be a prince in my eyes. You will always be my princess, no matter what the Sultans of Gharnatah might say."

"Would a real princess have endured this exile from the age of six?"

Lubna's near-skeletal touch gripped Jazirah's hand with fervent strength once thought long absent. "A Nasrid princess would survive many trials."

"Even the execution of her father? Muhammad does what his father would not. Why couldn't Yusuf's son have left us alone to our misery?"

"You should go to your father. If this is indeed Prince Ismail's last day upon the earth, he should have you beside him."

"I will never leave him." Jazirah looked to the horizon, where the seabirds became faint dots against the sky and the galley's sails billowed. Such an easy escape did not await her father.

She left Lubna on the ramparts and ducked beneath the arched entryway of stones. As she had blossomed into womanhood, her limbs lengthened until she stood taller than her father once had.

"Mind your head."

Upon first sight of the jailor Harun, she straightened. He lounged at the bend in the corridor. At almost his height, despite the thirteen-year age gap between them, she no longer cringed or looked up with a watery gaze at the odious tyrant.

While he scratched at his scraggly beard, her lips twitched. Fleas plagued him without mercy, as he deserved. She missed their old jailor Samir, released from service seven years ago, and wedded to a bride thirty years his senior. Sultan Yusuf had shown more pity for the aged Samir than he demonstrated for his own brother Ismail.

Harun ambled toward Jazirah. Dark waves of his hair brushed the ceiling's wooden beams. A wide grin upturned the corners of his mouth. He could have mesmerized any female with his green eyes. Only Jazirah and Lubna perceived the danger he posed.

Jazirah stiffened and placed her hands behind her back. With a furtive touch beneath her woolen sleeve, she fingered the pommel of a sheathed dagger lashed to her forearm.

He angled his head and looked past her. "The whore has told you of your father's fate?"

Jazirah edged closer to the wall and blocked his view of her slave. "Do not look at her! Lubna is free from your treachery. Leave her be!"

"I have had her countless times. Do you believe you could stop me if I wished to take her again? I am the warden of this fortress and all who live here do so by my leave. Never forget, Jazirah. If I wanted Lubna again, she would not refuse me. As it is, I do not desire your scraggly slave."

He slowed in the middle of the passage, but not so far away for Jazirah to escape the stink of wild onions and garlic on his breath.

"Ready to watch your father die? Will the Sultan's guards leave you here alone with Lubna? Shall you join your traitorous father in death, eh? I could help if you let me. Would you like me to do so for you, Jazirah?"

How could one man be so callous, yet attempt to cajole at the same time? Her fingers tightened around the bone hilt of the concealed weapon.

Black brows flared over Harun's emerald-eyed stare, but whether malice or triumph dwelled in his gaze, Jazirah could not guess.

He said, "You do not answer. You were always a little too proud for your own good. Nasrid pride was your father's downfall. It will be yours."

She drew the blade. "My ending may come one day, but yours shall be sooner than you think if you try anything."

He raised his hands, the palms facing out. "Careful before you cut yourself, princess. You won't need your little dagger with me. I'd never hurt you."

Her jaw tightened. "Lies! You're a pig, Harun. One day, there will be justice for Lubna. If you think I will let you do to me what you have done to her, you are mistaken. Whether my father lives or dies this day, I won't stay in your power forever."

The smile faded and his mouth twisted. Then he chuckled. "Allah shall grant me a better fortune and I shall have all I want from you. You will understand when they take your father's head, when there is no one else here to help you. Then you will think of Harun."

He peered beyond her again before he spun on his heels and sauntered away.

A ragged sigh whistled between her lips. She pressed her palm against the wall and drew deep breaths, before slipping her weapon back into its leather hold. She turned back to Lubna, who faced the sea.

Jazirah said, "He's gone."

The slave whimpered. "Forgive me, my princess. I was a fool to think Harun would have treated us well if I let him—"

"Never mind Harun. I'll never let him hurt you again. Come with me."

Jazirah held out her arm. After a few hiccups and sniffles, Lubna joined her, and they clasped hands.

Lubna brought Jazirah's long fingers to her lips, pale and abraded. "I have shamed you and your father."

"Only his last hours matter. Now come."

Jazirah drew Lubna down the hall. The first narrow door on the left stood slightly ajar. Within the cell, a hunched figure knelt before an iron-barred window. He had set his stubby fingers on his knees. A streak of water leaked from a seam in the bowl beside him and fed the dank straw.

Lubna whispered, "If only prayer might aid him at this hour."

"Prayer is all I have left, woman." Jazirah's father straightened with a groan.

Jazirah bit back a sob. Tears would not help. She scrambled to him and crouched at his side. "I won't let them take you away from me!"

A stranger might have mistaken him for her venerable grandfather. Eight months in the dungeon at Gharnatah and ten years here had transformed him. He appeared almost double his age of forty.

He raised a withered hand to her chin. "My brave daughter. If you had been a son, you would be a formidable warrior for Gharnatah."

"Not Gharnatah under the tyrant's rule."

Dark hair flecked with gray streaks fell over his bloodshot eyes. He had not slept during the night. Whenever Jazirah had turned on her straw mat, coughs and the shuffles of his footfalls penetrated the uneven brick wall between their cells.

He whispered, "Do not worry for me. If my nephew Muhammad's guards are anything like the ones his father Yusuf once commanded, they shall grant me a quick, merciful death."

She clutched at the neckline of his tattered tunic and the thin cloth tore. Lubna could mend it in the morning... but then, Jazirah remembered there would be no need.

His hands covered hers. "You must let me go, my child. Your future awaits."

"Not without you!"

"Your destiny shall be greater than mine, Jazirah. You must believe."

Harun's bellowed summons shattered the moment between father and daughter. She shuddered and burrowed against his chest. His kiss alighted on her hair.

"I did not want you to see this, but you would defy me even if I told you to stay here." He raised his head. "Lubna, fetch her *hijab*. Cover your hair with a veil as well."

The slave pressed trembling fingers to her mouth. Rooted to the floor, tears coated her cheeks again.

He sighed. "Lubna. Please. You must be strong for Jazirah."

With a whimper, the Greek slave fled to the adjacent room. Her loud sobs echoed.

Jazirah said, "She's been in love with you since I was a little girl."

Her father patted her shoulder. "I know. You must be strong for her as well."

She helped him stand. By the time Lubna returned, Jazirah had brushed the straw from her father's clothes.

He chuckled, a rasping rumble. "Your fastidiousness is unnecessary, my child. I will be dead soon. Allah, the Compassionate, the Merciful will not care about my dirtied clothing."

Jazirah could not fathom his levity or composure in their desperate hour. With a sigh, she veiled herself, the dingy *hijab* frayed at the edges. She and Lubna clasped fingers again and followed her father. They mounted two flights of stone stairs. Waiting guards ushered them out into the golden light over Shalabuniya. Jazirah shaded her eyes with a hand and lingered on the steps between two rows of sentries at the balustrades.

Their jailor stood in the courtyard among lemon trees set against walls the color of burnished brass. He awaited the slow progress of a group on horseback. Sleek Arabians colored chestnut, dappled silver, and dark bay topped the crest. All the stray cats in the forecourt scattered before iron-shod hooves. The horses neighed and flecks of froth lathered their coats. They clip-clopped across the rough cobblestones before the riders slowed near Harun, who waved over three stable boys idling at the base of the steps.

As one, Jazirah's father and Lubna gasped when the lead rider dismounted with help and raised a pale, gracile hand to a gold headcloth. A fold in the fabric revealed fine-boned features coupled with copper-colored eyes. The woman stared across the shaded courtyard, her focus on the trio atop the stairs. She ignored the jailor's greeting and spoke with the lone figure who had alighted from his horse beside her.

Jazirah recoiled from the sight of a livid, pink scar bisecting his face. The warrior in a scarlet cape pinned her to the spot with a sharp glance before he bowed to the woman beside him. She left him and approached Jazirah's family. Harun trailed her, but she glanced over her shoulder and muttered something unheard to him. Patches of red crept up the jailor's bull neck. The lead guardsmen drew his curved sword against Harun and held the warden back while his mistress continued to the steps. The hem of her brocaded garment trimmed with black fur swept the dust.

Lubna joined her master at the base of the stairs, both blocking Jazirah's descent from the top step. Even before she uttered a ready protest, the slave commanded, "Stay there!"

Jazirah stiffened. "Father?"

Over his shoulder, he whispered, "Do as Lubna said, daughter."

She glared at both of their backs. Why had they shielded her from this woman?

At less than a hand's span away from them, the new arrival stopped and regarded Jazirah's father in silence. Then she offered him the traditional greeting, her words muffled behind silk. Despite wobbly knees, Jazirah's father managed a stiff bow before he straightened with Lubna's discreet aid.

Their unexpected guest said, "I am pleased to see you, Prince Ismail. It has been too long."

"I remember our first meeting. Much has changed since then. Now your son sends you, his most ardent supporter. Some say you are his best assassin in the harem."

A fire sparked in her brilliant gaze. "My son is no cruel murderer! Do not speak of Muhammad ibn Yusuf with such disrespect. He is your Sultan as he is mine."

Jazirah quivered before the *Umm al-Walad*, the mother of Sultan Muhammad. Gharnatah's queen shifted the same enigmatic stare bestowed on Jazirah's father to his daughter. With deep, even breaths, Jazirah slowed the furious beating of her heart.

The Sultan's mother addressed her. "I am Butayna and you are Jazirah. Will you speak with me alone?"

How rude! She had not even asked for permission from Jazirah's father.

Jazirah pressed her shoulders back and lifted her chin. "Surely, my father should attend our discussion."

Butayna pursed her lips. "When I require his presence, I shall send for him."

"My father should be aware of matters concerning his future."

"Prince Ismail's fate has not brought me to Shalabuniya this morn. Rather, your destiny intrigues me. You will lead me to a place where we may talk in private. I will not ask again."

Jazirah would have balked at the command, but her father faced her in full and shook his head. She clamped her lips together and clenched her fingers.

"Daughter, take the *Umm al-Walad* to the battlements for our view of the White Sea. She would enjoy the sight."

"As you wish." Jazirah unfolded her hands and waved to the entrance. "If you will follow me, my Sultana."

Butayna hefted her brocaded skirts. Jazirah led her inside the fortress, all too aware of the woman's steady gaze on her back. No one else had ever unnerved her except Harun upon first sight of him. Her labored breathing filled the narrowed halls. The swish of silk along the stone steps irritated her as Butayna tracked her footfalls down into the bowels of Shalabuniya's castle. The rough stone of the walls closed in around her. She raced toward the light beckoning from an open door.

"Ouch!" She cried out as her forehead smacked against the low ceiling at the exit. She massaged the flesh and staggered out into the daylight.

"Are you hurt badly? Shall I fetch your maidservant?" Butayna reached for her arm.

Jazirah stumbled away. She gripped the parapet and steadied herself. "I don't need help! Not from you!"

"Your sentiment may change with time."

Jazirah gave Butayna a withering glance and received a smile as odd as the woman's statement.

Butayna strode the length of the stone causeway. With thin fingers, one dotted by a luminescent pearl ring, she unwound the cloth from her head. Sunlight shimmered across dark brown hair pinned up and festooned with jeweled combs. Not a strand out of place.

Jazirah pressed against the wall behind her, aware of her own wrinkled and tattered garments. She touched her sun-bronzed features and wished they could have conversed indoors, far from the glare of the light, which revealed her pitiable state.

Butayna gazed out on the tranquil waters of the White Sea and heaved a languid sigh. "Your father rightly assumed I would approve of this place. Yusuf would have enjoyed it, too."

"Humph. Then mayhap he should have traded places with his brother. Would dear Uncle Yusuf have liked Shalabuniya much then?"

Butayna's perspective on the serene seascape never wavered. "Bitterness sours your tone. You appear far too young to be so sullen. What is your age?"

"I am sixteen."

"Ah, much too young for such sourness."

"Your husband's decree robbed me of childhood contentment. I take no joy in my captivity."

"There is beauty outside of these walls, Jazirah. Life is never without its delights. It is a lesson I discovered in too short a life at Yusuf's side. I am still learning it. You could do the same if you allowed yourself the opportunity."

Jazirah swallowed, straightened, and moved away from the wall. "How can a prison ever be considered beautiful?"

Butayna's gaze returned and rooted Jazirah to a spot along the ramparts. "A harem can be a gilded prison. There is no escape for its occupants."

Jazirah sneered. "Confinement has suited you well enough as the mother of the Sultan! Even in this place, tales reach us of your power. The gossips tell how your son does not make a decision, even about his daily meals, without consulting you."

When Butayna giggled, Jazirah had not expected the girlish sound or the amusement in her tone. "They also say I send a steady supply of women to my son's bed while plying them with pennyroyal seeds to keep control of the harem, rather than ceding my power to the mother of Muhammad's eventual heir. Rumormongers tell of how I directed my son in the murder of his father to keep his younger brother, whom Yusuf must have preferred, from the throne. These nameless, faceless gossipers know much about harem life in the palace of *Al-Qal'at al-Hamra*, don't they? My son can make decisions without his mother's influence. Muhammad is a man of eighteen years. He has precluded my interference, lest his ministers say he clings to his mother's skirts. I have no more power than he may grant. You and I share the same limits. Whether we are subject to the whims of a husband and son, or a father as in your case, our will is not always our own."

Jazirah studied Butayna's visage. A high brow, coupled with an aquiline nose, pronounced cheekbones, and thin lips. Butayna turned sideways as if to offer a better view of her slight frame. She possessed rather large feet splayed beneath the silken *jubba*. She had average attributes. Naught to have stirred unending devotion in a man. Only those eyes compelled attention. Had she ensnared Yusuf's heart with their beauty?

As Butayna smiled beneath the scrutiny, Jazirah scoffed at her. "You stand in all of your glory and fine silks and speak to me of imprisonment. You don't have the right!"

"Don't mock me, princess. You have not earned the privilege. Nor do you know enough about my past or current circumstances to judge me."

"I already perceive some truths about you. You admire my father for one. Second, your men are not here to kill him. Even a heartless despot such as Muhammad would not send his own mother to witness a man's execution. After word had arrived from Gharnatah, I was so certain Father would have met his end today."

"There is never a warning before the executioner arrives, Jazirah." A hitch subdued Butayna's voice before she turned and looked out to sea again. "As it is, I understand you well, better than you may think. I had reason to be bitter when I was your age. Captivity will do so to anyone. Life altered when I learned of love and bore my son. In time, I regained my freedom. You could have the same opportunity."

Jazirah closed the distance between them. "Why are you here?"

"To grant your wishes and my own. Do you want to be free of this place?"

"More than anything, but I desire the same fate for my father and Lubna. We will leave Shalabuniya together or not at all. I will not abandon my family."

"You could regain your liberty within days, never to see your puffed-up jailor again. Ridiculous man! He dared suggest guiding me to the steps. Am I crook-backed with old age? I may be Yusuf's widow, but I am hardly feeble."

Jazirah laughed. She could not help it. Harun had colored when Butayna rebuffed him earlier. He deserved more than reproach for his presumptions.

Butayna favored her with warm regard. "You are taller than any Nasrid woman I have ever known, but your height is no disadvantage. You have inherited the beauty of the females in your family. Even life at Shalabuniya has not tempered a natural tendency toward prideful behavior. I find you well-suited."

"For what?"

"I offer a bargain, a means to seal the breach, which has existed since my husband jailed your father. My son Muhammad would marry you. You would become his Sultana, a queen of Gharnatah."

Jazirah closed her mouth and drew back. Time slowed. Even the ships at sea ceased bobbing on the waves. She could not have heard right. Marriage to Muhammad? A life at the side of the man whose father had imprisoned her father?

She asked, "You want me to trade one prison for another? To perpetuate a tyrant's line. Yusuf's callous decision ruined more than just my father's life."

"You have lost much because of my husband, but he is not among the living and cannot atone. My son Muhammad could restore your losses."

"You do not know them!"

The wind whipped up and ripped at Jazirah's veil, exposing the unruly mass of black curls atop her head.

Butayna peered at her. "I thought you had red hair, like your mother."

Jazirah muttered, "My sister had red hair! Six years younger than me, a babe who entered the world in the months before my father's imprisonment. An innocent child lost forever, consigned to misery and death by your husband."

With her mouth agape, Butayna recoiled. "The child died? I didn't know! Yusuf never told me of your family's fate."

"Then consider yourself fortunate for having avoided the brutal truth! You did not have to watch my mother and sister in agony as the milk dried up. Unable to nurse her baby, my mother willed herself into the grave and joined the daughter who had perished in her arms. Before doing so, she gave her paltry rations to my former nurse Lubna, so she and I might survive. You ask me to wed the son of the man who ruined lives most precious to me. What would you do, given such a choice?"

"You cannot place the blame upon Muhammad. He is not his father."

"Isn't he as cruel as Yusuf?"

Jazirah panted as she released pent-up fury against the kin responsible for her misery. Until her father's imprisonment, she had lived in ignorance, unaware of a legacy of murder and betrayal among the Nasrids, which had oft pitted father against son and brother against brother. Her uncle Yusuf's acts shattered more than her idyllic happiness. He had ruined the certainty of safety and comfort among family members. For if relatives could condemn each other, what hope could be held for kindness from strangers?

Butayna could not alter the past. Her husband had condemned Jazirah, an innocent girl at six years old, and her sister, a tiny babe, with their mother to the cells below the citadel of *Al-Quasaba* in Gharnatah. No matter the suspicions surrounding his brother, Yusuf had been reckless and needlessly cruel. Despite his death, Jazirah would never forgive him nor accept this sham of a marriage with his heir.

"Then, you are refusing to wed Muhammad?"

"I am."

"A union with my son would mean freedom for your father. You won't consider the possibility even for Prince Ismail's sake? The years have altered him for the worse."

"Ten of them have been spent in this place, the last seven at the mercy of Harun and his moods. What did you expect would happen when your husband confined his brother here? I can set all my father's current troubles at Muhammad's feet. When your son became Sultan, he could have at least inquired after his uncle in a gesture of kindness. Instead, he sends you with this jest, but I find no humor in his loathsome proposal. I will never become the wife of Muhammad ibn Yusuf."

Butayna's lips tightened, as if incredulous at the idea of someone rejecting her precious son's offer, but Jazirah remained unmoved. Let this proud Sultana find some other wife for her wretched offspring. Jazirah would not have him.

Butayna gazed steadily at her. Determination enlivened her stare. A woman accustomed to acquiescence from others would not relent easily. "Never is a long time, Jazirah. Does your father have the benefit of time?"

Chapter 2
The Garden Favorite

Sultan Muhammad V

Gharnatah, Al-Andalus or Granada, Andalusia
Dhu al-Hijja 756 AH or December A.D. 1355 or Tebeth 5116

Winter's wind rustled layers of parchment strewn across the writing desk of Sultan Muhammad V of Gharnatah. A quick perusal of the untidy bundles would have revealed messages addressed to Muhammad from the courts of Christian Spain and the Arab lands. None of these missives disturbed him, despite the terse demands for tribute from Castilla-León and the return of Aragónese and Catalan captives. Of even lesser concern were entreaties bearing the signatures of potentates from as far as Jumhuriyat Misr, the land of the ancient relic with the body of a lion, which the Greek historians called the Sphinx. In his eighteen years, Muhammad had never added a lion to his menagerie. Mayhap in response to the Mamluk Sultan Badr ad-Din al-Hasan, who sought trading rights between Gharnatah and Jumhuriyat Misr, Muhammad would demand a pair of lions in consideration.

As far as he knew, his mother had never seen a lion either. Yet, Butayna had called him such for longer than he could remember. She believed he possessed the strength of those majestic creatures roaming free in Ifriqiyah, but upon this winter's evening, Muhammad did not share the opinion. If anything, he remained caged like a lynx in its enclosure.

His father Yusuf's advice came to mind. *'One must first recognize the trap to avoid it.'* Survival was not possible without acknowledgment of the prevailing danger.

Was it possible to evade destiny? How could Muhammad have eluded his fate, one affording him mastery of all Gharnatah? The throne belonged to him by birthright, a sacred duty. Yet, he would have surrendered it gladly if his father could have taken his place upon the dais again.

Muhammad closed his eyes and slumped over the desk, forehead cupped in his hand. Fourteen months after he had suffered cruel treachery, the pain of loss still plagued him. His world had crumbled on the day his father's blood seeped into the bedclothes. Muhammad had not cried then. His mother and his beloved sister Aisha had wept enough for all three of them. He sobbed now, in the dim, dying light of the room where one reign had ended too soon, and another begun.

Faint breezes ruffled the hair trimmed short at Muhammad's nape, stirs reminiscent of the softness of a feminine caress. A shiver ran down his spine and he raised his head, scrutinizing the shadows. He sat alone in the austere room. However, sometimes at night he glimpsed shades or heard the unearthly peal of a woman's laughter. He did not speak of such things to anyone, not even his mother, for who would have believed him? If uneasy specters haunted his palace of *Al-Qal'at al-Hamra*, they did so with good reason. Too many had met premature deaths here at the hands of traitors. Rumors swirled around the court even now, of how Butayna had encouraged her son to order the assassination of his father.

Muhammad never wondered at the source of the gossip about him and his mother. His glare fell on the parchment atop the stack closest to him, the sole missive causing him the most trouble. As he reached for the crumpled letter, his sinewy fingers cast a long shadow across the page in the lamplight. He reread the cursive calligraphy penned with a fine hand.

'My noble Sultan, I beg you not to refuse my humble entreaties again. You ignore me, a lowly woman of the harem who lives only by your gracious goodwill. How has my request offended you? My only wish is to live the remainder of my days in the comfort and companionship of my beloved daughter Fatima and her husband. How can you refuse me? My younger daughters, your honored sisters Sultanas Khadija, Shams, Mumina, and Zoraya, grow each day. Our quarters where I have languished since the last days of your noble father, my beloved husband Yusuf, are now inadequate. The Raïs Muhammad the Red, in his capacity as your loyal governor of Malaka, has offered us larger accommodations better suited to our increasing needs. I plead with you to let us go free for the sake of the daughters beloved of your father's heart, sisters of your own blood. I await your favor. Your stepmother, Sultana Maryam umm Ismail.'

He slapped her words onto the pile with a grunt. Some of the other correspondence fell, but he let the wind have the sheaves.

"Humble! Humph! Lowly. Hah!"

Muhammad propped up his chin with a hand. Where was his mother? Courtiers would have mocked his concerned query in secret. A Sultan of Gharnatah could never appear dependent on his mother, especially a Christian. The semblance of Muhammad's relationships with those in his harem mattered most outside of its gilded walls.

At his feet, the Persian cat Thalj flicked her long white tail and peered up at him with yellow-green eyes. Her three kittens were much like her, the color of newly fallen snow. The smallest among them, a female that Muhammad called Nawar, jostled with her brothers Hamza and Usaamah for positions at their mother's teats. Cats prowled every corner of *Al-Qal'at al-Hamra*, but Muhammad held a particular fondness for Thalj. She had appeared at his doorstep on the morning after the loss of his father and slinked beside him, where she purred and rubbed her fur against his ankles. Her presence bolstered his spirit in the aftermath of Yusuf's murder.

Even Thalj's quiet comfort could not ease his current travail. The dilemma had plagued him for months since Maryam made her first request. An inclination to dismiss her pleas outright gave way to practical concerns. Would it not be better for all, especially his mother, if her rival left the harem? Should he banish his stepmother to the house of her daughter and a son by marriage, risking the advancement of the plots Maryam must be nurturing? If Maryam remained at *Al-Qal'at al-Hamra*, Muhammad's spies could monitor her. Still, her lingering presence affronted his mother daily.

Just over a week's worth of bitter days had passed in Butayna's absence. She went to Shalabuniya with a stated purpose of securing a wife for her son. Butayna wanted more than grandchildren to keep her company as her years lengthened. She believed a marriage would repair the rift caused by Yusuf's imprisonment of his brother. The intended bride remained the daughter of a traitor, Muhammad's own paternal uncle. If Father had believed in his brother's guilt, reason had guided him well. Yusuf's decisions had always derived from careful consideration, a trait inherited by his heir.

For his part, Muhammad wished another woman might be the sole mother of his offspring. Allah had blessed him with a treasure beyond compare, whom he prized above all others. He remained devoted to her since their first meeting two summers ago, after which she had become a treasured companion.

He whispered her name. "Haziyya al-Riyad."

The appellation meant the 'garden favorite' in Arabic, a whimsical choice evocative of the place where he had first met his *kadin* in the Nasrid summer palace of the *Jannat al-'Arif*. His chief minister Ridwan gave him the gift of the beloved concubine. On this evening, Muhammad anticipated her pleasurable company, far from the concerns of his rebellious stepmother or the demands made upon him as Sultan. In Haziyya's arms, he could forgo his troubles.

As if his words had summoned her, a knock came at the door. Muhammad's eager reply did not bring Haziyya into the room. Only a hint of her fragrance wafted through the double doors of his chamber. Instead of his favored concubine, his personal captain, Pero Ruiz entered and bowed. A long shirt of silver chainmail reached the top of his boots. Dark brown hair covered his brow.

When Pero first gained the position as commander of the royal bodyguard, less than a score of men answered to him. Now the corps numbered just under two hundred, all Christians, and former captives taken by the Moors from every region of Spain outside Gharnatah, like Muhammad's mother. As with the first guards whom she had selected in Muhammad's boyhood, each man had regained his freedom and had pledged his sword in service. Thus far, Muhammad had not tested the extent of his men's loyalty.

He waved to their leader. "You may rise."

Pero flung back a scarlet cape fastened at his neck. He began, "*Rey de mi reino,*" before he paused and cleared his throat. "My Sultan, the *kadin* is come."

Muhammad's chuckle rumbled in the back of his throat. He would never ridicule his captain, who crinkled his brow in a characteristic gesture oft adopted whenever he misspoke.

Pero tried his Arabic again. "My Sultan, your *kadin* has come."

Muhammad nodded to the man whom he had entrusted with his life since the age of eleven. "You do well with the lessons my mother imparts. I am happy you and the rest of my Christian guards decided to learn the Arabic language."

The captain gave a stiff nod. "It was time, my Sultan."

"Indeed. Send my Haziyya. After she has entered, close the door."

Muhammad rose from his writing desk and the legs of the stool on which he had sat scraped across the marble floor. Thalj opened her jeweled eyes and lifted her head again before she yawned and stretched out. Muhammad rounded the low table at the center of the room where he took his evening meal with courtiers or some of his trusted ministers among his council, the *Diwan al-Insha.*

Just then, his favorite entered the room. He paused as though thunderstruck. He always did at the sight of her. Magnificent would be an inadequate description for Haziyya al-Riyad. Coils of reddish-brown hair enhanced with henna and plaited into wiry braids fell to her generous hips. Crimson circles dotted her cheek and the apex of her brow line. Three silver bracelets affixed with tiny bells around her wrists jangled with each footfall. The blue and yellow silk *rida* hid curves as familiar to Muhammad as his own body. Leather boots peeked beneath the hem. From a blue beaded necklace, a four-pointed silver pendant hung. Haziyya refused to don the *hijab*. Tuareg women, like her mother, abhorred the restriction of the veil.

She bowed as custom dictated, the sole concession she had made since Muhammad claimed her. He reached for her rounded chin and she rose. They stood the same height. He stared at his reflection in her almond-shaped eyes, the color of dark, moist clay. Something flickered in her stare before a frown marred her brow. She never hid her emotions and rejected all display of false pretenses or affected moods, unlike his other women.

"You are troubled tonight, *Amanar*." Only in private had she ever uttered this secret name for him. Moorish astronomers called the brightest cluster of stars *Al-Jabbar*, the giant. The ancient Greeks referred to the same brilliant lights as Orion. For the Tuareg, Orion meant the warrior in the desert, *Amanar*.

Muhammad caressed Haziyya's flesh. "I am never worried when I am with you."

The furrows of her brow deepened. "I have eyes to see otherwise. Your own are reddened and downcast. You were thinking of your father earlier."

He nodded. "I can hide naught from you."

"Why would you wish to?"

She pulled away and sat at the table without his permission. Then she looked up and held out her hand to him. "Will you let me comfort you?"

"As only you can." He stretched out on the carpet beneath the table, his head pillowed in her lap. She stroked his nape first before her fingertips strayed to his temple. She drew concentric shapes across the surface, while humming one of the Berber songs he did not know. He peered up at honey-brown skin stained a pale shade of indigo and inhaled her unique fragrance of sandalwood and cinnamon.

She murmured, "Tell me of your troubles."

"Where shall I begin?"

"Start at the beginning."

A wearied sigh escaped him. "Maryam wishes to leave the harem and live with her daughter Fatima at Malaka. The wretched second wife of my father has pestered me for months. I am tempted to allow her departure, so these pleas will cease."

"You would permit her leave-taking because of the *Umm al-Walad*, your honored mother who does not hide her hatred of Maryam?"

"I'd allow her to go for my own comfort! Maryam's absence would benefit my household. However, it would also leave her free to scheme for her eldest son's ascendancy. She wants him to rule in my stead. She will never stop seeking the throne for him. My throne."

"The *murabit* of my village would say 'trust in Allah but tether your camel' in this instance." When a frown pained his brow, she added, "Your decision will determine your destiny, so choose wisely."

He sat up and gazed at her. "Are you saying I should leave naught to chance concerning Maryam? Should I eliminate all threats against me? Do I move against a woman whom my father loved and her children who share my Nasrid blood?"

"The answer is before you, but you do not wish to see it. I cannot tell the Sultan of Gharnatah what he should do. Even your own mother does not dare."

He held her chin again. "She does, and more. I expected candor from you, not these Berber riddles by your holy men. You have never hidden your feelings. Why do so now?"

"I fear for you."

Her admission surprised him and stirred a desire to reassure her. How could he provide more than meaningless promises she would not believe? Instead, he pressed his head to hers.

She expelled a ragged breath fragranced with mint. "I will love you forever, Muhammad, no matter the path you choose. Wherever fate may lead you, only let me walk by your side."

"To be my guide in the wilderness, as the only person in whom I may place my complete trust. Do you know why? You never lie, even if your words will displease me. I shall love you always, Haziyya. No one else may ever claim my heart."

"Even the cousin whom you must marry? Mayhap this princess shall grant you the children I cannot. You will love her then. You'll be a good father someday, *Amanar*."

He lifted his head before he cradled hers against his shoulder. A shudder passed through her, but no warm tears blotted the neckline of his *jubba*. If Haziyya ever cried over their mutual disappointment, she did so in secret.

They had been together for two years in which no child had appeared, not even the false prospect of one. She bled at regular intervals each month. Just as troubling, no other *jawari* of his had become pregnant before or after Haziyya's arrival. The possibility of Muhammad's failure, not those of slave concubines, taunted him. His doctor had found no cause, but Muhammad could not dispel doubts. Would the Nasrid line end with him?

He whispered, "Don't worry. We will have our children when Allah ordains it." Mayhap he said so to soothe his growing concerns and assuage hers. Even as she shook her head, he hugged her closer. "Listen to me. Jazirah bint Ismail could give me a thousand sons and daughters, but she will never hold my heart. It is yours."

When she glanced at him, he continued, "My mother alone clamors for this union. I do not want the wife foisted off upon me, but my mother believes Jazirah and her father will become pawns in a game for my enemies. My uncle betrayed my father's secrets to the Marinids. I have seen no proofs to convince me otherwise. Jazirah's father betrayed my father. I will marry her if I must, but I will never trust her."

"As you no longer trust your mother."

His jaw tightened. "Years of the intrigues in this harem have altered her. Her alliance with Hisham, a man whom I have long suspected is untrustworthy, troubles me. My mother knew better in her youth. Nonetheless, her reliance on him increases daily."

"Yet, Hisham remains your chief eunuch."

"My mother protested his proposed removal as a betrayal of Ridwan, whom I need as my chief minister. I do not need his snake of a brother. I cannot fathom how my mother could have found common ground with Hisham. He is always in her chamber, even late at night. If Hisham was not a eunuch, I might think my mother dishonors my father."

"She would never do so. Your mother loved Sultan Yusuf, may Allah preserve his memory. She loves him still, as she adores you. If she believes this union with your cousin in Shalabuniya is the best course, mayhap there is good reason."

He inhaled the fragrant sandalwood in Haziyya's hair. "No further talk of my marriage or my mother's wishes, only our desires."

"We speak no more, not with words."

Light kisses across his collarbone stirred a heavy groan. His grip tightened and he crushed Haziyya against him. His touch strayed to her hair and fisted the thick coils. A lesser woman might have whimpered, but his possessiveness always emboldened her. She nipped along his jaw, while her hand slipped beneath the neckline of the silk tunic. Her heavy, silver bracelets clinked together. At every instance where the smooth pads of her fingers splayed across his chest and stroked the fine pelt of hair, a strangled moan tore through his lips. Her other hand curled at his nape and he bent his head toward her. In another breath, he opened his mouth and her tongue teased his. Their lips met and he quickly deepened their embrace. Each kiss drove hot stabs into the pit of his stomach. She threaded fingers through his hair and gripped the back of his head.

His name on another's lips penetrated the red haze of his lust. The door handle of his chamber rattled. Insistent protests vied with the gruff responses of his captain.

"My honored Sultana, the Sultan has retired for the evening."

"At the side of Haziyya, no doubt. The Sultan will see me tonight, Pero, regardless of what you say!" Pounding followed. "My lion, I must talk to you!"

Muhammad groaned. "My mother shall send me to an early grave."

Haziyya caressed his hairline. "Or protect you from one. The *Umm al-Walad* is devoted. She would not have sought you out at this hour unless she deemed her visit of great importance."

He gazed at her. "You think I should let her in."

She nuzzled his temple. "It is not for a concubine to tell you what to do."

He laughed and buried his face in her fragrant hair. "As if you were just a mere concubine. Stay. This will not take long."

She settled back on her heels while Muhammad stood. He closed his tunic's neckline and brushed wrinkles from the legs of his linens. On bare feet, he crossed the room and opened the door. Butayna stood framed in the entryway with her eyes aglow. She veered from casting her most heated glare at Pero to frowning at Muhammad in silence. He missed the woman she had been, one who favored him with open smiles and the utter truth.

Behind her, Pero's younger brother Alfonso abased himself before Muhammad, who acknowledged him with a wave before he told his mother's trusted guardsman to stand. Then Muhammad recalled his customary duty and bowed before Butayna.

"Peace, *Ummi.* The sight of you is pleasing."

"My Sultan gladdens my heart with his greeting."

Her sullen, low tone gave voice to the lie and her lingering annoyance. He ushered her into the room. Pero mumbled some words, which sounded like an apology, but Muhammad dismissed the man.

Haziyya rose and clasped her fingers to her belly. No flush colored her face, nor did her chest rise and fall with impassioned breaths. Muhammad envied her composure. She bowed low and held the position.

His mother did not acknowledge the concubine's deference. Instead, Butayna turned to him. "Please, let us speak alone, my Sultan."

He cocked his head. "I would prefer it if my *kadin* stayed."

Butayna grimaced. "Our discussion should occur in private."

"I have naught to hide from Haziyya." He approached his favorite and touched her shoulder. "You may stand."

When she did so, her gaze narrowed and remained on him. In the space of two breaths, her displeasure etched across lips thinned like his mother's own. He frowned. Why had she directed her annoyance to him? His mother was the culprit requiring Haziyya's departure.

Then she muttered, "Truly, I should leave you, my Sultan."

"I do not want you to go."

"As my Sultan knows, life does not always bend to our will."

He looked from Haziyya to his mother. Butayna lifted her chin and met his stare with the same reserve as his *kadin* held in her regard. Then Butayna nodded almost imperceptibly to Haziyya and a tight-lipped smile softened her severe expression. By the time Muhammad glanced at his favorite again, she offered a mirrored smile to his mother. If he did not know better, he might have suspected some silent collusion between the pair. Odd when they held no common ground. Haziyya respected and admired Butayna, but his mother maintained a boundary between them, which Muhammad suspected had nothing to do with Haziyya's status in the harem or his love for her. What was the source of his mother's reticence?

Muhammad reached for Haziyya's chin a final time. She sniffed but did not bridle as he stroked the skin. "When my mother has retired, I shall call you again to my side."

"I will come to you no matter the hour of your summons."

With great regret, he lowered his hand. She bowed before approaching his mother and repeating the gesture of humility, which Butayna left unacknowledged. His mother's pride subverted her kindhearted nature. When Haziyya left him in Butayna's company, the sounds of jangling metal and all warmth in the room went with her.

Muhammad sighed and raked a hand over his face. "You picked a poor time to interrupt me, *Ummi.* I looked forward to a night in Haziyya's arms."

"I shall not keep you from them for longer than necessary. Your *kadin* is astute, even for one so young. If I had held even a scrap of her wisdom when I attained her age, my adjustment to life in Gharnatah might have been less... troublesome. I admire her. She is a worthy companion for you."

"I believe this is the first praise you have ever offered her."

She rolled her eyes and moved toward him. "My lion, you must not think I question your attachment to Haziyya—"

"It is not mere attachment! I love her." His voice rose louder than he had intended. "I would marry her if I could. Our sons and daughters shall have her hair and eyes."

"You cannot wed a concubine who has not borne you a child."

Muhammad scowled at her. "I am Sultan. I can change the rules."

"You will not, my lion. Never forget—"

"I don't need reminders about the conventions of this harem, especially from you."

"I don't understand your meaning."

"My aunt Leila, may Allah preserve her memory, once said you disdained the rules of this place. Now, you adhere and demand I do the same."

"Adversity has taught me acceptance, my lion. Haziyya cannot be your wife. Not until she proves capable of bearing heirs to sustain your line."

He waved his mother to the low table. "Then I suppose we should speak of the bride you have chosen for me, whom you imagine shall grant me the required heir. How soon must I wed Jazirah, so I may have my happiness with Haziyya?"

Butayna took a seat across from him. She smoothed nimble fingers over folds of cerulean blue silk wrapped around her head. Her pearl ring glistened, a token from his father granted in the months after Muhammad's birth. The lamplight revealed tiny lines and dark circles around her eyes, which had appeared in the months after his father's assassination. Life held little joy for her in Yusuf's absence.

Muhammad leaned forward and clasped the hand nearest to him. He covered her fingers with his and recalled the days when only her familiar touch soothed away his concerns. A time when he knew little of a Sultan's cares, only the everlasting bond between a mother and son.

"Have you slept at all, *Ummi*?"

The hard line of her lips relaxed. "You must not worry for me. Your concern lies with Jazirah bint Ismail, who has rejected the marriage bargain."

A mirthful rumble filled Muhammad's throat. "She doesn't want me?"

"There is no humor in her repudiation. She refused you, even though the match meant liberty for her father."

Muhammad sobered in an instant. "I did not agree to his freedom when you first proposed this union. I still do not."

Butayna touched her pale mouth. "You would have married Jazirah and kept her father imprisoned? You are a Nasrid, my son, but I never raised you to be so cruel."

"Shall you tell me again of the merits of compassion?"

"Do you need another lesson? This union would... it could bolster the family. The bonds between its members are the basis of strength. Your blessed father understood the value of unanimity among the Nasrids and imparted it to me. *'Asabiyah*, the bond between us is all important. Discord weakens us."

He squeezed her fingers, honored by her devotion to Yusuf. "Us? You have never counted yourself among us."

"I am the mother of Nasrids. Where else should my loyalty lie? Through this union, you would have found a suitable wife, a princess of your own bloodline. Better her than a bride from the Marinids or their Hafsid enemies. We do not need further strife."

"True, for there is enough contention within these walls. For you, a union with Jazirah would be better than an alliance from across the White Sea. Few among the *Diwan al-Insha* would agree."

"Your councilors see only the Sultan. They care naught for your future, only the riches and honors they may gain at your side. I see my blessed son, whom I have vowed to protect against his enemies. Free your uncle and you do more than deny your foes a pawn. You are not heartless, my lion. I raised you and your sister to have sympathy for others, particularly those struck by ill fortune. Take pity upon Prince Ismail. Captivity does not befit him. He is a prince of Gharnatah."

When had she developed this strange attachment to his uncle? The question mystified and troubled him. What were her motives? For Muhammad's sake and to all outward appearances, she must appear above reproach.

He removed his touch upon her hand. "No Nasrid prince has ever benefited from time at Shalabuniya. My father sent his brother there for mercy's sake. Instead, Father could have had my uncle and his family executed. Every member of this family knows of my uncle's letters to the Marinids, which earned him exile along with his family."

"I am more concerned about the views of this harem's occupants. Your brothers Ismail and Qays remain unmarried. Maryam has pondered the future for her sons. She knows your uncle has a daughter of marriageable age."

He mused, "Maryam thinks of little more than my throne. What would she gain if one of her sons weds the daughter of a man bereft of the governorship he once held?"

"Some think your uncle endured needless cruelty. He has friends at court and in the provinces."

"My uncle is an old cat without claws. A pact with him through marriage won't interest anyone, least of all Maryam's sons."

"Maryam has longer claws than Thalj, or have you forgotten?"

"I forget naught! When I would have eliminated your nemesis upon Father's death, you urged compassion on behalf of her children. Your pity may be my undoing."

"You cannot have the blood of your siblings upon your hands, which will be the result if you remove their mother. There must be another way to thwart Maryam. One means is by this marriage. In traditions long held, your forbearers have always chosen at least one wife with kinship ties—"

"Shall I have lessons in family history this night as well, *Ummi*?"

Butayna rushed on as if he had not spoken. "There are few Nasrid princesses whose ages make them suitable marriage partners for the bearing of heirs. Your relations will not overlook Jazirah. You must marry her! You need a son."

"I will sire sons with Haziyya. *Ummi*, my uncle's daughter does not want me. I certainly have no wish to wed her."

"If this is about your Nasrid pride—"

"I will never force Jazirah to marry me! If any among my cousins or brothers wishes to have her, I shall gladly give my consent."

Butayna slapped the table. "Then you are a fool! I did not raise a fool."

His jaw stiffened. "You did not raise me. Aunt Leila did. Now I am Sultan, and a proud one. Be mindful of the respect I deserve, *Ummi*, and your position in this harem. You are a woman, a Christian, and a former slave."

"The dangers you face are real, Muhammad. Even a mere woman, who is a Christian and former slave can perceive them. Threats emanate from the walls of this harem, from Maryam and her sons! Your infatuation with your Berber beauty blinds you to peril. While you luxuriate in pleasure, Maryam plots your downfall!"

Thalj interrupted their argument with a yowl before she scurried across the floor and out of the chamber, flicking her tail. One by one, the kittens darted after their mother.

Muhammad assessed Butayna in silence. Always a passionate woman, she was never more ferocious than when a threat to her loved ones, especially her children, arose. Like a lioness, she protected her offspring.

In a clipped tone he stated, "I cannot help but be aware of the risk. You and Maryam have divided this harem for too long. This conflict cannot continue."

She drew back. "What do you intend to do with her?"

He waved away the latent fear in her tone. "Be at ease, she will live. I have not decided about Maryam's persistent requests. You should seek your rest, *Ummi*."

"If my Sultan wishes to dismiss me for the comfort of Haziyya's body, I will comply." She rose and swept the mantle from her shoulders.

He stood also and grasped her fingers, gazing deep into her eyes for truths he might discern there. Before Yusuf's death, mother and son had braved the perils of courtly life together, united against Maryam's attempts to undermine Yusuf's regard for them. When had Butayna grown comfortable with keeping secrets from Muhammad?

She blinked and looked away. Courage born of misfortunes had always fortified her, but now, the light in her eyes faded. "Why do you stare at me, my lion?"

"You seem overwrought by more than the return from Shalabuniya. Mayhap you should remain indoors tomorrow, instead of your usual visit to Al-Bayazin."

The arrogant tilt of her head, which he admired in secret, returned. "Do you fear I have grown frail in a short absence from Gharnatah? I assure you, my lion, I am myself. Tomorrow, I shall enter the quarter as usual."

He asked, "Where do you go in Al-Bayazin each month?"

Her nails raked against his palm, fingers clenched. His hold tightened, mayhap too much, for she winced. Her stare flicked up and beyond him, drawing his deep sigh. He probed for a truthful answer, one he might never receive.

"To the merchants' quarter, my lion, to inspect slaves."

He could not resist correcting her, even if it meant rousing suspicions he should have held at bay. "You mean the Jewish merchants' quarter, for the residences of Gharnatah's Moorish slave sellers are to the south."

A tic along the jawline appeared when she must have gritted her teeth. "Have your guards been following me, Muhammad?" She tugged her hand away before he could reply.

"You know they have not. The good doctor Al-Shaquri mentioned how he saw you in Al-Bayazin during the month of Dhu al-Qa`da this year. I recalled your visit in a prior month and realized you must enter the Jewish merchants' quarter at regular intervals. Despite your stated purpose, the number of slaves has not increased. Hisham's accounting remains the same. Do you always find captives unsuited to a life of servitude in the Sultan of Gharnatah's household?"

She sniffed and twirled her pearl ring. "Why should the number of slaves grow? You have rejected every other *jarya* in the harem for the favor of Haziyya. My choices of your pleasure slaves would not suit you, so I leave those unfortunate people as I find them."

The certainty of her lies stirred fury inside of him. He struggled against the urge to strike her. He had sworn never to touch any woman in anger again, not since Maryam had drawn his ire in the aftermath of his father's murder. Instead, he fisted his hands at his sides and considered his mother. Proof of her mischief did not exist, not yet.

"May I leave you, my lion?"

He relented with a silent vow and permitted her departure. One day, he would uncover the full truth of these fruitless visits she undertook each month. Alone, he swept a hand over his hair. Mayhap not even the companionship of his garden favorite could quell the unsettled nature of his mood. Turmoil had ensnared the harem for too long. How could he end the rivalry between Butayna and Maryam, an enmity aged almost two decades, without claiming the lives of innocents?

Lisa J. Yarde

Chapter 3
Pledges

Princess Jazirah

Shalabuniya, Al-Andalus or Salobrena, Andalusia
Muharram – Safar 757 AH or February A.D. 1356 or Shevat –
Adar 5116

Two months after Butayna's visit, Jazirah still avoided the battlements. In the first days afterward, she had lingered by the doorway at the edge of the cobblestones. Memories of Muhammad's mother filled her mind, so she soon ceased all attempts at venturing out. Her father and Lubna noticed. Jazirah's assurances of her wellbeing and good spirits did not ease the furrows etched across her father's brow. Blatant lies about the abnormally cold weather drew quizzical frowns from Lubna. Jazirah did not know why the two people who knew her best in this world permitted her these untruths. Mayhap they waited for her to speak, although she vowed she would never mention the proposal from Gharnatah's ruler.

Jazirah held no romantic notions of love or hopes of a fortunate alliance through marriage. Any would-be suitor of hers would have to overlook the false accusations against her father. No one would dare, for the act would be tantamount to questioning Sultan Yusuf's decision. Who would risk his heir's displeasure for her father's sake? Another marital offer might never come, but Jazirah would rather endure a life of spinsterhood, never knowing the possibility of love or the joy of a babe suckling at her breast, than become the wife of her cousin.

If her father perceived the nature of the conversation Jazirah had held with Butayna, his views remained unknown. Lubna suspected something. She flicked surreptitious glances Jazirah's way whenever she thought her former charge would not notice. Much like the look Lubna gave Jazirah now while they sat together in the dank, windowless cell they shared. In silence, they patched the holes of frayed woolen tunics. Their proximity to each other warded off frigid air, which penetrated chinks in the masonry. The lone brazier Harun had provided burned in her father's cell. He needed the warmth more than the women did.

The tunics once belonged to a kindly guardsman, rare among Harun's men, who had no further use for his old clothes. He had succumbed in recent days to a lingering bout of fever coupled

25

with red pustules on his hands and face. At his earlier request, Lubna had offered aid during the prior week, having garnered some respect among the men for her effective advice against the black plague six years ago. Still, the death of the sentry occurred along with two of his children. His widow had given over the garments in meager thanks for Lubna's help, regardless of the outcome. Lubna washed the tunics and ensured the absence of fleas, but powerful odors akin to garlic and onions, and sweat and horse leather clung to the fibers. In truth, the clothes were too large for Jazirah and her father, but Lubna insisted upon the needlework.

Jazirah's hand cramped and she stabbed her forefinger again. Reddened prick marks dotted her flesh. She stifled a groan, lifted the finger to her lips, and sucked at the tip. Coppery blood tasted of salt on her tongue.

"Be careful, my child! Why don't you let me finish? Sit with your father this evening. It would cheer him if you recited some of your lovely poetry again."

"Will the verses fill his belly? We have had little to eat since early this morn and it is almost time for the evening prayers of *Salat al-Maghrib*."

Lubna bent her head, pushed hair away from her face, and squinted hard at her sewing. "You have to accept, my princess, there may be no rations for us tonight. The fare Harun sends is not fit for a Christian's dog, much less Nasrids of Gharnatah."

"I learned long ago to stop questioning the source of the stringy meat floating in the broth. Now, I wish we had some. We cannot survive on brown water in our bowls or moldy bread, harder than the stonework."

"Harun means to starve us, my princess, as punishment. It's my fault. If I had not accepted these castoffs—"

"Our warden wants us, me specifically, beholden to him. Since no one will tell him who gave us the tunics, he punishes us along with his men. He lies when he says there is no salted meat for the broth. He does not appear to be starving, but my father is. Oh, he's so thin, Lubna. A good wind could carry Father aloft. He can't—"

A cough echoed through the wall. Jazirah jerked forward, but Lubna's bony fingers gripped her arm. "Wait, listen."

Both of them held their breaths and released them at the same time when no rasping wheezes occurred.

Lubna pinched the bridge of her nose and blinked, her eyes reddened from lack of sleep. She jabbed the needle into the tattered wool again. "Prince Ismail improves. We must believe. This fever will not claim his life."

Jazirah sighed and set her work aside. She drew up her outstretched legs, hugged them, and rested her chin at the apex of her knees. "What if Father cannot survive without aid? I may have to ask Harun for a doctor's help. I will go to our jailor myself. You shouldn't do it."

Lubna gave a bitter laugh. "You waste your time, sweet child. As if our warden would take pity upon Prince Ismail. Harun does not know the meaning of mercy. He will reject your plea."

"I have to try for my father's sake."

"Harun does little without the promise of recompense! I should know. You are never to seek him out. Do you understand me, Jazirah?"

"What would you have me do while my father remains in his sickbed?"

"Naught where Harun's aid is required! You will not take the risk. I shall do it. I will go to him after I've had a wash this evening."

Jazirah scowled at her slave. "You will not whore yourself for me—"

"I've told you never to say such words!" Lubna's stinging slap cut off the rest of Jazirah's speech. She stared at the palm print on her forearm. Lubna dropped the needlework and buried her face in her hands.

If Jazirah's father possessed his former strength, he would have plied the whip against Lubna's back himself for the offense. He could never know.

Jazirah draped an arm over Lubna's shoulders. "I'm sorry. Please forget my hurtful words."

Lubna blubbered, "Oh, it is not you who should be asking for forgiveness!" She tugged Jazirah closer and they hugged each other.

After her former nurse's sobs subsided into soft hiccups, Jazirah raised her head. "What are we to do then? Neither of us can trust Harun, but to whom can we turn when my father must have a doctor?"

Lubna patted her back. "Do not distress yourself. I will think of something." When Jazirah bridled, Lubna added, "The plan will not involve Harun. I swear, I will not go to him, nor will you. Let me finish the sewing so you and Prince Ismail can have these miserable coverings."

"But what of you? How will you keep warm this winter?"

Lubna swiped at her gaunt face. "I will survive by the grace of God."

"Do you think we have Allah's favor even after all of these years?"

Lubna cupped Jazirah's chin. "Does doubt bedevil you?"

"It is harder with each year spent in misery to remember Allah ordains all. If He chose this fate for us, what did we do to deserve it?"

"Do you still believe in a world where only the wicked are punished? If so, I should never have told you such stories when you were a child." Lubna drew back, her shadowy gaze suddenly turned sharp. "But then, you are no longer a child, are you? No more of the tender babe I once suckled in the weeks after I lost my first boy."

"The first boy?" When Lubna nodded, Jazirah added, "Then your second child was also male? I didn't know the babe had formed enough to detect the sex."

"He would have lived except for Harun. I would have been happy with the baby. Children are faultless for the sins of their fathers."

Jazirah turned aside, not quite willing to agree. If Lubna spoke true, Muhammad did not bear the blame for his father's mistakes with Jazirah's father.

Lubna said, "I've broken my vow. In her last words, your mother begged me to ensure your comfort. I have provided none. I did not protect you from cruelty. You've seen horror and misery, and known hunger and cold, which no Nasrid princess should have ever endured. I cannot fail your father. He shall have a doctor's aid."

"How? You promised you would not go to Harun."

"I meant those words. Trust in me."

"I do. I always will."

Jazirah embraced Lubna's ragged form again, little more than sinewy flesh stretched over bone. They could not continue this way, not without some help. What could they do when no one in Al-Andalus would risk the venture?

Lubna said, "Leave the sewing and see to your father."

"You're certain you don't need me?"

With a frown directed at Jazirah's uneven stitches, Lubna shook her head. Jazirah rolled her eyes, but a smile tugged at the corner of her mouth. Then she kissed Lubna's brow.

"Why did you do so, my princess?"

"Thank you for the sacrifices you have made for us. I will never forget them."

Splotches colored Lubna's cheeks, as noticeable as the birthmark on her face. "At least not until your usual insolence rears itself again. Now go and comfort your father."

Jazirah rose and strolled across the cell. At the doorway, she paused and stared at Lubna, who groaned and said, "What is it now?"

"I meant my words, too. Sometimes, I struggle to recall my mother's features. You and Father have always said I resemble her, but I remember red hair only."

"Her spirit dwells within you, Jazirah. She was not born into a life of servitude. You should be proud of your ancestry and the bloodlines of both your parents."

"I know. Father told me. It's just, even if I can't summon the memory of *Ummi*, I remember your face above the crib. In my heart, you are my mother."

Lubna's chin dipped as she sniffled and folded her hands in her lap. When she raised her head, she maintained steady eye contact despite a watery stare. "And you, sweet princess, will always be the child I shall never have."

Jazirah turned away and went to the adjacent door. She pushed against the wood studded with rusted iron rivets, which raked at her palm. She ducked beneath the lintel and stood within the small room. Uneven seams in the timber slats of dilapidated shutters could not prevent a draft. Her father rested on grubby straw beneath two fusty wool blankets. A *shashiya* clung to his head, the threadbare skullcap exposing gray-streaked hair. She stared hard at his chest for a time until it rose and fell with labored movements. She crept closer and knelt beside him. Was it just her imagination or had the shadows beneath his bulging eyes darkened?

"Father?" Jazirah touched his forehead, feverish and dotted with beads of perspiration. She called to him again. "Father!"

Although his eyes did not open, he lifted a gnarled hand, and reached for hers. She grasped his fingers. Cold and crinkled, not the hands of the prince who had swept her up in his arms during her childhood and twirled her around the gardens at Wadi-Ash. Youthful recollections of him had sustained her in the darkest hours of their sojourn. Where would she find solace after his death?

He cleared his throat. "I did not want to awaken. I was dreaming of you."

She stretched out beside him on the floor. "Why envision me when I am here?"

"Not just you. There were children. They played in a courtyard. Four fine boys surrounded you, while a girl tugged on your skirts."

Jazirah patted his chest. "I would have to marry to have children, Father."

He murmured, "You will remember what I told you of my dreams. Sometimes, they come true. Besides, you should have happiness."

"If people received all they deserved, then we would not be here."

"Allah chooses thus. Do not despair. Another offer of marriage may come in time."

She raised her head and peered at him. Shafts of evening light illuminated the creased skin around his eyes above the sunken cheekbones. His dark lashes flickered and he returned her determined stare.

"You knew the reason for Butayna's visit, Father?"

"Of course, I did. Even if she had not shared her aim with me before she retired from Shalabuniya, I already anticipated her purpose. Lubna suspected as well. Muhammad did not need to send his mother to me. Butayna gained his assent to the proposed union, but I believe the idea originated with her, born of natural kindness."

Jazirah shook her head. "She should have asked your permission first."

"Why should my feelings matter more than yours? You answered with true intent?"

"You've taught me to always reveal the truth, Father, even if I might cause others displeasure. Butayna may be the *Umm al-Walad* of Gharnatah, but you are my parent. Decisions about my marital prospects are yours. She showed bad manners."

A broad grin exposed two pits in his mouth. "You think so, hmmm? Butayna is an unconventional woman by your standard, but she always shows the utmost respect to those who deserve it. She behaves in ways contrary to your expectations of Moorish women because she is not a Moor. She is a Christian born in the north of this peninsula, like your mother."

While Jazirah absorbed the information, he added, "Do not think too ill of Muhammad's mother. She has a woman's heart. She did not dare to hope I would allow you any alternative except compliance. Jazirah, I am not long for this world—"

When she would have protested, he hushed her. "Listen, for this may be the last days in which I will speak as your father. The future is ahead of you. This is your life to live, not mine. Butayna deferred to you because she believed as I do. Union with Muhammad was your choice to make. You have made it."

She clutched the edge of the coarse blanket. "But, Father—"

"Jazirah, do not doubt yourself now. You are a woman in form and mind. In equal parts, you have inherited the best qualities of your mother's proud people, the Basques, and my Nasrid forbearers. Allah has blessed you with grace and discernment. Such traits would fill any would-be husband's heart with pride. You see the world around you as it is, enough to tell Butayna what you thought of her son's proposal in your usual forthright nature. Still, I caution you against the bitter resentment you hold toward your cousin. Muhammad is not Yusuf."

"His mother said the same."

"She was right. My brother was never the man Muhammad has become."

"How would you know, Father? You have not seen your nephew since he was a boy."

"What I knew of the child portended well for the man. Even a glimpse of him would be needless, when he surely remains as much his mother's son as he is a Nasrid. People do not change their true nature. Muhammad had Butayna's pride and passion coupled with our intellect and intuition, almost from birth. Like you, he gained the best traits from his parents. Blessed with a mother like Butayna, Muhammad has reason to hope. He is not his father's son in every respect. The intrigues of Yusuf's court led him to doubt. It was not his fault."

"You always speak well of my uncle Yusuf, even after all he did. You never resented how the council ministers passed you over in the succession?"

"Not once. Our own blessed grandmother Fatima thought Yusuf better suited to the role and the *Diwan al-Insha* chose him with her blessing. My brother knew burdens as Sultan, which I could never imagine. With age comes wisdom and the loss of childlike innocence, but falsehoods are hard to discern and at times, preferable to the truth."

"How can you say so? Look at how Yusuf treated you based on a lie!"

Long lashes concealed her father's stare. "Jazirah, in all the years we have been at Shalabuniya, you have never asked if the allegations against me were indeed false."

She had never allowed the possibility to enter her mind. "A man who abhors lies as you do could not have betrayed his own brother's secrets. I trust you."

His arm came around her shoulder and gripped with uncommon strength. "I pray you may never have reason to doubt me."

"I could not." She sat up and his hand slid away. "Though I must now wonder if you have misgivings about my choice." As she continued to stare, the realization of his opinion dawned. "Oh, Father, you think I was wrong to refuse the offer."

"Jazirah, it is done."

"Still, you fault me for the decision."

"I held a father's wish for his daughter's happiness."

"And you think I could have been happy at the side of a man who has let you linger here? Even if my uncle believed he behaved justly, where was his son's pity after he ascended the throne? If Butayna felt any concern for our plight, enough to suggest marriage as a means to our freedom, I can guarantee her son did not share the sentiment. His inaction has told me all I care to learn of Muhammad ibn Yusuf. A man so indifferent to the plight of his family long imprisoned would not be a match for me."

"He cannot know how we suffer under Harun. Butayna will tell him."

Jazirah hated how his voice warbled. "Father, do you expect your optimism will comfort me when you leave this world? When Lubna and I must deal with Harun's brutality alone? You said Muhammad has his mother's pride. Will such emotion allow him to overlook my refusal? I think not. I have no reason to trust in the generosity of our Nasrid relations. You should have surrendered those expectations long ago."

He reached for her again. "My child, you are too young to be so embittered. Do not close your heart. It is the path away from love and the future."

She swiped at hot tears before they fell. "I have awaited our freedom for too long. This hope you cling to will not avail us."

Her father closed his eyes. "Yet, hope remains."

***

The weather worsened over the next five days, as did Prince Ismail's condition. Despite cold cloths on his brow, his fever remained unabated. Infusions of chamomile, mint, and crushed almonds brewed in a tea by Jazirah did not produce the results Lubna intended. Neither of them knew the cause of the illness, which had claimed two more lives in the interim. At first, everyone feared the plague had returned, but no black boils appeared on the bodies of the afflicted.

Following Lubna's directions, Jazirah gave her father sips of sesame oil to ease the burning pain in his throat, although she could do naught for the fiery sensation beneath his skin. Raised, red bumps dotted his forearms. Soon she could not even rely on her companion, for Lubna sickened. She complained daily of aches in her head and a fever sapped her strength.

The role of caretaker fell to Jazirah. When guards opened her cell each dawn, she tended to her family until her eyes burned and watered, and her head drooped from sheer exhaustion. She returned alone every night, the clank of the iron crossbar behind her an ever-present reminder of her entrapment in circumstances she could not control. During the short hours before dawn, she stared at the ceiling while sleep eluded her. Would freedom ever be hers? In rare instances where she slept, horrible nightmares followed in which Harun dragged her from her cell and displayed her father's lifeless body. She missed Lubna's nearness above all on those nights, having never been alone before.

At the end of a week, she resolved to break the vow made under duress. She washed her face in a basin of chilled water and dressed in the same clothes she had worn for the week, complete with the billowy tunic. The neckline scratched at her skin, which had developed a rash she chose to ignore. With her hair covered, she mounted the first flight of steps. Fatigue seeped through her limbs, but fear of losing the only people who loved her drove Jazirah down the hallway.

The first pair of sentries stationed on the landing displayed lascivious grins while they snatched at her clothes. She batted the questing hands away. Harun's men posed little threat to her. They feared his wrath more than they lusted for her.

Soon she stood at the corridor's end before a closed door. Harun usually ate his first meal of the day within the room.

She peeked at guards on either side of the entryway. "I want to see him."

The squat man closest to her shrugged. "Why should I care? I'd like to bend you over and see if your backside and legs are scrawny like the rest of you." His companion who stood nearby gave a raspy chuckle at the crude words. "But you wouldn't want that, would you?"

She bit back a sharp retort. Her fingers curled beneath the wide sleeves of the tunic, the tip of the dagger so close. If the fat toad tried anything, he would soon learn from his error.

She insisted, "Open this door now and let me speak to Harun."

"Are you mad? He's eating. No one bothers him in the morning. You forget?" The man punctuated each phrase with a poke in her chest. "No one, not even—"

She slapped his fingers away. "Don't you dare touch me, you ignorant boor!"

His beefy hand clamped on her arm and he shook her. "I'm touching you now. What will you do? You think you're still some princess in a castle. Would a princess have to scream for help? Cry out and see who'll come to you."

Sprays of his spittle struck her in the face. The door opened with a creak of the hinges. Her tormentor displayed yellowed teeth in a wide grin. His fellow guardsmen laughed, pitiless.

"She doesn't have to utter a sound. You never will again."

In an instant, Jazirah tasted gobs of copper in her mouth. She looked down in mute horror at the red blobs splattered across the black wool. Blood. She raised her gaze to the source. A metallic silver tip protruded between the sentry's gaping lips, from the wrong direction. His eyes bulged wide in their sockets. He gurgled and twitched before his grip on her loosened. As his hand fell away, she tumbled and scrabbled backward. His companion pressed against the wall in mute horror, mouth agape.

Harun peered past the dead man's shoulder and looked down at Jazirah. "I warned them all of the consequences if even one touched you. This fool did not listen."

The jailor twisted and wrenched a curved dagger from the base of his victim's skull. The body slid to the floor, where convulsions ceased. Harun gripped the *khanjar*, mired in gore and mayhap as long as Jazirah's forearm, by the hilt. He wiped the bloodied blade on a cloth spattered with grease stains, which he discarded next to the motionless figure. Harun sneered at the viscous pool forming beneath the head and shifted his stance as the blood edged toward his leather boot. He stepped over the body and approached Jazirah, a final command issued to the guard at the doorway. "See to the removal. Send a eunuch to clean this filth."

The three remaining men rushed forward and bore the murdered sentry away.

Harun crouched over Jazirah, hair falling over his eyes. He stank of onions and garlic as usual. His slow smile from him softened features she detested. "Are you injured?"

She flicked her tongue at the corner of her lips and drew his stare to her mouth.

She whispered, "I'm not hurt." After two deep, calming breaths, she forced a measure of steely resolve into her voice. "He did not harm me."

"Do you see how I would kill for you, if only you would be mine?"

Harun was a foul murderer. He had done her no special service by dispatching one of his men. He relished the act and the terror he inspired in others.

With a shudder, her gape strayed to the dagger he brandished. "You need no excuses, including defense of me, to act according to your nature—"

He bared his teeth in a vicious snarl and reached for her. She yelped. "Don't!"

With the stained tip of his forefinger, he lifted her chin. Tremors coursed through her limbs. A gentle touch from this brutal man terrified her more than his coldblooded method of dispatching a subordinate. "I have told you before, I would never cause you pain."

She was not so desperate as to believe him. Like her father, Jazirah despised liars. "You've hurt Lubna! You used and discarded her after you no longer wanted her body. When you discovered she carried your child, you raped and battered her."

He stroked her jawline. "You are pure, not like Lubna. If you would only come to me, I could keep you safe. I tired of the tricks your slave learned in bed. Where is she? Have her exertions of late worn her out?"

"Lubna has the same malady my father suffers! What are these exertions?"

He fondled her flesh and sighed. "So sweet, so fair. How could I ever want her when I could have you?" She could not correct him for he continued, "Most of my men have had your slave in the last few days. What promises has she extracted from them after she spread her legs? She is like most whores, always desiring something. Thinks she can get it, too."

Jazirah recoiled. What had Lubna done for their sakes?

He asked, "Why did you seek me now? Are you ready to give me what I want most?"

His black brows knitted together. Vanity would not allow him to consider whether she held any other purpose.

She blurted out, "My father needs a doctor!"

His hand fell away. Her gaze darted between the *khanjar* and his expressionless face. He stood, towering over her in silence before sheathing his weapon. She heaved a ragged breath. Her stomach pitched at the thought of pleading with him, but if he required it, humbling herself would be no trouble. For her father's sake, she would do anything.

"Harun, I beg you! He is so frail. At any day now, he could draw his last breath. I will do whatsoever you ask... even... I would give myself to you if only he might live!"

The moment the words issued from her lips, Jazirah clamped her hand over her mouth. Then her fingers slid away. She had vowed to do anything for her father and she meant to keep the oath. What did her virginity matter? If she exchanged brief pain for the misery of her father, the sacrifice would be well worth the shame. Without the prospect of marital joy, what difference would it make to her future if she submitted to Harun now?

He never spoke, only stared at her. Then he bent and offered his hand. She hesitated for the space of two breaths before she pressed her fingers against his palm. He hauled her to her feet. The moment she stood upright, he released her and bowed. She stared at his exposed neck and wished she might stab him just there.

"Did you hear me? Harun, this is my solemn vow and I will hold to it if you'll agree to send for a doctor. Please! Say something. Just give me a sign of your pledge!"

He straightened and gave her a brusque nod. "Your father and Lubna will have a doctor's care. I want Prince Ismail to live long enough for the day when you are mine. You will give me what I want, Jazirah. You will be my wife."

Her belly fluttered. He could not mean it. "Harun, I did not say I would marry you." One thing to submit to him in a moment's disgrace. Quite another to endure a life with him for her husband forever.

His fingers fastened on her wrist. She cried out.

"What did you think I wanted, Jazirah? I will have you for my wife. Now, take off your *hijab*. Let me see your hair. After we have married, you shall wear it unbound in my presence only. Do as I command if you want me to summon the doctor now."

He let her go. Her fingers trembled as she raised them to her head. With a quick pull of the yellowed cloth, she whipped the veil away.

Harun stretched out his hand, while she stood rigid. He lifted the thick tresses and raked his fingers through the length of her hair.

"If you ever allow another man to see the glory of you, he will writhe in unimaginable pain. Never you, my beauty, but your tender heart could not bear pains endured for your sake. Put on your veil. Never remove it except by my order."

She nodded, rendered mute as when she had first met him, and his barbarity frightened her. She replaced the veil atop her head. He tugged a corner and ensured the cloth covered her hair.

His smile returned. "Go. You should be with your father when the doctor comes."

She spun on her heels and raced down the steps. She did not stop even when she reached her doorway and the adjacent cell where Lubna's pitiable groans echoes beyond the walls. Instead, Jazirah fled to the parapet facing the White Sea, bent over the wall, and heaved until bile soured her breath. Then she sagged on the floor and cradled her head in her hands.

Chapter 4
The Doctor

Princess Jazirah

Shalabuniya, Al-Andalus or Salobrena, Andalusia
Safar 757 AH or February A.D. 1356 or Adar 5116

Alone in her cell, Jazirah untied the two leather straps knotted around her forearm. The small weapon she carried, half the length of Harun's *khanjar*, clattered on the cobblestones. How could she ever pick the blade up again?

An ice-cold rinse of her mouth left her teeth chattering. A fetid aftertaste from the well water lingered. She wrenched off the veil Harun had soiled with his bloodied hand and pulled the splattered tunic over her head. She sat back on her heels and drew a lungful of air before dunking her hands into the water basin. Although her fingers clenched, she scrubbed at the flesh. No blood coated her hands, but they were just as unclean as if she had wielded the *khanjar* and taken the life of Harun's guardsman.

How had her existence altered so soon? The well-being of her father and Lubna meant much, but a life at Harun's side would be unbearable. A shudder drew a pain-filled gasp from her and she clutched at her side. In mute disbelief, she shook her head, unable to fathom the words her jailor had uttered. He did not wish to abuse her body as he had done with Lubna. Instead, he intended to make Jazirah his bride. Her stomach knotted and another dry heave overtook her. Head bowed, she waited for the spasm to pass.

After the agonized ending of her mother and younger sister, death held no surprises for Jazirah. The specter of it had haunted the grounds of Shalabuniya's fortress from the start of Harun's term as her father's jailor. Guards disappeared at random and bodies washed ashore, throats slashed. No one questioned the source of these injuries, not within Harun's hearing. How would Jazirah bear the touch of such an evil man?

"I cannot do this. If God is in heaven, don't let this be the road I must tread."

She cradled her forehead. Gharnatah held hope for her. Was there still time? Could she send word to Muhammad, an acceptance of his proposal, if only to escape Harun? The jailor would have to let her go if the Sultan demanded it. Muhammad would receive her desperate appeal for help and he would.... She rubbed at her temple. He would laugh at her and consider her a fool for having spurned him in the first place. How he must have blustered, red-faced when his mother brought news of the refusal. Jazirah's foolish pride had drawn her into this difficulty. How could she undo a stupid mistake?

"Anything would be better than a union with Harun, even marriage to Muhammad."

Except she would never be able to convince the Sultan of her need now. Only he could shield her from Harun's attentions, but she had spurned Muhammad's interest. Even if she held the faintest prospect of gaining his aid, how would a letter reach him? Unless ink, reed, and vellum miraculously appeared in her cell, she could not compose the contents of any message. Harun would never send a dispatch, especially when the contents of the missive undermined his plans. She could not persuade any guard to go to *Al-Qal'at al-Hamra* in secret, not without some shameful promise or action on her part, as Lubna would have done. Why had her slave taken ill so soon, especially when Jazirah needed her the most?

Jazirah's eyes watered as hopelessness weighed upon her shoulders. Her plea would never reach Gharnatah. For the first time, neither her father nor Lubna could guide her actions. She had to find the means to escape Harun by herself.

From above, his thundered orders intruded on her thoughts. Mayhap he summoned a doctor after all. A weary sigh eased between her lips. The savage might keep his pledge in anticipation of her acquiescence alone. How could she give in?

She rose from the ground, hands immediately brushing at the muck on her skirt. A quiet hush descended on the hallway as she stepped out and crept to her father's cell. Inside, Lubna rested on a clean bed of straw Jazirah had scattered earlier below the wall. Her father kept to his usual spot near the window, where he shivered and murmured in a deep torpor. She knelt and stared hard at his chest area, willing it to rise and fall beneath the blanket. He shuddered despite the brazier placed between the window and his position. Each shallow breath required all his energy. The bumps on his face had crusted over and white fluid seeped from them. A cough wracked his body and his head lolled toward the adjacent wall. If he should die, he must face the opposite way toward the *Qiblah*, the direction of prayer oriented to Makkah.

She sat back on her heels beside Lubna who opened her eyes. A cluster of red pustules obscured the slave's features. Jazirah bowed her head and tried to stifle her sobs.

"Don't... cry." Lubna's thin, pale lips had cracked and peeled. "Your father?"

"He is with us," Jazirah whispered.

'He will… live. Help… will come."

Courage had departed Jazirah, but she would not squash Lubna's hopes.

***

A doctor arrived in the midst of the noonday prayer time at *Salat al-Zuhr*. When Harun brought him, Jazirah welcomed the interruption.

Harun said, "This is Pharez ben Abraham ben Zarzar. All of Gharnatah knows his reputation and of his son, Abraham ben Zarzar, two of the most skilled physicians in Al-Andalus."

While she had never heard of either man, Jazirah acknowledged a Jewish physician in attendance to one Muslim patient and his stricken Christian slave would be better than no care at all. She stared at the doctor's black robes emblazoned with a yellow star at the left shoulder. His hood encompassed all but a few grizzled curls. A whimsical smile, almost hidden behind a drooping mustache and full beard, perplexed her more than his presence.

She donned gloves on her fingers and linen for her face as Lubna had advised. Then Jazirah led the doctor into the adjoining cell. He took methodical care in setting down a small casket borne by leather straps atop the lone stool. With deep-veined hands, he opened the box. A strong aroma of mint permeated the room. Glass vials clinked as he inspected and rattled a few filled with dried herbs and powders. He returned four bottles to the box and replaced them with others. He had not looked at the patients. Instead, he hummed or muttered to himself. Just when Jazirah could bear no more of his inattention, he straightened with a grunt and rubbed the middle of his back.

He flashed a gap-toothed grin. "Let's see what we have here. Hmmm. Ah."

The doctor shuffled to her father's side, gave a cursory glance, and then shook his head. What did his action mean? Then he moved to Lubna. The same worrisome gesture did not follow. Was Lubna on the mend with hope fading elsewhere?

"Can you help them, doctor?"

Pharez wiggled a gnarled finger at her. "Patience is required, hmmm. And time."

She rolled her eyes. Given his aged appearance, he might not have the benefit of time. Then she eyed Harun. Where had he scrounged up this relic?

The warden gripped the doorpost and perched like a vulture eyeing a carcass. His lips parted as if he planned to speak, but Jazirah turned and ignored him. His possessive gaze bored into her back. How long did she have before he revealed his absurd intentions? Her father would refuse consent, of course, but terrible costs would ensue. No one thwarted Harun and lived. A reminder Jazirah did not need.

Her father groaned and his head rolled away from the eastern-facing window again. Jazirah moved to him, but Pharez stopped her. "The light disturbs him. A common response in cases such as these."

"Then you know what ails him? Please, can you help?"

The doctor did not answer. Instead, he looked beyond her. "Jailor, have you a large piece of colored cloth, hmmm? Preferably dyed red. Linen or cotton would do."

Before Harun could answer, Jazirah asked, "What will you do with it?"

Pharez's lips twitched. "Ah, I remember youthful curiosity and the desire to know everything all at once. Mastery of the spirit will be difficult for you—"

Jazirah's chest tightened and her nails dug into her palm. "You do not know me. Do not speak above your station again." Her muscles quivered as she restrained herself from slapping the man for his insolence.

The physician lifted his tufted eyebrows and offered her a conciliatory nod, before his mouth relaxed again into a warm, wide smile. "Ah, as you say. The cloth is a covering for the window. I'll need two poles to hang the material. Jailor, if you please."

Behind Jazirah, Harun sucked his teeth. Soon his footfalls resounded down the hall and faded. Jazirah breathed a sigh and pressed against the wall.

Pharez took a pair of gloves and two vials. "Have you some water?"

Jazirah nudged the half-filled bowl beneath the window with her toe. A little of the filmy liquid inside sloshed over the rim. The doctor stared at the puddle, creases etched in his brow.

Then he regarded her. "What relation do you bear this stricken man?"

Jazirah answered, "He is my father."

"Ah. And the woman?"

"Lubna has cared for me since birth. She is the only mother I can recall."

"Then for love of the sole parent remaining to you and one whom you think of as your mother, get them fresh water. It must be clean, hmmm."

"The well has been polluted since the sickness befell this place."

"Water from the sea can be refined for my purpose."

"Harun will not let me leave this place to go to the shore."

"I will go in your stead."

"But you'll take forever!" Despite his deepened frown, she rushed on. "You are an old man and I'm not sure my father or Lubna can wait upon your return. We must get other help."

"There is no one more qualified in Shalabuniya. Why do you think your warden summoned me from my daughter's wedding, hmmm? He must have some great stake in saving these lives for he threatened my failure would ensure death."

"Harun said so?" By the Prophet's beard, he intended to guarantee Jazirah's father lived, if only to see Harun's triumph. There could be no other cause for his insistence.

She swallowed. "For how long will you be gone?"

"No longer than necessary."

"If my father dies, you will be sorry, not just because Harun swore retribution."

Pharez's irritating smile returned, broader than before. "Ah, you certainly have the impetuosity of your age. Delay will not endanger your father or trusted servant. Remain here with those whom you love. Believe me, your presence provides more comfort than I ever could."

She pressed a hand to her chest. "Are you saying you can't help them?"

He went to the doorway and paused beneath the lintel. "Calm yourself. A preliminary examination requires careful scrutiny, but I have seen this sickness before. You did well to wear gloves and cover your face, hmmm. The red plague spreads easily without such precautions."

"The red plague," she repeated. "What is the red plague?"

"Can your father afford to wait while I explain?"

"Then go and hasten back with your water. Hurry!" She turned her back on him.

He added a soft chuckle to his response. "You possess such an imperious tone, but I see it is part of your nature. I should have recognized the source before now...."

Before she could demand an explanation of his puzzling statement, he withdrew.

She sank beside her father. "You must give battle to this red plague, whatever it may be. Fight, Father, as you have never fought before."

***

The muscles in Jazirah's legs had cramped by the time the doctor returned. His effervescent whistling stirred her from a fitful slumber. Brilliant orange sunlight streamed through the tattered window screen. She raised her drooping head and rubbed a crick from the back of her neck. Then she observed her father and Lubna, both of whom drew labored breaths.

Two of Harun's men entered the room. They put down a steaming pot set on wooden shafts pushed through the vessel's handles. A third guardsman idled in the doorway, a bolt of red cotton wrapped around his hands. He flashed Jazirah a gap-toothed grin. She ignored his leer.

She asked, "Doctor, what hour is it?"

"I have heard two of your calls to prayers since my arrival. It will be dusk soon."

Jazirah shook her head. Had she slept for so long?

The doctor took the cloth from the man in the doorway and shooed the rest of Harun's mercenaries. A grunt escaped him as he drew the first of the poles up. Jazirah stood and rushed to his side, helping him to lift the olive wood.

"You should have told Harun's men to do this before you dismissed them. An old man such as you should not strain his back with such a task."

"Ah, your care and interest in my well-being is welcome." With her assistance, he propped the two rods along the wall, neither piece of wood taller than Jazirah stood. Then he draped the length of the cloth over the upright end, so the material shielded the room from the fiery glare of the setting sun. He rubbed his hands together.

"As I've said before, those who suffer the red plague indicate some sensitivity to light. This cloth covering helps."

"Tell me more of this red plague. I have never heard of it."

"Among my fellow physicians it is at times called the small pox, to differentiate from the larger pockmarks left by other virulent diseases. It mars the body with reddened pustules. Survival is rare after two weeks, and results in small, pitted scars. I suspect you once had the red plague as a child. Will you allow me to inspect your hands?"

"I'll permit it."

He clutched her left hand. "Ah, here it is! Did the woman who served you never explain these marks? Do they range further?"

Jazirah looked at the thin line of whitened indentations extending upward from the apex of her thumb and forefinger. They had marred her flesh from childhood. As a result, she kept even her forearms covered during the hottest summers in Al-Andalus. Now she pushed the sleeves of the wool tunic and her *qamis* back, revealing the skin beneath the cotton shirt.

Pharez smiled and nodded, but the source of his amusement eluded her. Then he frowned and glanced at Lubna.

"It is as I suspected. You were a victim of the red plague in your youth. Something vexes me though. If, as you say, this woman has been with you from childhood, she should not have become sick again."

"I don't understand."

"Those who endure and survive the red plague do not suffer in subsequent exposures. Are you certain this woman has never left you for any length of time?"

"If she did so, I'm unaware of it."

"Ah, as you say. I'll tend to both patients now."

First, he removed the blankets atop her father and Lubna. Jazirah covered her mouth and stifled a cry at the thick clusters of pustules on their palms and soles. The doctor took the bowl of fetid water, went out of the room, and returned with an empty vessel. He tipped the iron pot slightly, poured some of its contents in the bowl, and swished the water around before he exited the cell again. Upon his return, he added vial after vial of substances into the cracked bowl. He lowered himself to the ground with a heavy grunt and stretched out his legs, while he sprinkled water over crushed dried garlic, sandalwood paste, ground lemon peel, and a drop of honey along with other fragrant spices she did not recognize. Pharez retrieved a pestle from the box and pounded the paste with a sprightly, nervous energy despite his obvious age. He even hummed to himself as if his patients faced no grave circumstances.

After an interminable time passed with only his mutterings to break the monotonous silence, Jazirah groaned. "What are you doing?"

"Making medicine for the scars. Have you a beaker or a cup, hmmm? When the purified water is cooled, these people must drink."

She went to her cell and came back with the wooden mug she and Lubna typically shared. It clanged on the stone ground, harder than she intended, for the physician flinched and stared wide-eyed at her.

She mumbled an apology and bolstered herself beside the window.

Pharez said, "You should rest. If you are overwrought, you cannot help."

"Still, I'll remain here, doctor."

He mused, "Stubbornness, too. Another trait I should have anticipated."

"You speak as if you know me although you do not."

"We have never met before, but I know your family in Gharnatah. Hmmm. My relatives have served the Sultanate of Gharnatah since the days of your ancestor Sultan Muhammad *al-Fakih*, blessed be his name. My father was a physician before me, my son undertook the training and, if *El Dio* will allow, his son Moses ben Zarzar shall be an apprentice. Most Nasrids bear the distinct features common in your family. Ah, always the dark hair and the sharp-eyed gaze." He jerked the pestle in her father's direction. "This man, he is Prince Ismail ibn Ismail who was the *Raïs* of Wadi-Ash. Despite the ravages of time, I would know him as the former governor of the city, a son of Sultan Abu'l-Walid Ismail, blessed be his name. Your father bears the likeness of his brother Sultan Abdul Hajjaj Yusuf, blessed be his name."

A momentary jolt stymied her breath. Then she leaned forward, intent. "If you know the Nasrids, you are also aware of how Sultan Yusuf imprisoned my father by an unjust decree. Yusuf's son keeps my father here unfairly."

The doctor waved his hand. "Squabbles among the Nasrids are a mystery to me."

"I'm telling you the truth! My uncle is dead, but Muhammad retains my father as his prisoner, never inquiring after—"

"If you will forgive my interruption, Sultan Abu Abdallah Muhammad, blessed be he, is a just and wise ruler in the image of his father and his ancestor Sultan Muhammad *al-Fakih*, blessed be his name. Our Sultan will not overturn his father Yusuf's decree without just cause. Would you go against your own nature, hmmm?"

When she did not answer him, Pharez attended to his duty again, adding, "You may not wish to hear it, but you are the same as your royal cousin. The past influences both of your perspectives. Mayhap one day, misunderstandings may be resolved."

Jazirah sighed and pressed back on the cold stone. As a Jew in the Sultanate, the doctor would remain beholden to his Moorish masters, never risking the loss of their patronage even to help a young woman and her stricken father.

Then Pharez asked, "Will you tell me your name, princess of Gharnatah?"

"I am Jazirah bint Ismail. I have not held a title for a long time."

Pharez stopped the pounding. "You are a Nasrid. You will always be a princess. Royal blood will always bear out." Then he added, "This poultice might reduce the scars. Will you apply it to the woman's skin, while I do the same for your father, hmmm? The mix will ruin your gloves."

"Pieces of cloth mean little when compared to my family." She stood with him and tended to Lubna, coating the afflicted areas with Pharez's remedy, while he worked on her father.

Afterward the doctor took a cup of water and sprinkled some dried green herbs into it. "Now, they must drink. The woman first."

Jazirah coaxed Lubna from her fitful sleep. "You were right. Help did come. There's a doctor here. Open your eyes and see."

Long lashes fluttered as Lubna opened her red-rimmed eyes. With a vacant, unfocused stare, she scanned the room until her gaze rested on Jazirah's face. She opened her mouth as if to speak, but Jazirah placed a finger to her lips.

"There's no need to talk. Rest and drink this medicine."

Jazirah held out her hand for the cup, which Pharez tendered. "Half a measure in small sips will do. No more."

Jazirah cradled the slave's nape and lifted her head. Lubna gagged as the vessel touched her lips, but Jazirah encouraged her. "It will help. You must drink."

Lubna could bear no more and pushed the vessel away. Jazirah handed it to the doctor who went to her father. Despite several attempts, Pharez could not rouse him.

Jazirah sprang to her father's side and whispered in his ear, "Please, Father. There is life left in you, and hope. You told me so. You must awaken."

His shallow breaths stirred Jazirah's greatest fears, but she warded off despair. "Father! Open your eyes! You will not die today. The cells at *Al-Quasaba* did not kill you in the first days of your imprisonment. The journey here did not ruin you, not even when the soles of your feet blistered and your lips cracked. You survived the loss of my mother and your child. You will endure this! You are a Nasrid, a prince of Gharnatah. A warrior's spirit dwells inside of you derived from your proud ancestor Muhammad *al-Fakih*. We who number among his descendants, we are fighters, we never surrender. Do you hear me, Father?"

A groan escaped him. "I... hear. Not... deaf, my child."

Jazirah could have wept copious tears, but she held them at bay and raised her father's head, while Pharez pressed the cup against her father's parched lips.

"Slow sips as the doctor has ordered, Father. Drink. Drink and live."

When her father finished, Jazirah permitted him to rest undisturbed again. She looked at the physician, who smiled at her.

"What happens now, doctor?"

"We wait. Hmmm."

In the evening, Pharez packed up his box and prepared to leave. "I will come again in the morning after your second *Salat*. Remember, more of the water with the herbs I have left. Once when your last call to prayer occurs and then again before dawn."

Jazirah leaned against the doorpost and nodded. "You must do something for me. I need you to send word to Gharnatah, to Sultan Muhammad."

The doctor's fingers hovered over the latch before he closed his medicine chest. "Ah, my princess, I am not a courtier or a confidante of the Sultan. A brief introduction from Abraham does not merit the privilege of intimacy with the lord of Gharnatah. However, my son—"

Jazirah waved away his concerns. "Yet, you will do this for me, so I, and mayhap my father, may be in your debt."

When he stared at her in silence, Jazirah knew she had gained his compliance. "Tell my royal cousin the offer is acceptable and he should send an envoy to Shalabuniya."

"Shall I write no more than these two vague lines? Will he know your meaning?"

"He will. If you do this, and my father lives, we shall both owe you a great deal."

"How do you intend to pay?" Pharez cast a weary glance around the shabby cell.

"You shall see, doctor." When he raised his eyebrows, she added, "I am a Nasrid. My word once given is good enough to establish faith between you and me."

***

Pharez came each day and with every visitation, Jazirah's father and Lubna improved. After Harun learned the news from the doctor, the jailor accompanied him always. Jazirah chafed inside. She could not determine whether Pharez had sent her message while Harun hovered and waited to execute his horrible plan to claim her for a bride.

As the pustules on her father's face scabbed and dried up, little by little his normal features returned. The physician warned the pockmarks would likely be permanent, but Jazirah did not care as long as her father remained among the living.

While she sat beside him, applying a poultice to his hands, one of Harun's men entered the cell. He spoke in hushed tones with the warden.

Harun's lips thinned and an irritated grunt filled his throat. "The Sultan's soldiers? Here? What message have they brought?"

"Their captain did not tell me." The guard hung his head, sheepish.

"Did not or would not? Wretched bastards!" Harun sucked his teeth and glared at Jazirah.

She tended to her father and prayed Harun believed she had not overheard. She dared not lift her gaze to find Pharez seated against the wall with his pestle, making more medicine and muttering to himself as usual. He did not know the relief his swift actions afforded her, but after she married the Sultan, Jazirah would ensure Pharez received an ample reward. She would convince her new husband of the duty.

Harun shoved his man through the doorway. "Well, find out their purpose!"

With a final frown cast over his shoulder, the jailor left as well. Once his footfalls faded, Jazirah set aside the bowl of poultice and rushed to Pharez. When she grabbed his shoulders, the Jew cried out.

"You did it, doctor!"

"Hmmm. Did what, my princess?"

"You sent the missive to Muhammad and his men have come! Didn't you hear what Harun said before he left?"

Pharez's brow crinkled beneath his black hood. "But I have not addressed the Sultan. I told you, I could not dare make such a serious breach. I wrote to my son in Gharnatah for his advice on the matter only yesterday. The herald could not have reached my Abraham by now."

Jazirah shook her head. "What are you saying? It is impossible. Why then are the Sultan's soldiers here?"

"Hmmm, I do not know, but I could not have summoned them, my princess. Mayhap you misheard Harun's conversation."

"I did not! I know what he said."

From behind her, Jazirah's father called out, "What... what is it, my child?"

She crouched at his side. "Muhammad has sent his soldiers. I will go to them and convince them to free us from this place."

His frail hand brushed hers. "Daughter... do not endanger yourself... for my sake."

She looked from him to a sleeping Lubna and back again. "Oh, Father, to whom do I owe a duty if not you? Rest. I will not come to harm. I mean to find Muhammad's soldiers. We cannot remain here any longer. Muhammad may demand any price he wishes for his favor, but I will have it today!"

This time, she evaded her father's furtive touch and stood. "Stay with them, doctor."

"You should not leave, my princess. Do not give your father cause for worry."

She ignored Pharez and moved to the doorway. At the opposite end, Harun spoke with four of his men. When she appeared, he glanced beyond the circle of mercenaries. She met his gaze and held it. To reach the Sultan's soldiers, she would have to get past the man, and to the upper landing. She drew a deep breath and steeled herself for desperate action.

Two of Harun's men left him and approached Jazirah. She delved for her dagger within the billowy sleeves of her tunic. Dismay summoned a gasp. She had not tied the weapon by leather tongs to her forearm, not since the day after Harun had stabbed his guardsman.

The mercenaries bypassed her and went into her father's room. Jazirah frowned as they took up positions at the wall just inside the doorway. "What are you doing?"

Harun closed the distance between them in rapid strides. "They are following my orders, for the protection of those within."

His hand clamped on her arm and she jerked away. "Don't touch me!"

Harun squeezed, and she clamped her jaws together, stifling a pain-filled wince. He leaned close, peering into her eyes. "You are mine. I will touch you when and where I like."

Her father wheezed, "Harun... take your filthy hands... from my daughter!"

Pharez colored. "Jailor, the ill treatment of those in your charge is a dereliction of your duty. I insist you release the princess."

Harun let go of Jazirah and stepped inside the cell. He stomped to Pharez's side and stood over him. To his credit, the doctor neither cowered nor shrank away. Harun grabbed Pharez by the throat and slammed his head against the wall. Jazirah screamed and covered her mouth with her hands.

"What concern of yours is it? I could choke the life from you, old man."

Jazirah yelled, "Don't hurt him!"

Harun glanced over his shoulder at her. "Worry for yourself, princess."

"Run!"

Jazirah needed no prompts from her father. She dashed down the corridor, even as Harun cried out, "You two, stay here! Keep them inside!"

His heavy footfalls spurred Jazirah on, but the other pair of guardsmen blocked her path. Even before she reached them, Harun's fingers closed on her arms and dragged her backward. She twisted and struck out at him with a free hand, which he caught in midair. He hauled her up against him. Her chest constricted, but still she pummeled her captor.

Pandemonium had set in above stairs. Loud curses and grunts, and the clang of metal against metal echoed. Harun hauled Jazirah in a steady retreat to the opened door of her cell.

"You men, guard this door. Don't let the Sultan's soldiers inside."

Harun shoved her into the room. A metallic gleam caught her eye. Her dagger! Harun pushed the door closed. The iron bolt on the outside slammed into place.

His breath hot and harsh against her neck, he murmured, "The Sultan has sent his men to claim you. He will never have you."

"You can't keep me here, Harun! Let us go."

"You promised you would be mine!"

She twisted in the circle of his arms. "I did not! Muhammad made a proposal of marriage, accepted long before you professed your intent. Release the others and let us leave. Muhammad's men will have your head if you don't."

He reached between their bodies for the brass fastener of the belt around his cloak. "If I cannot have you willing, I'll have you all the same. We'll see if the Sultan wants you then."

He could not mean to do it. Regardless, she would never let Harun rape her.

Harun wrestled with the belt and his hold loosened. She pushed away and dived for the edge of the blanket, the dagger hidden beneath its folds. Harun fell upon her in an instant. A wild beast, he covered and pinned her body to the ground. She gripped the hilt, but his hand closed on her thin wrist and squeezed until she let go. Something hard pressed against the back of her thigh before Harun ripped her skirt and exposed flesh to the cold air in the cell. He wrenched away the *hijab* and his fingers fisted in the thick curls beneath her veil. He nuzzled her neck. Disgusted, she reared up and smashed the back of her head against his nose, but other than a heavy grunt, he remained undeterred. With a free hand, she clawed at his ear, but he gripped both her wrists in a merciless hold. With the other hand, he pushed aside her skirt and pawed at her thighs.

Then the door thudded and shook on its hinges.

Jazirah screamed as he rolled and twisted her on to her back. Finding Harun's forearm exposed, she bit him hard. His yowl of pain gave her a moment's respite. She grabbed her dagger once more and aimed wildly. His fingers closed on hers. He forced her on to her back again and straddled her, pressing his full weight atop her body. He backhanded her twice, before he gripped the edge of the blade. Blood seeped from his closed palm, but he held on. She would not release the weapon until Harun slammed his first against her right cheek. Red spots spiraled in a haze. Her dagger spun away and clattered in some far corner, too far to be of use to her now.

The doorway splintered and swung back on its hinges with a terrifying thud against the wall. A curved ax protruded from the shattered wood. Red-caped men burst into the room. The lead man brandished a bloodied sword. A fearsome scar split his features in half. She had seen him before.

"Get up!" he ordered, his weapon poised at Harun's back. "I won't tell you again."

Harun aimed spittle at the guard. His grip on Jazirah's wrists loosened. "She's mine! If—"

In the instant of his distraction, she tugged Harun's dagger from him and drove it into the middle of his chest. Blood spurted and covered her. A long shudder ran through him. He stared with widened eyes. She heaved a deep breath. Tears trickled. Between their bodies, the tip of the Gharnatah warrior's blade had pierced Harun's back and protruded from his belly. Skewered on both weapons, the jailor breathed his last. He crushed Jazirah beneath dead weight.

Her rescuer wrenched his blade from the body and rolled it aside. "Princess, I am Alfonso Ruiz, captain of the guard for the honorable Sultana Butayna, the *Umm al-Walad* of Gharnatah. At the behest of her son, our great Sultan Muhammad ibn Yusuf, I have come to take you and your family from this place. Are you hurt?"

She whispered, "I am not. The blood is... was... it is not mine."

He nodded and proffered his hand, while averting his gaze from her half-naked form. "Rise, my princess."

She tugged down the skirt over her bloodied thighs and accepted his help.

"My family?"

"They are safe next door with a contingent of my men and the doctors."

She repeated, "Doctors?"

"The *Umm al-Walad* has rendered the services of the royal physician Muhammad al-Shaquri, in response to your request for aid. When your letter arrived a week ago, the Sultan ordered Al-Shaquri to join my men in the journey to Shalabuniya."

"My letter?" Jazirah shook her head.

"Yours. Come, my princess."

He led her into the next room, where Jazirah's father and Lubna sobbed upon sight of her. Pharez stood close by, attentive to a younger, dark-bearded man. The two guards whom Harun had left behind now knelt beside the doorway, with swords pressed at their neck by men from Gharnatah. Both doctors bowed and straightened.

Pharez asked with a trembling voice, "My princess, are you hurt?"

She looked down at the blood. "I am well. Harun is dead." Then she knelt beside her father and looked to Lubna. "We are free of this place forever."

Chapter 5
Homebound

Princess Jazirah

Shalabuniya, Al-Andalus or Salobrena, Andalusia
Safar 757 AH or February A.D. 1356 or Adar 5116

Lubna clasped Jazirah's hand. "Oh, my princess. Did Harun try to…?"

"He did not rape me. I would not permit it. Instead, I—"

"If you will forgive the interruption, I killed the man when I discovered him atop the princess." Captain Ruiz bowed beside Jazirah. "The Sultan charged me with her protection. The warden's life became forfeit after what he did."

Jazirah raised her gaze to his. "I told you, captain, he did not harm me. I'm sure I will have bruises to bear, but Harun did not achieve his aim."

His brusque nod warned of his doubt. While she glared at him, the captain withdrew and spoke to the men who guarded Harun's mercenaries. Then Ruiz led his warriors out of the room. Huddled in a corner near the door, Pharez spoke with the Sultan's physician. At times, he gestured to the patients while Al-Shaquri listened and nodded.

Jazirah's father brushed her hand and drew her attention. He coughed and cleared his throat. "What will… what happens to us now?"

"I don't know, Father, but our days here are numbered. The captain came to take us to Gharnatah at the Sultan's command."

"Why?"

Jazirah shook her head. "I hope to understand Muhammad's purpose soon."

Time remained before their departure for discovery of the truth. For now, the enormity of their altered circumstances left Jazirah pensive. Harun dead at her hands and the long nightmare of captivity ended with Muhammad's decree. He had sent his men to retrieve her and her family because of a letter he believed Jazirah had written.

She could not fathom a logical reason for Muhammad's misperception, except one. She glanced at Lubna, who had closed her eyes. There would be an end to all suspicions later. For now, both patients needed rest.

Jazirah patted her father's chest. "I will return soon."

She rose and stepped out into the hallway, lit by the sun's glare from the door to the battlements, which the Sultan's bodyguards must have propped open. Their leader lounged against the wall at the opposite end, cleaning his bloodied blade with a wadded cotton strip. She plodded in his direction, avoiding even a surreptitious glance beyond the doorway of her cell. She could never enter the room again without the memory of the assault. Even now, she closed her eyes as the shade of Harun's presence reared up in her mind. His clawing fingers under her skirt. His fetid breath. She shook her head, opened her eyes, and banished all thoughts of him.

"Captain, I did not have the chance before now, but you must allow me to thank you for saving me from the warden of Shalabuniya."

He looked up from his task. "Your gratitude is unnecessary. I am a warrior for Gharnatah and its noble Sultan. I will slay all those whom he directs me to kill and defend anyone to whom he has granted his protection."

"Surely, you are more than your sword."

He grunted. The fearsome scar across his face twitched.

While unsure of how she should interpret his manner, Jazirah insisted, "I am also grateful for your... discretion with my family." She clasped her bloodied hands, forever marred by Harun's murder. "May I ask why you took full blame for the jailor's death? The blade with which I pierced his heart killed him as surely as the one through his back."

He pushed himself from the wall. He sheathed his sword before regarding her. "If I may question you, my princess, do you believe the man intended you grave harm?"

"He would have raped and ruined me. I could not have stopped him by my means alone."

"Do you have remorse over his death?"

"I would regret the loss of any life, but not his in truth. He was a vile dog."

"Then why should it matter how he met his end? He is dead. Forget him. Live."

"I intend to." She resolved against ever thinking of Harun again. "In the meantime, I'll require your help."

"You shall have it, my princess."

"My father and Lubna will need food."

"The meager stores my men found are rotted and mold-covered. Fit for pig slops."

Then Harun had not lied. He had not kept excess food. Still, how had he eaten each day?

"You will not find pigs in this land, captain."

"I noticed. We discovered a mass of coin within strong boxes inside the warden's quarters."

Harun had kept money to buy provisions. For himself, no doubt, but where had he obtained the funds?

"I'll give the money to you, my princess, all except a few *dirhams* for meals each day. I shall send some of my men with these copper coins to the marketplace for fresh fish now."

"Thank you, captain."

He waved away her appreciation with a sigh laced by irritation. "We cannot remain here for long. The Sultan expects us in Gharnatah. I shall not keep him waiting."

"My family needs a period of recuperation as much as the food."

He held up a forefinger. "I give one week. One. Then we ride for Gharnatah. Ready your family for the journey home."

She sighed and nodded. "I shall prepare them."

His stiff-necked bow followed before he mounted the stairs.

After his abrupt leave-taking, Jazirah sagged against the wall. With the benefit of the doctors, her family would have no difficult adjustment. A harder task awaited her, the journey to reclaim her past.

***

Jazirah's father thrived from the attentive care of two fine doctors and showed an improved state with each passing day. Jazirah's confidence in Pharez increased as she witnessed how his younger counterpart deferred to him and inquired about treatment of the red plague, while taking copious notes. By the third day after the arrival of the Sultan's men, Jazirah helped her father as he sat up and took broth on his own. He stood of his own willpower on the next day. Within hours, he staggered to the door of his cell and back again, although fatigued by the effort. Al-Shaquri trimmed his scraggly beard and aided him to the bathhouse at the fortress on the morning of the sixth day. Before noon, he sat outside despite the chill on the battlements. Jazirah stood and held a silver gilt mirror before him. His fingers traced the pockmarks, craters no bigger than a quarter of a *dirham.*

Then he laughed. "Do you think women will still find me handsome?"

Jazirah bent and kissed his brow. "You shall always be, Father. Besides, as a prince of Gharnatah, the title alone is enough to recommend you."

He chuckled again. In truth, she had no idea of his status. Would he govern a city again? What did the future hold for them? What did Muhammad expect of her, what would he demand? More importantly, could she bow to his wishes?

They went inside well before *Salat al-Zuhr.* Al-Shaquri awaited them, having brought fresh water in a basin along with prayer beads.

He bowed. "I thought we might prepare for midday prayer together, my prince."

"You are kind, doctor," Jazirah said. She ushered her father to a pallet, which the Sultan's men had brought from above stairs. She asked Al-Shaquri, "Have you seen Lubna?"

"I believe your slave may be embroiled in a vigorous discussion with the captain. I passed them on my way down, my princess."

Jazirah rubbed her forehead. In the days since Lubna's steady recovery, she had returned to her former state, which brought as much trepidation as joy. Her renewed vigor accompanied a sharp tongue, oft used against the captain.

Jazirah rose and said, "Again, thank you, doctor. I shall find Lubna."

The task did not prove difficult. Voices raised in mutual annoyance echoed as soon as Jazirah reached the landing. The captain and Lubna stood framed by sunlight at the castle's exit door, a steaming bucket of water discarded and ignored at both their feet.

Lubna upbraided the man. "Would you ruin all of her hopes? Are you an ignorant ass? What do you think the Sultan will say when he hears these words?"

"Woman, peace! I will not turn from my duty. My Sultan will ask about the events here. I shall not keep the truth from him."

"Including what you think you saw?"

"I know what I saw!"

"You know naught of what Jazirah has endured. Harun would have raped her six years ago when she was a child if I had not submitted to him."

Jazirah hid at the base of the steps where she might remain unnoticed. Had Harun set his mind to claiming her for a wife from the age of ten years old? Some brides in Al-Andalus married in early youth. According to Jazirah's father, her great-grandmother Fatima had done so, bearing her firstborn many years ago after a childhood marriage.

The captain continued the conversation. "Then it is as I have said to your princess, he received a just fate as should all rapists and molesters. None of this changes the incident in the princess' cell. I told you what I saw. The jailor had held the princess down and pressed himself between her legs. Her skirt gathered around her hips. When I killed him and pushed his body aside, there was blood on her thighs—"

Jazirah released her pent-up breath in a huff. He thought she had lied about her state. He planned to share his opinion with Muhammad.

"Stupid oaf! I saw her in the aftermath and there was blood everywhere! If you repeat this story of yours to the Sultan, imagine what he will believe! Jazirah comes to him untainted. I swear, if you cause the Sultan to presume otherwise, if your recklessness jeopardizes my princess' future, I'll have your balls!"

The captain chuckled. "The Moors took those long ago. Did you think the Sultan would allow any men except eunuchs in his harem?"

"Your master must have stolen your brains as well. I have warned you—"

"I am warned! Now leave off and let me carry this bucket along the stairs for you. Despite your fierce nature, you are a woman weakened by your ordeal."

"Just a weak woman, eh? Put it down! I don't need your help."

"If you are not weak, you have a woman's silly pride at least. Why does your mistress allow you to behave this way? You do not have the temperament of a slave. I suspect Prince Ismail and Princess Jazirah have never chastised you, as you deserve. Humph, no husband either, for a man would not permit such upheaval in his household."

"Mayhap you have not been a man for so long, you've forgotten how a real one would behave!" Despite the laughter ensuing from her brazen insult, Lubna continued, "I'm not your concern. Only know this. I will safeguard Jazirah's future with my life. I have failed her for far too long—"

"You bear a needless burden, woman. The princess survived her years here and escaped the cruel attentions of her warden because of you."

"Be quiet! You think to understand in less than a week what our lives at Shalabuniya have been. Consider my advice, captain, and the consequences for Jazirah if you do not. You will not ruin her! I won't let you!"

The captain's soft chuckle followed before his heavy-booted feet stomped away, their impact lessened with each step. Jazirah took to the stairs, preceding Lubna, and fled out to the ramparts.

"Jazirah?" Lubna called to her later. "Where are you?"

She answered, "I'm out here!"

Lubna joined her. Both of them looked out to sea in silence before the call to prayer resounded in a rich timbre. Empty boats bobbed on the water absent their crews. Not far from the escarpment's base, a lone figure rolled out his prayer mat, little more than dried reeds tied together.

Jazirah closed her eyes as the muadhdhin's voice summoned the faithful. The prospect of communion with God provided no comfort.

Lubna said, "Time for your ablutions."

Jazirah looked at her. "I will not neglect them, but we must talk first. Doctor ben Zarzar seemed to think I had experienced the red plague before. Was I ever sick like you and Father?"

"When you were six years old, your father went to Gharnatah with your mother, sister, and me. Your mother did not want to leave you behind, but you had developed a cough two days before. I remember the prince's assurances as we left Wadi-Ash. I begged to stay behind, but your mother needed help. She was carrying another child, only three months along. Mayhap the long-desired son of Prince Ismail."

Jazirah blinked back tears but kept her silence. Another innocent life lost to Yusuf's cruelty. Why had Allah allowed such anguish for her family?

Lubna continued, "A messenger arrived within the week after we reached Gharnatah. You were ill, as was the governess who cared for you in our absence. I returned to Wadi-Ash within a day to find those faded white marks on your flesh. The governess was dead in the antechamber next to the nursery. You had survived on the rotting remnants of your last meal, locked behind barred doors. The prince's cowardly guards must have ignored your cries. By the end of the following week, you showed no signs of sickness, only the scars left as a reminder. No one knew what had happened or if it would reoccur. Your father dispatched men who executed those who had abandoned you. Your mother insisted upon my return. She wanted you at her side. You appeared unaffected, just so happy to be with your parents again. They agreed no one would ever speak of the horrific period within your hearing. You never spoke of it again. They told me to forget. As a result, I vowed never to leave you again. The evening after my return to Gharnatah, Sultan Yusuf invited your father to dine with him. Later, I learned of the prince's arrest when the Sultan's soldiers came for us."

Jazirah sighed. One mystery uncovered and another awaiting resolution.

"Are you ready to tell me why Muhammad directed his soldiers to come here?"

Lubna shrugged. "I would have thought you knew the reason by now. I sent a letter to Gharnatah in your name, addressed to the *Umm al-Walad*. A pledge to accept the Sultan's marriage bargain if he would send his men and a doctor to save Prince Ismail's life. The guard whose tunic you wear has a brother who was always fond of me. When your father worsened, I decided to act. The brother helped."

"His last act. He is among the dead who fought against the Sultan's soldiers."

"He served his purpose. I regret his loss for his last kindness alone, naught more."

Jazirah shook her head. How many times had Lubna sold her body for the sake of a favor? "You have given Muhammad and the *Umm al-Walad* false hope."

"You never thought of marrying the Sultan to escape Harun?"

"I did in recent days, but now, you have made the choice for me! I cannot accept!"

"You would not dare refuse the union! Not after all I have won for you."

"With a lie."

"A lie born of love for you and your father."

"Is the act excusable now? A falsehood crafted for the greater good is no less an untruth. What am I to say when we arrive in Gharnatah?"

"Your marital vow. Wed Muhammad. Bear his children and love them. If you can, learn to love him, too. We must all make sacrifices in our lifetime. This is yours."

***

Gharnatah, Al-Andalus or Granada, Andalusia
Safar 757 AH or February A.D. 1356 or Adar 5116

Jazirah's first sight of the ochre plains of Gharnatah came on a damp morning. Her party paused at the top of a hillock. A heavy mist enshrouded the distant mountains, but one jagged white peak pierced the gray veil. Bleak clouds kept the sun at bay, so the hour remained uncertain.

"Home. Just as I remembered it," her father whispered.

Jazirah glanced at him before her gaze returned to the panorama. She recalled little else except the redbrick walls, naught of the pennons and flags unfurled from turrets atop the battlements, or the orchards and trees below the city's fortifications.

The captain urged their descent on the slope. He had kept to the strict intent of his words, permitting one week before their departure. Thereafter he set a furious pace, stopping only when Jazirah demanded he allow them to eat and pray at the proper times. They had spent the nights under the stars before resuming the northbound journey each day. Throughout the ride, Jazirah glared at the captain's back for the sake of her father and Lubna. Ruiz lacked compassion for even an old man like Pharez, who groaned at every jostle.

Her father waved his hand and pronounced, "The *Bab Ilbira*."

He indicated the main city gate. Jazirah smoothed a hand over her veil and ensured it remained in place against the high wind. Just then, the sun peeked through the canopy. Jazirah lifted her gaze and found the orb nearing its zenith. Little activity occurred outside of the walls, except for the sheep and cattle

57

turned out on the plains. The animals clustered together and braved the cold.

Jazirah ducked her head, grateful for the warm, hooded mantles the Christian warriors had provided. Beneath hers, she wore her usual threadbare clothing. What would Muhammad think once he saw her garments? A soft chuckle escaped her. Would embarrassment plague him at the state of his future bride? Good. Let him see all his neglect had wrought.

Her father asked, "What amuses you so? Are you happy to be at home?"

Her mare bumped against his and Jazirah tightened her grasp on the reins. "Oh Father, this could never be my home. I was born at Wadi-Ash."

"Jazirah, Gharnatah will always be our Nasrid home. It is where we return to, the abode of our ancestors, where they lie buried. One day, we will join them in the sacred earth of this place. While we live, Gharnatah shall always call to us."

She remained silent as they arrived at the city gate. The sentries did not question the Sultan's soldiers. Jazirah kept her head down for the rest of the journey, uncompelled by any desire to reacquaint herself with the overcrowded and noisome place. If her father recognized some irresistible appeal about Gharnatah, she did not. He had been born here. The city would never be her home.

Soon, the riders came to a bridge across a shallow river where again they crossed without questions from the patrol. Only when they began the ascent along a steep incline did she take in the vista of whitewashed houses across a sharp ravine and the gate ahead. Wood and iron groaned as the large double doors swung open. A smaller portal carved into the right side would not do for their horses. The curtain wall, also to her right, revealed cracks. Since her childhood, her father had repeated stories of their forbearers, the great rulers who rose against their enemies and claimed the Sultanate for themselves. Tales of civil war, strife, and blood, which her father took pride in, held no allure for Jazirah. He might see the majestic abode of their ancestors, but she viewed *Al-Qal'at al-Hamra* with a child's terror.

As they entered the precinct of the citadel, Jazirah closed her eyes. She and Lubna had spent one night in a dank basement cell of *Al-Quasaba* after Yusuf's soldiers came for them. None would tell her the whereabouts of her father, who had kissed her earlier in the day before he left their quarters for dinner with her uncle Yusuf. Her mother had taken Jazirah's fussy sister for an evening walk in the hopes of calming the babe. They never returned. Jazirah would not see her family again until she reunited with her mother the next morning, bound for

Shalabuniya. By the time of her father's arrival in the spring, Jazirah's mother and sister had been dead for over half of a year.

Tears threatened, but she sniffled and swallowed her sobs.

Lubna touched her arm. "Are you well, my child?"

"It's just the cold. I never want to feel a chill again."

Lubna patted her. "You will always have a warm brazier in your room."

They crossed a stone bridge and the environs altered. Redbrick walls gave way to sleek marble and paved cobblestones. A light dusting of snow covered the ground. No one waited to greet them as the captain dismounted, removed his gloves, and slapped them against his palm.

He approached Jazirah's father and bowed. "My prince, we go on foot. Can you manage it?"

"I will walk in the palace of my forefathers, Alfonso Ruiz."

With a grunt, he swung his leg over the stallion's back and alighted on the ground. He rubbed his hips as he did so but straightened quickly. He reached Jazirah first. She slid down, caught in the circle of his gangly arms. Her thighs burned since she had not ridden in years.

Her father's kiss brushed her brow line. "Are you ready for this trial?"

Her gaze met his. "I am not scared."

He released her and she locked arms with him. Lubna and the doctors joined them.

Pharez and Al-Shaquri shared a hearty embrace and exchanged the kiss of peace.

The younger man asked, "You will not join us? Prince Ismail owes his life to your diligent care. Our Sultan will surely wish to express his gratitude."

"Hmmm, no doubt, but I would be ashamed to stand before him, travel worn and weary. I am for home in the Jewish quarter, a bath, and the embrace of my grandchildren."

"Then allow one of the captain's men to escort you on the mount you rode here. He can always lead the horse back."

The elderly physician patted his hip. "Ah, not so soon again. I would prefer the walk. Blessed be thee."

"*Wa-'alayka,* Doctor ben Zarzar."

Pharez came to Jazirah and her father, cradling the wooden box of vials and medicines against his hip. He favored them with a bow, groaning as he stood. "*Shalom.* My prince, my princess, it has been my honor."

Jazirah spoke up before her father could. "It has been our privilege to know you. Captain, bring the saddlebags with the coin from Shalabuniya."

She delved inside the satchel Ruiz tendered and pressed a fistful against the doctor's hand. "This money can never amount to the full measure of my gratitude."

He looked down at *dinars* glittering in his palm. "My princess, this is too much."

"You gave my father and our trusted servant back to me. There is no sum equal to my family's worth."

"I thank you for your favor. Blessed be thee and joy to your house."

As the old man shuffled off, Jazirah breathed a sigh. "Go with God, doctor."

Her father tugged her arm. "Come, we must not keep the Sultan waiting."

The captain led them across the cobblestones to the guarded entrance.

Jazirah called out to him, "What day of the week is this?"

"The fourth day, my princess," he yelled over his shoulder, as sloped steps led them past façades with doorways on either side, down into a darkened room where faint light penetrated.

Jazirah's father said to her, "Public audience already occurred if your royal cousin has kept the traditions of his father. You must learn about court ritual and the ministers here. They are influential, even more so than the Sultan's family. The greatest among the councilors is a Christian convert, Ridwan. He resides in one of the largest houses within *Al-Qal'at al-Hamra*. He was Muhammad's tutor in his boyhood. At the Sultan's side is also the minister Ibn al-Khatib, a great friend of Yusuf when they were young. Learn what you can of these two men. If Muhammad's plans for you remain the same, you cannot hide behind harem walls, daughter. This place can be dangerous if you do not perceive the rules, which govern all conduct here. Due to my disgrace, many will view you with like-minded suspicion, your would-be husband among them. You will not have a friend here, Jazirah. Do you understand me?"

She replied, "I do."

He paused just inside the entryway. "Why have you brought us to this room?"

Jazirah squeezed his forearm. "Father, what is it?"

He did not answer. Instead, he challenged the captain. "This is the *mashwar* of my great-grandfather Muhammad *al-Fakih*, the council chamber where the Sultan judges his people. Why must we wait here? Are we to be judged?"

The captain's jawline twitched. "You will await the Sultan until after he has concluded his prayers. You stand here because it is my noble master's wish."

Before the exchange could continue, he bowed again and left them. Jazirah's father turned to Al-Shaquri with a questioning glance, which the young doctor returned by way of a nonchalant shrug.

Jazirah exhaled and leaned against one of four slender marble columns at the center of the space. Tiles in a zigzag pattern of blue, green, red, and white covered the lower half of the walls. Through a doorway behind her, golden light streaked through thin seams of the dark wood.

She read aloud one of the lines inscribed in the room. "Do not be afraid to ask for justice, for you will find it."

She turned to her father. "Is it true? Will we find justice, recompense for all losses?"

"None of us knows the future, my child." He went to the shuttered door leading out to a garden oriented to the west and the citadel beyond it.

Jazirah studied the glass lantern at the center of the room while Lubna joined her. All maintained a lengthy silence, until Al-Shaquri cleared his throat. "I'm certain there is good reason for the delay, my prince and princess."

Footfalls slapped the tiles, just before the *Umm al-Walad* rounded the northeast corner through another door. Black skirts swirled around Butayna's legs, as she halted and gripped the stucco wall.

"Prince Ismail, you're alive! I had feared the worst."

The doctor bowed in her presence, as did Jazirah's father, who cast a glance filled with meaning at his daughter. She mimicked his movement alongside Lubna.

Butayna said, "Please stand as you were. My slaves Jawla and Hafsa shall bring dates, cups of water, and pomegranate juice."

She had not released her grip on the wall. Her knuckles whitened, and her thin fingers shook, the pearl ring Jazirah saw at Shalabuniya still worn on the woman's left hand. Jazirah would have speculated as to the cause of Butayna's apparent disquiet, but two red-haired women provided a distraction as they distributed the light refreshments. Jazirah noted the absence of slave collars, but then Lubna had not worn one in her years of service.

Jazirah's father demanded of Butayna, "Does your son intend to keep us waiting?"

She approached him. "The captain of my guard is still talking with him." As she spoke, Lubna glanced at Jazirah. Butayna continued, "I am certain the Sultan shall not be much longer."

Indeed, he was not, as she predicted. Shadowed by six escorts draped in the same short, red capes as the captain and his men, a heavyset young man with a dark beard to match his thick hair preceded the others through the door Butayna had entered. Jazirah recognized him as the Sultan by his facial features alone, as if a younger version of her father had come into the chamber. His green brocaded *jubba* fit him neatly, revealing a slight paunch beneath the robe, no doubt the result of a life of luxury and comfort. His dark-eyed stare rose above full, high cheeks and flitted to Jazirah's father before he noted her presence. Then frown lines marred his brow. At a wave from her father, Jazirah and Lubna bowed before the lord of Gharnatah.

Butayna's captain accompanied the Sultan alongside a honey-colored woman whose silver bracelets clinked while she walked. With thick braids bared for all to see and one blue or silver bead affixed to the end of each plait, Jazirah would have taken her for a Sultana by her mantle dyed indigo and trimmed with ermine. Muhammad had a sister according to Jazirah's father, but the female at his back was no Nasrid. Up close, the bluish-purple sheen on her face became evident. One of the Berbers by the ink stains coloring her skin, likely a concubine of the Sultan.

For her part, the Berber female met Jazirah's stare with a curious, measured regard before she bowed. Jazirah sniffed and lifted her chin.

The Sultan neared while his entourage gathered with Al-Shaquri at the entrance. Muhammad held out his hand and the *Umm al-Walad* crossed the room and joined him. Side by side, mother and son shared a similar height, but little else.

He said, "At last they have come, *Ummi.* It seems Al-Shaquri arrived in time. Rise, all of you. Allah, the Compassionate, the Merciful, favored you, allowing my physician to treat whatever illness befell you."

"If my Sultan will permit," the doctor edged closer to him, "the honor is not mine to claim. Certainly, Alfonso Ruiz must have noted the services of Pharez ben Zarzar."

"Bah! A Jew!" Muhammad gave a dismissive wave of his hand.

Jazirah huffed. Beside him, Muhammad's mother released his hand and clasped her fingers. Her lips became a thin seam.

The Sultan looked from her to Jazirah. "Well, is this her? Come into the light, cousin, where I may see you better."

For the space of several breaths, Jazirah did not move from her position, even when Lubna pinched her arm through the mantle. Jazirah's father took her hand. He led her to the center and drew back her hood.

Muhammad said, "She is taller than I am."

Small satisfaction rippled through Jazirah to look down her nose at him.

His mother stated, "She has the grace and beauty of women in your family, my Sultan. Why should her height matter?"

He flicked a glare at her, and continued, "Humph, I see black brows. Remove the *hijab*. I want to know the color of her hair beneath the veil."

Unsure as to whether he meant the odd request for her or her father, Jazirah stood motionless. Would Muhammad inspect her before all?

The Sultan's frown returned. "Is she mute or simply ignorant?"

While Jazirah bristled, her father grasped her elbow, and squeezed. "I assure you, my Sultan, my daughter is an intelligent young woman. She understands you well."

He unpinned Jazirah's veil and stepped back. Curls cascaded to her waist.

A tic pulsed along Muhammad's jaw. "She has black hair as well."

His mother rushed to say, "Why should the color matter? Many, including you, have the same shade of hair. Mayhap she might dye the locks with henna."

"I will not!" Jazirah's pronouncement rang through the chamber.

She and Muhammad exchanged severe glances before he turned to his mother. "She gives her opinion without hesitation or shall I say, inflexibly?"

"If my Sultan will forgive, why would you wish otherwise, when you value truth?"

His scowl deepened. "The mark on her face will fade with time, I suppose." Then he added, "*Ummi*, I may overlook any defects if—"

"Why do you speak of me as if I am not here?" Jazirah demanded. Despite the collective gasps from everyone in attendance, she continued, "We may address each other as equals for we are both the grandchildren of a Sultan of Gharnatah."

Her father admonished, "Jazirah, you are not the equal of a man, least of all the Sultan! You will apologize and beg his forgiveness. Now!"

Muhammad raised a hand. "Let her keep false words behind her teeth. I would not believe them. What else could I expect, but this conduct from the daughter of a traitor to his people and my father?"

He glowered at Jazirah. "Foolish girl! I could have ignored your letter after your initial rebuff."

"As you overlooked my father's plight all of these years? I did not want this farce—"

"My Sultan, Princess Jazirah, please! This is a most inauspicious beginning. Please, please," the *Umm al-Walad* implored, "we should not raise old arguments again. By her

consent and the agreement of the Sultan, Jazirah will wed and—
"

"Not so fast, *Ummi*. If what your captain has told me is true, there must be some reasonable delay in the union."

A stricken cry from Lubna matched Jazirah's pain-filled wheeze. Muhammad knew about Harun. She pressed a hand to her bosom and stared across the room at Butayna's captain. He never flinched, but the fearsome scar contracted.

Butayna said, "You cannot mean to disgrace us all by a refusal now."

If he did, Jazirah would bear the indignity. To be the bride of the insufferable peacock before her might be the utmost trial she had ever known, greater than exile.

The Sultan regarded his mother with a deepening scowl. "Did I say this was my intent? I require a postponement of the nuptials, naught more. As your captain told me, the warden attacked my cousin and sought to claim her innocence by violence. If I wished to embarrass my future bride, I would demand a physical examination. Instead, we will wait three consecutive months in which her womanly time must occur. My Haziyya is the daughter of a midwife. She shall come to Princess Jazirah each day and determine when her link with the moon has occurred. The delay serves a second purpose. It allows me time to know the princess before we must wed. Although we are cousins, we have much to learn of each other. None of my courtiers would question my wish. I will wed Jazirah if my terms are met."

He turned to her father, whose throat bobbed. "They will be, my Sultan."

A sharp ache stabbed Jazirah's chest. She glared at her parent, whose gaze slid away. He would not acknowledge her silent fury. How dare he concede to Muhammad and surrender to his humiliating demands? Didn't her father trust her word?

The Sultan turned away and held out his hand to the concubine. "Come, my Haziyya. The day shortens with each passing hour. I would ride horses into the hills with you and my guards."

When she pressed her fingers against his palm, he raised her flesh to his lips. As one, they departed the columned chamber. Al-Shaquri made his excuses, mumbled some farewell, and left, too. Only the Sultan's mother remained with Jazirah's family.

The *Umm al-Walad* drew closer to Jazirah. "You did not send the letter about conditions at the fortress. You could not have written in such desperation, promising your hand in marriage, to behave so now. You had not planned to marry my son after all."

Jazirah clamped her lips together and gave no affirmation or denial.

Her father began, "My Sultana, whatever was said—"

"Is a promise your daughter must fulfill! Muhammad can never know the truth. Whether Jazirah wishes to or not, she shall wed. The Sultan has pledged himself based upon a vow he thinks she made. The words cannot be undone."

To Jazirah, she added, "My captain and I shall escort you to the estate Muhammad provides for your father's comfort. You will live there until your marriage. Prepare yourself. In three months' time, you shall be a bride and a Sultana of Gharnatah."

Chapter 6
Anew

Princess Jazirah

Gharnatah, Al-Andalus or Granada, Andalusia
Safar 757 AH or February A.D. 1356 or Adar 5116

Rigid, with hands fisted at her sides, Jazirah plodded across the rounded cobblestones beside her father in silence. Each stepping-stone pressed against the calluses on her feet through worn-out soles. She, her father, and Lubna followed the *Umm al-Walad* and her personal guards through the courtyard outside the council chamber. The captain found his men and beckoned the one closest to the horse with the satchels of coin collected at Shalabuniya.

Courtiers gathered, and in the guise of offering reverent bows to the Sultan's mother, inspected her companions with blatant curiosity. Gasps and whispers of recognition followed. Jazirah heard her father's name. Soon pointing began, but Jazirah held her head higher. She would not allow strangers to deride her or her family for their reduced condition. Blame lay elsewhere.

Muhammad's mother proclaimed, "Isn't *Salat al-Zuhr* fast approaching?"

Although she seemed not to be speaking to anyone in particular, her captain answered, "It is almost time for the Muslims' noonday prayer, my Sultana."

"These people do not seem to know. Moors have always prided themselves on their piety, saying it exceeds Christian faith. A debatable matter, which I shall speak with the Sultan about, as the devotion of his people is a chief concern. Do remind me to mention the names of those whom I saw loitering here as examples for my son."

"I shall remember, queen of queens."

Butayna's words had the desired effect, as those milling about the courtyard made hasty farewells to their companions and dispersed.

Jazirah might have expressed some gratitude, but the speculation of nameless courtiers held no meaning for her. She seethed inside, but kept her jaws clamped together. Her father seemed oblivious to her frustration, walking beside her with a hitch in his gait. Whatever aches he experienced did not diminish the obvious joy he took in being at *Al-Qal'at al-Hamra* again. Redness suffused his dimples. A wide grin creased the corners of his mouth while he strode the cobblestone streets of his home.

She could not share his happiness, not when he had permitted Muhammad to question her assurance. Although she cast furious glances at the captain's back while they traversed the cobblestones, in truth, she could not summon anger toward him. The man had done the duty his master required. Ruiz's forthright nature permitted no concealment of the events he had witnessed at Shalabuniya. If he thought Harun had claimed her virginity, the warrior held a duty to convey the concern to the Sultan.

Yet, how could her father have surrendered to Muhammad's demand so easily? The stab of betrayal left Jazirah embittered. She would have submitted to a midwife's examination, rather than endure the farcical interrogations of the next three months, in which Muhammad's Berber lover inquired about bloodstained cotton bands. The Sultan sought to avoid speculation from the courtiers about his motives, but he gave no thought to how they might interpret a marital ceremony delayed by months.

Mired in her thoughts, Jazirah slammed into the captain's iron-muscled back. She stumbled away and waved off her father's help. She gave the captain what she hoped was her most baleful glare. He returned the gesture, lines furrowing his brow as if irritated by her failure to note when they had stopped. No servant would have dared a display of annoyance, but then these Christian warriors were not hers to govern.

Lubna asked, "Are you well, my princess?"

Jazirah's curt nod preceded a brusque response. "Do not coddle me like a child."

Lubna lowered her gaze. Color seeped across her face.

Jazirah's throat tightened, but she swallowed and avoided all stares. Her temper showed itself at the worst times. She would apologize to Lubna later, but not now, while Muhammad's mother eyed her in silent bemusement with a twitching mouth.

Let the woman have her entertainment, but soon she and her son would understand Jazirah's nature. She would never bow and concede to anyone again, least of all Gharnatah's ruler and his mother. Jazirah bore a Nasrid's pride, the same as Muhammad. She vowed he would never forget the heritage they both shared.

Behind his mother, a quartet stood before the redbrick façade of a two-storied house at the southern edge of the courtyard. They could only be slaves, by their downcast, red-rimmed gazes, plain dress, and bare feet as much as the thin iron collars encircling their necks. A reed-thin boy huddled beside a portly woman whose hazel eyes matched his. Their copper-colored flesh contrasted with the pale skin of a woman with yellow hair and her male counterpart, who did not resemble her. Their proximity suggested more than mere acquaintance.

Adjacent to the residence, the curtain wall restricted the southern view. The opened doorway afforded full observation of the citadel of *Al-Quasaba* to the west, the council chambers to the north, and the gardens of the east, where the road coiled past the unseen frontage of other buildings.

An apparition garbed in pristine ivory glided beyond the door. It took two blinks before Jazirah recognized a man approached them, rather than some unearthly wraith. She had never seen anyone so pale. Wind tugged at a sheaf of parchment held between his white-gloved fingers. With a free hand, he shaded his dove-gray eyes from the midday sun. Bloodless lips thinned in an imitation of a smile directed toward Muhammad's mother.

He bowed before her. "All is in readiness, o queen of queens."

"Thank you, Hisham," Butayna replied, tilting her head. "Prince Ismail, Princess Jazirah, this is the chief eunuch of the harem, Abdullah Hisham. At my command, Hisham has acquired slaves for your household. Both males are eunuchs. The elder woman can cook and bake, while the younger may serve as a seamstress and laundress. Details regarding age and origins are within the bill of sale Hisham bears."

Something in her clipped tone and furrowed brow stirred Jazirah's interest. The *Umm al-Walad* seemed displeased about the slaves. Jazirah shook her head. She was wrong. Butayna found no fault with them, for she would not have provided their services if she had believed them incapable. What other cause for vexation did she hold?

Jazirah's father nodded. "We appreciate your generosity."

His daughter did not share the sentiment and crossed her arms under her breasts. "Do you believe four slaves will be enough even for our small household, Father?"

Butayna nodded. "The coins found at Shalabuniya. Where are they?"

She beckoned the guardsman who held up the bags and when he loosened the strings, she dipped her hand inside the leather. She withdrew some money and opened her palm. Sunlight reflected off brilliant gold *dinars.* The die engraver had etched *Naskhi* script, the calligraphic style of the court, around the margins. Within an incised square the Nasrid motto 'None victorious save Allah' appeared.

Butayna continued, "The jailor must have hoarded the monies my Sultan and his noble father provided for your upkeep. By the gracious command of my son, these funds are yours now to purchase more servants."

Jazirah shook her head. The unexpected overture, when the coins belonged to the Sultanate, did not startle her. Rather the prior generosity of Yusuf and Muhammad rendered her speechless. Both Sultans had made provision for them at Shalabuniya. Why consign a family to hell only to support them? Mayhap father and son had done so to ease their burden of scruples. Familial devotion could not have motivated them.

"Yusuf provided for us? Muhammad, too?" Her father made the inquiries Jazirah refused to utter. The high pitch of his voice betrayed similar shock.

Butayna lifted her chin. "The capricious nature of relations within your family makes you wary of even a measure of kindness. You must believe my husband did not cast you into the depths of Shalabuniya without some regret and concern. He sent funds each year to ensure you were clothed and well-fed."

"In exile," Jazirah muttered. "In a place where we almost died."

Butayna scowled. "You did not die. My son continued his father's attempts at upkeep. Muhammad rescued you from captivity. Both men intended to secure your comfort. I do the same with the provision of these slaves."

"I do not want them!" Jazirah shuddered with rage. Comfort indeed! How could she even say such a word?

"Daughter, think of what you're saying."

She avoided her father's meaningful glance, her stare fixed on Muhammad's mother.

Butayna's wide-eyed gaze and trembling lips hinted at her distress. She broke their eye contact and cast a glance at the slaves.

At first, Jazirah gloried in the small triumph, certain the Sultan's mother had intended to place spies within the household, persons loyal to her who would monitor the occupants. What other purpose might there be for her generosity?

However, the low, almost mournful tone with which Butayna addressed the yellow-haired woman and her close companion dispelled Jazirah's initial presumption.

Puzzled, she looked for clarification from her father. "What does she tell them?"

He said, "In her mother tongue, the *Umm al-Walad* expresses some regrets because she cannot place a young husband and wife with a kindly master and mistress. She explains why they must return to the *corrals* tomorrow."

Ashen features and watery gazes met Butayna's speech. The couple clutched hands and the man murmured words, revealed by their pitch as tokens of solace. Meanwhile, Butayna crouched before the little boy and took his small hand. As she spoke, tears streamed down his scrawny face. He peeked at Jazirah before he covered his eyes.

Afflicted, Jazirah leaned closer to her father. He added, "Now, Butayna explains the same circumstances to the cook and her boy in the Persian language. Whomever should buy them will likely separate these two families. Each slave would fetch a high price at auction. Who knows if a new master will care about the severance of bonds between family members? The *Umm al-Walad* could bear the burden of multiple slaves at any price, but no one is as rich as she, or the Sultan."

In her youth, Jazirah would not have concerned herself with the future of slaves. What did the lot of those who served her family matter to a child? Age brought reasoning. Where would she be today without Lubna's steady guidance and care? As her attachment had grown and her understanding of the fragile nature of familial bonds increased, she no longer thought of slaves as meaningless fixtures of her life.

Butayna must have shared the sentiment as well, for she once existed at the whim and will of Yusuf before he had claimed her for his own. She clearly pitied these slaves. After a pat upon the boy's head of stringy hair, she rose with her captain's help and made a listless gesture to the white eunuch. "There is no reason to keep them out in the cold, Hisham. Return them to the pits—"

Jazirah ordered, "Wait! The slaves may remain upon the fulfillment of a condition."

She had never expected to find common ground with the Sultan's mother, but as Butayna lifted her gaze, gratitude reflected in her glistening stare.

She asked, "What is your wish, Princess Jazirah?"

"Let me view the bill of sale."

The chief eunuch flicked a sloe-eyed look at Butayna, who nodded before Hisham stepped forward and bowed before Jazirah's father. He accepted the parchment without scanning its contents, while his daughter huffed and glared at Hisham until he backed away. She held out her hand for the document.

In truth, she only wished to verify one notation, the date of the sale. It had occurred on the seventh day in the month of Safar, exactly a week ago. Hardly enough time for Butayna to bind the loyalty of the slaves if she had wished.

"Thank you. I accept the gift of the slaves and promise to treat them well." Satisfied, Jazirah returned the parchment to Hisham, who rolled up the document.

He addressed her father. "If you wish to purchase more slaves, I can advise you on the best merchants in the neighborhood of Al-Bayazin—"

Rumbles of laughter interrupted Hisham. "You may make your recommendations to my daughter. She has charge of our household."

While the pale eunuch stared in mute horror with his mouth agape, Jazirah added, "A duty I'll share with my Lubna, who shall be our stewardess in the interim."

At Lubna's quiet gasp, Jazirah turned and placed a hand upon her shoulder. "I cannot lighten your burdens. I shall always trust you above any other. Chief among your tasks is the duty to find a counterpart to take on your role in Father's house after I have wed. I want you by my side wherever I may be. After my marriage, Father cannot be without help. Choose from among these slaves or others we may acquire. You'll make the right decisions."

"I'll never give you reason to doubt me, my princess."

"You never have, Lubna."

Hisham sputtered, "My prince, you grant mastery of your house to... women?"

Jazirah did not give her father a chance to answer, although she guessed at what his response might have been by the spasm across his lips. She said, "Don't you bow and scrape before the Sultan's mother, eunuch?"

Hisham pressed his lips together, impossibly pale.

Butayna's face flushed and she ducked her head before she whispered, "It would be my pleasure to show you the residence." She waved to the doorway.

Jazirah found her arm tucked with her father's own. In a pique, her nails raked his forearm under the woolen tunic. He did not seem to mind.

He said to Butayna, "Lead on, my Sultana."

A mosaic of red, white, black, green, and golden tiles stretched from the entryway along a short vestibule, brackets for torches fixed to the walls. A master artisan had inlaid the ceiling with fretwork panels painted in brilliant vermillion. Ushered through a horseshoe arch, Jazirah came to the colonnaded gallery, which opened on to the courtyard. At its center, water spilled from a pale marble fountain and flowed along a channel running east to west between flowerbeds devoid of any vegetation.

In the recesses of Jazirah's mind, a child's laughter echoed. Would her children with Muhammad play in this garden someday?

Her father inhaled deeply and sighed. "In this place the brother of my grandfather Faraj, a grave man named Muhammad, lived before he became a provincial governor. In those early days, he and my grandfather were orphans who arrived in Gharnatah in the wake of their father's death at

Malaka. A rivalry existed between the brothers born mere months apart and never ended until by Muhammad's own folly, he predeceased my grandfather. Afterward, Faraj raised his brother's children, wedding the eldest boy to my great-aunt Leila. Through dynastic marriage, we Nasrids have always reconciled strife. It is a lesson my grandmother, Faraj's wife Fatima, imparted to us. The family is all-important. In our union, we are strong."

Jazirah released his arm and strolled into the garden. She trailed her fingertips through the frigid water in the fountain's basin. "A pity your generation, especially my uncle Yusuf, did not listen to your grandmother's teachings."

From her peripheral vision, she noted her father's frown.

Shrill laughter from Butayna followed before she said, "You have a sharp wit, princess. Muhammad shall find a remarkable match with you for his Sultana."

Jazirah cast a withering glance over her shoulder. She did not care for the high-minded opinions of a man who had doubted her personal honor. Mayhap he believed women held none.

She dismissed thoughts of him and slowly whirled, studying the frontage of the courtyard. Lattice-covered windows overlooked the space, the view from some of them blocked by juniper, carob and olive trees bounding the oleander and rosemary bushes. Her ancestors had ruled Gharnatah for over a century. What events had occurred here in the shadows to alter the dynasty? After all, divisions between brothers had affected the Nasrids even in her lifetime.

When she turned, Butayna's bemused expression remained. Jazirah's father had moved beside the Sultan's mother. Some exchange must have occurred between them during Jazirah's distraction.

She asked, "Will you show us the rest?"

Butayna indicated the cedar double doors at the opposite end of the garden. "It would be my pleasure, princess."

They crossed the gardens and entered a series of six rooms arranged around the courtyard. A damp chill penetrated Jazirah's mantle and boots. Lime wash commingled with a hint of turmeric or expensive saffron covered the walls. She smeared the tip of her finger across a freshly patched, golden-hued portion of the plaster. A streak came away on her flesh. She envisioned her father taking his meals, reading correspondence, and issuing commands to his servants in these spaces devoid of fixtures, except for rusted iron braziers. The kitchen at the south contained a cold oven mired in ash with faded lusterware stacked in one corner. A mouse scuttled from behind the oven and disappeared into the adjoining corridor.

Lubna said, "There are still a few hours of daylight in which I may purchase cooking pots from the marketplace of *Al-Qaysariyya*. We can make this into a suitable home."

Over her shoulder, Jazirah commanded, "Take our new eunuch with you to the city's marketplace. I doubt you will require guards to prevent his escape. He seems unlikely to abandon his woman."

To the young man who stood beside his wife, Jazirah asked, "What is your name?"

Butayna cleared her throat. "He does not speak Arabic and has no slave name. Gonzalo and his wife Beatriz arrived here from the city of Jayyan or Jaén, as I knew it, a month ago."

Jazirah remembered little of her childhood lessons in the Castillan tongue, having no reason for practice and no tutor at Shalabuniya. She recalled her Latin and Greek well but doubted Gonzalo or Beatriz would know either language. "This cannot be. How am I to instruct him if he will not understand?"

Her father said, "You will relay your commands through me, daughter." He approached the couple in the doorway of the kitchen.

He held up splayed fingers. He began speaking while Butayna moved beside Jazirah and translated the words into Arabic. "I will not harm you. I am the *Infante* Ismail." He waved to Jazirah and Lubna. "There stands my daughter, the *Infanta* Jazirah, who is your mistress, and our slave Lubna, the stewardess of the house. Serve us well and we will not harm you. Our great Sultan's mother, *la reina* Butayna has informed me your names are Gonzalo and Beatriz. You are from Castilla-León?"

Beatriz cowered beside her husband and clasped his arm, dirtied fingernails against the white tunic he wore. The eunuch's surprise grew evident in his widened gaze and the redness suffusing his pale face. He exchanged a weary glance with his companion before he answered, "*Sí, señor.*"

"Since we have made introductions, my daughter wishes you to accompany our stewardess Lubna to the marketplace today. Can you do this, Gonzalo?"

The eunuch peered at his spouse again, a frown marring his youthful brow.

"No harm shall come to Beatriz in your absence. My daughter will give her a task."

Gonzalo gave an audible sigh. "I will go to the marketplace as you command, *señor.*"

Jazirah turned to Butayna. "How am I to instruct the wife in anything if she can't understand me?"

"I shall remain with you throughout the day if your father wishes to rest. You must communicate with Beatriz and her, with you. If you would like, we could begin your lessons in

Castillan tomorrow, alongside hers in Arabic. The slaves will learn as they surrender their old lives and begin anew."

Jazirah took some comfort in the possibility she was not the only person in the room who held uncertainties about the days ahead. She directed a smile in Beatriz's direction. The woman looked at Gonzalo before she returned the gesture half-heartedly. Jazirah suppressed a shudder at the young woman's yellowed teeth.

Butayna said, "I'll show you the bedchambers and storage rooms above stairs before your Lubna leaves for *Al-Qaysariyya*. The private *hammam* where you may bathe is below this...."

***

Hours later, Jazirah reached for a gilt tray perched on a shelf. She brushed the cobwebs away. Then with a ragged strip of silk in hand, she beckoned Beatriz, who moved closer to the natural light the sole kitchen window provided. Gesticulation had worked quite well with Beatriz over the last two hours. Jazirah smiled and nodded each time the young woman did exactly as her mistress intended. Then she bent toward her task, all the better to avoid the sour stench of her companion. She should not have expected better from anyone who had spent time in a slave pen, but by the Prophet's beard, the stench proved almost unbearable. Upon completion of the work, she would ensure Beatriz followed her to the bath.

For now, the slave held a faded lusterware pan of salt sprinkled with lemon juice. Jazirah dipped the material into the mixture and rubbed the tray until it gleamed, akin to the other silver objects rescued from neglect. She paused and stared at her reflection in the metal. Unkempt hair framed her glistening features. The reddened splotch on her right cheek, a remnant of Harun's violence, contrasted with her olive-brown skin. She swiped at bands of perspiration and pushed curls away from her face.

"What are you doing?"

Jazirah peered over her shoulder and found the Sultan's mother in the kitchen doorway, her devoted captain at her back. Jazirah's father had retired and Butayna had remained with him. Jazirah imagined the topic of conversation revolved around their respective children, but she had given the matter no further thought, not when the house required her attention.

Butayna asked, "You clean the silver while your slave stands idle?"

"She is not idle. She is assisting me. I would not have her ruin what silver remains. It is enough for her to watch and learn of its care."

The spicy scent of Butayna's perfume masked a little of Beatriz's odor. Muhammad's mother glided across the tiles, which Jazirah and Beatriz had scrubbed and washed in the interim. Jazirah refused to look up, even when Butayna's feet came into view.

"The slave boy Dhanu caught two ducks along the banks of the *Hadarro* River."

Jazirah frowned. "Duck?"

"Don't scowl. Duck is *halal*. As you may eat the flesh, Dhanu's mother Jyoti roasts the birds for dinner. Her son is a good hunter. Dhanu learned from his father before slavers took them from the Deccan Peninsula. Jyoti's husband did not survive the castration."

When Jazirah's silent stare met her words, Butayna added, "These slaves owe you loyalty and their lives. Whatever you may suspect of my motives, I would never interfere with them. You will come to know them better than I ever could."

"What did you and my father speak of when you were upstairs?"

"I asked him to tell me the full truth of conditions at Shalabuniya."

The tray slipped from Jazirah's grasp, clanged, and rattled on the tiles. She reached for it and resumed polishing as if no disturbance had occurred. Still, her hands shook. Beatriz stared at her with a widened, pensive gaze.

Butayna crouched at her feet and withdrew the metal from Jazirah's hold. Then her smooth fingers encompassed Jazirah's own. For the space of two breaths, Jazirah permitted the contact, but then she tried to pull away.

Muhammad's mother would not relent. "The past can no longer trouble you."

Tears threatened as Jazirah whispered, "Did you cast your history aside so easily?"

The sigh from Butayna filled the room. "I accepted the bad with the good. Neither solely defines who I am today. I chose my future. You will do the same."

She stood. "Your Lubna will return from *Al-Qaysariyya* soon. I hope among her purchases, she has found silks and woolens for you. You are a Nasrid princess, Jazirah. It is time for you to dress as befits the future wife of my son. Join me in the morning after you have had your meal. Bring Beatriz with you. The lessons I have promised will begin on the morrow."

***

Jazirah mounted the stairs to her father's room in the evening. Bronze candelabras illuminated each landing. Beatriz followed, bearing the silver tray with a plate of roasted duck drizzled in date sauce, and accompanied by dried figs and flatbread alongside a copper cup. Jazirah carried water, and sweet and sour *sekanjabin* drink in two pitchers. Her father reclined on a

75

bed surrounded by sheer indigo curtains, a copy of *Al-Qur'an* in his hand. The stool Butayna must have occupied stood beside his bed.

He set his book aside. "Ah, so this was the delicious smell wafting through my window from the courtyard. Why did you not summon me to the dining room?"

"You should rest." Jazirah waved Beatriz toward him. "The slave will remain."

He said, "I would rather enjoy your company. Or, are you still furious with me?"

Jazirah's arms trembled as she laid down the burden of the pitchers.

"You do not have to deny it, daughter. I have disappointed you."

She rounded on him. "Why did you allow Muhammad to delay our nuptials?"

"I did not know you were so eager to wed him."

"I want this charade to end! No doubt, the Sultan's court is rife with speculation. The courtiers will want to know why you have returned, why I am with you, and what Muhammad intends to do with both of us. We could have avoided gossip if the Sultan announced our betrothal."

She stepped away from the bed and toward the window. Her grip alighted on the *shimasas*. The top of the latticework window screen pressed into her hand. She gulped deep breaths of the evening air.

"Jazirah, haste invites idle conjecture as much as delay. If you think the gossip will cease when Muhammad makes his pronouncement, you are wrong. Questions shall remain. The ministers will wish to know whether I may reclaim a governorship and a position of influence. Others will ponder why Muhammad chose you for a wife. None will question the Sultan's wisdom if he wishes to learn more of his bride before he weds. It would seem a prudent choice, so he may discover our allegiances. This postponement benefits you, too. Show the people of Gharnatah our loyalty to Muhammad and you may well convince him."

"You heard him! He has no more desire to wed me than I have in marrying him."

"He has not refused the honor. He could have brought true shame on your head as he cast us out of his palace. He might have left us to rot in prison. Yet, my nephew did not do either. Allow him time, Jazirah. He shall discover you are more than he imagined."

She turned and glared at her father. "Oh, he shall, Father. I swear it upon the blood of my mother and sister. Muhammad shall remember I am a true Nasrid."

Chapter 7
A Meeting

Sultan Muhammad V

Gharnatah, Al-Andalus or Granada, Andalusia
Jumada al-Ula 757 AH or May A.D. 1356 or Sivan 5116

On the first warm day of spring, Muhammad trod the cobblestone streets of the royal *madina* in the company of his *hajib* Ridwan and half of the royal guard. Within the palatial city, courtiers and slaves alike bent double as Muhammad followed the route from the *mashwar* to the harem. He took no more note of his people and their esteem than he would have at any other time, not when he placed greater importance on an exchange with his chief minister, a man whom Muhammad had respected from boyhood. Sunlight's fiery golden glow cast a patina on Ridwan's baldpate. Too many times, Ridwan flicked the tip of his pink tongue over thinned lips. Muhammad wished he would stop, for the action recalled Ridwan's hateful brother, the snake of a chief eunuch Hisham whom Butayna relied upon with increased fervor.

"You shall be the first to know if my plans change, but they will not. My intent to wed Jazirah bint Ismail has not altered my opinion of her father. A prince he may be, but my uncle shall never again hold a governorship of Al-Andalus. I want him here, close to me where I may observe his activities."

Ridwan's face reddened even more, impossibly so, and he appeared on the verge of an apoplexy. He held too much respect for the Sultan who had raised him to the highest position among the ministers to interrupt, but Muhammad rushed on.

"You must convey my words to the *Diwan*. I will not have foolish dissent among my council members over fears of my uncle's influence. I have shown him more mercy than he deserves. I'll wed his daughter as promised, but no more than this. Now, cease these groundless fears and trust in me!"

When he fell silent, Ridwan released a pent-up breath, as if grateful Muhammad would finally allow him to speak. "Great Sultan, your council of ministers means no disrespect in consideration of the arrangements for your uncle—"

Muhammad halted and glared at his former tutor. They once stood at equal height, but in the last two years, Ridwan's back bowed and his spine curved. Muhammad could no longer deny his childhood tutor had grown old. Sparse gray feathered his temples and his visage betrayed more lines than Muhammad remembered.

"Ridwan, they are my plans. This does not mean I reject the concerns of my council. Their fears are groundless. Above all ministers, I value your opinion most. What do you believe of my words?"

Ridwan averred, "I have watched a proud boy grow in the image of his father Yusuf, may Allah preserve his memory. If you say your uncle will have no place in your government, it shall be so. I place my faith in you as I have since the earliest days of your youth, my Sultan."

"Good. You may retire, Ridwan. I am certain your family would welcome a rare opportunity to share the afternoon meal and prayers with you."

Ridwan's mouth gaped, before he recognized the easy dismissal. Hiding whatever he might have said behind a smooth smile, he grunted, bent, and reached for the hem of Muhammad's ceremonial robe, the *khil'a*.

"Come, no need for formality." Muhammad embraced Ridwan and pecked both cheeks. As they drew apart, a wide grin split the elder man's face. Muhammad did not have to look beyond Ridwan's sloped shoulders for signs of shock from his courtiers. Gasps followed. Muhammad shared Ridwan's amusement, but for a different reason. Let his subjects think what they would of the encounter. Appearances mattered more than truth to them. What could they know of his esteem for the man before him?

"You are always too kind to me, my Sultan," Ridwan stated.

"No more than you were to me. You took a proud young boy and made a prince of the faithful out of him. Mastery of the throne did not come to me alone by birthright. Your teachings influenced me. They still do."

"Then I have done naught more than my duty to your ancestors who raised me up, a frightened Christian child, from the slave pits. *Al-salam 'alayka*, my master."

"And peace be with you and yours always, my teacher," Muhammad answered in Ridwan's native Castillan.

The chief minister's rheumy gray eyes glistened before he released Muhammad and turned away. Ridwan shuffled across the courtyard until his bald-pated head disappeared behind a dense copse of myrtle trees.

Muhammad entered the harem through its one access point, oriented to the southwest. Indoors, he immediately removed the black and gold *khil'a*, and handed the robe of state to Pero, who stood at his back. Muhammad smoothed his hands over the white *jubba* worn under the robe. The captain and his men followed him through a dim corridor, until they emerged in the garden courtyard, flooded by afternoon sunlight. All the guards and servants in the perimeter ceased their activities.

To the west, outside the quarters Muhammad occupied, an unexpected sight awaited him. His mother and his favorite leaned against opposing columns. Haziyya, garbed in her traditional blue, appeared as a glittering sapphire. His mother wore green and gold, which enhanced the warm amber light in her eyes. Whatever purpose had brought them together puzzled Muhammad.

He reached his mother first and bowed before he took her hand. Then he clasped Haziyya's fingers and raised them to his lips. "The joy of my life is complete in the company of those women whom I love best. I am surprised to see you, *Ummi*, for it is your Christian Sunday."

Butayna lifted her chin. "Prayers and Mass may wait upon my son. You have spent too much time at Ridwan's feet. My Sultan has acquired his teacher's silvery tongue."

"Better than Ibn al-Khatib's sharp wit. He thinks to browbeat me in my dealings with Castilla-León and Al-Maghrib al-Aksa. He would have me bend before him. I would rather let the Castillans and Marinids overrun Gharnatah than submit authority to my father's servant."

"Your *katib sirri-hi* forgets your Nasrid pride. I do not."

"Have you come to lecture me about my failings as the personal secretary did, *Ummi*?" When she huffed, he held up his hands to stave off an argument he would lose. "Do not answer. Come and take refreshment."

The trio entered the central chamber with Pero following, while the rest of Muhammad's personal guard aligned themselves beneath the columns and along the walls of the courtyard. Nestled in a corner with her nursing kittens, Thalj raised her head and peered at Muhammad. He whistled and called to her, but the cat did not move. Her sparkling gaze took note of his companions before she stretched out again.

Pero went to the Sultan's robing room and laid the costly embroidered garment out on a chest for the personal launderer's retrieval.

Then Muhammad said to him, "Summon slaves with food and drink. The day is warm and my council meeting lasted longer than I had anticipated."

His captain bowed and then swept his cape back before he withdrew.

Muhammad gestured for his *kadin* and Butayna to sit at the low table in the center of the room. Butayna's slim fingers smoothed across the polished cedar and a slow smile summoned her dimples. Muhammad realized her thoughts must have drifted far away to some pleasant interlude at dinner with his father.

She caught him staring and cleared her throat. Her gaze darted to Haziyya, who folded her hands in her lap. Muhammad's nape prickled and he rubbed the flesh at the hairline.

Haziyya said, "My Sultan, I last visited with Princess Jazirah's stewardess this morning. The link with the moon has severed. The princess has completed three cycles of her woman's blood. If she had been with child, you would have known by now."

Muhammad asked, "Did you examine Jazirah?"

"She allowed it, although she grumbled to her slave woman of my cold hands."

Butayna said, "Jazirah comes to you a virgin."

He mused, "How long has it been since I had a virgin?"

Butayna sniffled. "Not since you bedded Haziyya. Now all of your other women languish untouched in the harem." She snuck a glance at the favorite before she added, "You have little reason to put off the marriage, my Sultan, except for one cause." When he arched his eyebrows, she added, "In these three months since Jazirah's arrival, you have not spent time alone with her. You have visited her household once and inquired after the health of her father, but never talked to her."

"How do you know?" He regarded Haziyya as he said so. How could he ever want another when she held him enraptured?

His mother said, "All within *Al-Qal'at al-Hamra* are aware. Would you have your courtiers believe something is amiss? Shall they wonder why you have brought guests here and granted them a living only to ignore them?"

Snared by the simple beauty of his favorite, Muhammad hesitated before answering, "I don't care for the thoughts of sycophants and courtiers."

"You should, if you intend to remain Sultan."

Both Muhammad and Haziyya glared at Butayna, who twirled the pearl ring on her finger. "I know of no direct plots against you or any immediate danger. More than the eyes of your subjects remain ever watchful. For instance, I am aware of Maryam's visits with your uncle, which have occurred each week."

Muhammad stiffened at the news. "Has Jazirah met Maryam also?"

"It is certain. Jazirah never leaves her father's side."

All within lapsed into silence as slaves entered, bearing trays covered in steaming dishes, breads and cheeses, and fruits. After his servants presented the generous meal, Muhammad dismissed them, He spooned *'tharid* of lamb on his mother's flatbread and fed Haziyya chunks of chicken in mint sauce from his own plate. Afterward the conversation resumed while the slaves returned with bowls of fragrant rosewater and warm towels draped over their arms.

Muhammad washed and dried his hands before he regarded Butayna. "What would you have of me?"

"Dine with Jazirah tonight and on the morrow announce your intent to wed. The court perceives your purpose, for there could be no other reason you have released your uncle and brought his marriageable daughter here. End the gossip."

He swerved toward Haziyya. "What is your opinion of my future Sultana?"

Butayna's nails raked the wood as she clenched her fingers. "Who cares what your favorite bed slave thinks of one who is to be your wife?"

Muhammad shot her a withering glance. "Haziyya's thoughts are as important to me as your own." He waved a hand to his favorite.

"She is proud as any Nasrid should be, my Sultan. She does not deign to speak to me directly, only through her servant. She is beautiful, although she could benefit from a few smiles."

Butayna harrumphed. "Would you be content to simper if the Sultan ignored you?"

Haziyya broke eye contact with Muhammad at last. Her dark brows flared before she replied, "I would not, my honored Sultana."

With a curt nod, Butayna's fingers curled around Muhammad's forearm. "Summon your cousin tonight and know for yourself whether she shall be a suitable bride."

He covered her hand. "I was to dine with Haziyya this evening."

When she withdrew her touch and her gaze narrowed, he did not fault her. Even to his own ears, he sounded like a petulant boy instead of the master of all Gharnatah.

Haziyya said, "This evening must belong to the one you will wed."

He reached for her fingers and took his mother's own again. "Truly, I am blessed to have you both at my side."

Butayna's eyes glittered. She sniffled and looked away, as if she did not deserve his praise. Muhammad promised to consider her reticence later. For now, he would have to prepare himself for an encounter with a wife he did not want.

***

Regrets magnified as Muhammad sat at table again, awaiting Jazirah's arrival. First, he should not have dressed so well. He tugged at the silver sleeves of another brocaded *khil'a*. Such an ostentatious robe suited the arrival of foreign dignitaries, as had occurred earlier in the day when he and the council of ministers met with the delegation from Fés el-Jedid. Jazirah deserved no such honors, although his *kadin* and mother had insisted upon it. Second, he should have never allowed his mother to order so much food from the kitchen. He glared at the wasteful spread.

His third regret ensued as Jazirah appeared at the opposite end of the garden courtyard. His doorway opened onto the pavilion and the vista beyond. He should not have sat to receive her, not when she already stood taller than he did.

She approached with a sure-footed stride, navigating the garden's water channels with ease. A yellow-haired servant and a collarless woman trailed her, both with bowed heads. A detachment of Christian guards under the Basque warrior Zabala brought up the rear. Butayna had insisted Jazirah and her father necessitated the same protection the royal family enjoyed.

As Jazirah reached his doorway, the muscles of Muhammad's abdomen constricted. He hardly recognized his guest. The unkempt female in frayed dress had given way to a figure attired in the manner of any Sultana of Gharnatah. Arrayed in silks, she also wore no cosmetics and needed none. By the Prophet's beard, she was perfect. Even her face, once so gaunt, had filled out. As had the rest of her, by the way the materials flared around her hips.

She stopped at the edge of the carpet and ceased staring at some indeterminate spot on the wall behind him. When she condescended to regard him, her narrowed, brown-eyed gaze mirrored the same resentment roiling inside him.

He pressed his elbows atop the table, clasped his hands, and rested his chin in the apex. The woman behind Jazirah whose hair and features resembled a rodent now coughed. She had the grace to cover her mouth with her pockmarked hand even before his glower shifted to her. Then Jazirah bent so stiffly, Muhammad could not suppress a chuckle.

"You will not break if you bow before me."

In an instant, she straightened, and her eyes became slits. Any hesitancy faded as she squared her shoulders. "I do not intend to break, my Sultan. Ever."

He extended a hand, indicating the low cushion across from him. In truth, looking up at her any longer would have produced a cramp in his neck. "Sit."

She raised her chin a little higher at his curt tone but complied. The skirts of the *jubba* spread wide at the rounded hips and revealed the cloying white fabric of the *sarawil* clinging to shapely calves and ankles. Fragrant rosewater clung to her. Her companions knelt beside her, while her royal guard blended in with their companions responsible for Muhammad's protection. Their captain Pero bowed and grasped the handles of both doors, prepared to close the portal.

"Wait!" Muhammad studied Jazirah's companions before he regarded their mistress. "Send them away. I shall serve us tonight."

Jazirah blinked rapidly and she licked her lower lip, drawing his regard to her mouth. Tinged pink and full, a woman's lips.

The longer he stared, her agitation increased, evidenced by the flush creeping up her neck. She opened her mouth twice but failed to speak.

On the third try, she uttered, "I don't think it is proper for me to be alone with you."

He gripped a silver goblet and poured *sekanjabin* into it, before he took a sip of the sweet and sour liquid and soothed his parched throat. "I am Sultan. I say what is proper."

"You don't understand. I have never been alone with any man, but for my father. Except for when...."

Muhammad guessed at what she would have said before her voice trailed off. "I am to be your husband. Do you think me no better than your warden? I would never bring such dishonor upon my head or yours!"

"But—"

"You will be silent when the Sultan speaks." When she clamped her mouth shut, he continued, "Did you not anticipate moments where we would be alone together? Do not trouble yourself. I am no brute nor are you such a lovely temptation to make me come upon you as an animal. I will not claim you before the marriage occurs. You shall remain untouched until our wedding night."

If his request had dulled her fires, the rest of his words diminished them entirely. A sigh whistled between her parted lips and his stomach clenched in response. Her chest rose and fell in time with each swift intake of breath. Upon first sight of her, he might have deemed any attraction to his cousin impossible. Faced with the revelation of her beauty and a pride mirroring his own, he could not help but consider how sweet her surrender might be. His body responded to her innocence.

He would have understood his reaction if he had been without a woman in days. Instead, Haziyya had pleasured him last night once she knew the certainty of her broken link with the moon. Jazirah was no rival for any other woman of his harem. Yet, her proud manner enflamed his most passionate desires. He wanted to do more than subdue her willful nature. His fingers twitched with an impulsive need to trace a thumb across her lips, to still her quivers with a kiss.

Beside her, Jazirah's woman whispered, "My princess, I can—"

"Leave us!" Jazirah snapped. "Please Lubna, take Beatriz with you." She turned to the yellow-haired slave and whispered in halting Castillan, "*Esclava*, you... can... go."

Both women stood and departed. Pero closed the doors and the resulting thud resounded. Muhammad said no more. He averted his gaze and poured *sekanjabin* for Jazirah. He spooned cold, vinegar-infused fish in a *skibaj* stew next to a slice of the flatbread and offered her roasted lamb and a *zirbiya* of hens cut up and boiled down in honey, sugar, and rosewater, which she declined in a soft murmur.

He took his own food and ate in silence. When he looked up from an almost empty plate, she had moved the lamb dish around and eaten some of the *skibaj.* He grimaced at the rest of the squandered food and tore a piece of *dafair* bread. He bit off a chunk and licked away the honey and cinnamon coating the loaf.

At her gasp, his gaze flew to her face and he frowned in puzzlement. She stared at his hand before she swallowed, a hint of fear and reserve he would not have guessed at upon their first meeting. He found her uncertainty offensive. She was a Nasrid, like him, unlikely to hold inhibitions.

He demanded, "Is the food distasteful, Jazirah?"

"It is only—"

He snapped, "It is only what?"

Nimble fingers tightened around the rim of her drinking vessel. "I am unaccustomed to such rich meals. We never ate so well in prison. My adjustment—"

He swirled the last of his drink, swallowed it in one gulp, and slammed the goblet on the cedar wood. "You will never cease, will you? At every opportunity of our lives together, shall you remind me of your confinement at Shalabuniya?"

Her silent regard turned dazed before she fanned her fingers against her breastbone. He imagined his hand there instead. He truly wished she would not touch herself, which only served to fire lustful musings. He should not want her, not when he had Haziyya.

"My Sultan," she began, "I did not speak of Shalabuniya."

"You do not have to! It is what you do not say, which offends me."

She cleared her throat. Her jawline pulsed. "I shall endeavor not to disturb you with my history. Even if it is a truth you would deny."

He cast down the piece of bread and poured more drink. He had never tried wine, although his mother enjoyed it. He wished he had some to imbibe now.

She skewered a pink piece of lamb and chewed it. "My father sends his felicitations for your continued good health. He prospers as well."

"Yet, the Jewish doctor attends him still."

Her black brows flared. "I did not know you were aware of Doctor Pharez's visits."

"I am aware of all occurrences in my domain."

"I see. Father has chosen Doctor Pharez as his personal physician."

"When there are other qualified doctors?"

"You mean Moorish doctors, of course. There is no one Father or I trust more. We cannot all have the services of your esteemed physician."

When he nodded, she continued, "Father dines this evening with Sultana Maryam and her eldest son. It is a little amusing when she says Prince Ismail. Both my father and her son look up in confusion."

Muhammad took no delight in the mention of his stepmother, brother, or frankly Jazirah's father. "You would do well to keep far from Maryam."

Her lips pursed. He groaned and snatched up more of the half-eaten bread.

She asked, "Why should I ignore her? The visits cheer my father. He has little to do except shuffle around the house you have provided."

Accusation underlay her tone, but he chose to ignore it.

"Prince Ismail, I meant your brother this time, excels at poetry. Has he ever recited verses before you?"

"He has not."

"You should let him. He is talented."

"How wonderful to hear he has some skill."

They lapsed into another strained silence, while Muhammad devoured a portion of the *zirbiya* with gusto. Jazirah picked at the *skibaj*. He slammed another emptied goblet atop the table. Mayhap the syrup of lemon would soothe him. Jazirah looked up from her plate but made no comment. Her refusal to show any outward awareness of his discomfort frustrated and fascinated him in equal measure. Didn't his nearness bother her? As his fingers closed around the cup, he wished they might have fisted in her hair instead.

He took secret pleasure in her sighs of delight as she turned her attention to the bread and pastry. She liked sweet foods. He would ensure the cooks always prepared honeyed *dafair* bread and almond-scented *khushkananaj* pastries for her at every evening meal... he halted such foolish thoughts. He could not allow a repeat of this night. It would not be best for both their sakes if they were alone together again before the marital ceremony occurred.

One task remained. He must choose a wedding date and consult with the court astrologer, but Muhammad found he did not wish to wait for an occasion determined by the stars. The sooner he wedded and bedded Jazirah, she might give him a son. His palm itched at the thought of touching her, but desire alone could not compel him. Her beauty would ensure handsome features in their child. Would their son inherit her nature or his?

"My Sultan, may I ask another question?"

Interrupted in his musings, he looked up from his almost emptied plate of *zirbiya*. She peered at him over the rim of her cup. He swiped a hand across his face. "Speak."

"How are we to have a true marriage when so much remains unsure? You question my heart and words. I consider whether you will be a fair husband. Too many uncertainties plague us. Your mother was right. This is not a favorable start. Mayhap we need more time—"

He blurted, "I intend to marry you before month's end, with a full week of feasting prior to our union. There is no reason to wait."

As she stared, agape, he reasoned there would be time to consider his excitement at his impulsive choice. In the meantime, her question deserved an honest answer.

"Make no mistake, Jazirah. We shall have a true marriage. You shall be my Sultana and I shall be your husband. I will wed you and share your bed upon our nuptial night. I plan to continue sharing a bed with you until you have quickened with my child. Give me an heir, one whom we may both treasure. Mayhap from our union, an understanding may grow."

Her fingers trembled. Her opal ring banged against the table before she gripped the wood's rounded edge. Stricken, she pressed her lips together until they paled.

He perceived her worry. Her earlier boldness had irritated and intrigued him, but it retreated with the possibility of the virgin's pain. He vowed on their wedded night to grant her pleasure, to show her no basis for fear would ever dwell between them in the marital bed. Haziyya had made a tender, compassionate lover of him. He savored the opportunity to awaken Jazirah's desire. The thought of how he might stir her hidden passions thrilled him.

She asked, "You require little more than duty from your wife?"

The question took him aback, given the nature of his carnal thoughts. Beyond wanting her in his bed and an heir to ensure the royal line, what else did he need from her? Loyalty, although he doubted he would ever get it when she blamed him and his father for her past predicament. More than mere tolerance. Somehow, when he gazed into her eyes, he found himself lacking in her opinion, a perception made truth by her narrowed stares and frowns. Of love, he anticipated nothing. Love required deeper trust than loyalty did.

As she eyed him expectantly, he cleared his throat. "Duty and an heir will suffice."

A tic at her jawline warned he might have given her the wrong answer. She looked away, her regard again intent on some spot behind him.

Then she asked, "What about my own wishes?"

He supposed she had them. "You may have whatever you seek, within reason."

"Except of recompense."

He glowered at her, his patience and good humor at an end. He had tried to put aside the past between their fathers, but how could he when she insisted upon dwelling on it? "Why did you come to Gharnatah, Jazirah?"

"You know my father's health prompted me. I take no more pleasure in the expectation of a life at your side than you do in consideration of me."

Not entirely true. Up until a moment ago, he imagined a boy with her features and his hair. Jazirah had ruined his mood with her contentious nature.

He plunked his spoon into the remnants of the *zirbiya*. "You will suffer me as I must suffer you. Our union serves to settle discord within our family, naught more."

Except the pleasurable prospect of the bedding was not a requirement of peace.

"What purpose will my father undertake in your kingdom?"

"I will decide. Do not concern yourself with my government, Jazirah. Your sphere shall be the harem—"

"Where the *Umm al-Walad* rules," she finished for him. "You would have a wife who is no better than a slave, subject to your whims or those of your mother. I have lived in captivity, but I assure you, I will not be as one of your bed slaves."

He gritted his teeth and clasped his hands. The urge to strike or kiss her into silence contended with equal intensity. Instead, he grunted and picked a few olives.

She broke the quiet. "Would you prefer if I did not speak for the rest of the meal?"

"I would." Although he doubted she would oblige him.

Her lips pursed before she moved her hands to her lap and stared at her half-eaten meal. He could not have been more shocked than by her acquiescence. Still, he did not relish the stillness between them. Why? Her stubborn quietness perturbed him more than their disagreements. He did not truly want her taciturn reserve... he just... by the Prophet's beard, he did not know what he wanted where Jazirah was concerned. Against his better judgment and wishes to the contrary, he wanted her. The taste of cinnamon and sugar on her lips, her sweet sighs, the feel of her hands at the back of his neck, those slender calves pressed against his thighs. Allah! How had she undone his resolve in one evening?

***

The hour was late when Muhammad strolled beside Jazirah with his hands clasped behind his back. His fingers twitched as an endless war raged inside him, a battle between violent and carnal thoughts, all revolving around her. Intense longing vied with equal mistrust. Would she be loyal to his interests or her father's own after marriage? He must regain control and prevent his would-be bride from altering his moods in the future. No woman should ever hold such sway over a man's emotions.

She adopted a respectful, almost companionable tranquility despite the clenched fingers fisted in her skirts. He did not doubt a similar conflict raged within her as well, her rebellious nature vying with the need to submit as his wife.

A desire to rid herself of him still governed her tongue. "Truly, I can find my way to the house of my father in the company of the guards you have assigned. You need not accompany me to the harem's exit."

Muhammad halted and peered over his shoulder, noting the discrete distance her escort of Zabala and his nine cohorts kept. All the eunuch-guards paused when their master did. Each man milled around an orange tree and studied it as if in awe. Muhammad chuckled at their poor attempt to appear unobtrusive and resumed his easy stride.

To Jazirah, he said, "My father raised me with the virtues of responsibility and courtesy. Lest I diminish further in your eyes, permit me some small show of...."

Raucous laughter forestalled his last word. A familiar, throaty tone set his brow pounding just before his stepmother came into view with her hated son.

Maryam bought with her the scents of *ghaliya*, roses, and lavender on the night air. Her features remained unaltered in her fortieth year as in previous decades. When her regard fell upon Muhammad, *kohl*-lined, dark eyes twinkled. Like Jazirah, she stood tall and could look down upon his head, but she did not do so this evening. Instead, she fell into a deep, well-practiced prostration. Wavy black tresses absent a streak of gray spilled from beneath a sheer veil lined with pearls. Ismail made the same gesture as his mother, although his broad back remained too stiff for Muhammad's liking.

Little more than ten months separated the brothers. Muhammad shared his mother's short stature, but Maryam had granted her son great height. He had his stocky build from his Nasrid ancestors. Whereas their mothers had once been friends, the young men would never be such. Ismail had inherited more than his mother's coloring and her hair, which he had taken to

88

wearing long and plaited with a silk ribbon. He had also garnered her sense of entitlement. Last month, he had dared demand a governorship, which Muhammad rejected in an instant. He wanted his rival and the prince's mother close by.

Despite a multitude of rejections, Maryam continued to plead for larger quarters outside the harem each week. Muhammad did not mistake her display of humility now as anything less than subterfuge designed to sway him. He remained unmoved by her gestures. The woman was a viper, always coiled and ready for attack. He would not permit her to catch him unawares.

In their red robes shot through with gold thread, mother and son would be well worth admiring glances. Muhammad ordered them to stand, his tone brusquer than he had intended. Best to get them gone from his sight.

"My great Sultan, Princess Jazirah. I trust you have enjoyed a pleasant evening." Amusement saturated Maryam's tone and suggested her thoughts to the contrary. How could she have guessed at the truth so easily?

Instead of stirring the old annoyances, her words made Muhammad glare at Jazirah. What had his intended bride confided in his mother's hated rival?

If Jazirah held any awareness of his suspicions, she showed no interest. A wide smile, so unexpected, graced her lips as she favored Maryam and Ismail with a warm greeting. The exchange of pleasantries between the women annoyed Muhammad almost as much as his brother's casual banter with his future wife.

Then Jazirah said, "My noble Sultan honored me with his invitation. This night forged a strong understanding between us. No doubt all of Gharnatah shall equally rejoice in the union of our family as we do."

Muhammad's brow throbbed a little deeper. What jest was this? Why had Jazirah chosen to tell Maryam some ridiculous untruth?

The glow in Maryam's gaze did not lessen, but tiny crinkles formed around her eyes. "I am well pleased for both of you. If I may ask my gracious Sultan, when will he permit the celebration of the nuptials?"

He muttered, "I hope to wed within the month." Why did she care?

Maryam's smile ebbed. "Is this Jazirah's wish as well?"

The question suggested the depths of Maryam's perception, but before he formed a reply, Jazirah said, "I share the same desire as my future husband on the matter. We wish to wed as soon as may be and end the old divisions forever. Surely, you shall take your place among my guests during *Al-laylat al-henna* and at the wedding feast."

Maryam pursed her full lips. "I would not miss the occasion. Of course, my two sons shall be on hand to witness their brother's happiness on the day of your union."

Shared scowls between Muhammad and his brother spoke volumes of their mutual displeasure at Maryam's words, but Ismail answered first. "I cannot speak for my brother Prince Qays, but it would be my honor, *Ummi*."

Muhammad noted how the platitude addressed Maryam, not the rightful recipient. No matter. Ismail's petty foolery aside, Muhammad could not deem his brother worthy of the honor he sought. Despite sprigs of hair on his pointed chin, Ismail's voice still croaked as one of a boy on the cusp of manhood.

Then Muhammad said, "Allow me a final interlude with my bride."

"I would never interfere, great Sultan." Maryam saluted him, then kissed her son and departed. Ismail bowed again and left for his own house in the royal *madina*. Two pairs of boots slapped the marble tiles before quiet descended again on the harem's garden courtyard.

When Muhammad stood beside only Jazirah, his fingers closed on her wrist. "What foolery is this? Why did you adopt any pretense before Maryam?"

She sighed and shook her head. "Duty has set me upon this path. I will follow its course. Maryam need never know the truth of your lack of regard for me. We wed to seal a decades-long rift, but I am always mindful this shall be a marriage between us. No one else should be involved in our troubles."

Her astuteness intrigued and surprised him. Had Maryam been fomenting discord already, which Jazirah forestalled with her pronouncement? If so, she had shown him more loyalty than he dared hope for in their union.

He assessed her in silence, while she looked down at where they touched. "Please release me. I don't wish to bear bruises on my wedding day, marks to invite speculation neither one of us can countenance."

He let her go, almost reluctantly. "Forgive me, I...."

The appearance of a fluffy white tail forestalled Muhammad's apology as Thalj joined them. Instead of greeting him, she slinked around and rubbed herself against Jazirah's ankles. Muhammad gaped as Jazirah bent and retrieved the cat.

She murmured, "A friendly one. I have seen her prowling the courtyard of the *mashwar* with kittens in tow. The three little ones always shy away from me, even when I offer flakes of fish. Their mother is not so reticent."

Until now, no one else had ever held or fed this cat to Muhammad's knowledge. Thalj purred while Jazirah stroked her coat before asking, "Is she yours?"

Muhammad replied in a clipped tone, "She is a favorite of mine. Her name is Thalj."

Jazirah glanced at him and then deposited the cat in his arms. "Then, I shall not keep her from her master."

With a bow, she took the men he had assigned to her. Muhammad lingered in the passageway long after Jazirah retired. Sweet rosewater scent remained in her wake.

Chapter 8
Rites

Princess Jazirah

Gharnatah, Al-Andalus or Granada, Andalusia
Jumada al-Ula 757 AH or May A.D. 1356 or Sivan 5116

Three days prior to her marriage to Muhammad, Jazirah bolted upright and pushed aside the coverlets of *cendal* on the bed. She shivered beneath the silk in the unexpected evening chill. Lubna rose from her pallet almost at the same time, crisscrossed the chamber, and soon brought a candle sputtering to life.

She asked, "Bad dreams again?"

Although Jazirah shook her head, Lubna replied, "You will forget Harun and the terror of life at Shalabuniya." The light revealed her angled features and bloodshot eyes. She had not slept well either.

"When will he ever stop plaguing my mind? Each time I close my eyes, his visage taunts me. I recall his breath and his hands upon me, and I am back in the cell again."

Lubna said, "Think no more of him or that terrible place. You should be resting, my Sultana. The *Umm al-Walad* and the harem women will come for you at moonrise. Servants of the Sultan's mother have told me the henna night is the longest of a bride's life."

"Somehow, I doubt it." Jazirah stretched with a loud yawn and swung her legs to the floor. "I am not Muhammad's wife. Do not call me Sultana yet. Allow me to be just your Jazirah for a little longer."

Lubna set the candlestick on the cedar wood table beside the bed and sat next to her charge. "Oh, my sweet, you will always be my Jazirah, but now you must share a life with a husband and I should grow accustomed to your title. Others would deem it unseemly for me to be informal with you, even if you were to allow it."

Jazirah grabbed Lubna's hand. "How can I surrender to Muhammad in the marriage bed, when I do not know or trust him? A Sultan must be accustomed to women who obey his wishes without hesitation."

"You believe your husband-to-be has such dutiful women within his family?"

Lubna's upraised eyebrows hinted at the truth she and Jazirah knew. The Sultan's mother was no weak-willed female ensconced behind plaster-daubed walls, nor did Muhammad enjoy the easy acquiescence of his father's second wife Maryam, if her tales of his intractable nature were true.

"How do I give myself to a man such as him?"

Lubna mused, "It would not be difficult to find pleasure in one such as Muhammad ibn Yusuf. He is handsome with his dark hair and eyes. There is something rather sensual about his mouth, meant for kissing." At Jazirah's shocked gasp, Lubna smiled. "No doubt he has a man's appetites as well. Shall you lie to me now and say you find him abhorrent? You would not answer when I asked the same after you had dined with him. Your silence told me all I needed to know, as did the color across your face when you spoke his name."

Jazirah recalled how the sight of Muhammad licking his fingers during dinner had stirred an ache in her belly. Without ever having experienced desire before, she understood her response as instinctual, the natural reaction of a woman to an attractive man.

She said, "My cousin is handsome. I would never deny the fact. So was Harun."

"The Sultan is no beast who abuses women. I have made discreet inquiries and learned from all those whom he has bedded before the *kadin* claimed him."

"Oh Lubna, you didn't. Everyone will think I set you to such a shameful purpose!"

"Should a bride-to-be remain ignorant of all aspects of her husband until the wedding night? It was not as if I asked about the size of his manhood." When Jazirah scowled, Lubna giggled. "Though I was told no woman would find cause for concern."

"Lubna!"

"His women leave his bed well-pleasured, but many become bitter afterward because he has never summoned them again for the *kadin's* sake. You will not endure such complaints as those of the Sultan's concubines."

Jazirah raked one hand through her abundant curls, sweeping hair across her shoulder. She did not care about Muhammad's *jawari,* or even the Berber female who held his heart. "Only those who have not given him sons are sorrowful."

"There is genuine resentment. Some believe Haziyya has bound him with some Berber love spell. They say God curses her womb as recompense."

"I will have to give Muhammad sons." To secure his cruel father's lineage, but they would be her children. Surely, such knowledge must comfort her in the future.

Lubna smoothed the pads of her fingertips across Jazirah's brow. "Don't frown. The getting of sons may be pleasant. Trust your body to respond. The Sultan remains a stranger, but I believe he will seek your pleasure as much as his own. I remember when I first wed a stranger. My husband held more fear of the marriage bed than I did. When he first tried to kiss me, our noses bumped together so hard. The blood on the sheet later was as much his as my own."

As Lubna chuckled, Jazirah joined her. Then the slave said, "In those ten short months together, we discovered each other. We learned of pleasure and love, before the Balkan slavers took me from him forever. He never even knew I was carrying his son. When our infant died in the slave pens, I wanted to join him, but then your father found me. He gave me purpose again when he put you, a little babe, into my arms. A child who needed me as much as I needed her."

As Lubna paused and heaved a sigh, Jazirah squeezed her fingers.

"Trust your instincts with Muhammad, my sweet, and touch him as you would be touched."

Heat bloomed across Jazirah's cheeks. "What if he is impatient with me? What if he behaves more like Harun... than your husband?"

"Your royal cousin is not cruel. I know the ilk and he is not among them. On the night you met him for dinner, before his dismissal, I saw how the Sultan watched you. I remember the thrill of such regard bestowed on me. He wants you for your pride and beauty. I suspect his yearning surprised even him."

After her evening with him, Jazirah had fled to her father's home in time for *Salat al-Isha,* but even the prayer hour had not calmed her. Dinner with Muhammad had stirred so many emotions. She had vacillated between exasperation and amazement, fury at his bold commands and fiery need to challenge him. Amid those turbulent feelings, desire to know more of him, including the manner of his touch and the temptation of his lips, had also dwelled.

Instinct told her Lubna spoke the truth. Muhammad would not be a cruel beast to her in the marriage bed. She understood so little of his moods, but somehow, certainty of how it would be between them stirred her curiosity and willingness to accept his attentions. Where Harun's despicable demands and authority had made her feel naught but abhorrence, the prospect of a night with Muhammad roused the opposite emotion.

Lubna prodded, "Tell me what you are feeling, my child."

"I can hardly describe it, mostly anticipation coupled with uncertainty. Fear, but not the kind you may suppose. Our future frightens me. Will we ever come to the accord I told Maryam we shared? May Allah forgive me for such an untruth."

"You did well to dispel Sultana Maryam's misguided attempts to warn you away from marriage to the Sultan. You perceived her sly comments at those dinners with your father as no more than words meant to sow enmity between you and her stepson."

"Were Maryam's statements misguided? She sought to warn me of Muhammad's true nature." Just as Jazirah believed he would be tolerant in the marital bed, she also suspected Maryam's overtures. Something warned her away from the woman.

"What new information did Sultan Yusuf's old queen share with you? Sultan Muhammad is proud, intractable, and unforgiving, dominating with the force of his will. He is also lord of Gharnatah. How else should he act? Mayhap Sultana Maryam thinks her eldest son would be more amenable in the role...."

"You're speaking treason, Lubna. It would be best if no one overheard you. Even better if you did not speak such words at all. Father warned me, there are ears and eyes everywhere in *Al-Qal'at al-Hamra*. We must be cautious."

"We learned vigilance at Shalabuniya. Why should this place be any different?"

"It is, Lubna. Believe me. Even I, never having lived in *Al-Qal'at al-Hamra* before now, know enough to be circumspect. The man I must marry does not rely with faith upon me any more than I may believe in him. I won't give Muhammad reason to deal unfairly with you, as his father did with mine."

Jazirah rose from the bed, taking the damask coverlet with her as she strolled to the southern-oriented window. She peered through the lattice shutters. The aperture of the small bedchamber she occupied faced Yusuf's great gate, completed in the second year of her father's exile. In the dying light, sunset cast its fiery glow against the redbrick walls of the *Bab al-Sharia*. The Hand of Fatima symbol carved just above the gate's archway held special significance for brides, a sign of prosperity. Would such blessings come to her as Muhammad's wife?

Lubna joined her and rubbed Jazirah's shoulders. "Will you eat anything before *Al-laylat al-henna*? I can tell Jyoti to prepare stuffed dates."

"The almond paste and rosewater inside would go to waste, for I am the only one who likes stuffed dates. Jyoti need only cook for herself, Dhanu, Beatriz, and Gonzalo since Father is not here."

"His absence worries you."

Jazirah pressed against the adjacent wall. "Where were these friends, who've called upon and feted Father in these last three months, when he needed allies in his exile? First Maryam, and then the governors of Lawsa and Al-Hamma visited him. Even the commander of the Volunteers of the Faith, who holds Wadi-Ash in Father's stead, has come. Now, Muhammad the Red of Malaka has arrived for the wedding and dines with Father."

Jazirah had mistrusted her cousin's intentions from the moment he appeared at her father's doorstep. Ruddy skin and hair the color of a firebrand had surely earned him the epithet. His red-rimmed eyes troubled her, as if lack of sleep or some sickness plagued him. He seemed a restless soul, one who glowered at everything around him. When her father had introduced them during the night before, the *Raïs* of Malaka had looked up at her and frowned as if her height displeased him as much as it had the Sultan. Throughout the exchange as they ate with her father, the governor's stark stare returned several times to her face, a gaze of assessment rather than covetousness. His brow crinkled as if he sought to unravel a mystery. Only when her father cleared his throat and dismissed Jazirah had she avoided her cousin's glare. Now her father shared a meal with him at a house the governor owned in the capital.

"Muhammad the Red troubles you more than most," Lubna guessed.

"Not just for the strange behavior he showed, pivoting his head from side to side as if he could not control its movements. Mayhap it is naught more than an overanxious mind, but my thoughts lead me toward suspicions about the man. I cannot help but fear Maryam's interests may align with his, too. After all, Maryam's eldest daughter Fatima is married to him."

Lubna pressed her lips briefly to Jazirah's shoulder. "Then you know what you must do, my sweet. Keep your father far from any schemes. Wed the Sultan and ensure none within this household arouse his misgivings."

Jazirah trilled, "Oh Lubna, you make it seem so easy! I am about to marry a man who has little regard for my cares or me. Muhammad's desires aside, he would sooner consign Father to the depths of *Al-Quasaba* again, than wed with me."

"Then you must allay the Sultan's concerns. Even a union born of necessity and burdened by mistrust, can bind partners. Trust and love can still flow."

Unshed tears at the corners of her eyes, Jazirah cast a bitter laugh into the wind. "Trust and love? I would hold more hope for an easy bedding and a son within the following year, than for trust and love with my would-be husband."

***

Jazirah went to the *hammam*, from which she later emerged refreshed and perfumed, in time for the arrival of the Sultanas. Arrayed in red and gold silks with her hair unbound and Lubna at her back, Jazirah stepped out alone into the night air. The full complement of household guards under Zabala's command protected her father instead of her.

The women of the Sultan's family and their servants awaited her. Chief among the royal household, Butayna and Maryam stood side by side, each with their personal attendants. Jazirah acknowledged bows from the red-haired Englishwomen Jawla and Hafsa, who served Butayna, as well as the dwarf Nazhun, whom Maryam kept close.

Jazirah had never seen Butayna and Maryam together before. The contrasts between the two women could not have been starker. One tall and clad in silver with dark tresses gleaming like heavy, brocaded silk in the torchlight eunuchs carried. The other shorter, dressed in lavender and gold, but plainer only in comparison to her counterpart. Maryam's wide, welcoming smile held more warmth than Butayna's lackluster attempt, more a grimace. Had she dreaded this night beside her rival?

The Sultan's mother approached. When Lubna tapped Jazirah's arm, she remembered her courtesies and fell into a deep bow. At the light touch of Butayna's hand on her shoulder, she straightened.

Butayna said, "We, the Sultanas of Gharnatah, sisters, daughters, aunts, and wives, embrace you. You will never want for care or comfort. We are your family."

A brown-haired, elfin young woman who bore a striking resemblance to Butayna stepped forward and pressed brief kisses to either side of Jazirah's face. "I am Aisha, sister to Muhammad, now your sister as well."

Another took her place, lithe and tall beneath her black *jubba* with eyes to match Maryam's own. In a velvety tone, she whispered, "I am also your sister, Fatima."

The rest of the women crowded around, each greeting Jazirah with the same effusiveness. Younger princesses, who could only be Muhammad's sisters, had joined four ladies who looked older than Butayna or Maryam. Jazirah stared into the faces of strangers and discerned features akin to her own or those of her father. Nasrids all.

Maryam pecked her cheeks. "May you know only the joys of marriage."

"God's blessings upon you and my son forever," Butayna murmured while she and Jazirah embraced. When they drew apart, Butayna hesitated before releasing Jazirah. What was the cause of this pool of tears welling in the *Umm al-Walad's* eyes?

Muhammad's six younger sisters led the way, chattering merrily together as their silks rustled the shrubbery along the walkway from the house of Jazirah's father. No one else except sentries monitored the route the women took, entering the harem before proceeding down a hallway painted with red, green, and blue pigments. They exited and took stairs to a north-facing garden, where the heady scents of flowers greeted Jazirah.

Tendrils of fragrant incense drifted from braziers and floated on air currents, swept up toward the canopy of twinkling stars. Female musicians struck up a lively tune. When Butayna joined the music in song, Jazirah thought it the most beautiful sound she had ever heard, until Maryam took up the refrain. Butayna cast a narrowed glower over her shoulder at her rival, but her voice never wavered. Together she and Maryam ushered Jazirah into the center of the garden, where a wizened crone sat on a plush carpet bounded by striped pillows, brushes, pots of henna, and a cedar wood footrest.

Jazirah traded a glance with Maryam, who nodded and helped her settle before the aged woman. Retainers fanned out with glasses of cut rock crystal filled to the brim with fruit juices or water laced with lemon or orange rinds. Other servants fueled the braziers, which dispersed thick, warming steam. Lubna joined Jazirah on the ground and offered a platter of date balls soaked in honey and caked with sugar crystals. Lubna winked at Jazirah, who nodded so Lubna could pop one of the sweets into her mouth. Rosewater coated Jazirah's tongue.

Then everyone from the lowliest slave in attendance to Muhammad's mother crowded together and looked on in rapt amusement, while the henna artist moistened the tip of the thin bristles with the end of her tongue, before she dipped the fibers into a green mush. The old woman began with Jazirah's nails first, painting each a deep green. Then she moved to the fingertips and drew three bands of perfect circles up to the knuckles. A linked diamond-shaped pattern followed. Despite rheumy eyes and gnarled hands, her delicate brushwork produced intricate images. A depiction of the crescent moon, stars, birds, pomegranates, and flower petals soon colored Jazirah's palms and backs of the hands up to the wrists.

"Exquisite," Butayna murmured.

Nestled against her, Aisha said, "*Ummi,* I wish to have my hands painted as well."

Butayna nodded. "You may, daughter. We all may, for it is extraordinary artistry."

Seated between her eldest daughters Fatima and Khadija, Maryam commented, "I am amazed you would think so as a Christian, Butayna. Among the *dhimmi,* such an act would be despicable. Wouldn't your priests say such hands are filth-stained?"

Butayna did not even deign to raise her rapt gaze from the henna application. "A Christian can appreciate true beauty. I do not know what the priests of a Christian country would say, when my abode is in a Moorish one, ruled by my son, the master of all Gharnatah."

Pride laced Butayna's answer. Surely, she had not needed to remind Maryam of her queenly status. As this was Jazirah's first occasion in the presence of both women, she proposed to learn all she could of their interactions, but thus far, Butayna seemed overly proud compared to Maryam.

Before slaves brought platters and salvers, they distributed water for washing from bird-shaped vessels crafted of bronze, along with towels for the drying of hands. Then Lubna offered Jazirah every delicacy the slaves displayed. By tradition, the guests would eat cold appetizers first. Jazirah refused all but the lemon-marinated chickpeas with ginger and cinnamon.

Although Lubna chided her lest she draw Butayna's ire, Jazirah silenced her with whispered words. "I don't enjoy tart foods! Give me a little more of the flatbread, please. At least it makes this purée more enjoyable."

A *'tharid* of ground spring lamb tasted of fennel, fresh coriander, and flecks of cinnamon sprinkled atop the broth. Lubna spooned a wrinkled bulb along with some of the crumbled bread of the *'tharid* from a ceramic bowl, painted and glazed with gold.

Jazirah crinkled her nose. "What is that?"

Lubna's shrug followed, but Butayna answered, "It is a truffle. It tastes good."

Maryam chimed in. "Christian pigs enjoy them, I'm told."

Butayna scowled at her counterpart and rejoined with, "My Yusuf, God defend his memory, told me of a *hadith* of your Prophet, in which he stated truffles were like manna from heaven."

How did Muhammad's mother know of the Traditions?

Maryam echoed Jazirah's thoughts. "You understand too much of a religion you have long disdained, even for your son's sake. Have you finally converted to Islam?"

Butayna snapped, "If I had, I would make no secret of it! I would be true to my chosen faith, unlike others who abandoned theirs for expediency alone."

The barely disguised insult to Maryam, who had converted to Islam after bearing her first son, drew frowns from the eldest daughters of both women.

Aisha leaned toward her mother. "*Ummi,* can we forgo the arguments for one night? A moment's peace, I pray."

Butayna sniffed. "I will permit it, if Maryam will."

Maryam's daughter Fatima said, "This night is for our sister, Jazirah. Petty squabbles of the past should not taint her happiness."

Jazirah ducked her head. While she lauded the younger Sultanas' efforts, she could never escape her history any more than Butayna and Maryam might put aside theirs.

She accepted the truffle Lubna offered. While chewing, Jazirah thought poorly of the earthy flavor. She almost spat it out. The taste reminded her of when Harun had once mashed her face in the ground when she refused to eat the slop he provided them, fare not fit for a Christian's pig or dog.

Looking around at the brightened faces of the guests, she reminded herself there would never be a repeat of such indignities. If only for tonight, she could be safe. For the first time in life, family might come to include more than her father and Lubna. She never knew how much she had missed in the fellowship of her relations.

Unbidden, her father's words upon their arrival came to mind. He had warned her there would be no friends in Gharnatah. Should she never trust any of these women?

Lubna drew her attention by offering more of the lamb. The food at the feast evoked every color and flavor of Al-Andalus. Sugar-sweetened and dried apricots, bananas, and figs between two layers of flat bread sprinkled with yellow saffron. Bitter oranges with chicken browned in almond oil. The arrival of spring meant shad had spawned in the *Xenil* River. Jazirah enjoyed the fried fish, pepper and garlic seasonings lingering on her tongue after the meal. She bit into honey-soaked, flaky layers of sweet cheese and pastry, only to have a little melted cheese cling to the corner of her mouth. Butayna smiled at her, but Jazirah looked away.

Throughout the feast, the musicians played. In turn, Butayna or Maryam sang for the entertainment of all, though it seemed to Jazirah the blending of their voices produced the best harmony. The discord between them remained evident while they traded sharp banter as the evening wore on. A deeper meaning dwelled beneath the thinly veiled arguments. Sharp words spoke of profound hurt and betrayal. One day, Jazirah resolved, she would discover the history of these two quarrelsome Sultanas.

Muhammad's sisters chased each other around the oleander bushes. Despite the hatred between Butayna and Maryam, neither woman had prevented the happy interaction of the younger Sultanas. If the daughters had reached an accord, mayhap the possibility for peace between their warring mothers remained in reach.

***

Sultan Muhammad V

100

As the morning of his union with Jazirah dawned, Muhammad stood with his personal attendants inside his dressing room. Like his mother with her cadre of servants at her disposal, he relied upon a core group for his personal needs. In his eleventh year, when his father had granted him a residence outside of the harem, Muhammad also received the Nubian female slaves Bahar, Qamar, and Suna, who were of an age with him. They had always greeted him with smiles each morning and wished him the joys of evening before he dismissed them.

Now he met Bahar's somber expression and the watery gazes of her companions with puzzlement. While she belted his plain white robe over a brown tunic, her hands shook. He stilled her cold fingers, and with a free hand, lifted her face for his examination. The same full features and wide mouth set in skin almost as dark as *kohl*, but her reddened eyes were unexpected. He looked around at Qamar and Suna with their downcast expressions.

Then he said, "I would think you were prepared to mourn at my funeral."

Suna sniffled and shook her head. "Noble master, please do not think us foolish. We are just so happy for you!"

A torrent of tears followed. She dropped his white leather slippers and sobbed behind her hands. Qamar kept a steady hold on the basket of Muhammad's personal bath implements, but she patted Suna's arm.

Muhammad shook his head. "If this is a show of joy, I can't fathom your sadness."

"Please don't mock Suna, noble master. You know her tender heart," Bahar said.

Muhammad grazed her rounded chin. "What of your tender heart, my lovely?"

"It is filled with praise and delight for you, as always," she replied.

Qamar added, "We, who have been at your side for seven years, we know the meaning of this moment. We wish you eternal happiness with your Sultana."

He reviewed their familiar faces, recognizing sincere expressions of pleasure on his behalf. "Smile for me then. No more tears, even if they are an outpouring of joy."

He left Bahar and joined Suna at the edge of the carpet. When Muhammad drew her into his arms, the sobs remained unabated. He permitted Suna these tears until she sobered and raised her head of cropped hair, granting him a fleeting smile. While he kissed and embraced her again, Bahar answered the knock at the door.

Pero saluted Muhammad. "Great Sultan, the honorable minister Ibn al-Khatib."

Muhammad released Suna, who bent and helped him don the slippers, while he said, "Is Ibn al-Khatib here in another vain effort to alter my plans? He wastes time."

Pero bowed, but stayed silent. Even Muhammad's women averted their stares.

He swiped a hand over his face and mumbled, "Still, I will speak with him and hear his words. I owe him such."

As Pero withdrew from the chamber, Muhammad tightened the belt around his thick waist. "Is all in readiness? Then let us leave."

He preceded the women out of his chambers. Bahar followed with his vestments draped over her arms including new robes of state, a red *jubba,* and a gold and green *khil'a.* Suna brought the long boots made of the finest leather in Christian Córdoba by Moorish hands, a gift from the Castillan monarch Pedro. She also carried an ebony jewelry box under her arm. Qamar had a basket of bathing scrubs, towels and cloths, oils, and implements.

When Muhammad opened the doors, his personal guard ringed the harem's garden courtyard. At its center, the minister Ibn al-Khatib stood with crossed arms. He gave Muhammad his most direct, probing stare. Aged forty-three years, Ibn al-Khatib had served the chancery of Gharnatah from his youth. With his back ramrod straight, his thick, dark locks immaculately curled and oiled, and his silvery robes of the best silk woven on Gharnati looms, he had become the epitome of a political leader in the court.

"You've come to wish me well on the morning of my marriage?" Muhammad stepped out from beneath the shade offered by the pavilion and approached Ibn al-Khatib.

The minister bowed and Muhammad tapped his shoulder. "Rise, for I do not have much time before I must meet my uncle at the bathhouse of the great mosque."

"This meeting brought me from the *mashwar.* I still advise against it, my Sultan."

Muhammad resumed walking and Ibn al-Khatib fell into step beside him, with the slaves in their wake. The heavy-booted footfalls of a score among Muhammad's personal guards followed. All other servants paused in their duties and bent their backs as Muhammad bypassed them.

He said, "The arrangements have been made and the meeting will occur. What is your chief objection? Is it my choice to bathe in the *hammam* of the great *masjid* with my uncle or my refusal to allow high ministers like you to join our private discussion?"

"Both actions are equally ill-advised. The Muhammad I helped educate would know better. Do I detect the persistent influence of Sultana Butayna upon her son?"

Muhammad halted at the doorstep, his fingers curling into fists. "Do you think I cannot act without the *Umm al-Walad's* direction? Mayhap we both misunderstand. In your words, I hear the arrogance of one who forgets I am no longer the child who sat upon his knee and for instruction about our laws. Odd, when you know I am a man of almost nineteen years."

"Almost nineteen." Ibn al-Khatib clasped and stroked the length of his beard. "You should not need to remind me of your age, my Sultan."

No other ministers would have dared take the liberties he did. All of them, even Ridwan, would have deferred by now.

Muhammad ground his teeth together. "Mayhap I need to remind you of other facts in your advanced years. I am Sultan by birthright and the will of our people. You may have proclaimed my ascension to the throne, but you do not rule me. No man or woman ever shall, least of all a servant of mine."

The elder statesman bowed. "I beg your favor. You are a young ruler, unaware of how some may view your actions. You retire to a public bath, rather than the lavish one your grandfather built to share the water with a man whom your own wise father didn't trust. I meant to offer good advice on—"

"Good advice? Instead, you have forced a hastily formed opinion on me. I am to wed my cousin. It is only right for me to meet with her father and discuss mutual expectations. If you could see beyond petty fears of his rise to power again, you would recognize my goal. I purposely chose the public *hammam*, not the family one for this meeting so my uncle would perceive his place. A prince in name only. He shall never regain the distinction of a Nasrid! As to your other scruple, I know enough of my uncle not to trust him. I do not need your advice about my family!"

Muhammad pushed through the double doors and stepped out into the mid-morning light. The denizens of the royal *madina* stopped their activities when he appeared. Their bows and salutes went unacknowledged. The slaughter of his father instilled a deep aversion in Muhammad against mingling with his people. He would not risk a blade through his back as his father had done with his murderer Al-Sagir.

A portion of his guard awaited Muhammad before the *hammam* attached to the mosque built in the time of his mad great-uncle, the third Sultan of the dynasty. In a circle of the sentries stood his uncle and beside him, a male slave and the Jewish personal physician.

All bowed, the doctor's grizzled curls tumbling from beneath his black hood.

Muhammad reviewed the state of his uncle when the man straightened with a grunt. Same hooked nose and incisive gaze, features of the family for generations. The lines of the weathered expression had not faded, but the dullness of his eyes had receded, and the cheeks were no longer hollow, even if forever pockmarked. A ruddy glow brightened his visage. He even smiled, as though pleased at their reunion.

"Uncle. Thank you for joining me."

"You honored me with your invitation. This is my doctor, Pharez ben Abraham ben Zarzar, who tended me with great care at Shalabuniya when—"

"I know the man!" Muhammad snapped at the mention of the fortress. If only he could tear it down so no one might ever speak of the accursed place again! He refused to ponder why reference to it bothered him so much. Such concerns led in a direction he would not go, stirring questions about his father's conduct and his own.

The doctor's face reddened. He bowed again, but kept his gaze averted.

A twinge of regret at his sour tone nagged at Muhammad until he dismissed the Jew from mind and addressed his uncle. "Shall we enter?"

Ismail said farewell to his physician while Muhammad proceeded down a slight slope and went to *Al-bayt al-maslakh,* the changing room of the bath. Other members of the royal bodyguard stood there, four at each corner and two on either side of the doorway into the next room, where Muhammad would relax at intervals in the bathing ritual. Muhammad removed his clothing with help from Qamar, who withdrew an ample towel from her basket and wrapped it around her master's waist. The linen fell to his ankles. The eunuch with his uncle did the same. The quartet went into the next room, where benches lined the walls of the first floor. More of Muhammad's men gathered around the balustrade of the second level.

His uncle peered at them. "Are so many required? Is it because I am with the sovereign? I assure you, I am as harmless as my Gonzalo." He patted his slave's arm.

"If you say so, uncle. Still, the soldiers will stay."

Muhammad sat on a wooden bench. Qamar removed her tunic and bared herself to the waist. The shocked gasp of the eunuch followed. Qamar settled at Muhammad's feet, a scoop of aromatic almond scrub cupped in her hands. She grasped his, kneading his palms and fingers in a deep, circular rhythm. Then she did the same with the soles of his feet. His uncle retired to the lavatory and re-emerged while Qamar continued the massage.

Muhammad summoned Pero. "Send for drinks and a light repast."

The captain nodded and bowed. "As you wish, my Sultan."

Seated across from Muhammad, his uncle enjoyed the ministrations of the eunuch. Muhammad leaned back against the tiled wall and closed his eyes, blotting out the sight.

Ibn al-Khatib's words stung most for the element of truth within them. Muhammad should have bathed in the *hammam* of his paternal grandfather, attended by trusted high ministers and his hated brothers. Instead, impulse directed him to send a messenger to the house of his uncle on the previous evening. He had thought better of his actions in the night, but even then, he had not rescinded the invitation. An occasion to sit alone with the man would allow Muhammad the opportunity to engage his uncle and learn of his thoughts. Did he still possess a traitor's heart?

Muhammad opened his eyes and began with, "Is my future wife growing nervous? I'm told all brides are as the union draws nearer."

"My daughter anticipates the wedding, little more."

An enigmatic answer, one Jazirah might have told her father to say if Muhammad asked. He recalled her words spoken during their dinner. *'I am always mindful this shall be a marriage between us.'* Not the speech of one who quaked with fear.

His mother had failed to provide any insight when he saw her at the end of *Al-laylat al-henna* two nights before. According to her, Jazirah had been her usual self during the ceremony, which evoked more questions than answers. How was he to gauge his bride's general manner beyond her haughty displays? Butayna had insisted the night went well, despite Maryam's unwelcome presence.

The proximity of his stepmother and Jazirah troubled him further, despite the latter's attempt at solidarity with him upon his announcement of their marriage. With each day, he grew more certain of Maryam's attempts to ferret out discord between him and Jazirah.

In the meantime, he needed to control his bride, but more importantly, his reactions around her. They had not seen each other since they dined together, but her proud features typically appeared in his mind as on this occasion. Her sweet, succulent mouth and lips he longed to kiss. He wondered about her taste and touch. He would have to charm her to discover whether she would be softer than silk in his arms. He grinned in expectation of the challenge.

"I see my nephew the Sultan looks forward to the marriage as well."

The voice forced Muhammad back to the present. He scowled at his uncle and rose from the bench before Qamar had finished.

"I do not wish to linger here. Come."

The men washed their hands and feet in the small basin, before they entered the bathing room of *Al-bayt al-barid*. On the left wall, a tub of water awaited them. Qamar brought her basket and set it on the floor. She removed her *sarawil*. The gossamer trousers pooled around her ankles before she stepped out of them and cast aside her sandals.

Muhammad laughed at the eunuch's paled face before removing his towel and hanging it on a peg along the wall. His uncle stripped, too. He and Muhammad stepped into the tub. Their slaves stood behind them, the eunuch aghast as he removed his clothes. Qamar paid his altered state no attention. Her nipple grazed Muhammad's arm. Before Haziyya, the movement would have stirred a lustful response. Then a more pleasant thought came to mind. If Jazirah had stood naked in his bath, he would have shown no such restraint.

Her father leaned forward as the eunuch soaped and lathered his back. "You have never favored pretense, my Sultan. Would you have me believe, when you saw my daughter the last time, she failed to stir your interest?"

"Jazirah is beautiful to be sure. There are several like her in my harem."

"I vow, my Sultan, you have never known anyone quite like her."

Chapter 9
The First Night

Sultan Muhammad V

Gharnatah, Al-Andalus or Granada, Andalusia
Jumada al-Ula 757 AH or May A.D. 1356 or Sivan 5116

After the visit to the *hammam*, Muhammad went to the *mashwar* in the company of his uncle. Together in the council chamber amid stony-faced ministers, the royals sat with a rustle of silks at a low table and reviewed the marital contract for a final time.

As rays of noonday sun pierced the slats in the doorway and fell across the pages, Jazirah's father said, "The terms are extremely generous to ensure the comfort and security of my daughter. I thank you also, my Sultan, for including the provision forbidding divorce if Jazirah should prove barren. My daughter will always have a place of honor in your harem."

Disgruntled snorts followed, but Ridwan, chief among the men who served the council, silenced them with a stern look. He alone stood between the signatories, a vantage point permitting him a view of everyone gathered in the recesses of the square-shaped chamber, just as Muhammad intended. Ridwan would report all he had seen within a day.

Golden light illuminated the delicate *Naskhi* calligraphy drawn by Ridwan's gnarled fingers. The chief minister had rightly suggested the divorce stipulation to which so many of his compatriots objected. A childless wife might be worthless in the opinion of others. Yet, an enemy required no more than Jazirah's link to royal blood to seek the throne for himself through marriage to her.

Muhammad also discerned his mother's guidance in the script written on smooth vellum. Upon Butayna's swift return from Shalabuniya, she had spoken about the need to keep Jazirah from the hands of Muhammad's enemies. Not a difficult task for Butayna to have influenced Ridwan, when she relied so much upon the chief eunuch Hisham, brother to the chief minister. All suspicion aside, Muhammad acknowledged the correctness of the move. He would keep Jazirah at his side no matter the cost, and thus, her father's activities could remain monitored.

Muhammad took a reed in hand and dipped the tip inside the inkpot. He held the reed out to his uncle, who signed first.

Muhammad's signature followed, then those of Ridwan and Ibn al-Khatib as witnesses. In his capacity as secretary of the ministerial body, the latter stamped the document with the seal of the Sultans in red ink.

Given the approval and signatures on the contract, the ceremony to follow before the *imam* of Gharnatah, the *walima* or wedding feast, and the bedding afterward were mere formalities. The vellum provided all the proof Muhammad needed. Jazirah belonged to him. He should not relish the thought so much.

He stood and extended his fingers to his uncle, who did not grasp them. Instead, he rose of his own will. Muhammad cupped his hands and the elder man placed his fingers within them, the formal style by which one person swore his oath of loyalty to another.

Ridwan applauded and at his baleful stare cast around the chamber, the assembly joined in, Ibn al-Khatib the last among them.

The bride's father said in a low whisper, "Jazirah is precious to me, my last and best hope for our family. A husband would treat her well, especially a Sultan."

Muhammad perceived the implicit demand in his uncle's tone and replied, "So long as she behaves in the way a Sultana, my wife, should act, I shall never dishonor her."

He received a nod, affirming mutual understanding of each charge. The applause would have drowned out their exchange from all except Ridwan.

As he gazed into his uncle's eyes, Muhammad viewed the stir of emotions in the man's features. A mix of concern, echoed by the furrowed brow, and resolve, set in the full lips. Pride also dwelled in the depths of his steady regard, but Muhammad wondered at its source. The approval of a father as his only child married or a prince's vanity regarding a marital alliance with the lord of Gharnatah. What mattered most to his uncle, a daughter's security, or the profitability of her union?

***

In the early evening, the wedding banquet occurred within the garden courtyard of the harem. Muhammad entertained the guests, including his male relations among the provincial governors, along with his chancery, high officials of the judiciary, and the *imam* of Gharnatah who had presided over the marriage ceremony at noon. Jazirah and her female guests were relegated to the harem's upper floor, where her bridal trousseau, the *addahbia* would be on display in his mother's chambers. Peals of laughter from above evidenced the women's enjoyment of their portion of the feast.

To Muhammad's right, the preeminent ministers Ridwan and Ibn al-Khatib occupied positions of honor alongside the *imam*. To

Muhammad's left, his two younger brothers gorged on a *madira* of minty lamb in yogurt, tender roasted kid, and the smoked flesh of a peacock presented in all its plumage. With each measure of fulsome praise or benediction offered by the guests in celebration of the marriage, the sons of Maryam raised their glasses of *sekanjabin*. Neither of them made any pronouncement or blessed their brother's unions.

Seated directly across from Muhammad, the husband of his eldest sister Fatima, the *Raïs* of Malaka stroked the thick beard, which had partly earned the governor his nickname. Then he reached inside the folds of his *jubba* before he bellowed for a eunuch who held a water pipe. Muhammad detested the practice of smoking, but he put aside his personal abhorrence. Although he exchanged banal chatter with Ridwan or the *imam* at times, he kept close watch on his cousin, also made a brother by marriage.

The kinship ties between them dated back to the days of the family's powerful matriarch, Muhammad's great-grandmother, who had died eight years before. Her first son was the paternal grandfather Muhammad had never known, a ruler stabbed to death over a concubine by his own cousins. Her second son had inherited the governorship of Malaka and sired an heir who then fathered Muhammad the Red.

The substance he drew upon so deeply from the pipe emitted a pungent, herbal odor, immediately recognizable. Although some inane advice on a happy wife made most of the guests laugh, Muhammad seethed deep inside. How dare his cousin smoke *hashish* in the midst of their assembly! Within an hour, Malaka's governor had reddened eyes to match the color of his beard. The final summons to prayer went up, but none of the attendees rose, not even the *imam* who spooned *madira* into his mouth.

Then Muhammad the Red cleared his throat and called attention to himself in a gruff tone. "What entertainments shall our Sultan provide? I have eaten and drunk my fill! What of the beautiful, young slave girls rumored to exist in the harem? Will we have no women tonight?"

Hisham, who stood at the opposite end of the courtyard near the harem's entrance, had hired dancers and singers for later in the evening. Muhammad waved to him. The musicians played, seated in the corner near the bathhouse access.

The dancers entered from the eastern portico in a flurry of red, yellow, and green gauzy silks, which left little to the imagination of the guests. Muhammad the Red grabbed at one buxom woman, but in his drug-induced torpor, she easily evaded him. He slipped back on the pillows, barely able to control his flailing limbs. His relations shied away from him as he cackled like a lunatic.

Muhammad's head pounded in time to the drumbeats. A look passed between him and Jazirah's father, one of mutual displeasure at the antics of the dazed fool in their midst.

At the height of revelry, Hisham glided beside Muhammad. He bent low and whispered with a white-gloved hand over his mouth, "The honored *Umm al-Walad* has escorted your wife to her chamber, where she awaits the Sultan's desire."

Muhammad rose and wished the *imam* and his ministers well.

"Does the Sultan leave us to bed his bride?" Muhammad the Red moved his head from side to side but found none others amused by his question. Still, he guffawed as he tapped his pipe. "Can he trust she has not slipped a knife between the sheets? Mayhap the mighty sword between his legs will not be the only one to do a little stabbing tonight!"

If Muhammad carried a blade, he would have thrust it between his cousin's teeth. Instead, he ignored the crude attempt at humor and strode with Hisham along the walkway. He mounted the narrow, marble steps two at a time. His heart thrummed in anticipation. Jazirah's guards, Zabala and his men, waited atop the landing. Muhammad dismissed them for the night. Too many ears to hear any sounds echoing from behind his wife's chamber doors.

Just outside the portal near the end of the vestibule, Butayna stood with Jazirah's maidservant, the rat-faced woman she had insisted on bringing from her father's house. The slave bowed while Muhammad's mother welcomed him and grasped his hands. Her eyes glistened like amber stones in the torchlight illuminating the long corridor. Butayna wore gold brocade with pearls sewn everywhere. Never had she appeared as elegant as on this evening.

"God's blessings upon you and your marriage bed, my Sultan." She raised his fingers to her mouth and kissed his skin.

"Do you entreat your Christ for a grandson conceived this night, *Ummi?*"

"As always, I pray for your bright future, my Sultan. I have placed a square of white linen atop the bedding. After you have consummated your union with Jazirah, at your summons, I shall retrieve the cloth, so it may be displayed before your guests."

"A shameful custom I would abolish if I could."

"There can be no question as to whether you have claimed Jazirah for your own."

"Be assured, *Ummi,* I will have her tonight."

With Hisham's aid, Muhammad removed the robes of state until he stood in a long white tunic paired with *sarawil* on his legs and fine goatskin slippers. He swept hair back from his forehead and reached for the door handle.

Butayna's light touch on his forearm stopped him. "Please, be gentle. Jazirah has a fierce wit and tongue, but she comes to you a maiden. She deserves your kindness as your kinswoman, as your wife, and a Sultana of Gharnatah."

He chuckled. "Would you have me believe she cowers beneath the bedclothes?"

The statement earned him a barely subdued "humph" from Jazirah's freckled slave. As one, he and his mother turned and scowled at her, while she averted her gaze to the cedar floor.

Then Muhammad said, "I know how to charm and woo a woman, *Ummi*."

"A pleasure slave is not a wife, my Sultan. Please remember."

She released him and drew back, standing beside Hisham with the slave behind them. The trio would remain until Muhammad provided the bloodied bridal sheet. He sighed and pushed the double doors inward.

He entered the room and closed the door behind him with a soft thump. Candlelight glowed in Jazirah's antechamber. Cushions lined the western wall, along with pillows. A low square table at the room's center bore a pitcher provided for refreshment, beside a platter of fruit. Someone had provided two cotton cloths next to a basin of water. Rose petals skimmed the surface. Sexual intercourse required *ghusl* or a full bath afterward, but Muhammad loathed the idea of visiting the bath at such a late hour or disturbing the rapport he hoped to achieve tonight. *Wudu* or the minor ablutions must be enough.

A night breeze filtered in through the window, which faced south toward the *rawda* where several ancestors lay entombed. In the marriage to Jazirah, Muhammad would seal a long divide, beginning in physical union with his wife. In Paradise, would his father Yusuf and his great-grandmother Fatima be pleased?

With one hand, he parted the deep indigo curtains leading to the bedchamber. Oil lamps burned low in the corners on two tables closest to the doorway. Latticework permitted only the faintest moonlight into the room, dominated by the bed. A large square of white linen fell on either side of the mattress. A glimpse through the opened curtains did not reveal his new bride awaiting him with the bedclothes drawn up to her chin.

Instead, she stood in the shadows between the two windows, clad in a voluminous *rida*. The green, almost black, robe with gold fringe revealed little of the form beneath it at first glance. His gaze skirted up its length until he found Jazirah regarding him in silence. Her mouth tamped down, she turned her head away, and looked through the window screen. A smile softened her profile. Stupefied for a moment, he contented himself with the sight of her and the appearance of quiet serenity she exuded.

"Is the Sultan frightened of me now?" she asked into the darkness.

He clasped his fingers before him. "I wonder what you find so amusing, Jazirah?"

She beckoned with a wave of her hand. "Come see."

As he approached, her rosewater scent incited his longing. Closer inspection and faint light drew his gaze to where the neckline of the *rida* ended in a deep V. A *khamsa* nestled between the valley of her breasts. The hand-shaped pendant sparkled with opals, diamonds, and emeralds set in gold, worn on a necklace of the same metal. Another necklace of gold filigree worn with an oval ruby pendant shaped like a pomegranate fell to her waistline.

She pointed to the lantern-lit street below. "Look, just there."

He admired the deep orange henna designs painted up to her wrist before he followed the direction of her hand.

Thalj prowled the night and flicked her tail. Behind her came a large cat with orange, gray, and white fur. He arched and rubbed his body against Thalj. She yawned and paused beside an oleander bush, her ears cocked. The other cat took this as a sign of invitation. Thalj twisted away, while she hissed and batted at his face. He scurried out of sight.

Muhammad and Jazirah shared a chuckle before he said, "My Thalj will not surrender too easily. He must do a better job of wooing her."

Jazirah glanced at him. "He's been at it for days now."

They waited for a few breaths until the male slunk into view again, his belly low to the ground. Thalj gave him a look and traipsed through the hedges. He followed.

Jazirah observed, "At least he is persistent."

Muhammad said, "Males oft must be."

When Jazirah turned to him slightly, at last he discerned part of her slim body. The *rida* fell upon sloping shoulders, enveloping Jazirah's long arms to the wrists, where the sleeves tightened. Two circles atop her rounded breasts protruded from the cloth. The rest remained in shadow.

He cleared his throat. "Did you enjoy your portion of the *walima*?"

She said, "The number of guests was the only difference between the marital feast and *Al-laylat al-henna*. With the wives of our cousins and the governors, along with your sisters, aunts, and your stepmother, all crowded into the *Umm al-Walad's* chambers, I could not breathe!"

"And what did you think of your bridal trousseau?"

"I am grateful for your gifts of silk, leathers, and jewels, especially from among them, these." She toyed with the two pendants and lifted them to the moonlight.

"Your joy in the wedding presents pleases me, Jazirah, for they are yours for life. The jewels you wear are part of our family history. The *khamsa* belonged to our great-grandmother Fatima. She received it on her wedding day to her husband, Prince Faraj. The ruby is even older. Fatima's mother had it as a wedding gift from her husband, our ancestor Muhammad the Lawgiver, the second Sultan. Afterward, he gave it to Fatima's daughter Leila on the eve of her nuptials. As Leila did not have any daughters, it came to her namesake, my beloved aunt, whose intended husband died before they could wed."

Jazirah looked away from him and something sparkled in the corner of her eye. He recalled the bruise shadowing her gaze from when they first met, but it had faded. Her skin was luminous, from the high, smooth brow to her sharp nose, a feature of their shared ancestry. Her full lips beckoned him. Beautiful. His.

Then her fingers closed on the jewels. "I will never take them off, unless we should have a daughter. Then she shall wear both at her wedding, my Sultan."

"I am your husband. In private, you'll call me by my given name, for I am yours."

She rested her temple along the wall. "Can a wife call the Sultan of Gharnatah hers? He belongs to his people first, but she must also share him with other women."

"Our religion allows me to wed three others, of which you shall always be the first."

"Should this fact improve my hopes for our marriage? These unions you spoke of, Muhammad the second Sultan and his wife, their daughter Fatima and her Faraj, and Princess Leila and her husband, I assume they were arranged as is our custom." After he nodded, she added, "Did any take joy in their marriages?"

"I never knew the personal history of any of our ancestors. Why do you ask about their happiness? Is it normal to anticipate wedded bliss when two people are strangers on their marital day?"

"Something Lubna had said about unions of necessity prompted me."

"Lubna? Who is she?"

Despite the dimness, her frown became evident. "The slave who waits at my door."

"Why do you keep her at your side? She has an ill-favored look with the marks on her face, brown hair and those gaunt features, like a mouse."

Jazirah crossed her arms under her breasts, which jutted and tempted him. Each no more than a handful... he forced his mind back to the present and her mood, suddenly turned sour as she glowered at him.

He put up his hands. "Forgive me. I never intended to insult your choice of servants."

"Lubna is a capable stewardess in my service. She may not be as attractive as the slave you cavorted with inside your bath—"

"Cavorted? What foolishness! How would you know of what occurred in my bath?"

"Father told me of your Nubian women and the one who attended you in the *hammam* near the public mosque this morning. I believe he used the word 'nubile' for a description of the naked woman washing you."

Incredulous, he wagged a finger at her. "You have been my wife for less than half a day. It is too early for jealousy."

She brushed aside his hand. "Jealousy? Do you think I care how many women you take into your bed? You forget I knew such a way of life from childhood. My father had other concubines, although he favored my mother. I never hoped to marry and never expected, if I did, to find a husband faithful solely to me. Such are the wishes of ignorant or foolish girls! I am neither."

He seized her shoulders. As she shook, he could only guess at the rage coursing through her body. She turned to the wall, denying him the spirited fury in her gaze, but at least she never shrugged off his hold. His nearness allowed him to inhale her fragrance deeply.

"Jazirah, will you delight in vexing me each day of our marriage?" Despite his words, irritation never beset him, not since she had stirred other, stronger emotions.

"If you wish me to stop, then you must cease being such a source of annoyance!"

He laughed, unable to help it, and released her. She never softened, although she no longer withheld her regard. Instead, she looked down at him from a narrowed stare, her face framed by thick curls. "Do I amuse you, my Sultan?"

"Muhammad," he corrected. "I shall answer to no title when we are alone together. We are married, Jazirah. I have no wish to fight with you on our wedding night."

She dropped her hands and mumbled, "I do not want to argue with you either, husband. Muhammad."

He fingered the tip of a tendril tucked behind the curve of her ear, so soft as the rest of her glowing skin.

Out in the darkness, the yowls of cats echoed. Mayhap Thalj had surrendered. Would Jazirah do the same for Muhammad given time and patience?

He glanced at the bed. "Do you know the reason for the linen square?"

In the ensuing silence and the space of several breaths, the revelry from below stairs reached them. Jazirah swallowed before nodding. "Your mother said our traditions require a display of the sheet with my virgin's blood upon it."

She shuddered and he gripped her shoulders once more. "Jazirah, I wish you to believe me. I would never take joy in hurting you, especially on this night."

"I don't fear the virgin's pain. Lubna told me it would not last."

"Did she speak to you of pleasure as well?"

"She said it is possible."

He smiled and slid one hand down her slender arm to her elbow. "It is more than possible. I would spare you pain and embarrassment if I could, but I promise you will remember only joy in my arms after tonight. I will please you."

She lifted her chin. "How can you know what I will like, if I don't even know?"

Her brazen words roused an answer to her challenge. She could not have understood the effect on him, or she would not have spoken so boldly.

She broke the intervening quietude first. "If the guests require proof of our marriage, let us give them what they want."

As she moved toward the bed, he tugged at her fingers, so slim in his hold. She frowned at him. "Why do you delay further?"

He whispered, "We have all night."

Her eyes widened. "The bedding will take all night?"

He could have laughed again at her artlessness, but thought better of it, lest she mistake the reason. Instead, he drew her to the bed and sat, gesturing for her to join him. Moonlight fell upon them, revealing even more of her body under the thin cloth. The curvature of her waist and the sleek thighs he had envisaged for weeks.

He coughed and said, "Your fingers have known toil."

Since she refused to speak, he lifted his gaze to hers.

She murmured, "If I mentioned the reason, you would be displeased."

He nodded. No more references to Shalabuniya. "Will you allow me to kiss you?"

"You are my husband. It is permissible."

So stiff and formal, yet he sensed the hesitation and uncertainty in her answer. If it took him this night or the entirety of their union, he vowed to prove there would be no cause for restraint in their marital bed. He desired the exact opposite.

She pursed her lips and closed her eyes, waiting.

Muhammad subdued a laugh. "What are you doing, Jazirah?"

She kept her lids squeezed tightly. "Is this not how kissing is done? When I saw the guards with their women, or sometimes Lubna… well, all had their eyes closed!"

"Indeed. Look at me, please."

As she did so, he caressed her hand with his thumb, pushed back her billowy sleeve, and ran his hand over pitted marks on her forearm. "Hmmm, these little scars."

She wriggled in his hold. "I thought the henna would have covered them. Doctor Pharez said the small pox afflicted me as a child, although I don't remember. The marks do go further up my arm, but do not be troubled. I shall always keep my limbs covered…."

He released her and drew up his legs, sitting akimbo. He tugged the edge of the *sarawil* and pointed out similar indentations, visible in patches where the hair on both of his legs did not cover them.

"I had the pox at the age of five after the disease first afflicted both of my younger brothers. You must never be ashamed of your body in my company."

With her delectable mouth agape, he forgot what he had planned to say next, until she pressed her lips together. She truly had the sweetest mouth he would ever dare kiss. Still, he must cease staring at her or he would forget his vow not to frighten her away.

He lowered the leg of his trousers. "Maryam alone seemed to know the remedy for the red pox. Even my doctor Al-Shaquri had seemed perplexed by its appearance. It forced Butayna and Maryam to share a room and care for their sick children together. The sole time in which I cannot recall any argument between them."

Jazirah sighed. "Maryam told me of her wish to leave your harem. Why won't you let her go to Malaka?"

"She stirs rebellion against me. She wants the throne for her eldest son."

"Name any woman who defers her wishes for her children to the offspring of a rival. Maryam is no different. Muhammad, how long have you been Sultan of Gharnatah?"

"For nineteen months." No day since had ever ended without thoughts of his father. Yusuf should have remained among the living, seated on his throne. Jazirah did not need to know of Muhammad's secret wish. He would not share bitter truths of himself with her.

His marriage encouraged long-hidden desires, buried so deep, he had not known they still existed. He recalled from childhood the sight of his mother and father deep in conversation. Yusuf had withheld little from his first queen and Butayna always listened, offering advice even when her husband never asked. As much as Muhammad favored Haziyya, a *kadin* could not know all of his burdens, not in the way a wife, a kinswoman would. As a Nasrid, Jazirah would understand. Could she ever be his confidante, a true companion?

"Muhammad, are you even listening to me?"

He blinked and glanced at her. "I'm sorry. I was lost in the past."

Despite her frown, she repeated the words. "I asked, in those nineteen months, what proof has Maryam offered of her disloyal nature?"

"She is always ensconced with the governor of Malaka for one. He is among the malcontents, who grumbles about my demands for a proper accounting of taxation revenues, including the poll tax Jews and Christians must pay, as well as tolls and ransom, all from which the Sultanate must derive a share. Unlike our cousin, I have served on the *Diwan* and learned from the council of ministers how good governance requires a strong administration. Muhammad the Red knows naught of the burdens of my rule. I keep him at his post for the sake of our family. We have had enough internal squabbles."

"I question his interest in a friendship with my father. He never visited Father when we were... away from Gharnatah. I do not know what to make of his new-found amity."

He studied her features, half-cast in shadows as clouds rolled in. She held something back. The certainty of it grew inside him with each passing moment.

She continued, "You should let Maryam leave Gharnatah and live as she chooses. I do not want the governor of Malaka around my father. If Maryam goes, Muhammad the Red will have no reason to come to the capital."

Muhammad had arrived at the same conclusion days ago. Equally troubled by reports of meetings between Jazirah's father and the *Raïs* of Malaka, Muhammad had surmised the best course would be Maryam's removal from court to her own house. He intended to announce the decision on the morning after the wedding, once he had spoken with his mother first.

"Let me think on it further, but not tonight. This night is for you."

"For us," she whispered.

He took her hand in his again and pressed his lips to her fingertips, tasting the remnants of sweet almonds. *Khushkananaj* again, most likely.

She asked, "What are you doing?"

He murmured against her flesh, "Kissing you all over... as I would wish."

"Oh. Does kissing... make the bedding easier? More enjoyable?"

"You will tell me, Jazirah."

Her skin, so different from the experience of touching Haziyya, was warm and rosewater clung to it, even her palm. He flicked his tongue against the flesh there and she rewarded him with a soft gasp. He trailed up her arm, until he could no longer push the sleeves of her robe any higher. Then he turned his attention to her other arm, nuzzling at her wrist and the inside of her elbow. Whereas his *kadin* tasted of salt, only sweet and the aroma of roses filled his nostrils in Jazirah's company.

He tugged aside the silk, setting a path his lips continued. While they met the curvature of Jazirah's shoulder and neck, her nails pressed into his arm. He could not restrain the bolt of lust piercing him. His kisses became fervent. He even nipped at the flesh, knowing it would leave a love mark. Her sighs first told of amusement and curiosity, but a hint of her awakened feelings came to vivid life in her moans. She scooted nearer to him. He resisted a desperate urge to drag her on to his lap. *Slow, slow,* he repeated to himself, as he recalled pleasurable hours of tutelage at Haziyya's hands.

Jazirah drew him closer with a breathy sigh. "Muhammad...."

"Hush now. No fear." He raised his head and their gazes locked. A storm brewed in Jazirah's bewildered stare, widened as if caught unawares.

She said, "I am not afraid."

Her lips hovered so close. He longed to taste them, but restrained himself again.

She asked, "How is it possible? Why am I fearless in your arms?"

He bent his head again, kissed her neck, and stroked the tender flesh of her inner arm with his fingertips. The base of her throat pulsed madly beneath his lips while he said, "We recognize each other, our true selves. We have... the same pride. Deep inside, we know each other... as only Nasrids can."

He focused on the other side of her neck, wanting to elicit the same response as before. Jazirah did not disappoint. Despite his best efforts, she tried his self-control with her moans and furtive caresses. Her hands had moved to his nape. He ran his fingertips across her exposed collarbone until they dipped beneath the neckline. His mouth followed the same route. Even as the moonlight receded and the candles flickered, all he could not see, he could touch and taste. He swept over a rounded breast and waited breathlessly for her reaction. Her fingers covered his and her heavy sigh encouraged him. His thumb rounded and teased at the little nub beckoning from the cloth. Sensing her anticipation as her hands fisted in his hair, his mouth took the place of his fingertip.

Jazirah moaned so loudly, the others in the corridor must have heard her, but he did not care. She arched her back, pressing her torso against his. Instinct alone must have guided her. The nipple pebbled beneath his tongue before he turned his attention to its counterpart. Her sweet response aside, the silk prevented him from truly tasting her. If he ripped the garment from her body, fear would overtake her, so he fought off the powerful impulse.

Instead, he swept his fingers down her taut abdomen. "Lie back amongst the pillows."

Tonight, he might put a babe into her belly, a son whom he wished might suckle at his mother's breast. Royal custom dictated the use of wet nurses, but Muhammad did not want the services of strangers. His children would derive their strength from Jazirah if she alone nursed them.

Old fears encroached upon him. In the seven years since he had bedded his first slave girl, none of his women had ever conceived a child. What would happen to his family's legacy if he could not father the next generation?

He cast aside those concerns and attended to his bride's awakened needs. Jazirah's heavy-lidded stare seemed unfocused and dazed, but she reclined in the center of the bed. He stood and in a swift motion, kicked off his slippers and removed his tunic. He stretched out beside her and she turned to him in an instant.

"Warm me. There is no brazier in the room and the night grows cool."

He smiled and touched a thick coil of her hair. He sniffed and stroked it between his fingers. The aroma of almond oil filled his nostrils as he buried his face in it and pulled her toward him. He kissed her temple and bestowed light sweeps of his lips, closing her eyelids. He even pecked the tip of her nose.

"Shall I cease?" he murmured against her skin.

When she did not answer straight away, he lifted his head and looked down at her. Heaving breaths whistled between her parted lips timed to the rise and fall of her chest.

She swallowed before she shook her head. "Not yet."

He smiled and caressed her chin. Her fingers covered his before she urged him close.

The first sweet taste of her mouth tinged with honey brought forth a deep sigh from him. She exceeded his dreams. Her furtive response proved her purity and roused a thrill inside him. He would ensure she enjoyed his passionate attentions as much as he relished her burgeoning introduction to pleasure. With a deep moan, he parted her lips and gathered her to him, hands under her hips as he dragged the folds of her garment up.

She aided him, though mayhap unwittingly, by refusing to stay still. Her hands roamed from his nape down across his back and around his waist, where her nails raked at and tickled his belly. Whether trailing through the coarse black curls, which dipped under his waistband, or gripping his hips, she withheld none of the passion he had only guessed at while they had dined together.

She made up for her lack of skill with great enthusiasm. He bared one pale breast to feast upon the soft flesh. She raised no objection, except for when he shifted his attention to her other puckered nipple. No maidenly protest followed while he bunched the edge of the *rida* around her thighs.

Then he nuzzled and nipped her earlobe. "Remove it. I want to see all of you."

"I would prefer to keep my robe on."

He looked up and smoothed a hand over her brow. He guessed at the insecurity warring with her curiosity. "Why this fear? Don't ever be reluctant to show yourself to me, not when you have seen how your presence stirs me. You must know I desire you."

"I do. I can feel... it... on my leg."

"Your leg?"

He masked rumbles of laughter in her almond-scented hair. In the absence of light, even its color did not offend him so much. Mayhap not at all. The texture proved luxurious, like the finest silken samite.

"I'm still cold, Muhammad. Please don't make me remove the *rida.*"

Her low murmur in his ear fired his blood, but the night ahead still required his patience. One pleasant interlude would not be enough for her to abandon all inhibitions. She had already allowed him much more than he dreamt possible.

"As you wish." He nibbled her lobe and kissed along the length of her neck again in the way she delighted. Jazirah twisted and moaned beneath him. He could not have guessed how Allah would have blessed him with an innocent, whose sensuality matched his own.

He moved to her breast again and smoothed a thumb over the hardened nipple. "You have enjoyed my attentions so far. Shall I still continue?"

Her answer came in the form of fingers tightening at the base of his skull. He gave a low chuckle. His queen, too proud to say 'please' would be begging for more of him before night's ending. He moved from her breasts down to her abdomen, planting more kisses as he went. His fingers stroked over her hip and under her thigh. Folds of the robe gathered beneath her, allowing him full view of the lower half of her body. He draped one thigh over his hip and tugged down his trousers. Nestled between her lean legs, he covered her body in full. His fingertips skimmed her hips and grabbed them. He drew her closer. She clung to him, distracted by his lips on hers.

The first thrust made Muhammad gasp. The second caused him to tremble. By the third, pure bliss ran the length of him. His mouth swallowed the sound Jazirah uttered. He rose up on his elbows. Through a haze of pleasure, he became aware of a burning sensation on his back, where Jazirah had dug her nails. She had stilled beneath him, her breaths shallow and uneven. The darkness hid all from him except the contours of her face.

"No," she whispered on the night breeze.

Chapter 10
Ways of the Harem

Sultana Jazirah

Gharnatah, Al-Andalus or Granada, Andalusia
Jumada al-Ula AH or May A.D. 1356 or Sivan – Tammuz 5116

A monstrous distortion of Harun's features rose above Jazirah. Cold green eyes glowed with a fire deep within their centers. Jazirah squeezed her eyes closed, but she could not blot out the terrifying visage. The shock from the invasion of her body frightened her into rigid stillness, like the day Harun had pinned her beneath him in the cell.

"Jazirah...." His cruel voice taunted her.

She shook her head. It wasn't him! Harun's corpse rotted away beneath the waters of the White Sea where the Sultan's men had cast him. His iron grip no longer imprisoned her. His hips weren't driving against hers now. He was not in her bed. Muhammad held and caressed her, her lawful husband. Not Harun.

Try as she might, she could not banish him from her mind. She drew in a deep, shaky breath and whispered, "Stop."

"Not... now."

She opened her eyes and saw little of the man who covered her, only his shadow reared up above hers along the wall. "I said stop."

"Jazirah... I can't."

His full weight smothered her and pressed her into the mattress. Desperate, she bucked against him, but his grip tightened. He quickened his thrusts and the burning sensation between her legs intensified. Then his body jerked once and stilled. A long, drawn-out groan escaped him before he rested his dark head against her shoulder. He panted like a dying man.

Fighting for every breath as well, she waited while her heart slowed its frantic rhythm. Atop her, Muhammad did not seem to notice as he kissed her skin.

"So sweet. I am... sorry. Next time, it will hurt less. The first time is always difficult for women. I knew it would be like this with you. Passion dwells inside your body. You will learn not to let it overwhelm you."

Tears trickled beneath her eyelashes and weaved a path across her face into the pillow. The task accomplished,

Muhammad's wedding guests could assure themselves he had deflowered her and affirmed their union. Her husband could have no further use for her on this night. She tugged at her lower lip while regrets overshadowed her. At first, all had seemed well. More than well. She had enjoyed Muhammad's tender approach, the thrill of his passionate kisses, and the gentleness of his touch. Why had the specter of Harun returned on this night to ruin it all?

"I hate to disturb you, Jazirah, but the others await the bridal sheet." Muhammad's voice echoed in the dark, intruding on her morose thoughts.

She said, "Then, please get up."

His rich laughter rang round the chamber. "You act as if I'm crushing you. Well, I have a little more belly than I might like, but our rich foods are to blame. I won't indulge so much at mealtime, lest my weight becomes burdensome to you."

As he withdrew from her, Jazirah stifled a wince and bit her tongue. They rose from the bed together. A stiff breeze buffeted her and she rubbed her arms against a chill.

Muhammad said, "I have the linen. You may rest again. I'll return shortly."

She sank down on the mattress and drew her knees up to her chest, while she tugged her garment around her ankles. A dull throb pulsed between her thighs.

She murmured, "You should leave."

He gave a bark of laughter. "Why? Jazirah, you cannot tell me you did not enjoy the greater portion of this night. Until the pain came, you... you found joy in my arms. You liked my kisses. I did not deliberately hurt you."

He had not injured her at all, in truth. The violence of the past had encroached on her initial joy with Muhammad. If she spoke of her feelings, he would not understand. He had demanded she make no further references to Shalabuniya. He was right in saying she should forget the place, but how could she ever do so?

"Jazirah?"

After she did not answer, footsteps padded around the bed. A hard thump followed.

"Ouch! By all the Christian dogs...." Muhammad cursed and muttered under his breath. Then his large hand found hers. She closed her eyes again.

"Jazirah, please. At least, let us cleanse our bodies. There is a bowl of rosewater. Afterward, I can lie here beside you if you wish and not touch you again. I would not even hold you if you did not permit it. The hour grows late and we should both get some sleep. In the morning, we can talk. You'll see, you have no cause for concern."

"Just send Lubna with the water to tend to me. You can go, Muhammad."

"Wait... what? Are you... are you dismissing me as one would a slave?"

"I am! I'm sorry, but this night has been... difficult for me. Please send Lubna."

"Your nursemaid? Are you a child again or the woman I just bedded?"

"Please get out!" She burrowed her face in the pillows.

He dropped her hand and stomped away. His hard grunts and rapid fumbles echoed. She listened for the swish of silk and then his heavy footfalls. When silence enveloped her, she looked up from the bed. The oil lamps had extinguished. He stood framed in the doorway with his shoulders hunched, one hand fisted in the curtain while the other dragged the bridal linen. He looked over his shoulder. In the adjacent room, the candles had also burned down, but she would not have needed light to guess at the anger reflected in his features.

"I will go, Jazirah, but not because you wish it. I could not spend another night in the arms of a petulant child crying for her nurse because of a pain all new wives must bear! Lie there and sulk for as long as you like. See if you gain any comfort."

How could he be so selfish? Couldn't he see her miserable state? Mayhap he just didn't care, not since he had taken what he wanted. She grabbed one of the pillows from under her head and flung it in his direction. He swung toward her, but never released his grip on the door hanging. Without another word, he left. She released a pent-up breath as hinges creaked.

"My Sultan! Is... all well?" The *Umm al-Walad*'s voice warbled. Silence overcame the harem's upper floor, allowing Jazirah to overhear every word.

"Here, *Ummi*, is the proof our customs require. Two spots of blood on the sheet. I have wedded and bedded my wife for all the good it did us both."

"What happened? We thought... it seemed... rather, we believed the bedding seemed, um, satisfactory to both of you."

Muhammad answered, "I suppose you all did with your ears pressed to the door, huh? My wedding night is not your concern!"

"Muhammad, you must make some allowance for Jazirah's age as it affects her temperament. She is but sixteen, my lion—"

"At the same age, you gave birth to me! Had you disgraced yourself in my father's bed, he would not have called for you again."

"Do lower your voice! Would you summon Jazirah's father with fear in his heart?"

"Great Sultan, is... Sultana Jazirah... sleeping?" Hesitance filled Lubna's voice.

Muhammad muttered, "Your prideful charge is mewling into the bed covers like a ridiculous child. Go to her!"

Lubna raced into the room. Jazirah covered her wet face with her hands and shuddered. What must Lubna think of her after she had learned of such immature behavior?

Her features impassive, Lubna knelt beside the bed, while Jazirah strained to hear Muhammad's response to his mother. "Neither of you will ever interfere in my marriage! Do you understand me? I have claimed Jazirah's maidenhead as required, but I could never be satisfied with such a bride! Hisham, you will bring Haziyya to my bed. Now!"

"At your command, my Sultan."

Pairs of slippers slapped the floor outside.

"My lion? Muhammad, please wait!"

Inside the bedchamber, Lubna's thin arms came around Jazirah, "Oh, my sweet child! It's over, it is over."

Jazirah shook her head. The terror of her nightmarish visions of Harun might never end.

***

Lubna crooned softly in Jazirah's ear. Nestled beside her slave atop the bedding, the dulcet tones would have lulled Jazirah to sleep, but not on this long night.

She pillowed her head against Lubna's chest. "How could Muhammad have been so cruel? He summoned his *kadin* on our wedding night."

"A man of sensual appetites will fulfill them where he may. I must remind you of a hard truth. You rejected him. Men do not like rebuffs, least of all from their wives. He might have been content to remain at your side instead of with the favorite, my Sultana."

Jazirah sighed. "Please, can't I still be your Jazirah?"

Lubna patted her shoulder. "I have said it before. You will always be my Jazirah, but my Jazirah is also a Sultana of Gharnatah with a husband who, if I understand correctly, brought her intense pleasure until she dismissed him. Why did you do so?"

Jazirah sat up and found Lubna's hands in the darkness. "Harun. When Muhammad... entered me, I could think of no one, but Harun."

Lubna squeezed her fingers. "Oh, no! Why, my child?"

"I could not help it!"

"What did he do to you?"

"Muhammad? He was kind, even considerate."

125

"I do not mean him. You have never spoken with me, nor your father, in detail of what happened with Harun in the cell at Shalabuniya. Tell me. Ease your burden."

Through a flood of tears, Jazirah shared her pain-filled recollection. When her sobs ceased, Lubna gathered her close and kissed her cheek. Then they drew apart.

Lubna said, "Harun is dead. He can never hurt you again. You must explain your behavior to your husband. He should know the cause."

"Any hint or outright mention of Shalabuniya stirs Muhammad's ire. Shall I tell him how the memory of Harun plagues me still? How I dreaded the nighttime hours months after my leave-taking for fear of how Harun haunted my dreams? When the nightmares stopped three weeks ago, I thought I had banished him forever. Memory of Harun returned at the worst time. Speaking of him would rouse Muhammad's wrath."

"He would also know your true feelings and mayhap gain a better understanding and appreciation of you, because you did not withhold secrets. Such an act could be the basis of trust in your marriage. Don't you want to inspire faith in your husband?"

Jazirah settled back against a smooth pillow and rubbed her left temple where the flesh pounded. What did she want from Muhammad? What could he ever offer as a balm for her wounded heart, which had learned too soon about the vagaries of love and the fragile bonds of family?

When she examined recent revelations about the generous acts he had committed on her father's behalf, she acknowledged Muhammad was not half the ogre she once imagined. He could be tender if he wished. He perceived a deep connection with her through their shared blood, one she could not deny. He was passionate, but also patient. Lubna could be right. If she gave Muhammad a measure of her trust, not only could he prove worthy of it. He might also learn to rely upon her, too. They could not remain adversarial to each other forever.

Lubna prodded her. "Your husband sought your pleasure tonight. Beyond the pain of your joining, did you not find happiness in his arms?"

"I did. At times, the intensity frightened me. I have never known the like."

"Sensuality is a new experience for you, my Sultana."

A pleasurable one as well, even with a husband she hardly knew and did not like. The memory of calluses on the pads of his fingertips as they teased her flesh and his warm breath on her bare skin made her shiver. With each one of his kisses and caresses, she had soared, before the nightmarish visage of Harun sent her spiraling down through a pained, dark haze.

Her companion interrupted her thoughts. "Build upon the discoveries of tonight. You may not like each other much, but you have both found a measure of what awaits when lovers share in equal delight."

"He is no less a stranger to me. I do not know his moods, little of what will anger or please him. How can I gain any rapport with him after tonight's disaster?"

"Do you think you have to love or trust someone to desire his touch? The heart knows what it wants, but so does the body. Passion's fire dwells inside of you. Your husband stirred its embers. Now, you will never forget. When you see him again, speak the truth. Tell him about Harun. Thus far, the Sultan has only heard from the bungling oaf of a captain, Alfonso Ruiz. A husband should know the facts from his wife. Share your fears with him as you share your body. Desire may be the path to the meeting of two embittered hearts."

Jazirah swallowed. "I am not sure I'm ready for desire again."

"You may find you want your husband's touch after having known it. Even if you are not eager for him, seek his forgiveness. Go to him in the morning and explain your emotions during the bedding. The hour is too late now."

"And he is with the *kadin*."

"You are well aware of the reason for his choice. Besides, Muhammad's hours with Haziyya have never bothered you before."

"I was not Muhammad's wife before."

"Then as his wife, you shall go to him and resolve this matter in the morning."

"I cannot."

Lubna thumped the pillow behind Jazirah's head. "You are too stubborn at times!"

"This is not about me. Public audience occurs at mid-morning. I do not know how long Muhammad may take to resolve his people's grievances and I have no wish to sit through hours of their complaints just to speak with him afterward."

"Then I could keep watch below stairs for his return."

"You would endure hours of useless waiting just for me?"

Lubna kissed Jazirah's forehead. "Don't you know already? I would do anything for you. My love and loyalty are unending."

***

Fitful hours of sleep and cruel visions tortured Jazirah in the night. She dreamt of Muhammad's hands upon her. In her dreams, whenever she looked into his eyes, they were the green of Harun's own, not Muhammad's dark brown gaze. The union of their bodies tore her asunder and when she stared in horror at the place where they had joined, he pierced her with the dagger she had driven into Harun's belly. Jazirah awoke twice with startled screams and cried each time upon Lubna's shoulder, while the slave comforted her.

Dawn came too soon and brought with it stark reality. She must confront Muhammad today. At the first call to prayer, echoing from the minaret atop the mosque, Lubna went out of the room. Later, she returned with water for Jazirah's ablutions.

"I threw away the rose petals in the basin."

Jazirah nodded. "There would be no further use for them."

She prayed in private while Lubna tidied the chamber. In the midst of *Salat al-Fajr*, slaves brought the bridal trousseau from Butayna's apartments. Jazirah smiled as Lubna gave terse orders. She had certainly taken well to her role.

"Not there in the corner where the brazier will burn at night! Would you set afire all of Sultana Jazirah's possessions? Out of the way!"

At the conclusion of her devotions, Jazirah exited her bedchamber and found Beatriz had joined Lubna. Together with the eunuchs of the harem, Jazirah's slave women had arranged the chests containing textiles and jewels. There were new damask curtains in flowing green and yellow silk for the windows. A leather-bound copy of *Al-Qur'an* lettered at the command of the *imam* of Gharnatah just for Jazirah rested atop the low table at which she might write her correspondence. A bronze water pitcher crafted in a shape of a stork accompanied glasses hewn of rock-cut crystal. Plush carpets covered most of the floor.

When Jazirah moved to help with a casket, Lubna waved her away. "You would do better to go with Beatriz to the *hammam*. I can finish here."

The yellow-haired woman had taken on the role of Jazirah's body slave or personal attendant. Despite their halting efforts to communicate with each other, a comfortable relationship had developed between them.

Jazirah said, "Since I am not needed," she signaled to Beatriz, "We'll go to *el baño*."

A wide smile splayed across Beatriz's mouth. "*Sí, mi princesa. Alteza.*"

Beatriz draped a black cloak over the *rida* Jazirah still wore. Together, they left the chamber. Half of Zabala's men stood bleary-eyed along the wall opposite the doorway. Jazirah giggled as one managed a half-hearted salute. She dismissed the exhausted sentries and led Beatriz down the stairs and across the harem's courtyard. Dawn cast a gold and pink sheen over the roof tiles and penetrated the detritus. Bees buzzed amongst fragrant petals.

Jazirah inhaled the aroma of oranges in the trees, before she looked to Muhammad's door, still closed. Had Haziyya remained with him? The captain Pero offered her a salute, while the rest of the royal guard along the walls bowed their heads. A eunuch walked along the northern wall with a gilded tray of cups and a pitcher emitting heady steam. He halted and set his burden down. He bent low, holding the position until Jazirah bypassed him.

A glass lantern reflected its light against the tiled walls. The bath superintendent met Jazirah and Beatriz just outside his chamber. He clapped his hands and a mob of attendants scurried from an adjacent room. They brought vials of scrubs, ointments, and oils, as well as towels and sandals. An assistant hurtled down the stairs with his supervisor's order for the slaves who stoked the fires.

The bath attendants ushered Jazirah to the changing room below. She removed her garments. Beatriz stood idle and unheeded, shuffling from one leg to the other, with the cloak and Jazirah's *rida* draped over her arm. Still, Jazirah kept her close by while sitting on the heated stone slab. A red-haired girl scrubbed her palms and the soles of her feet with ground apricot seeds. If all Sultanas of Gharnatah merited such treatment, Jazirah could grow accustomed to it.

Just before mid-morning, Jazirah returned with Beatriz to the harem, skin aglow beneath a plain white robe. Butayna stood at Jazirah's doorway, brilliant in lavender and gold. Jazirah's guards had changed, Zabala in command of four other men. Butayna's captain hovered at her back, while Lubna leaned against the doorjamb, her gaze oddly downcast. Even stranger, Alfonso Ruiz directed his stone-faced stare unabashedly at her, while she ignored him.

Apparently oblivious to the tension-filled scene behind her, Butayna said, "Dearest Jazirah, how pleased I am to see you appear well."

Jazirah smiled and met the stark stare. "Why should I not be?"

When she would have bowed, Butayna patted her arm. "Do not, I pray. You are my daughter by marriage. Harem customs accord me great rank, but a mother and the wife of the Sultan should be equals. A queen of your stature does not defer to any other, not even me."

Could Jazirah believe the words? A woman of Butayna's position, accustomed to subservience from all, might not share such power. If Jazirah bore the heir, she would attain Butayna's position upon her death. In the interim, wouldn't they become rivals for influence over Muhammad's decisions?

Jazirah stated, "I did not expect your visit this morning. We had no lessons in Arabic and Castillan planned for today." Then she turned to Lubna. "Why did you keep the *Umm al-Walad* at my door? This is no show of hospitality. You know better."

Butayna said, "Do not blame her. You're fortunate to find me here still. I just told her I could not remain much longer, as I must speak with Hisham before the public audience. I want to talk to you in private. Our servants may wait outside the doors."

She entered Jazirah's room without permission and scanned the chamber with all its new fixtures in place. She took to a cushion along the wall and patted the space beside her. Jazirah had no choice except to step over the threshold. Then she turned and closed the door. Her last sight was of a wide-eyed Beatriz in the corner, while Lubna and Alfonso Ruiz shared mutual glowers.

Jazirah took the seat next to Butayna and folded her hands in her lap.

Butayna began, "You must know why I'm here, the reason I wished to see you after last night's... unfortunate confusion between you and my son."

Jazirah settled back against the cushion. "I assumed your intent."

"The night appeared to have gone well. Then something changed. Muhammad will not tell me what happened. I come to you for an explanation."

"One my husband deserves to hear of first from my lips."

Butayna sniffed. "Are you saying you refuse to discuss the matter with me?"

"The concerns my husband and I share must be resolved between us."

The sharp huff from Butayna betrayed her pique. "I would be as a mother to you—"

"You are not! The woman whom your ardent protector glares at as though she were vermin is the only mother I remember or could ever want. You are Muhammad's mother. Respect the bounds of our marriage. Do not ask of our troubles again."

Butayna sighed and answered with a small nod. "I honor you and the right to resolve arguments with my son as you see best. You two are not so unlike each other as both of you may think. Muhammad behaves as stubbornly as you do."

"Oh?"

"Last night, he vowed he would not return to your bed unless you begged him. The getting of heirs will prove most difficult if the two of you remain at odds." Jazirah's harrumph echoed Butayna's words. "Your pride, his pride. *Madre de Dios!* One of you must give in to satisfy the other. I pity neither of you, only my grandchildren. They shall suffer from an excessive measure of arrogance inherited from both parents."

Then Butayna rose. Strained cords stood out beneath her neck. "I have intruded long enough. One day, I hope you may value our relationship and regard me as you would a mother. We are not competitors for my son's affection. I assure you, he views us with equal concern. Strong women oft disturb a man."

She departed. Through the opened door, her captain pressed his lips together and his hands curled into fists. Lubna darted inside, her cheeks flushed to match the mottled birthmark. A grimace crisscrossed Alfonso's face before his footfalls joined those of his diminutive mistress.

Lubna cleared her throat, her stare fixed on some indeterminate point on the floor. "I sent Beatriz to the kitchens for a meal. I thought you might be hungry by now."

"I am, and so should you be." All Jazirah's concerns fled as she leaned forward and examined Lubna's furrowed brow and her lips pressed together. In fact, she bore the same grim appearance as Butayna's captain had displayed.

Jazirah asked, "Why do you dislike Alfonso Ruiz so much?"

"What?" Lubna squeaked. She coughed and spoke again. "You know the reason, my Sultana. I have never cared for his interference and his callous conduct."

"You're still annoyed about events of three months ago? The concerns you held about his awareness of my troubles were unfounded. I am the cause for the current disquiet with Muhammad. You should no longer fault the captain for his duty to—"

"Jazirah, please! I do not wish to discuss this. I've had enough of the infernal captain and his behavior for the morning. I beg you, leave it be."

They sat in silence until Beatriz returned with her sweet smiles and the morning meal. As had become routine since Jazirah established her own household in Gharnatah, she ate with both of her retainers, Beatriz serving Jazirah before the slave took her food. Lubna's sour mood continued and she never met Jazirah's inquiring looks. Later, Beatriz cleared the table and Lubna departed to keep watch for Muhammad's return. Jazirah eyed Lubna's slumped shoulders without comment as she left the room.

The afternoon prayer came and went without soothing any of Jazirah's concerns. She turned her attention to Beatriz, who whistled while she folded laundered garments.

In Spanish, Jazirah began, "Beatriz, do you... love... *su esposo?*"

The answering blush on the slave's cheek and the glow in her eyes told Jazirah the truth, before Beatriz said in Arabic, "*Nam,* my Sultana. Gonzalo is... my only love."

"*Cuando*...eh, this is still so hard! When did you know?"

"Know? Of my love for him?"

"*Sí!*"

"*La primera vez que...*" Beatriz paused and shook her head. "The first time we... see the other. For wedding."

Jazirah smiled at her to show Beatriz she had switched to the correct words in Arabic. Could such a possibility arise? How might a man and woman love each other as soon as they had met? No couple could know this blessing from Allah. Mayhap Christ offered His followers better luck in marital choice.

"*Y sus... hijos?*"

Beatriz lowered her gaze. "*La,* no... children before... I could not have. The words...."

As her voice trailed off, Jazirah placed her hand over Beatriz's thin fingers. The poor slave, by some impediment, never had children and with Gonzalo made a eunuch, the opportunity would not arise.

"I understand, Beatriz. I know the words remain difficult. *Para mí, también.*"

When Jazirah could take no more of Lubna's absence, she dismissed Beatriz, so she could spend a few hours of the afternoon with her husband Gonzalo. Tears shone in the maid's eyes as she bent and kissed Jazirah's hands.

"Just remember, come back by *Salat al-Maghrib* this evening."

"*Nam,* my Sultana. I will come for your prayer."

As soon as Beatriz left, Jazirah clasped the talismans Muhammad had granted her as wedding gifts. She weighed the heavy ruby in her palm and brought the *khamsa* to her lips. She closed her eyes and struggled to recall the frail woman who had once come to her at Shalabuniya, the original owner of her heirlooms.

She sent an entreaty heavenward. "Noble Fatima, I was never fortunate to know you as my husband did. All I can remember is a visit in which my father embraced you. One moment where I stood bewildered in my great-grandmother's presence. Since then, Father has oft spoken of your enduring courage, the strength you said came to you from your own mother, whom I also never knew. Wherever you both may be in Paradise, watch over me. Guide my words and deeds henceforth. Show me what it truly means to be a Sultana of Gharnatah. Tell me how to heal the wounds within our family and inside of my heart."

She rose and exited the room. Her captain bowed as she paused beside him. "Zabala, have you seen Lubna above stairs since mid-morning?"

In a gruff voice, he answered, "No, my Sultana. Do you want me to find her?"

"Thank you, but I'll seek her out."

Jazirah passed five yellow-haired concubines huddled in a corner, a water pipe shared between them. Two tittered behind pale hands. Through the haze, the others cast Jazirah snide glances, which she ignored. Harem women and their thoughts of her were beyond concern.

As she reached the landing, voices drifted up.

"I have a duty."

"You think I do not know duty or love? I hold a man's thoughts and passions, despite what the slavers did to me. I can still love where I will. What about you? Will you pine forever for a proud prince? He does not look at you. He does not see you, the woman. For him, you are naught more than a servant for his daughter."

"A daughter who holds my loyalty. What you want from me is... impossible, Ruiz."

The agony in Lubna's tone sent Jazirah racing down the stairs as the answer came.

"Alfonso. I've told you my name countless times. My mother called me Alfonso. When I entered the service of Sultana Butayna, she preferred Ruiz for the son of Ruy, as Castillan custom would dictate. I want to hear you say my Christian name."

At the foot of the stairs, Jazirah clutched the banister. Her heart thrummed in a rapid rhythm at the sight of Lubna huddled within the exit to the garden courtyard, her head turned to the wall beside her. Butayna's captain stood in front of her, his sinewy hands gripping Lubna's arms. His lips hovered perilously close to her face, near the large, dappled blotch.

The intimate scene faded, replaced by one from the violent past in which Harun had shoved Lubna against a wall and violated her, all because he had discovered she carried his baby. As a tender child aged no more than eleven, Jazirah had cowered in the corner of their cell, unable to close her eyes even as Lubna pleaded for her to look away. Until then, Jazirah had never known a man could hurt a woman in such a way, the tenderness between her father and the concubines he once kept at his side having remained in her thoughts.

Now Jazirah demanded of Ruiz, "Take your hands from her! By what right do you presume to touch her? None!"

As she closed the distance between them, he released Lubna and stood aside.

Jazirah gathered her stewardess close. "Have you taken leave of your senses, man? If you ever attack my servant again, I won't await Butayna's consent. My guards will take your hands at my order!"

"No!" Lubna clutched the neckline of Jazirah's *rida* so fervently she almost ripped the delicate fabric of the robe. "Please do not harm him."

Jazirah turned to Lubna, "He could have hurt you."

"No, no, he would never. Oh, my Sultana, you don't understand, there are things I have not told you."

"I don't care! No man shall ever touch you again except by your leave." She glared at the captain. "Go now, before I do call for Zabala."

With a stiff nod and a mumbled apology offered to Lubna alone, he turned and mounted the steps leading to Butayna's section of the harem.

Lubna sagged, her head against Jazirah's shoulder. "Forgive me, my Sultana, but you were too harsh with him. He is not Harun. He could never be."

"You don't know, Lubna. Why are you so intent on protecting him?"

"Jazirah, I will tell you in time...."

"You will tell me now!"

"I cannot. The Sultan—"

"What does Muhammad have to do with any of this?"

"Look! He has returned."

Jazirah glanced over her shoulder. Muhammad stepped out from beneath the eastern pavilion among his guards. His haggard visage and red-rimmed eyes startled her, until she considered the cause. A night with his favorite.

A blur of shimmery blue silk darted across Jazirah's line of sight. Haziyya had raced from the direction of Muhammad's apartments and launched herself at him. He caught her in his arms and twirled with her before he kissed her lips.

"You told me to wait for you this morning." Haziyya's voice reached Jazirah even from across the garden.

Had the favorite been with him until he left for public audience? Jazirah stared hard at the concubine, having refused to do so during those shameful monthly visits before her marriage. The Berber woman's striking features, enhanced by the braids she had beaded and the exotic tattoos on her blue-tinted skin, would have been agreeable to any man. Muhammad buried his face in her neck and laughed while she must have whispered something to him.

Then he raised his head, his stare finding Jazirah's own in an instant. His gaze narrowed, like a predator having spotted the prey. She withdrew into the shadows.

Lubna murmured, "My Sultana—"

"Hush!" Jazirah snapped. She held her breath.

Haziyya's voice echoed again. "My Sultan, what is it? Your heart is beating so fast. Do I dare hope it is for my sake? No, it is not. Are you troubled?"

"No. Come, for I intend to spend the rest of the day in your arms."

A rush of footfalls pounded the marble walkway. Only when doors creaked on their hinges and slammed shut did Jazirah release a pent-up mouthful of air.

Lubna grasped her fingers. "There will be another time, my Sultana."

Jazirah forced a smile. "No doubt there will. Let us return to my room. There, you can speak to me about Alfonso Ruiz. Weren't you telling me just this morning about how much you dislike the man? You have me in a muddle, Lubna, as to the workings of your mind."

Lubna said, "This isn't about my mind—"

"Jazirah?"

As one, they stopped and looked across the grounds to where Maryam stood in the sunlight. Her constant companion, the slave Nazhun, peered out from behind her hip. Maryam's white cotton robe and wet hair clung to her body.

She said, "I thought you might have still been abed after last night's excesses."

Lubna clutched at Jazirah's forearm, but she shrugged her servant off and whispered, "We must not appear rude before Yusuf's widow."

They navigated the narrow walkway between fragrant flowerbeds, swatting at the ever-present bees, before they halted at Maryam's side.

Jazirah greeted her and then said, "Even a new bride cannot linger abed all day."

"I had hoped to speak with you. Will you join me now?"

"I would be happy to, but surely, you must wish to dress after your bath."

"There is no reason my dear Nazhun cannot robe me while we speak. Send your slave away, as I shall do with mine. We should talk in private."

Behind Jazirah, Lubna pinched her arm. Jazirah clamped her jaw tight before she turned, wishing there were some means to soothe the crisscrossed lines on Lubna's brow, to reassure her Maryam's wiles were of no concern.

Jazirah commanded, "Return to my quarters. I shall see you later."

Lubna mumbled, "As you wish, my Sultana."

Maryam led the way up to her quarters via a narrow staircase. At the second landing, they meandered down a corridor and passed three windows offering a cool breeze.

Through a carved doorway, Jazirah entered a poorly lit, but crowded room three times the size of her antechamber. Lattice covered the windows, allowing faint light inside. Dark red, green, and purple cushions lined the walls and plush Persian rugs carpeted the floor. Thick incense burned. In the dimness, servants placed jewels and clothing into chests, and stacked wooden bowls swathed in cotton and bronze vessels into crates.

"Forgive my inquiry, my Sultana, but are you going somewhere?"

Breathless, Jazirah awaited verification of the answer she wanted to hear, while silently thanking Muhammad for the fulfillment of his promise made yestereve.

Maryam turned, her dark-eyed stare narrowed. "So formal still when I have said we should not be. You outrank me now. Besides, I thought you knew Muhammad's plans for me. Has your husband still not taken you into his confidence?"

Before Jazirah could answer, Maryam's pinched façade relaxed, although the smile she adopted seemed insincere. "Before Muhammad retired to public audience, he sent word. He has given his consent to my departure. I shall have a house of my own near Yusuf's *Bab al-Sharia*. I shall be a close neighbor to your father. Won't this be nice?"

Chapter 11
Warnings

Sultana Jazirah

Gharnatah, Al-Andalus or Granada, Andalusia
Jumada al-Ula 757 AH or May A.D. 1356 or Tammuz 5116

Within Maryam's room, Jazirah perched upon a stool and kept her gaze trained on the floor, while the slave Nazhun anointed her mistress' body with fragrant oils and perfumes. The scents of musk, ambergris, cassia, and jasmine comingled, an odor Jazirah found repellent. She turned away slightly, not trusting herself to speak without heaving up her earlier meals.

Maryam observed, "You fared well during the night. Although your face is pale, your eyes remain bright, no shadows beneath them. I am surprised you are not exhausted for Nasrid men make excellent lovers. Is the Sultan deficient?"

At the rude, abrupt question, Jazirah glanced at Maryam while she pulled a cotton *qamis* over her head. The thin shift covered the rounded pouch of her belly and fell around her hips, but one glance revealed olive-brown flesh beneath the material. Jazirah gasped, unable to conceal her unease while Maryam chuckled at her expense.

"Are you so discomfited by nudity? Flesh is oft on display here, so I suggest you become accustomed. Did Muhammad let you keep your clothes on? His father never did with me."

Maryam turned away and drew *sarawil* up her slender legs, while Nazhun belted the trousers with a red and green band of cloth. Slippers dyed crimson in the shade of thick blood went on Maryam's feet and a *rida* with gold trim covered her. A necklace of onyx beads encircled the neckline of the robe. Bracelets of the same gemstones completed the attire.

"Leave us, Nazhun," Maryam ordered. "Don't stray too far. I won't bellow for you through the harem. I'll want my rubies after all. Find them among the chests."

The dwarf mumbled some response Jazirah could not overhear and scuttled away.

When Maryam sat, the bed frame creaked even under her trim figure. "Forgive me if I am blunt, my dear, but I know something of husbands, having had two of them."

"You were wed before you married Yusuf?" Jazirah's father had never told her.

"I was married, to the former apprentice of my goldsmith father. I endured Gedaliah's clumsy fumbling for three years until his death. The first time Yusuf took me into his bed was... unexpectedly pleasurable. Did Muhammad satisfy you? It was his duty."

Jazirah sensed the woman searched invariably for means to harm Muhammad's reputation. Despite Jazirah's doubts about him, she would not allow anyone else to influence her opinion of her new husband. She would learn his ways on her own.

"He did please me." She would have said so even if he had not.

Maryam's throaty laugh followed. "Indeed, you have had no one else to compare Muhammad with, so what else might you say."

Jazirah folded her arms across her chest. "Do you have a reason to doubt me?"

Maryam sobered immediately. "I do not. Forgive me, Jazirah, I did not mean to imply anything untoward about your husband's talents. Between the ages of eleven and thirteen, Nasrid boys receive their own households and slave girls. Among them are those who have obtained particular training in how to please a man. The slaves who taught my husband the ways of love did their duty well. I suspect Haziyya had similar influence with Muhammad. If you delighted in his loving, then he took to her lessons well. Haziyya is perfect, isn't she?"

"I would be a fool and liar to deny it."

"I did not think so upon first sight of her. I have never understood why the Tuareg people insist upon this indigo dye for clothing, which stains their bodies from head to toe. It makes them look dirty. Still, there is a certain exotic appeal to Haziyya. She has enthralled your husband. It would take another equally remarkable woman to capture his heart. I do not rely on this gossip about Berber love spells. Do you?"

Jazirah gripped the stool. "I do not believe in sorcery. Haziyya is devoted to Muhammad. I am a grateful recipient of the lessons she has granted him. My husband could not have been more patient or tender than he was on our first night."

She regretted her cold dismissal of Muhammad. She should have let him hold and comfort her as he had asked.

Just then, a shriek followed by husky male laughter rang through the harem. Maryam's smile returned, while a stony sensation weighed down Jazirah's stomach.

Jazirah's chest rose and fell with a heavy sigh. Was everyone in the harem mocking her even now, as those *jawari* she had encountered near her chamber door? Did all within the gilded harem walls know Muhammad still preferred his Berber concubine above a wife of royal blood?

Maryam said, "I believe Haziyya is with your husband now. It is oft his preference to waste hours at her side. Husbands can be fickle in their attentions, especially Sultans. Although Yusuf had me, and Butayna I suppose, he still took other women."

"It is Muhammad's right to have his favorites or any other woman he chooses. Mayhap you remain unaccustomed to harem ways because you were not born to this life. I was." Jazirah tossed her hair back and fingered the necklaces from her bridal trousseau. "Besides, I might need a respite from Muhammad's... attentions at times. Otherwise, I would be pregnant each year, which must be dangerous. Concubines serve their function in the harem."

Maryam's black brows flared and her mouth crinkled at the edges. "How generous of you to think so. I wonder if the sentiment will continue as the days of your marriage lengthen. Mayhap in time, you will accomplish what even Haziyya has not done and give Muhammad the son he craves. A grave responsibility for one so young."

Jazirah swallowed. "A duty all wives must endure."

"I certainly did. Ten times."

"Ten, but you have only seven children, not..." Jazirah's voice faded as she recognized tragedy underlay Maryam's words. "Forgive me, I spoke without thought."

"There is naught to forgive. You could not have known how Butayna has stolen from me." Maryam looked away. A tic pulsed beneath her sharp jawline.

Jazirah's heart hammered. "I don't understand." Except she feared she already did.

Maryam eyed her again. "Surely, you are aware of the great divide in this harem. Such was not always thus. In our childhood, Butayna and I were faithful friends, her father a prominent physician who served within my father's community at times."

If Jazirah had not held on to one side of the stool, she might have slid to the ground. Dazed, she stared at Maryam in silence and then gave a slow shake of her head.

Maryam continued, "I see the surprise in your gaze, but no shame tainted the association between a Christian physician and Jews of wealth and respected status. At least, not on my father's part. The link lasted for many years, until our families journeyed east together, and our caravan came under attack. More intent on other matters than escape, Butayna cost me two precious lives, a daughter no more than two years old and the son I carried within me."

Unable to speak, Jazirah only nodded. No wonder Maryam hated Butayna so much.

Maryam took slow, deliberate strides to the northernmost window. She spoke in a dull tone. "It would not be the last time Butayna ruined my joy. I entered this harem first and she followed some weeks afterward. Then I saw her again prior to the night I first bedded Yusuf. Butayna's owner, your aunt Leila, pushed Butayna into Yusuf's bed where she captured his attention for some time, although he never forgot about me. In the interim, memories of the joy I found in his arms sustained me. By contrivance with your aunt, Butayna bore Muhammad and his spoiled sister, Aisha. Despite the interference, my children arrived in succession. Then an eighth pregnancy occurred, one the court astrologer predicted would result in a third boy.

"My last babe never drew the first breath of life. I never saw or held him. Some days after Yusuf had announced our happy news to his court, I bled and sickened. I existed in a dreamlike haze, more a nightmare as events blurred and time stretched. Afterward, I remained weak for months. None could explain what had happened, but I realized the truth. Butayna must have poisoned me."

Maryam's slim fingers gripped the sill until her knuckles whitened. A breeze blew in. Thick locks of hair billowed behind her.

Shocked, Jazirah whispered, "Why would she have done such a heinous act?"

Maryam tossed her head, curls twisted like coiled snakes. "Insecurities bedeviled her. In her frailty, she had only given Yusuf two children, while he had seven of my body. Yusuf favored me and our babes over Butayna and hers."

Jazirah bristled. Some great truth eluded her. If Maryam spoke the truth, why would Yusuf have picked Butayna's son to follow him? Jazirah could not discern any other reason except her uncle's prevailing wish for his heir.

She blurted, "My husband is the Sultan!"

Maryam turned her head and lowered her chin as she muttered over her shoulder, "Your dear husband entered the world first. A mere ten months separated his birth from my Ismail's arrival. Those meddlesome ministers Ridwan and Ibn al-Khatib decreed Muhammad's rule. Yusuf never proclaimed an heir before his death. Mayhap he feared what Butayna might do to me or my children if he had chosen our son."

Jazirah nibbled at her bottom lip. It could not be true. She should have known Butayna for a vile schemer from the moment she had met her at Shalabuniya. How could Muhammad's mother have been so clever as to hide a deceitful nature?

"I can't believe you. Poison? The Sultan's mother could not have done so!"

When Maryam turned in full and glared at her again, the woman's eyes were darker than her onyx beads. "If you think Butayna is above the use of poisons to eliminate her rivals, then you are a fool, Jazirah. You do not appear to be foolish, so take my words as fair warning. Do not trust Butayna. She killed Yusuf's mother five years ago and might have done away with me by the same means. One morning, after I had shared a meal with the old *Umm al-Walad*, we both became violently ill. She died in agony. I could have succumbed, but for quick thinking. I vomited up the hemlock seeds, which looked so much like anise on the bread. Nazhun, who served Yusuf's mother, ran to fetch my husband. Do you see why I keep the slave close to me? I owe her my gratitude and more.

"During my recovery, the baker killed herself, or mayhap, Butayna's men killed her. Yusuf must have known. For months, he consigned Butayna to *Al-Qasr Xenil* south of the river of the same name. Why would he have done so if he did not believe in her guilt? Muhammad must have pleaded for his mother's return. When she did come again, I vowed to protect those in my household from her intrigues. Yusuf should have executed her, but love stayed his hand. Not concern for her, but their children. What man could murder the mother of his babes? Even one as cruel as Butayna."

Niggling doubts about Butayna returned in full force. Jazirah's father had oft spoken of his own grandmother's encroachment upon the power of his father's wives. He and his siblings received their education from their grandmother, who ruled the harem during Yusuf's rule, despite the presence of his mother. A woman Maryam claimed had perished at Butayna's hands. Would she attempt to supersede Jazirah's role?

Jazirah pressed her hand to her breastbone. An ache swelled within her heart. She had lived with the harshness of her Nasrid relations for so long, no act of viciousness should have surprised her. Butayna's behavior, if true, left Jazirah stunned. She recalled how Muhammad's mother had welcomed her on the henna night into the companionship of the women of the royal family. Could Butayna have played her false? Jazirah did not want to believe it. She could not ask anyone else for the truth. Yet, persistent suspicion of Maryam's motives warned her not to accept the words as the full facts.

Maryam retraced her steps and crouched at Jazirah's feet. "I could extend my protection to you. Butayna will never be your friend if you give Muhammad his sons and gain influence over him. His mother guards her relationship with her son jealously. She will not soon surrender a role of authority in this harem. I will help you survive her in any way I can. I want to be your friend."

Upon their arrival, Jazirah's father had cautioned she would have no allies. As she stared down at Maryam, a question burgeoned on Jazirah's lips, which she could not utter without rousing suspicion. Why did Maryam offer friendship?

Maryam whispered, "It pains me to tell you more, but as one who would be your friend, I cannot hide the truth, not even about your husband."

"What of Muhammad?" Jazirah eyed Maryam, searching for the core of truth in the depths of a murky stare. She found only blackened emptiness.

Maryam sat back on her heels, fingers clasped again. "I fear he inherited more of his mother's cruel ways than his father's nature. When my Yusuf died, I wanted to perish with him. However, our children would have remained alone and defenseless against Muhammad's power. I could not abandon them for my love's sake. I came to the bedchamber where my Yusuf breathed his last to be with him, but Butayna was there first. The ministers had already declared for her son. When I cried out for consideration of my eldest son's inheritance, Muhammad slapped me twice across the face. I blame the lure of his newfound power. What could I have done, a feeble widow, against it? You must never anger Muhammad. I have oft heard him rail at Butayna as well. Once a man becomes violent with women, it is only a matter of time and circumstance before cruelty escalates."

As Jazirah took in this last unexpected pronouncement, Maryam rose and returned to the bed. "You know the truth of men, for you have experienced the vileness of your jailor at Shalabuniya. Yet, there is doubt in your eyes. You wonder whether my words are true."

A flurry of thoughts blossomed in Jazirah's mind. Muhammad had criticized her for any hint of her misery at Shalabuniya. His dissatisfaction with her remained evident in their private dinner. Two weeks later the same man had caressed her pockmarks in the moonlight and kissed her with such tenderness and reverence, the like of which she had never anticipated. No one could be so contradictory. What was the truth of her husband's nature?

She licked her lower lip. "I have only known patience and kindness from my husband during the night we spent together." Even as she spoke, she recalled his callous leave-taking and the summons for Haziyya, who entertained him even now. "It is hard for me to reconcile your words with what I have seen of Muhammad."

"The truth is hardest to bear. Lies are easier to believe."

Jazirah bent forward and willed tears away. Muhammad had not lied about his desire for her, or even his wish to spare her physical pain in their joining. Yet, he had not cared about her turmoil when he sent for his lover.

Such a man, cursed with such a changeable nature, would be unpredictable. Mayhap Maryam had cautioned her rightly. Muhammad would never understand how she could have equated him with Harun, no matter the explanation she offered. Still, if she never clarified the previous night's conclusion, how could she ever forge a bond based on compassion with Muhammad?

Maryam's husky voice intruded on her bedeviled mind. "Oh, my dear, you look stricken. Now, I must beg your forgiveness for having burdened you with this knowledge of your husband and his mother. I never intended to upset you."

Did she think she had accomplished her aim so easily? Jazirah would not soon succumb to gossip, no matter her private concerns. She must discover the truth of all Maryam had said and she knew just where to obtain the proof.

She straightened and cleared her throat. "I thank you for the cautionary words. I shall remain guarded in my interactions with Butayna, but you must allow, I cannot judge my husband by your tales of him alone. You view his ascendancy as an infringement upon your eldest son's claims to the throne. Still, Muhammad is Sultan and he is my husband. If I cannot have an easy accord with him, our dynasty will suffer. You must understand if I shall take these next months to form my own opinion of him."

Something flickered in Maryam's eyes, a momentary glint of some indiscernible emotion before the mask of her wide smile slid into place.

"Of course, my dear. Whatever you may think of me, I wish your husband naught but the happiness he deserves. I only pray for your sake you may never know Muhammad's cruelty."

Later, Jazirah staggered out into the garden on wooden legs. She gripped the plaster-covered masonry and drew deep breaths before she resumed walking across the courtyard. Sights and sounds faded.

"Jazirah? Dearest, are you unwell?"

She found Butayna beneath the southern portico beside the chief eunuch Hisham. He bowed to the *Umm al-Walad* and glided along the wall before he disappeared.

Butayna stretched out her hand, but Jazirah recoiled as Maryam's warnings filled her mind. Had those same fingers mixed the poison to rid Maryam of her baby?

With a nonplussed, wide-eyed gaze, Butayna blinked and withdrew her touch. "Shall I call for your stewardess or maidservant?"

Jazirah snapped, "I do not need them!" She swallowed. "What I require is the truth from you."

Butayna's regard jerked to some spot behind Jazirah, who turned and followed her stare to where latticework covered Maryam's windows. Had Butayna guessed at her rival's presence behind the screens?

"I shall try to tell you what you wish to hear, though I must wonder at what you may have heard of the same subject from Maryam. You just came from her apartment, did you not? She told you something to displease you. Now, you look at me as one would a stranger."

Butayna's voice shook. While she fell silent, her mouth drawn in a thin line, she never ceased glaring in the same direction.

Jazirah replied, "Maryam spoke to me of her conflicts with you. She also said my uncle Yusuf never chose an heir. The court's high ministers appointed Muhammad."

A spark flared in Butayna's eyes before she turned her glower on Jazirah. "It is true. Yusuf never decreed before the court the son who would follow him. This does not mean he had never chosen an heir. He wanted Muhammad to succeed him."

A mother would believe whatsoever, if it meant the ascension of her child. Jazirah could not fault Butayna's fidelity to Muhammad. A mother would do anything for her offspring, even inventing falsehoods for their benefit. She might also kill for them.

Jazirah added, "Maryam also told me of the aftermath of Yusuf's death. When she demanded the recognition of her eldest son's equal claim to Gharnatah, Muhammad slapped her. I would find it difficult to gain an attachment to a man who hurts women, especially one whom I must call husband. I saw enough of such behavior under Harun. Did Maryam speak the truth about Muhammad's behavior?"

Jazirah knew the answer even before Butayna lowered her gaze. Quivers parted her lips. A whimper came out. Jazirah backed away from Butayna's outstretched hand.

"Do not turn from me, Jazirah! I swear it was a momentary lapse. You were not there! You did not know the tribulations my son underwent at the hour of his father's death. It was a difficult time for all of us and...."

Jazirah clapped her hands over her ears and fled. The rush of her footfalls up the stairs and across the floor drowned out anything else she might have heard. On the landing, she slowed her steps and rubbed her chest, where her heart thrummed. At the doorway, Zabala and his men bowed before her, stone-faced. She mumbled a greeting, rushed inside, and pressed her back against the closed double doors.

If Maryam's caution about Muhammad merited belief, had she spoken the truth about everything else?

***

Gharnatah, Al-Andalus or Granada, Andalusia
Rajab 757 AH or July A.D. 1356 or Av 5116

Seven weeks afterward, the harsh glint of sunlight streamed through windows at the summer palace at *Jannat al-'Arif.* A loud bang jerked Jazirah awake. Her nails tangled in the silken coverlet of *cendal* as she pushed it back and swung her legs over the bed. The motion sent her spiraling through a wave of dizziness. She gripped the mattress until the faintness subsided.

Her husband's household still had not settled into their seasonal residence, although Muhammad had ordered the move twelve days before. Except for one chance meeting on the water staircase to the oratory, she and Muhammad had kept their distance from each other. Jazirah did not intend to break their unspoken accord, but she could not always avoid the sight or sounds of her husband. He met Ridwan, sometimes with Ibn al-Khatib, for the morning meal in the shadows of the portico. He escorted his mother and sister or Haziyya to dinner in his tower most nights. Before the last meal, he oft strolled alone through the upper garden just outside the eastern quarters where Jazirah, his sister Aisha, and Haziyya roomed. At times, he leaned against a slender, marble column and stared out on the expanse of the city to the north and *Al-Qal'at al-Hamra* to the west. He usually stayed until the sun retreated in a red haze. Hot winds rustled his garments and his hair, which had grown longer. Jazirah recalled its sleek feel between her fingertips.

Naked, she crossed the chamber and went to the window overlooking the garden. The summer's intense heat pervaded the palace even after sundown and encouraged the denizens to don scant clothing. Thus, Jazirah had taken to sleeping in the nude, a move Lubna always viewed with concern, while Beatriz's skin colored the reddened hue of rich saffron at the sight. Maryam had warned Jazirah how nakedness abounded here. Her servants would have to grow familiar with it, as she had done.

The scent from orange trees invaded Jazirah's bedchamber and flooded her nostrils. Although they were bitter, she craved the tart taste of the fruit since impulse made her pluck one from a tree one week ago. As she pressed forward, her nipples brushed against the lattice. She drew back with a wince. Why was her flesh so tender of late?

The hour remained unknown, but dawn had arrived. She had missed *Salat al-Fajr,* not the first time she neglected the earliest prayer hour. Lethargy weighed down her limbs. She leaned against the adjacent wall with a loud yawn and rubbed at her lower back, where a minor ache had troubled her each morning for a week.

The creak of iron hinges warned her of Lubna's arrival. Jazirah did not turn around, even at Lubna's wearied sigh.

"My Sultana, why do you stand unclothed? I could have been anyone, Zabala even."

"He would never enter my room without warning. Unlike you. Why didn't you awaken me early?"

"After you finally fell asleep in the late hours of night? I'm not cruel. Your nightmares have not subsided. Beatriz kept looking up from her pallet each time you tossed and turned, although I reassured her only dreams tormented you."

Now Jazirah looked around. "Forgive me for disturbing both of you."

Lubna strolled toward her with a smile, sheaves of parchment in hand, a probing gaze in her eyes. Then she bowed and grasped and kissed Jazirah's fingers.

Jazirah smiled and gave her a playful shove. "Why did you kiss me?"

"You have forgotten your seventeenth birthday has arrived?"

Jazirah turned away and looked out of the window again. "How could I? The first in eleven years I have spent outside Shalabuniya. I will go to the *hammam* and then visit with Father. There is no one else I would rather spend my birthday with, except you."

"Life for a queen of Gharnatah cannot be so simple. The *Umm al-Walad* knows the significance of this date. I believe she learned of it from your father. The Sultan's mother wishes to have a feast in your honor. Her maidservant Jawla informed me of the request. Your father would be welcome at the gathering, too. I suppose Sultana Maryam will receive an invitation as well. It would be impolite to ignore her and her children, although they no longer reside within your husband's harem."

The last thing Jazirah wished would be a repeat of the gathering at her marriage feast, especially in the company of Butayna and Maryam, neither of whom she trusted. She swept the hair back from her bare shoulder and rubbed her neck.

Lubna said, "Something has changed inside of you these last few weeks. You are reserved with the *Umm al-Walad.* I date the behavior from your afternoon with her rival. What became of your plan to speak with your husband about the discord between you? He is never far from your thoughts. You watch him in secret. Don't you realize he does the same when he thinks you're not looking?"

Except Jazirah had known each time Muhammad's hot gaze alighted on her, whether he stared at her in the garden from his northernmost quarters or anytime she had departed from lessons in his mother's southerly chambers.

Unshed tears pricked the corners of Jazirah's eyes. Try as she might, her husband's fervent touch, his warm lips, and the musky scent of him lingered. Her one night with him might as well have been a fleeting dream. Still, her recollection would never fade.

Lubna clutched Jazirah's forearm. "What did Sultana Maryam say to taint your opinion of your husband and his mother?"

Jazirah opened her mouth before she closed it again. For weeks, she had wanted to confide in Lubna of Maryam's tales. Jazirah never found the courage. She wavered between acceptance and disbelief, her mind mired in chaotic questions even now.

She drew in and then released a slow, deep breath. "Little of significance for me to rely upon, but do not press me further. I need time to sort the muddle in my mind. To determine the true nature of the man I have married and his mother."

"You think to do so by avoiding those whom you would know better?"

Jazirah shook off her hold. "Do not question me!"

From her peripheral gaze, she noted how Lubna raised her eyebrows before bowing. "As my Sultana wishes."

Jazirah rolled her eyes. "You always use my title when you are annoyed with me."

"When my Jazirah reminds me that she is a queen worthy of all due respect, I would be a fool to forget. Still, I would not ruin this day with disagreements. Instead, I came to offer my gift for your birthday."

She thrust the parchment at Jazirah. The frayed, curled edges of each sheet were coarse to the touch. A whiff of some musty odor rose from the pages.

Jazirah perused each page before she frowned at Lubna. "Is this some jest? I have parchment for letters. Besides, you have marked all of these with notations coinciding with months. What good is used parchment to me? What is this?"

"For two years, since you had your first bleeding, I have charted each incidence."

"Why?"

"To know whether you might be capable of bearing children. Since we came to Gharnatah, you have had your moon blood three months in a row, with the benefit of a good diet, rest, and comfort."

Jazirah rubbed the middle of her forehead. "And I bled last month in Jumada al-Thani, just after Muhammad's birthday. Lubna, why bother me about menses?"

"Your cycle has changed again. You bled only a little for two days last month. Now in this month of Rajab, naught has occurred. You are more irritable than usual, quicker to show your temper. You crave bitter foods. Honey has not touched your tongue in weeks. All since you first bedded your husband. Do you take my meaning?"

Jazirah trembled and blinked back a rush of tears. "Then you... you believe I am...." She could scarce give voice to the words scattered throughout her mind.

Lubna palmed Jazirah's lower abdomen. "I think you carry the Sultan's child."

Jazirah covered Lubna's fingers with a shaking hand. "But how? I mean, I know how! It's just... well, we were only together for one night, in one... interlude. How could Muhammad have sired a babe upon me so soon?"

Lubna buried her laughter against Jazirah's shoulder. "Only a moment's pleasure is required. There are also times when even such bliss as lovers may share is unnecessary."

When she drew back, her features suddenly downcast, Jazirah rested a hand on Lubna's shoulder and squeezed. The shadow of Harun still darkened both of their lives, souring even these tender moments between them. Lubna turned her head and placed a light peck on Jazirah's knuckles.

"Children are a natural occurrence between a fertile woman and a virile man, such as you and the Sultan. The timing must have been good. You had broken your moon link two weeks before your wedding night."

Jazirah looked down at her belly, which seemed no different in appearance. She pressed her fingertips inward. A babe might dwell within. Her baby.

Then a thought occurred. "Could you be wrong? It is too soon to hold hope."

"This is why we will wait another month before you tell Muhammad's mother."

"Why her?" Jazirah still feared the possibility of Butayna's interference.

"Only she or the Sultan can summon the midwife to verify your condition. Although I do not doubt it. A babe for my sweet babe. No one, not even your noble father, could be as proud of you as I am."

"I pray if I am with child, it will be a girl."

Lubna swatted Jazirah's arm. "Hush! A son would sit upon his father's throne."

"A son will belong to Gharnatah and his father's people. A girl would be mine for a time, at least until she weds."

With a chuckle, Lubna said, "A girl shall be her father's own, too. Princesses are always of importance to their fathers, especially when the father is a Sultan who needs alliances secured by political marriages."

Jazirah raised her chin. "If I have a daughter, she will not become her father's pawn. I won't allow it."

Lubna sighed. "We are all pawns, Jazirah."

***

On the tenth day after she learned of a possible pregnancy, Jazirah bled again in the mid-morning, enough to cause Lubna and her some concern.

Beatriz held Jazirah's hand, while Lubna hovered nearby. "You understand why we cannot keep this a secret any longer. Your husband's mother must be told."

"Told what?" Beatriz asked.

Jazirah sniffed and wiped at her wet face. "Lubna thinks I am with child."

Despite Beatriz's shocked expression, Lubna said, "Stay with our Sultana until my return. I must beg the *Umm al-Walad* to send for the royal midwife."

Butayna came with Lubna at midday. A pink flush colored Butayna's skin and her smile revealed little crinkles around her mouth. She sat next to Jazirah, but at a discreet distance, mirroring the diffidence Jazirah had adopted in recent weeks.

Butayna said, "Your stewardess has told me of her suspicions. I have summoned the midwife. You shall receive the best care. The midwife has delivered all babies within this harem, including my children. My captain shall bring her. I'll remain with you during her examination. Afterward, Muhammad must know. Soon, the entire harem will hear of it. There are few secrets in this place."

***

Late in the evening after the midwife's departure, Jazirah received word. Her husband wished to see her after *Salat al-Maghrib*. Her hands shook even as Lubna grasped and kissed her fingers.

"You should share this joy together. Come, you need to wash and prepare for him."

Just when Jazirah had finished her ablutions and Beatriz helped her dress, a knock came at the door. Lubna bowed and stood aside as Jazirah's father came in. She raced to him with tears in her eyes and he enfolded her in his familiar hold.

He said, "A message came from Muhammad. He called me to his chambers and said you would be there, so I came early to escort you. What has happened? Why are you crying, my sweet daughter?"

Jazirah sniffled and whispered in his ear, "Only tears of joy. You're going to be a grandfather." Then she drew back in the circle of his arms.

His mouth agape, he looked to Lubna, who smiled and nodded. Then he let out a loud whoop and crushed Jazirah to his side again. She laughed and hugged him before he released her a final time and grasped her hands.

"The blessings of Allah upon you and your child, always. How do you feel?"

"Frightened and happy all at the same time. I have bled, which is why Butayna asked for the midwife so soon. The woman thinks the child will thrive. I am also well."

He kissed her fingertips. "Let us petition Allah to favor both of you."

After sunset, Jazirah left her chambers accompanied by her father and Lubna. The trio followed the narrow path of the garden's outskirts north to her husband's quarters. Beatriz had frowned when told to stay behind and clean the chamber, but Jazirah reassured her they would return soon.

The red-gold glow of the heavens set the sky ablaze and a furious evening wind raked at Jazirah's veil. As she and her companions neared the doorway, guarded by Pero, Jazirah licked her lips and took deep, calming breaths. She had not spoken with Muhammad at any length since their wedding night. At any occasion where she deemed the time right to visit him and explain her behavior, Maryam's warning echoed in her mind.

Pero directed them up the stairs to the open-air landing. Jazirah clutched her father's arm, startled to find her husband did not wait alone on the plush carpets. To his left, his mother sat back on her heels with the chief eunuch Hisham crouched behind her. Beside Muhammad, his favorite concubine rested with her hands in her lap. She looked at Jazirah once before her stare flitted away.

Muhammad's intent regard pinned Jazirah to the spot, so Lubna could not help bumping into her from behind. She mumbled some apology, which Jazirah barely registered. She had not anticipated this cold reception from Muhammad. The table between them, laid bare, absent even a pitcher of water, suggested this would be no pleasant occasion.

Her husband waved them to the cushions directly across from him. When they sat, he began with, "The *Umm al-Walad* told me of the midwife's visit. The woman believes you are with child, Jazirah."

He seemed neither pleased nor dissatisfied, but his icy tone discomfited her nonetheless. She cleared her throat. "I think so as well, husband."

A tic pulsed beneath the flesh of his jawline. He flexed his fingers and closed them in a fist. Beside him, Butayna gave a slight shake of her head. In the tense silence, Jazirah looked from mother to son, before she peered at her father. His brow creased, and his mouth opened, but no sound came out.

Jazirah's attention returned to her husband. "I had thought you would be pleased."

Muhammad's fist thumped the floorboards so hard, the table rattled on its squat legs. "Why should I be pleased? How dare you attempt this farce and expect my joy?"

She placed her arm across her abdomen with concern for the future of the babe inside of her. "What are you saying?"

He ground out the next words. "Tell us the truth, if you can speak it at all. Who is the father of your baby? For it is certainly not my doing if you are with child."

Chapter 12
Wounds

Sultana Jazirah

Gharnatah, Al-Andalus or Granada, Andalusia
Rajab 757 AH or July A.D. 1356 or Av 5116

Rendered speechless by Muhammad's inquiry, Jazirah trembled. If she had been standing before her husband while he made his accusation, his next words would have sent her reeling in agony and disbelief.

"Tell me how it is possible for you, above all other women of my harem including my *kadin*, to have accomplished what none of them could. In seven years, I have never fathered a babe. You would have me believe on the first and only night in which we shared a bed as husband and wife, you quickened with my child? Some would call it a miracle, but I do not believe in happenstance. So, speak. Tell us who fathered your offspring. Lies will not avail you, for your spawn and its father's life are already forfeit."

Jazirah struggled for words. How could he have arrived at such an outrageous conclusion? What sort of man would disgrace his wife before their family? How could he reasonably believe the careless words he had uttered?

His mother peered at him with widened eyes. "Is this why your joy turned to displeasure after I had informed you of the midwife's purpose? Oh, my lion, you are so wrong! Jazirah has not played you false. She carries your heir. You have no reason to believe yourself a cuckold."

Muhammad glowered at her. "How could you know? Are you with my wife at every hour of each day and night? You were next to me this afternoon when I summoned Zabala. He admitted he was not always at her side in the baths or the oratory. What good are he and his men if they cannot give me a daily accounting of the activities of my bride and her father? Zabala is lucky I did not take his head in recompense."

With a broken sob, Jazirah shuttered her gaze. Although she should have suspected the guards spied on them at Muhammad's behest, proof of their real purpose knifed her heart.

Her father gathered her close to him and bussed her cheek before he said. "My Sultan, Jazirah came to you as a virgin—"

"She did. I will not deny the fact. I cannot affirm her behavior afterward."

"You dare disparage my daughter's good name!"

Muhammad replied in a cold monotone, "So speaks the traitor who betrayed my father's words to the Marinids. Do you think I am ignorant of your activities even now? Plots stir against me. You are at the heart of them. Why else should my most disloyal governors have dined with you in these intervening months?"

"Then why haven't you arrested me? Suspicion alone satisfied your father. Why should you require greater proofs?"

Jazirah clutched the neckline of her father's tunic. "Say no more!"

Her watery gaze darted to her husband's face. In his reckless state, he would not allow the challenge from her father to go unanswered. Indeed, fury contorted Muhammad's features. Jazirah did not know him anymore. Mayhap she never would.

Before he could reply, Butayna pleaded, "Prince Ismail, do not rouse Muhammad's bitterness! I'm certain your actions do not merit suspicion." She reached for her son's fingers. "You must listen to me! You have made a grave mistake. There is no reason for you to believe you are not the father of Jazirah's child."

He slapped her hand away. "I have every reason, *Ummi*, as you are well aware! Do not try to convince me of how she," he said, casting a furious wave of his hand in Jazirah's direction, "is the only fertile female in my harem."

Behind her, the chief eunuch said, "My honored Sultana, mayhap it is time for—"

"I know, Hisham! I will explain the matter to my son." Her gaze swept the room. "Leave us, all of you. Prince Ismail, take Jazirah to your house."

Muhammad's scowl deepened. "You cannot dismiss anyone when I have not given them leave to go. Do you forget who is Sultan here? I want my precious wife confined to her rooms until she gives me the answers I seek."

His mother replied in a mournful tone, "Only I can do so, my lion. Let the others depart so we may speak in private. I will allay your dreadful concerns."

"You may try, though I do not see how it is possible. Jazirah and her father must remain at *Al-Qal'at al-Hamra*. I want them guarded. Not by Zabala and his men! I have had enough of their incompetence."

"Prince Ismail and Jazirah have no other place to go. Do not dismiss Zabala. When the harem learns of Jazirah's condition, she must have protection. Her safety is more important than ever since she carries your heir."

"You have not provided this proof. I am waiting. Go from us, all of you."

Hisham rose first and with a flourish and bow left them. Jazirah's father squeezed her elbow and aided her as she rose on shaky legs. At the first footfall, she stumbled and might have pitched forward, but her father and Lubna steadied her. She reached for the wooden railing and looked behind her.

Muhammad's tight-lipped, grim expression met hers. They would never have peace. Deep in her heart, Jazirah mourned the loss of hope for a comfortable companionship or even friendship with the man she had married.

Through a tearful gaze, she found her footing on the first step. She staggered down the stairs, certain of how Muhammad's fiery stare followed her. As she emerged into the daylight again at the bottom of the landing, she paused and heaved a ragged breath before sagging on the marble floor. Her father joined her and hugged her tightly, while she pillowed her head against his shoulder and keened her heartbreak.

She had been such a fool. Before today, she had believed only fists and weapons caused real injuries. Words cut deeper than any blade.

A shadow fell over her and her nape tingled. When she looked up, Haziyya hovered beside her father. Lubna stood with tightened fists, a fierce scowl directed at the concubine. Just when it seemed Haziyya might speak, instead she turned away and disappeared through the eastern doorway.

Jazirah's father rose and extended his hand to her. "Come, daughter. We will go to my house and dine together. The welcoming smiles of Jyoti and her son Dhanu will cheer you, as will my cook's lamb stew."

When she gave no answer, her father bent and grasped her arm. "You must get up, Jazirah. You are stronger than Muhammad will ever know."

Still, he bolstered her as they left *Jannat al-'Arif* via the southern staircase, a route leading through the overcrowded storage areas. The high steward Mufawwiz struggled to bow before them, his large belly an ever-increasing impediment. His cheerful greeting went unanswered. In Jazirah's state, she could not trust herself to speak, even to the servants she admired in Muhammad's household. Suspicions plagued her. Were they all his spies, just like Zabala?

The trio deviated from the walled track between *Jannat al-'Arif* and *Al-Qal'at al-Hamra*. Instead, they took a well-lit path between alder and almond trees, lights in the distance beckoning them through their dim surroundings. The wind ripped at fragile pink and white blossoms, scattering them among the detritus of the forest. Guards permitted them entry into the royal *madina,* still bustling with denizens who strolled after evening prayer or ambled toward the market stalls, open even as shadows fell over the walls of *Al-Quasaba*. In the distance, Jazirah sighted the frontage of her father's house and Gonzalo's features cast in a golden hue by the torch he carried. His crinkled brow relaxed and a smile soothed his features once he recognized them.

Behind him, Zabala and a few of his men waited on either side of the entrance. The captain had been staring straight ahead, but as Jazirah's gaze fell upon him and persisted, he looked away. In truth, she did not fault him for the betrayal, just as she had not blamed Alfonso Ruiz for relaying news of Harun's attack. The Sultan's guards demonstrated their unswerving loyalty to their master, although Muhammad did not deserve it. He had proved himself a heartless and mistrustful man.

The road sloped downward, leading past Maryam's redbrick residence. Lights glowed beyond the curtains draped across the latticed windows, suggesting the family had settled in for the night. Here remained the sole place Jazirah might take refuge from prying eyes.

She pulled away from her father and paused beside the high walled fence, bounded by juniper trees and climbing roses. Lubna and Jazirah's father also stopped.

He asked, "Why do we stand here?"

Jazirah replied, "I cannot go further."

He glanced at the frontage before he reached for her. "Remember what I told you when we arrived in Gharnatah. There are no friends here, not within Maryam's house. Come now."

She warded off his touch. "I will not, Father. Please, just leave me be."

Jazirah ducked beneath the horseshoe arch, which served as the gateway. Faltering steps brought her to the double doors. She pounded the wood.

Behind her, Lubna called out, "My sweet child, do not do this! Give Muhammad time to know the truth from his mother. He shall regret this evening. One day, you will learn to forgive him."

Jazirah ignored the plea. Her fist struck the door again so hard, tremors shot up her arm. She cried out, "Maryam! I need you!"

Hinges creaked before the dwarf Nazhun peered out into the encroaching darkness. Jazirah pushed past her into the warmth of the well-lit antechamber. Maryam came around the corner and Jazirah broke into a run toward her.

Maryam caught her shoulders. "By Allah's grace, what is the matter? Why have you come?"

Jazirah wept and burrowed her face in Maryam's neck.

"Why are you crying, my dear? What has happened to sadden you so?"

The words echoed ones Jazirah's father had asked earlier, but now anguished sobs trickled over her cheeks. Her hope and joy spoiled forever by heartless words.

Through her tears, she said, "Oh Maryam, you were so right about Muhammad! He is so cruel. I was wrong... about everything!"

Maryam's kiss pecked her brow. "Come, my dear one, come into my chamber. The girls are in the *hammam,* so we may speak in private. Tell me all of what transpired between you and your husband."

***

Sultan Muhammad V

Muhammad seethed inside and gritted his teeth until his jawline pulsed. The certainty of Jazirah's betrayal left him embittered. She could not have conceived his child where all others had failed. At first, the news had sparked such joy within him. He had sat dumbstruck while the midwife reassured him Jazirah's bleeding posed no great risk to the well-being of his heir. He had called for wine for his mother and *sekanjabin* for himself, but the drink tasted even more sour than usual when he considered the implausibility of his role in the conception.

Something remained amiss, a hidden truth his mother claimed to know. He turned to her. Although she shrank away, he took no pains to hide the anger embroiling him.

"You will explain how I could be the father of Jazirah's baby. If your answer fails to satisfy me, I shall confine my uncle to *Al-Quasaba* and Jazirah to her rooms for the rest of this misbegotten pregnancy. My men shall discover the identity of the bastard's father. The executioner shall strangle him and the child."

Butayna's lips trembled and her hands shook, but her stare never wavered. "You will regret having threatened such violence against a babe of your own blood."

"How can you know the child is mine?" When the answer did not immediately issue, he shouted, "I'm waiting!"

She clasped her fingers and lifted her chin just a little higher. "Do not growl at me, my lion. Unlike the bride you have sent scurrying, your wrath does not frighten me. Your anger is unwarranted. Jazirah carries your heir, a child you have duly sired—"

"While no other woman of the harem has ever become pregnant?"

"There is a reason. Have you never wondered why I pressed for this marriage with Jazirah, why I insisted the mother of your firstborn should be a princess of Nasrid blood? Throughout your family's history, wedding cousin to cousin has always merited approval and assured strong familial ties. Your father broke with tradition when he married two slaves, a Christian and a Jew—"

"What do these unions have to do with me?"

She held up her palm. "If you would be silent, I will explain. Through your spies, you know what some courtiers of Gharnatah whisper about me. They say I am a vile Christian woman who has tainted her children with her idolatrous ways. My son is not fit for the throne because of the stain of my blood. Your friendship with the king of Castilla-León only exists because I have compelled it. Such grand schemes have your enemies lain at my feet, it is a wonder I find time for myself. Their words are lies, as well you know, but among them is another claim. They say I have prevented the birth of your heir. In this instance, there is some truth."

Muhammad shuddered. Rumors had bedeviled the harem for years of Butayna's undue influence, words surely springing from Maryam's lips, for who except she could have motive or information about his private domain. He had never considered the possibility Maryam spoke the truth, until now. Had he been a fool all along? Had he relied upon a mother who undermined him?

Dumbstruck, he listened while Butayna continued, "The rumormongers were right. I have interfered in the conception of your heir to safeguard all lives. Yours, the eventual mother, and child. For years, every woman of this harem, from the lowliest body slave to your *kadin* has drunk a decoction of pennyroyal and ground wild carrot seeds in all teas and juices. Hisham carried out my order and maintained the practice. The plants can prevent pregnancy or cause a woman who has conceived to bleed heavily and lose her baby. If ever any of your women had your child in the womb, they would not have known. They would have bled, thinking it naught more than a renewed link with the moon."

He did not doubt the stealth of Hisham, but Butayna's collusion with the eunuch stunned him. Her wan features now flushed pink under his scrutiny.

"You may well ask yourself why I have prevented your heirs from being born of slave women. There must be no question regarding the right of a son of yours to claim the throne. His mother had to be a Sultana of royal blood, not one raised from the lowly rank of slave through motherhood and marriage, as I was. For a year prior to your wedding, I went into the house of the Jew, Juan Manuel Gomero, a slave merchant who has served the needs of all noble families of Al-Andalus, to discover news of marriageable princesses."

Muhammad recalled the night of her return from Shalabuniya and his inquiry about her visits to the Jewish merchants' quarter. She had lied even then, as she did now, for those visits continued long after Jazirah's arrival in Gharnatah.

Undaunted by the exposure of her falsehoods, she looked toward the distant hills. "Your bride could not be a Berber either, not even one as perfect as Haziyya. Many among your ministers fear the claims of the Berbers garrisoned upon this land. The influence of the commander and his Berber Volunteers of the Faith extends beyond their fortress in the city of Wadi-Ash. The heir of Gharnatah could not be born from a woman of the Berber tribes. Jazirah was the best choice, a daughter of your uncle. Marriage to her ended the breach caused by years of captivity, gave her and her father the comfort and security long denied them, and granted you a bride who proved fertile. She has never imbibed the mix of pennyroyal and wild carrot seeds. Cease these groundless fears, and know with certainty, you are the father of her babe."

His heart and mind, both torn in two by Butayna's callous cruelty, could not encompass all she had done. One question remained unanswered.

"How could you have done this to me?"

Her amber and cinnamon-flecked stare returned to his. She demanded, "You can ask? Have you not lived in this viper's den," she flung her arm wide, "for almost as long as I have? Have you not seen the harem's sanctity breached and torn asunder by the discord I have shared with Maryam? The solution would have been one wife as the mother of the heir, but Yusuf had three heirs by two women. When those outside of the walls discovered the infighting between Sultanas and their sons with equal claim to the throne, how long do you think they reasoned before choosing sides? Even your father's ministers and servants chose! By God's grace, Ridwan and Ibn al-Khatib secured your right to the throne when Maryam would have crushed your claim by attacking me. You remember my exile to *Al-Qasr Xenil?*"

How could he ever forget? After his paternal grandmother's murder in his childhood, scandal had abounded, and whispers followed him through corridors. Gossip held the cause of death as Butayna's bold attempt to do away with Yusuf's reliance on his mother and his attachment to Maryam. Consequently, Yusuf had sent Butayna away. He never even let her say farewell to her children, left bewildered by her absence and the accusations.

"I see by the faraway look in your eyes, you do remember." Her next words drew Muhammad from troubles of the past to those of the present. "Everyone, including your father, believed I had poisoned your grandmother and Maryam, except for Ridwan and Hisham. The brothers knew of the baker whom Maryam had hired to taint your grandmother's food with hemlock seeds."

His brow began hurting and he rubbed at the flesh. So many plots, such deception surrounded him. Who could he trust except himself?

"The furrow across your brows betrays your disbelief. Ask Ridwan. You no longer trust me, but he has never lied to you. He would tell you of Maryam's schemes. Ridwan knows the truth."

He shook his head. "Truth. It is a wonder you can speak the word without choking upon it. All this truth you have kept from me, your beloved son."

"Not just my beloved son. Yusuf's heir, first and always." She bowed her head and her shoulders sloped as if weighed by burdens. "You never belonged to me, but to Gharnatah and its people. Your aunt took you into her arms from birth. She held you when you cried at night. Your first words and steps were hers to treasure, never mine. Instead, I gave you all I could of a mother's love, devotion, and defense."

A hollow laugh filled his throat. "Your protection did more harm than good!"

Her gaze returned to his. Her mouth quivered. "My lion. Please—"

"Stop! Enough of your lies and half-truths. You have had your say. Now I will have mine. You have always called me your lion because you believed I held the courage of such creatures. If only you could have seen into my heart and known its deepest fears. Had you been blessed with insight, you would have understood how I feared a proud line would end with me. Surely, I was to blame for having no sons, not the countless slave girls and concubines I had bedded—"

Butayna sobbed, "Oh my lion, you were never at fault!"

"No. You were."

"Muhammad." She reached for his hand.

He flinched and recoiled from her. "Do not touch me! Instead, listen well for the Sultan of Gharnatah speaks. What is a Sultan except he has sons to ensure his lineage and daughters to delight and care for him in his old age?"

Copious tears ran down her cheeks, but he sat unmoved by them. "Even on my wedding night, I worried whether I could sire an heir for Gharnatah. Now you affirm I have done so when I thought myself a bitter disappointment, all because of a practice you instituted. You held no concern for how your actions might have harmed me, not the Sultan, but the son who trusted you. In my heart, I have always been the child born of your body first, never just the lord of Gharnatah. You taught me the first and most important lesson of life. I knew love from you before I learned of laws, religion, and my father's expectations of me. As a child, I cried for your comfort in the darkness, and your arms about me, never my aunt's own! Your love bolstered me when my father died and in all the days since. Your love alone."

While she burrowed her face in the sleeves of her robe and wept, he gritted his teeth and closed his fingers into tight fists. "This is the Sultan's decree. Your foul practice ceases now. No more of pennyroyal and wild carrot seeds. I will order the fields around Gharnatah slashed and burnt. Your misguided attempt has deprived my *kadin* of the children we have wished for and caused us needless anguish. For the pain Haziyya has suffered, I will never forgive you. Go from me now and do not come into my presence again unless I require it. I cannot bear the sight of you! Before you retire for the night, you will fulfill a final command. Send Haziyya to me."

"Will you tell her of my actions?"

"I keep no secrets from the woman I love."

Except he would have to withhold the truth in this instance. His disloyal councilors and governors already believed his mother lay at the source of the kingdom's troubles. He would not give them the proof to destroy his Sultanate. A whisper in the presumed privacy of his quarters with Haziyya might reach those who spied upon him.

Even Jazirah, who had suffered needlessly, must never know. Regret soured in Muhammad's stomach. His gentle approaches to his wife had been for naught, all well-laid plans undone by his mother who had counseled the union.

She lifted her head and her red-rimmed stare met his. Never had she appeared so pitiable. She had called down his wrath. He would not relent.

"I said go!" His shout echoed, and birds took to flight, wheeling in scattered circles.

Butayna rose and stumbled before she righted herself. Her features swollen and downcast, she nodded to him. He closed his eyes, unwilling to offer his regard any longer. Near silent footfalls shuffled across the floorboards and paused.

She said, "I did this for you, my lion. Despise me for the deed, but one day, I pray you shall believe my good intent."

When he did not speak, her bitter sob echoed. The stairs creaked before silence fell.

He released his breath and spoke to the evening shadows. "I love you, *Ummi*. I always shall, but your betrayal wounds me deeply. How can I ever forgive what you have done, not only to me, but to any chance of the peace I longed for with Jazirah?"

***

Sultana Jazirah

Gharnatah, Al-Andalus or Granada, Andalusia
Dhu al-Qa`da 757 AH or November A.D. 1356 or Kislev 5117

The winter season brought snowfall on a bitter, cold morning when Jazirah intended to visit with her father. While she insisted on her plans, Lubna shot her dark looks.

"You are almost six months gone with child! Why must you always demand your way even when there is danger?"

Jazirah flashed a smile at Beatriz who aided her with a pair of boots. "I am a Nasrid. I have my pride."

"And your folly," Lubna muttered as she went into the bedchamber and returned with Jazirah's leather cloak.

After a conciliatory pat on Lubna's cheeks, Jazirah led her servants through the double doors of her room. The eunuch guards waited just beyond the portal, Zabala in command. The men bowed. Their number had doubled by Muhammad's order, ten protectors in the daytime hours, five of them always assigned to Jazirah and five for her father. The other ten would return in the evening, allocated in the same manner as the rest of their company.

Jazirah greeted her captain every morning as pleasantly as she had done when Muhammad first assigned him. Once he fell into step beside her, any conversation between them or chatter with her servants became banal as with today's talk of his family in Bilbao. She still liked Zabala, but she would never trust him again.

He said, "The memory of my mother, father, and sisters does not fade, but my life is here. I am no longer a captive. I am content. I have the great Sultan's trust. I have you to serve."

She took no trouble to correct him. He protected Muhammad's interests alone, a fact she could never forget. In pairs, she trod with him and the others, walking down the stairs and out to the portico, where she paused within its recesses.

Muhammad and Haziyya lingered in his doorway. He leaned forward and whispered something in his favorite's ear, which made her laughter echo to the rafters. He kissed her lips at his leisure, his hand cupping her lower abdomen, which poked out slightly through her clothing. Then he knelt and pressed his lips to her belly. She threaded slender fingers through his hair and smiled at him, while he gazed up at her.

Behind Jazirah, Lubna clutched at her elbow. "My Sultana, Haziyya is...."

Jazirah had never witnessed such joy on her husband's face, evident in the rosy glow of his apple-round cheeks and the wide grin splayed across his lips. Even as he stood, his fingers remained on Haziyya's belly.

Then he looked across the courtyard. The spark in his gaze slowly ebbed as his lashes lowered. Haziyya followed the direction of his stare. She drew back a pace and bowed in Jazirah's direction.

Lubna's hold tightened, sharp nails indenting Jazirah's sleeve. Instead of a wince, Jazirah patted the hand holding her. As Lubna released her, Jazirah bent as much as her expanding girth would comfortably allow, acknowledging her husband's presence. The clang of metal on marble informed her guards had done the same in obeisance to their true master.

Just then, Thalj slinked into view from behind a frost-covered bush. The cat paused and rubbed her body against Jazirah, who said, "Good morning, my lovely. I haven't seen you or your shadows since yesterday."

Muhammad cleared his throat and whistled for Thalj. Jazirah straightened and allowed a little smirk upon her lips as the cat sat on her hindquarters and cleaned snow from her paws.

All traces of Muhammad's amusement faded. The hand on his favored concubine's abdomen fell away. His fiery regard intensified, eyes narrowing. Jazirah would never know how she managed to withstand his fury.

Except for these rare glimpses of her husband beneath the pavilions separating them, she would not know of his presence in the harem at all. His neglectful cruelty divided them still. She had long awaited some word or sign from him, an admittance of the grave error on his part. No apology ever came. He had many opportunities but spent his daytime hours with his council and the nights with his preferred companion. For this, and much more, she would not absolve him.

In the aftermath, Lubna and Beatriz also brought confused tales of some clash between Muhammad and his mother, which resulted in a prolonged absence from her son's side. Any correlation between this occurrence and Muhammad's accusations against Jazirah remained unknown to her.

She turned to Lubna. "Come, I would not delay my visit with Father any longer."

A frown on Lubna's brow receded. "Indeed, we would not wish to spoil the outing."

They walked together, Zabala and the others at a discrete distance. A little yowl came from Thalj, but no more after Jazirah's entourage rounded the corner and plodded toward the exit.

Lubna whispered, "I shall discover what I can of Haziyya's condition."

"If you must." Jazirah brushed the voluminous folds of her head veil aside. Her shoulders shook, but she kept a steady pace. Just a little closer to the door and she would escape the harem, if only for a few hours. The unexpected sight of Muhammad's joy with his favorite had almost undone her, left her a quivering, whimpering heap upon the ground.

Lubna pressed her. "You cannot remain so uninterested in what we just saw. If Haziyya carries your husband's child, there is much to consider. The court astrologer has predicted you shall have a son. What if he is wrong? What if Haziyya bears a boy?"

"Butayna said the old man has never been wrong."

"If Haziyya has the heir instead of you, her son will rule Gharnatah."

"What would you have me do about it now?" When Lubna glared at her, Jazirah stopped and glanced at Zabala. He paused beside a brazier and studied it as if he had never seen a heater.

Jazirah pitched her voice low and asked, "You think I should act based on harem gossip? Speak to Muhammad's mother and seek her help? Even if I believed Butayna would kill a child in its mother's womb, I could never do so." She caressed her rounded belly as she oft did during nights she should have slept. "Not when I have felt the life of my own babe within me."

As they resumed their walk, Lubna said, "Do not presume others are so kind."

"I presume naught."

Lubna halted. "Then I may seek more information about Haziyya?"

Jazirah nodded. "You may." She patted Lubna's arm and declared, "Return to the harem and wait for me this evening. Beatriz shall stay at my side."

With a low bow, Lubna trod the path they had just taken. Zabala's crinkled brow and his watchful stare shifted to her, even after Jazirah gestured for him with an impatient wave. As he pushed back the doors, they stepped out into the sunlight glinting off a layer of snow.

Jazirah shaded her eyes with a gloved hand, all the better to hide a rush of tears. On their wedding night, she had vowed never to care how many women gained pleasure in her husband's arms. Not a lie, but not the entire truth either, as she must contend with the mothers of his other children. Haziyya's baby would be the first among many. The threat of rivals to the future of Jazirah's child was once a trivial concern now brought to vivid life.

Chapter 13
Princess

Sultan Muhammad V

Gharnatah, Al-Andalus or Granada, Andalusia
Safar 758 AH or February A.D. 1357 or Adar I 5117

In late evening, the sun cast its burnished glare across the hillside at *Al-Qal'at al-Hamra*. Muhammad climbed the curtain wall of the citadel's battlements. His guards, under Pero's command, dismissed the sentries and fanned out along the parapet. Muhammad looked south as merchants left the compound via Yusuf's great gate, the *Bab al-Sharia*. As a youth, Muhammad had ordered its opening. He had not known it then, but as Ridwan confided some months afterward, Yusuf had intended the act as the first official duty permitted to his heir.

Within the coming days, Muhammad anticipated his introduction to a new role as parent. The midwife had said Jazirah's baby would arrive in this month of Safar. Muhammad prayed for a healthy son and now looked to secure his heir's future.

Two others joined him along the wall, each under heavy escort. The Marinid Prince Yahya ibn Umar ibn Rahhu, known by the title *Shaykh al-Ghuzat*, served as the commander of the Volunteers of the Faith based at Wadi-Ash. Appointed in the reign of Muhammad's father, Yahya stood beside his young kinsman and the commander of the infantry divisions, Prince Ali ibn Musa Rahhu Badruddin. Seven Sultans of Gharnatah over six generations had endured the Marinid masters of the *Ghuzat* and their control of various strategic posts across Al-Andalus, in defense of Islam. Thus far, no ruler of Gharnatah, the sole remaining Muslim kingdom within the peninsula, had shown resolve against the Christians of Castilla-León, Aragón, and Portugal, without the help of their North African allies. Muhammad intended to be the first to stand alone against all, even the Marinids.

A soft peal of laughter drew his attention to the base of the wall. As if on cue, his younger sisters Aisha and Khadija strolled below. Their slaves and eunuch guards, hunched under the weight of heavy crates and satchels, followed the princesses. Both willful young women had discarded their face veils. Of the pair, Maryam's daughter Khadija appeared more beautiful than Muhammad's full-blood sister did.

As Sultan, he held the responsibility to arrange the marriages of his siblings for his kingdom's benefit. He had allowed his marital state to occupy him for too long. An opportunity to fulfill his duty with one of his sisters and sway the mind of the Marinid commander presented itself. Yahya already had two wives. He would not mind a third if she bore royal blood. The old man might soon find his loyalties divided. He would come to rank the demands of his young wife and his heart above those of his master in Al-Maghrib al-Aksa. Muhammad would ensure this outcome.

When he cleared his throat, Aisha rather than Khadija, looked up first. A sweet smile curved her lips in greeting for her brother. Beside Muhammad, Ali's thick, dark fingers gripped the wall. He leaned forward, his attention on the women below. Yahya stared straight ahead, unaffected. Muhammad groaned.

His sisters bowed and greeted him.

With a grunt, he called down, "Did you enjoy the excursion? Are there any *dinars* left in my coffers after your excesses?"

Khadija gave a little laugh. The corners of Muhammad's mouth tightened as he directed a sharp glance at her. She smothered the sound and edged behind Aisha, as if unable to bear the scrutiny. Muhammad's suspicions and dislike of Khadija's mother extended to all his siblings of the half-blood. Mayhap an unfair assessment in the case of Maryam's daughters, but he could not help it. His half-sisters might not have inherited their mother's nature. Aisha believed so.

She answered him. "Some, my dear Sultan, for the traders will return tomorrow."

Her smirk almost unknotted the tension roiling inside of him. He gestured toward Yahya. "This is the mighty Yahya ibn Umar, who has served us well since the days of our father. The Sword of *Jihad*, he is a great warrior for Islam."

Aisha took in the grizzled head of the elderly commander before she asked, "And his stalwart young companion? Is he also a worthy defender?"

As a son of the Rahhu clan and a slave from Ifriqiyah, Ali had inherited his Nubian mother's swarthy skin, coupled with the hawk-eyed gaze and aquiline nose of his Berber father. In his youthful prime, likely no more than six years Muhammad's senior, he also stood taller than Muhammad did. Ali's stout form and stance hinted at his prowess. Any woman would have judged him of interest, but Aisha's admiring stare discomfited Muhammad. His prideful sister did not practice humility or restraint, defects derived from their mother.

Muhammad coughed. "Yahya's kinsman is another fine fighter, quick with his bow."

The wind took Aisha's laughter aloft as it dragged her hair veil back from her shoulders and tugged at rich brown tresses beneath the silk.

She flashed a grin at Ali. "My brother would have me believe you bear no name, fine fighter for Islam."

Muhammad tugged at the neckline of his tunic. His sweet sister's appearance without a full veil was troublesome enough. She would have shocked the more conservative judges of his court, the *ulamas* armed with their strict Maliki doctrine. He permitted Aisha's whims along with almost every demand she made because he loved her, but this bold discourse with a stranger would not do.

Yahya's reckless relative thwarted Muhammad's planned interruption. "I am Ali ibn Musa. It is my honor to fight for Islam and to gain attention from the great Sultan's sister. I am undeserving."

When he bowed, Muhammad wished Ali had smacked his head on the bricks.

Aisha asked, "Why would you think yourself beneath notice when my brother praises you? He judges all people in fairness and is rarely wrong." Her generous comment aside, Muhammad cringed as she continued the exchange. "I have a name as well. I am Aisha bint Yusuf, sister to the Sultan."

Ali rose and his broad grin mirrored hers. "Aisha bint Yusuf. I shall never forget—"

Muhammad interjected, "It's grown windy, sister, and your mantle may not be enough to keep you warm. Mayhap you should return to the harem."

Aisha stopped staring at Ali long enough to acknowledge Muhammad. "I can deny you little, my Sultan, even after your poor attempt at dismissal." Her wistful sigh reached him before she looked at Ali again. Muhammad ground his teeth together.

Then she and their sister Khadija curtsied. Slow strides took them through the gatehouse and into the courtyard. Muhammad waited until they disappeared. He cast a spiteful glower at Ali, who remained in an ignorant daze, his regard fastened on the archway under which the young Sultanas had withdrawn. Even Yahya frowned at Ali's foolery.

Muhammad grumbled, "Come! Dinner awaits and I do not relish a cold meal."

Then another sight to the southeast made him pause at the edge of the parapet. His younger brother Ismail strolled from the forecourt of their uncle's residence and exited the gate. Jazirah followed, gloved fingers resting upon the high belly visible under her mantle. Muhammad would have known his wife anywhere, even beneath her black *hijab*. No other woman within the royal *madina* carried herself with such pride. She threw back her head and laughed, while the prince at her side shared her amusement.

***

Sultana Jazirah

"You cannot mean it! You believed such fanciful nonsense?" Jazirah exclaimed.

Ismail answered her in a soft tone. "I did believe it. *Ummi* said the midwife brought all new babies. Why would I ever have questioned a mother's words? I was a child."

She chuckled again. "You must have noticed how Maryam's belly swelled under her garments during each pregnancy with your younger sisters."

He shook his head. Silken hair like the texture of his mother's own fell on either side of his face to his waist. "My last sister Zoraya came into the world quickly. We elder children could no longer remain ignorant of the birthing process." He shuddered and his features crinkled.

Jazirah laughed at his expense. "A dreadful experience for one so young."

"Not soon forgotten." Then he sobered. "I should not say such to you, lest you grow frightened at the prospect."

"The birthing day fast approaches. For my part, I shall simply be happy to see my own feet again. I thank Allah daily for my Beatriz, otherwise I would not know if I wore a proper pair of footwear."

He looked down. "She has taken all due care. You always appear well."

As he raised his head and met her gaze, his mouth slackened. He did not blink, entranced. She broke their steady eye contact and looked at the frost-covered ground.

He erased some of the already slight distance between them. "Why do you look away at times when I regard you?"

In the waning months of her pregnancy, Jazirah oft preferred to share her morning meal with Maryam and dinners with her father. Muhammad's younger brother had become a fixture at each occasion. She believed he deliberately sought her out. His stares lingered for too long. His solicitude extended beyond mere courtesy or curiosity.

She withheld her regard. "I had best return to the harem, my prince. Lubna will wonder where I am. The sun has almost set."

"It is still early. Your stewardess worries overmuch."

"She has been as a mother to me for seventeen years."

Zabala coughed. "The hour grows late and my men are cold, my Sultana."

The guards had milled around during the conversation, shivering in short capes.

Before Jazirah could respond, Ismail snapped, "For your mistress' sake, you would stand outside and freeze to death if she wished! Ignorant slave!"

She pressed a hand to his arm briefly. "Zabala is no slave. Butayna freed him."

Ismail sneered at her eunuch guard. "Her folly. If I were you, I would take a leather whip to this one's back! Those who serve us have no other needs beyond their duties."

Jazirah did not think servants were mindless beasts. She would have told Ismail such, but a swift kick from the babe inside caused her to gasp.

As she panted, Ismail clutched her elbow. "Are you unwell?"

She shook her head. "Oh, never! It is the child. Lubna swears it must be a boy, for only a Nasrid prince would be so fierce with his mother. Please, release me."

The unwarranted touch lingered before his hand finally fell away. "Muhammad is lucky to have you for a wife."

She could not deny the effect of his compliments. "You have been so kind since our arrival. When others shunned my father, you hunted with him on the first spring day."

More than Muhammad had ever done. Since the announcement of her pregnancy, her father had seen even less of Muhammad than she did. Like Jazirah, her father could not forgive Muhammad's malice.

"Your father is a good man, Jazirah, despite what Muhammad may believe about him. I shall never abandon my uncle."

Where were such sentiments when Jazirah's family had languished in exile for so many years? For all of Maryam and Ismail's generosity now, neither of them risked such action before the release from Shalabuniya. What did Maryam and her son want?

Zabala sneezed, and in doing so, reminded Jazirah of her intent. "I should leave."

The tendons stood out in Ismail's neck. When he swallowed, his throat bobbed. "Before you go, may I beg a final indulgence?"

"What is it?" She strove against an edge of impatience in her tone.

"May I feel the child kicking? Please. It would mean much to me."

From Jazirah's peripheral gaze, she noted Zabala's frown. The request left her stupefied. Even the prince's mother Maryam had not asked for the privilege. If Jazirah believed the claims from

Maryam and Butayna, their rivalry extended to their sons. Ismail could not take genuine joy in his brother's imminent fatherhood.

Still, a brief touch could not hurt. It was not as if the prince laid his hands upon her naked form. Layers of cloth covered her. She grasped his fingers and drew them to her abdomen.

At the hard thud against his palm, he pulled back his hand, and regarded it with wonder. She almost smiled at his awestruck appearance.

"The baby does not hurt me. I do wish there would be less kicking in the evening and at night, so I might rest. The day will come soon, in which I may hold my child. Please, let me retire so I may prepare for the evening prayer."

He peered at her belly before their gazes met. "Shall I see you tomorrow?" Such hope buoyed his tone.

"I do not know. We must see how the day unfolds."

"I long for its arrival."

Jazirah left him then without further comment, her heart troubled. She admired Ismail's talents as a poet and musician. She thought of him as a brother gained through marriage, but his feelings had changed in an unseemly manner. She would not encourage them, even if her husband did not deserve loyalty.

Instead of the harem, she went to the ancestral mosque. By her uncle Yusuf's decree, women occupied space at the rear, apart from the male worshippers. Among the faithful, she hoped to find answers to her troubles or gain some quiet comfort. Neither came to her during the devotions. Her guards remained with her throughout *Salat al-Maghrib* although the men stayed by the exit.

By rote, she took the path to her father's house and collected Beatriz, who had spent most of dinner with Gonzalo. Jazirah noted a little resentment revealed in the slave's pout, as she had to leave her husband again.

Jazirah plodded across the cold cobblestones. Ice sluiced through the soles of her boots and she grimaced at every footfall. Indoors, Zabala guided her up the steps. Winded, she paused atop the landing.

His frown followed. "Are you well, my Sultana?"

She nodded, still too breathless to speak.

He ushered her along the walkway. "Just a few steps more and you may rest."

She never doubted his allegiance to Muhammad. He would report her earlier exchange with Ismail. Still, she held only gratitude for Zabala's service.

Beatriz led the way and opened the doors to Jazirah's chamber. Inside, Muhammad sat stone-faced on a cushion along the wall beneath the southern window.

Jazirah clutched the door handle. The metal dug into her palm. Beatriz drew back with a gasp, almost crashing into Jazirah.

Muhammad stood, blotting out the lantern light piercing the lattice window screen. He waved his hand. "Leave us, all of you. My wife will remain."

Beatriz fled as though her skirts were on fire. When the doors closed behind Jazirah with a heavy thud, she trembled. She had not stood alone with Muhammad in a room since their wedding night. How far away the evening beside him seemed now.

He removed the distance between them in rapid strides and forced Jazirah to retreat. She flattened against the door. He placed his hands on either side of her, palms flat against the wood.

She swallowed. "What are you doing in my rooms?"

"Should I have asked for your permission? Would you have allowed it, sweet wife?"

His reply taunted her and she was in no mood to bandy wits with him. "Please leave, Muhammad. I am tired and wish to rest."

"Why are you returning to the harem at this late hour?"

Her heart thrummed. Scant space between them drew the scent of mint and cinnamon on his breath into her nostrils. "Why should you care when I come and go?"

"I care when my wife spends her waking hours with those who conspire against me. My concern grows when she lets other men touch her in intimate ways. By other men, I mean my brother Ismail."

Her husband had seen her! There could be no other explanation. Zabala would not have had time to inform Muhammad.

She swallowed and drew a harsh breath. "You have no right to set spies upon me!"

He slammed his fist beside her head. The shock reverberated through the wood. "You give me little reason to trust you when you dine with my enemies! I promised your father I would treat you as you deserved. If your conduct with my brother invites mistrust, I must act accordingly. So there are no mistakes, wife, let me make my meaning plain. If I ever see Ismail's hands upon you again, I shall have them cut off. He must never touch you. Say the words. I want to know you believe me."

She lowered her moist gaze, but Muhammad grasped her chin. She cried out although he had not hurt her. His determined stare bored into hers. "Say them."

"Ismail will never touch me again," she muttered.

He looked down between their bodies. He released his hold and parted the folds of her mantle to reveal her robe under the wool covering. He laid his fingers upon her belly, where their child twisted and kicked. He smiled in response as his hand traced the contours of her flesh, his touch reverent. Then he looked up at her and she forgot to breathe. How could a cruel man be so gentle?

His dark eyes, shaded by long lashes, no longer narrowed in fury. He fondled the underside of her breast, as if testing its full weight against his palm. Her lips parted, but she held herself rigid. Their juxtaposition increased her awareness of him. Her responsiveness to even their simplest contact remained undeniable. His light touch roused emotions buried for long months of their absence from each other.

"Our child shall be glorious. Just like his beautiful mother." His voice hoarsened, while fingertips skimmed her robe again. Beneath the silk, her flesh tingled in every place he stroked. Unable to tear her gaze away, she trembled before him.

"You are mine, as is the babe within you." He reached for her cheek. His thumb glided along the corner of her mouth and the curve of her lower lip.

She breathed raggedly as his caress slid down her throat. With his body flush against hers, she could not ignore the evidence of his arousal or pretend he had not stirred similar wants within her. The husband whom she should despise.

His lips were so close she could almost taste them. He breathed, "Jazirah...."

Before she succumbed and lost herself in desire, she wrenched free of him. "Now you claim the wife you have discarded for long months and the child you once threatened! Never come into my rooms again. I hate you!"

She stumbled to the nearest cushion and knelt on the floor, limbs cradling her bowed head.

Muhammad said, "Think of me as you choose, so long as you heed my warning."

Bitter sobs overcame her. How could she bear this sham of a marriage? Her child would enter a home forever fractured by the unceasing disputes between its parents.

The door creaked once. Muhammad repeated, "Mine." Then he left her.

***

One full week later, Muhammad readied for public audience. Wearied and in desperate need of good sleep, the sluggish movement of his chief maidservants frustrated him more than his own lethargy. He had not slept well since the encounter with his wife.

He grumbled, "Where is Thalj? Have you seen my cat? She's gone missing for days."

Bahar ventured, "I believe she is above stairs with Sultana Jazirah, master. Thalj must be a great comfort to your wife as she awaits the birth of your son."

"Humph! Only if you wish to think so." His own cat had betrayed him. Had he not been the one to feed and indulge her always? Jazirah had usurped his role.

He stood and tightened the belt around his waist, shooing away Suna. Qamar turned from him at a knock on the door.

"If Pero is here, I am not ready!"

Instead of the captain as Muhammad expected, the pale visage of his mother appeared.

Near soundless footsteps brought her into his presence. She seemed diminished since her lengthy absence from his side, her visage haggard and her eyes red-rimmed, as if sleeplessness also plagued her. He had rescinded the order barring her from his quarters a month ago, as visits from the midwife for Jazirah's sake necessitated Muhammad's permission. He and Butayna never spoke more than required, their talks strained.

He muttered, "If you are here to bother me about the midwife, of course she may come. Her examinations of Jazirah do not warrant my consent each time."

Butayna said, "Good, for the need is urgent. Your wife's labor has begun."

Muhammad gaped at her. Then he said, "Are you sure?"

She rolled her eyes heavenward. "I have had two children if my Sultan will recall."

He revised his recent opinion. Not diminished at all given the sharpness of her reply. His brow hurt, but soon the source of annoyance faded. At last, the day had arrived and he would soon hold his child. The Nasrid line would not end with him.

He ran a hand over his head. Almost grudgingly, he asked, "What of Jazirah? How does she fare? Is she well? Does she need me?"

At the last moment, he chided himself for an ignorant fool. If his wife cried out for any man's comfort, it would be her father, not her husband. She likely wanted no more of him after their last encounter.

Pure, impulsive jealousy had directed Muhammad's visit to her room last week. How dare she have allowed Ismail to touch her belly when her own husband had not done so? His hands itched for the feel of his wife again. She had blossomed as a beautiful rose with his babe inside of her, impossibly lovelier than on their wedding night. As with his *kadin,* Jazirah had left her mark on their encounters. He could not forget them or her.

Butayna cleared her throat and he recalled her presence. She stopped regarding him with lifted brows as if he had become a lackwit. "The last thing any would-be mother needs is a man in the birthing chamber. Jazirah is well, but she is also frightened of the pain as any woman in her travail must be."

"She is afraid," he repeated, incredulous. "She said so?"

His mother's frown returned. "There are times in which I wonder if you shall ever know your wife as well as you should, my Sultan."

He held the same concern. How could they ever come together without rancor?

With a curt nod, Butayna said, "I shall have my captain fetch the midwife."

"Do not delay! Jazirah and our baby must have the best of care."

Butayna spoke in a clipped tone, "Never fear, my Sultan. Your wife and babe will be well."

When she turned and proceeded to the door, he called out, "You will stay with her and send word to me of her good health and the child's own when the time comes!"

Did he sound like an overbearing, worried father already? He had not asked a boon from his mother in many months, but he begged now as much as for Jazirah's sake as his own.

Butayna sighed. "You may be assured I shall not leave your wife's side. She is to be a mother to my first grandchild."

She continued to the doorway and then paused, her grip on the handle. "If you have a moment before public audience, Aisha awaits you under the portico."

Muhammad's scalp itched. His sister had tried to see him on the previous two nights, but he then dined with Al-Shaquri until the late evening and the following night with Ridwan. Most of the earlier week had found Muhammad in the company of the Marinid commander Yahya and his men. They were to depart for Wadi-Ash on the morrow at noon. Now Aisha dogged her brother, an unlikely coincidence.

He muttered, "I do not have a moment, *Ummi*. I'm late already."

"As if public audience might commence without you. The people can wait upon the Sultan of Gharnatah."

He ignored her evident irritation. "What does Aisha want from me?"

Butayna shrugged. "You would do better to ask her. I'll see to your wife's needs."

After she left, Qamar approached Muhammad. "If my master is concerned for his noble wife, I do not doubt his Sultana shall do well in the midwife's care."

Suna smiled and nodded to him. "We shall pray for the safety of mother and child."

As he still regretted his earlier behavior, he mumbled his thanks. The trio bowed and left.

At the doorway, Muhammad's hand closed on the handle. He rested his head against the wood. "Merciful Father, let Jazirah and our child be well this day."

With a heavy exhalation, he left the room. As his personal guards bowed, Aisha's petite form rose in their midst. The siblings dispensed with all formal greeting as she threw her arms around his neck and kissed both of his cheeks. He returned her embrace and reveled in their intimacy.

She said, "*Ummi* told me of this day's fine prospect. I shall rejoice with you, brother, when you hold your son at last."

He drew back. "But such is not the reason for your visit? Am I right?"

Her laugh resounded through the courtyard. "Not the sole reason."

Muhammad's arms fell away. "What do you want, Aisha?"

"Not what. Who. Give me Ali ibn Musa for a husband and I shall have all I desire."

He wiped his forehead, which swiftly pounded. "You met him but a week ago—"

"And I have spoken to him each day since." At his rushed intake of breath, she added, "Though always in the company of my Christian guards or my maidservants, lest I shame you."

He sputtered, "But... you do not know this man! How could... you cannot—"

She laughed. "What troubles you more, Muhammad? Is it because I have selected a husband or because my choice is not the man you wished for me?"

"Both!" He scratched his head while she pressed a kiss against his cheek.

"You cannot control every aspect of the lives around you, dear brother."

"It would seem not." He grasped her hands. "I had meant for you to wed Yahya—"

"An old man with two wives and a passel of sons?" Furrowed lines dug into her brow. "I thought you held a brother's love for me."

"I do! There would be great advantage in such a union."

"Not to me!" She pulled away from him. "Find another to wed your Sword of *Jihad*. I will have Ali ibn Musa or no husband at all."

"You do not know the man!"

"Our union shall give me opportunity. Who among us is fortunate to wed for love?" The embers of her hot glare banked.

"Happiness in marital choice is rare. Would you refuse me the chance?"

He shook his head. "I dare not, Aisha." He did not want his sister consigned to a miserable existence, akin to his union. "But you must see—"

She hugged him heartily, while he protested, "I did not agree in full! The matter requires due consideration and my councilors shall have their say."

"Ridwan and Ibn al-Khatib shall accept your decision." She pecked his cheek and released him. "Don't disappoint me. I'm going to tell *Ummi* the good news!"

"Aisha!"

She ignored him and sped away.

He shook his head at how tiresome women could be.

***

Sultana Jazirah

Hours after the initial pains jolted her from the first deep slumber in weeks, Jazirah sweated and groaned on the birthing stool. With Lubna at her back and the daughter of the midwife both offering encouragement, Jazirah gritted her teeth against the screams aching in her throat.

Lubna rubbed her back. "The pain will be well worth it, my Sultana, when you hold the heir of Gharnatah in your arms, the first of the Sultan's many sons."

"I'll kill Muhammad before I ever let him touch me again!"

Jazirah meant her words. Even if Muhammad and she desired each other still, she could never endure this ordeal again. No woman of sound mind would by choice.

Although bleary-eyed, she shook her head as the young apprentice midwife approached with the beaker, tendrils of steam spiraling past the lid.

Jazirah slapped the proffered hand aside. "I will have no more!"

"The medicine cannot harm you or my grandchild. It will ease your pain."

Jazirah rolled her head and found Muhammad's mother seated on a chair between her two silent maidservants. How dare Butayna offer advice from her comfortable cushion, while Jazirah toiled in agony, exposed before strangers with hair plastered to her temples! Another splinter of pain slashed along her swollen abdomen. She gripped the arms of the birthing stool. A series of cramps rippled the length of her stomach.

She muttered, "I have to push."

The midwife's daughter raised from her position between Jazirah's throbbing legs and said over her shoulder, *"Ummi,* she is not quite ready—"

175

"I am!" Jazirah protested. As she attempted to push, a burning sensation radiated outward from the center of her body. She screamed as if hellfire enveloped her.

"Stop!" the midwife ordered. "Of all the impatient Nasrids I have ever known...."

Butayna rose from her chair and knelt beside Jazirah. "Dearest, you'll tear and bleed. Would you endanger yourself to have this babe before your due time?"

The midwife's daughter surrendered her place to her mother, who lowered her hefty bulk to the floor. She balanced a small ceramic pot in her hand and gestured to Butayna with the vessel. "My Sultana, if you will. You are a part of her family and can comfort her in ways we cannot."

Butayna peered at Jazirah, who fell back against the stool. Then Muhammad's mother said, "If you believe so. I'll do anything for her sake." She took the pot and smoothed a thick and oily, but warm paste over Jazirah's belly.

Jazirah muttered, "You do it for your son and his heir, no more."

Butayna did not lift her gaze from her task. "We are women and this travail binds us. We suffer much as mothers for our children's sakes. Such sacrifice begins here when we bring them into the world."

Both of the midwife's assistants nodded before they dispersed to separate corners of the room, to heat water and fold clean cloths and blankets. Braziers kept the chill at bay, but the wind rattled the shuttered windows and set Jazirah's nerves on edge.

Lubna whispered, "It will soon be over."

Butayna finished massaging Jazirah's stomach and looked at Lubna. "Yusuf's sister attended Muhammad's birth. Leila became a great friend to me as the years passed, but when I first came into the harem, I had no one. Jazirah is blessed to have you."

Lubna nodded. "I'll never leave her side."

Time stretched and Jazirah's pains lengthened. The midwife pronounced the hour of delivery had arrived. She spoke to Jazirah. "My ancestors served the Nasrids from the days of Fatima, daughter of Muhammad the Lawgiver. My grandmother and mother delivered Fatima's first son in this harem. Have no fear. With my aid, you'll soon hold your son. I tell you the same words I said to the honorable *Umm al-Walad* as she prepared to deliver our Sultan. Now when you feel the pain most, I want you to bear down as you would upon your chamber pot."

Her daughter and granddaughter collapsed into shocked laughter, with exclamations of "*Ummi!* For shame!" and "Grandmother!"

Jazirah and Butayna gaped at the midwife. Finally, Butayna sputtered, "She should not have such an image in mind as she brings forth my grandchild!"

The midwife rolled her eyes while Butayna said to Jazirah, "The pain will arrive, intensify, and then retreat. At the first hint, hold your breath and then release it as the pain lengthens. Your stomach will clench and you will feel the urge to push as if to empty the contents of your... body. Have no fear. The midwife will help."

Not even Butayna's guidance prepared Jazirah for the intensity of her labor, where everything felt pulled and twisted into myriad knots. Through her delirium, she heard Lubna and Butayna's encouragements, and the midwife's admonishments. When she feared her child would tear her apart, she closed her eyes in surrender.

Butayna's hand grasped hers and guided feeble fingers between Jazirah's thighs. Tears streamed down her cheeks. Her palm cupped something round and slick.

Muhammad's mother rested her brow against Jazirah's own. "Your child emerges. Feel his head. It is time to welcome him to the world."

Jazirah swallowed and opened her eyes. New determination suffused her. Within agonized moments, the baby slipped from her body. She sagged again on the stool. Desperate for the sight of her child, she blinked rapidly. A thick stream of fluid ran down the pasty, wrinkled form. The birth cord bound the newborn to her.

Then the midwife said, "My Sultana, you have given birth to a fine son."

She placed the child against Jazirah's stomach, while her assistants hastily covered mother and son in layers of linen and rubbed the child. His piercing screech seemed the sweetest sound Jazirah had ever heard. Although weak, her arms came about her tiny boy and held him close.

The midwife intruded on her joy. "Your toil is not over. Let my granddaughter take the prince and tend to him, while my daughter waits for the afterbirth."

Jazirah did not want to relinquish her son so soon, but she did as asked.

Lubna's tears wet her shoulder. "He is beautiful, my Sultana."

Butayna patted Jazirah's arm. "You have done well. While the apprentice sees to your needs, the midwife and I must take your son to Muhammad, so he may proclaim the birth of your son and his heir before the court."

Jazirah gasped, but Butayna hushed her. "We will not be gone for long."

Cramps signaled the descent of the afterbirth. Afterward the apprentices withdrew holding a bloodied cloth, their heads bowed together before the elder said, "All is well. Can we get the Sultana into new clothes and on to a clean pallet?"

Butayna's maidservants Jawla and Hafsa helped Jazirah to dress. Then they guided her to the corner with the warmest brazier. She reclined on the pallet with its soft, cotton covering. Soon, Butayna and the midwife returned, with Muhammad in tow.

Jazirah studied the redness suffusing his face as he cradled their son in his arms. His bemused features betrayed his happiness and utter fascination with the tiny bundle nestled in his grasp.

She swallowed and held out her hands for their boy. "Please give him to me. I would like to know how to nurse him."

The midwife sputtered, "Surely, the Sultana would wish for a wet-nurse—"

Muhammad cut her off. "I do not object if my wife prefers to breastfeed our son. It is my wish as well. Mayhap your daughter or granddaughter might show her." He glanced at his mother. "Do you see a reason why I should baulk at the choice?"

Butayna's stare upraised, she whispered, "I would never interfere in a mother's love for her child. If Jazirah wishes it, she should nurse him."

Ignoring the midwife's shocked expression, Muhammad crouched and gave the babe over. "I thank you for the gift of him, Jazirah. He is perfect as a son of ours would be."

A Nubian girl stepped out from behind her master. She bore a gilded tray, on which glittered strands of lapis lazuli, turquoise, and sapphires amid gold.

Jazirah left her husband's present unacknowledged. Instead, she cradled her child close and pushed aside the folds of swaddling clothes, so she might see his face. With his rounded stub of a nose and puckered lips, he did not resemble a Nasrid.

Behind Muhammad, Butayna asked, "What will you name him, my Sultan?"

He rose and glanced at her before he proclaimed, "He shall be Abdul Hajjaj Yusuf, the second of his name, for my beloved, honored father."

As Butayna lowered her gaze, tears seeped beneath her lashes.

Jazirah returned her attention to her son. She had hoped to name him for her father, but she should have known better. The choice, as with other decisions affecting her life, belonged to Muhammad.

She hugged their child close, kissed the fuzzy black hair on his head, and whispered against his brow, "Yusuf."

Chapter 15
Of Kings and Vassals

Sultan Muhammad V

Gharnatah, Al-Andalus or Granada, Andalusia
Rabi al-Awwal 758 AH or March A.D. 1358 or Adar 5118

Within the throne room, Muhammad sat in a semi-circle of the most important men in his realm, his most loyal governors, ministers, and the commanders of Gharnatah's military. Courtiers gathered in the recesses of the chamber, including Muhammad's younger brothers whom he had summoned. Guards lined the walls. To the east, a large wooden screen obstructed the view of the closest doorway.

As Muhammad lifted his gaze from the unrolled parchment in his lap, he wished he might escape through the exit. Life for a Sultan of Gharnatah could never be so simple. Instead, he studied the faces of those gathered before him. Yahya grimaced and rubbed at his left hip, as he oft did lately. Beyond him, Ismail appeared bored while Qays seemed bewildered by the necessity of his attendance. At sixteen, Qays had never been to court, no matter how Maryam cajoled or insisted. His lower lip jutted, quivering each time his unsteady gaze met Muhammad's own. Ismail's mouth formed an ugly sneer, as he shifted his stance and scanned the features of the ministers. Mayhap he reviled their high position or apparent subservience. He would find other cause for dissatisfaction before the morning concluded.

Muhammad said, "I have decided to give the Castillans the aid they require in their war against Aragón. At Al-Jazirah al-Khadra, three armed galleys will await the arrival of King Pedro's fleet, which will sail down the *Wadi al-Kabir*."

Chatter followed from the courtiers, until Ridwan demanded silence.

Ibn al-Khatib queried, "Is it not enough for us to risk the lives of our men in forays through Aragónese lands for months? Must we give the Christians our galleys, too?"

His had not been the lone voice of dissent while Muhammad discussed the matter in his council chamber on the previous day. Only this proud minister had set himself apart before the full court.

Ridwan furrowed his bushy eyebrows and glared at his colleague. Muhammad raised a hand when the chief minister would have responded in his stead and leaned toward his rebellious personal secretary.

In a hushed tone, he said, "My men. My galleys," before he addressed the courtiers. "Shall I have my *hajib* remind us all of why we must send ships to the Castillans?"

Ridwan proclaimed, "Never let us forget the price we have paid to keep Gharnatah free from Christian interlopers. For more than a century, from the time of the first Sultan Muhammad, we have bled this land for Islam. Is there anyone who suggests we shirk the duty to preserve our dominion and the true faith? Do we wage a disastrous war against the Christians? Or do we survive as we have always done? Who here knows the right course for our future better than our great Sultan?"

Muhammad gripped the arms of the throne and awaited a challenger. No one disturbed the prevailing silence. King Pedro would have his three ships.

Ibn al-Khatib bowed his head before he sank into a kneeling position beside Muhammad, who settled back in his seat and nodded as if he accepted the conciliatory sign. He had forgiven past incidents too many times before, honoring his father's implicit trust in Ibn al-Khatib. One day, Muhammad would have Pero take the minister's head for his insolence.

Then Yahya groaned as he bowed. "The *Ghuzat* is prepared to serve you...."

Muhammad cleared his throat. The Marinid prince's dark eyes swept around the tower, as if the interruption had shocked him. Muhammad said, "The ruler of Castilla-León does not need mounted raiders, Yahya, as when you, Faraj ibn Ridwan, and I struck terror into the hearts of the Valencians last autumn. Sailors require the defense of bowmen."

Yahya craned his neck to regard his kinsman Ali at the same time Muhammad tilted his head to the young man and said, "Prince Ali ibn Musa Rahhu Badruddin, you shall join my admiral at the port of Al-Jazirah al-Khadra. You will leave Gharnatah at noon. There must be no delay. Ready yourself and your men."

Ali knelt and bowed his shaved head. "I hear and obey, great Sultan. My warriors and I shall prepare ourselves."

Of all the shocked gasps, only the echo from behind the lattice screen mattered most to Muhammad. A bolt of regret for his sister's pain shot through his heart. He closed his eyes for a moment and then reopened them.

"Prince Ismail ibn Yusuf. Prince Qays ibn Yusuf. You will approach."

Confused courtiers parted their ranks and gawked at Muhammad's brothers, whose expressions betrayed the same shocked sentiment. Qays hung back and only moved when Ismail did so. Both circumvented the sacred square in the center of the floor, inscribed with the ninety-nine names of God, and stood before Muhammad.

Qays did not have the courage to lift his stare, but Ismail glared as boldly at Muhammad as he had at the ministers. His hardened gaze reflected resentment and extreme pride. He would never bend a knee before his elder brother. At the age of eighteen, Ismail had not learned to mask his passions, a vital lesson for any prince at court.

Still, Muhammad refused to set aside his intended declaration. Ismail would never recognize the honor accorded to him. He would only begrudge the command, but he must learn a measure of duty to his countrymen. Mayhap the lesson would temper his contemptible pride.

Muhammad said, "Both of you require training in the responsibilities of Nasrid princes. Your lives cannot revolve around pleasures of the hunt and harem. I am the prince of the faithful and I have given service in battle during each of the sorties into the kingdom of Aragón. Warfare is a duty none of us can avoid. Each of you has a deft hand with a bowstring." Qays shuddered and tears filled his dark eyes even before Muhammad said, "You will join Prince Ali aboard the ships at Al-Jazirah al-Khadra and demonstrate your prowess in the service of Gharnatah."

Palpable emotions radiated in the faces of all assembled. Yahya scowled at his relative as if Ali had denied him a great prize. Muhammad would never have adjudged the Sword of *Jihad* for a petty fool. The few captives he might take for sale at market mattered little.

Even Ridwan and Ibn al-Khatib exchanged wary glances before both men stared at Muhammad. He chose to ignore the silent entreaty shining in their eyes and Ridwan's crinkled brow. As it was, Muhammad remained uncertain his brothers deserved the recognition, but of late, his lifelong treatment of his siblings caused concern. Doubts had plagued him from the day Khadija had stood with Aisha before the citadel's battlements. His half-sister had hidden away her smiles for fear of offending him. Mistrust of Maryam had long tainted his view of her children, but his half-sisters had never done anything to offend him.

If he found Ismail's pride unpleasant, well, a Nasrid prince naturally possessed an excess of conceit. Muhammad determined his younger brother should earn such a high opinion of himself. His skill with the bow rivaled Muhammad's own with a sword. Let Ismail prove himself worthy of accolades in the coming conflict. Redness suffused his face. Muhammad saw nothing reflected in Ismail's visage to refute the earlier belief about a lack of discernment.

Regrets seeped into Muhammad's mind. He should never have offered the chance for glory. He could rescind the directive now. Still, he clamped his lips closed, although his jaw ached.

Ridwan bent and whispered in his ear, "Shall you dismiss the court, my Sultan?"

When Muhammad nodded, Ridwan straightened and his voice boomed. "Withdraw, all of you! So speaks the prince of the faithful."

"Except for you and my brothers," Muhammad added, although his instruction faded beneath a multitude of shuffling and stomping feet. Ismail and Qays heard him for they did not exit the chamber along with everyone else.

Muhammad rose from the throne. He ignored a deep bow from the departing Ibn al-Khatib and instead, beckoned his brothers along with Ridwan. "There is much to discuss in this forthcoming campaign."

When Muhammad faced the lattice screen, beyond which lay the eastern exit to the harem, he swallowed an ache in his throat. Pero and the royal bodyguard fell into step beside him, shadowed by Ridwan. Muhammad paused as they reached the room divider, where the royal women sat without veils for their faces, a long-established custom. Still, a sharp intake of breath from Ridwan and his whispered apology followed. Muhammad glanced over his shoulder and found the man had turned away. In other circumstances, Muhammad might have found amusement in his prime minister's embarrassment, but this was no occasion for levity.

Aisha had burrowed her sorrow against their mother's neck. Butayna nodded to him in silent recognition of her assent to his plans. He never needed her approval, but the sign from her tempered some of his concerns. His sister's shoulders shook. Her soft sobs ripped at his heart, but he gritted his teeth. Of late, he had become a disappointment to Aisha and she no longer strove to hide her feelings. The pitiable sight of his sister and her refusal to acknowledge him spoke volumes of her resentment.

Despite her prevailing wish to wed Ali ibn Musa, Muhammad sided with Ibn al-Khatib and Ridwan, both of whom believed a Nasrid princess merited more than a young man with little acclaim. The provincial governors of Runda or Al-Jazirah al-Khadra might suit Aisha better. She would accept the reasoning if the object of her interest did not remain in Gharnatah, or so Muhammad hoped.

Hatred seethed and swirled in the dark pools of Maryam's gaze and simmered along the slashing line of her mouth as she glimpsed him. Jazirah joined her, a frown knitting her black brows together. Did she hold such concern over his decree or was she frightened for his eldest brother? He shook his head. No matter the course he took, someone would always find fault.

He broke eye contact with his wife almost at the same time as when Jazirah turned to Maryam and whispered something in her ear. Both women rose, as did Butayna, still supporting Aisha.

Muhammad looked behind him. Ismail and Qays stood rooted to the floor, unmoved from their positions before the throne.

A groan subdued in the back of his throat, Muhammad said, "Brothers, I cannot wait all day for you to follow me to the harem where we will speak."

Ismail's rigid stance did not alter. With hands fisted at his sides, he cleared his throat and haltingly spoke. "You... you think you have everyone within the court fooled about your real purpose? The actual reason you are sending Qays and me away?"

"Be mindful of your tone!" Muhammad's voice rang around the chamber. "We are brothers, but I am Sultan of Gharnatah, which you should never forget."

"I am no longer the child you can browbeat just because you are the eldest son!" Ismail's voice croaked as it rose a notch. "I was always Yusuf's favorite and you know it. Have you finally found the means to rid yourself of a rival? You have your heir with Jazirah and you want me out of the way. You talk of glory for Gharnatah... but you desire my death in battle. Deny it and let all know you for a liar!"

Muhammad shook with rage as he whirled and glared at Maryam, for surely, she had emboldened her son. She stood rigid and silent. Jazirah shook her head, but her watery stare no longer met his. She must have been gaping at Ismail. Jealousy embittered Muhammad. How dare she show any regard for his brother's foolery? Mayhap their relations were more troublesome than Muhammad had guessed. Hot fury roiled in his gut.

He gritted his teeth and viewed his siblings again. "Are you both refusing an order from a Sultan of Gharnatah?"

Qays grasped their brother's arm, but Ismail shook him off and spluttered, "Get away! It must be now or never. We can't let him dictate our futures and determine how we die."

Then he addressed Muhammad. "I refuse the command of a tyrant. I will not go to Al-Jazirah al-Khadra."

Muhammad observed Ridwan, who had offered his profile until now. Grim-faced, the elder man nodded. "You know what must be done, my Sultan. Only you can do it."

A dull ache swelled in Muhammad's throat before he declared, "Arrest them."

"No!" Maryam's scream echoed in the tower. While Muhammad studied her, she struggled against Jazirah's hold. "Let me loose! My sons!"

With steady strength, Jazirah did not relent. The tears swept down her cheek as she said, "Calm yourself. Do not endanger your sons further. You will have them back."

Muhammad turned from those cries shed for his traitorous brothers. Ridwan crossed the room with a contingent of the guards, who surrounded Ismail and Qays, the youngest of the brothers. Qays sobbed, but never resisted.

Maryam's shrieks followed her children. "Ismail! Qays!"

With a sigh, Muhammad finally faced his mother, who still gripped a sobbing Aisha. Butayna shook her head and never spoke before she and her daughter left the room via the eastern doorway. Maryam sagged on the cold marble floor and wept behind her hands. Jazirah knelt and offered comfort. The dark fringe of her long lashes hid her gaze from Muhammad, as he brushed past her and left the pair of women alone in his throne room.

***

Sultana Jazirah

Rabi al-Awwal 758 AH or July A.D. 1358 or Av 5118

Jazirah scrambled awake, bathed in perspiration, within her room at the *Jannat al-'Arif*. She shielded her eyes from the harsh glare of sunlight streaming through the eastern window. Her gaze flew to the ornate crib where she had earlier laid her son. Except Yusuf no longer nestled beneath the woolen coverlet Lubna had knitted for him.

"Yusuf!" Her plaintive cry echoed.

"Calm yourself. He is with his father."

Jazirah turned to the door, where Butayna's soft voice had emanated. Yusuf's grandmother sat on the low stool, which Lubna had occupied before Jazirah fell asleep. A shaft of light streaked across her mattress to the tiled floor, consigning Butayna to the shadows. Now she stood and approached the bed.

Butayna said, "Surely, you do not resent the times Muhammad wishes to hold his son, especially when you are asleep."

Resting on her elbows, Jazirah lowered her gaze. "Of course not. My child was beside me and I expected to find him there."

Uninvited, Butayna sat. Her hair coiled and fell beyond her shoulders like rivers of molten brass, burnished in the sunshine. Unable to ignore the intent stare cast at her, Jazirah returned it. Try as she might, she could not escape the sense of intimidation she experienced in Butayna's presence, as if this former Christian slave's current stature made her better than a queen of royal blood.

Then Butayna deflected her gaze unexpectedly, a faraway look in her eyes fixed on the window overlooking the garden. "We have not been alone together in some time."

For almost two years in fact, during the weeks after Jazirah's marriage, once she had cancelled the language lessons Butayna provided. After Maryam's revelations, Butayna and Jazirah drew further apart, until neither spoke more than courtesy required. Except for the date of Yusuf's birth, they had rarely interacted.

Ever afterward, Jazirah held some regret for her actions. She should not have let Maryam taint a nascent opinion of her mother-in-law. As it was, Jazirah did not entirely trust Maryam's disclosures, which she always attempted to cloak in the veil of good advice. Jazirah remained uncertain Butayna merited the cautionary words. Thus far, she had shown herself to be a devoted mother to her children, even if some inexplicable stiffness affected her interactions with Muhammad, or Aisha preferred the company of her younger sisters to the presence of her mother. Butayna also loved her grandson and showered Yusuf with almost as much affection as Jazirah did. Despite her fears, Butayna had never sought to contravene his mother's wish to nurse and raise Yusuf on her own, without the interference of nursemaids and governesses.

Jazirah lifted her chin. "We have not. Why have you sought me at midday?"

"It is my custom to keep to my rooms during the long summer, but I wished to speak with you. Will you walk with me?"

Eyebrows lifted, Jazirah scoffed. "You want us to venture outdoors in this heat?"

Butayna regarded her again. "There is a westerly breeze. I would not trouble you if I did not have an urgent need." Her voice took on an earnest tone. "Please."

The 'please' ensured Jazirah's assent, not because she liked the show of humility. Rather, she knew her mother-in-law would not have pleaded without necessity.

Waves of heat enveloped them as they stepped out an hour before midday. At Butayna's command, their personal guards remained behind. When Jazirah looked back, Alfonso Ruiz and Zabala wore frowns in unison, but both captains stood stationary between the summer palace's columns.

Perspiration glided along Jazirah's temple as she followed Butayna down the steps of the south portico and into the gardens, which gave the residence its name. Odorous flowers encircled them, as did the buzz of bees. Jazirah swatted at one when it flew too close to her nose and drew a chuckle from Butayna.

"Your father vowed you were fearless, or mayhap it was foolhardy."

Jazirah lowered her hand. "Knowing my father, it is possible he said both."

Butayna paused along a row of oleander bushes and surveyed the panorama. Jazirah joined her. In silence, the women took in the olive groves, fig trees, and vegetable gardens abutting the northeastern curtain wall of *Al-Qal'at al-Hamra.*

"This land offers a generous bounty to those who are willing to toil, Jazirah. It is unforgiving of others who do not take risks. At times, it requires a little foolhardiness from all of us who would stake a claim to life." With an odd glint in her eyes, Butayna turned to Jazirah. "Your ancestors did not take Gharnatah without grave risks. They did not lead cautious lives."

Where did Butayna intend this meandering conversation to go? Surely, she had not brought Jazirah out in blistering temperatures for a lesson in the family history.

Still, Butayna went on. "Your great-grandmother Fatima entrusted me with a secret, which I have shared with each of my children to ensure their survival. Despite the... difficulties you have encountered with my son, you are a vital part of his family because you are his Sultana and mother to his heir. Whatever you may think of me, I would keep you and Yusuf from harm, as I would do the same for Muhammad and Aisha. You are my family. I must share Fatima's secret with you. Keep all of what I will tell you from others, in particular, Maryam. I have seen your... regard grow for her."

"I do not favor dishonesty in my relationships."

"What about an omission, not only to save your life alone, but your sweet son?"

When Jazirah did not answer her question, Butayna turned to the vista again. "Consider the view and tell me what you see."

Sentries patrolled atop the narrow walkway, leading to the newest of the towers Yusuf had constructed during his reign. Below the battlements, the hillside sloped along the ravine bordering the *Hadarro* River. On the opposite bank, houses crowded the neighborhood of Al-Bayazin.

As Jazirah described the view, Butayna raised her palm. "No. Look closer."

One of the soldiers in the distance dallied along the parapet. He stared past the vegetation, a long, lingering look. Was it just Jazirah's imagination or had his gaze flicked over her before he moved on? A gardener just below them tilled a patch of earth beside an irrigation channel. He directed sporadic glances up to the oleander bushes. Once, his regard met Jazirah's own and held for longer than politeness allowed. She swallowed and drew back from his line of sight.

"Are these more of my husband's spies to report on my activities?" She glared at her mother-in-law. "Is this why you brought me out here?"

"They are not Muhammad's men. They are loyal to Juan Manuel Gomero. Years ago, when your ancestress Fatima returned to Gharnatah during the reign of your grandfather, she extracted a promise from Juan Manuel to watch over her family for all his days and aid her descendants to flee through hidden exits beneath the ramparts of *Al-Qal'at al-Hamra* if desperate need arose."

Jazirah repeated, "Secret exits? Who is this person to know of them?" She did not subdue the impatience in her tone. Her ire rose as a slow smile curved Butayna's lips. Was her mind addled?

"Do not frown at me so," Butayna whispered before she focused on the olive groves again. "Juan Manuel is the slave merchant who sold me into the harem here. A Jew." Despite Jazirah's gasp, she continued, "A dear friend and the only kinsman remaining to connect me to a hidden Jewish heritage."

Jazirah swayed slightly on her feet, but Butayna grasped her arm in a firm grip. "You will walk with me. To understand Fatima's secrets, you must learn mine as well. There are people here who do not spy for the benefit of those whom I love. They cannot know what I would tell you. Come."

As they walked, Jazirah recalled her arrival and Butayna's affront at Muhammad's dismissive tone when Doctor ben Zarzar received his due praise. While Butayna led Jazirah through avenues of myrtles and ivy climbing the stonework of gatehouses, she wavered between distress and disbelief as Muhammad's mother revealed her past. The midday call to prayer came and went, with Jazirah mesmerized by Butayna's story. Life for her began as a Christian, but her ancestors were Jews, even her own mother. She discovered the truth in letters this Juan Manuel had procured from her father, a man she once thought dead after her kidnapping on the plains of Castilla-León. She affirmed Maryam's story of their sale, but never spoke of her interactions with her former friend. Although somewhat disappointed by a lack of information to counteract the stories she had heard thus far, Jazirah could not deny the significance of Butayna's revelations.

Their rambling journey had taken them on a circuitous route through the palace complex, ending along a rampart near the northern entrance to the citadel. Below them, sunlight cascaded along the *Hadarro*, the river a gleaming, silver ribbon. The guardsmen on patrol offered deferential nods, but otherwise ignored the women.

Jazirah gripped the wall. "Does Muhammad know of his full heritage?"

Butayna chuckled, her profile sharp against the stone backdrop. "Of course not. I have not revealed it to him or Aisha. I tell you, so you may perceive the importance of Juan Manuel in all our lives and how he may help us." She spared a brief glance over her left shoulder before continuing. "My son has kept his brothers imprisoned for five months. He has not allowed their mother or anyone else to see Ismail and Qays. Maryam will want revenge."

With a rushed intake of breath, Jazirah prepared to counter the words, but clamped her mouth closed again.

Butayna said, "I know the certainty of Maryam's retribution. I have lived with its consequences for most of my years. I have told you of how her firstborn daughter died during the attack, which took us into Al-Andalus. The son Maryam carried also perished soon afterward. I did not say how she blamed me for those deaths, still holds me responsible. Maryam believes the deaths resulted because I would not abandon my father to the raiders. It is not in me to forsake those whom I love. Now, it is time you knew the rest, Fatima's secret."

She led Jazirah down the steps and along a footpath just below the walkway. A guard strolled by at the same time but seemed nonplussed by Butayna's actions. In fact, he nodded to her and continued his patrol. Jazirah released the breath she had not realized she was holding, at which Butayna laughed. "He is loyal to Juan Manuel also. You will come to know those who are as well as I do. They shall seek you out when necessary."

They halted beside a section of the wall covered in ivy. Butayna brushed clumps of vines aside and revealed the rusted, iron grate covering an aperture. Jazirah lifted her hands to the large hole and felt the rush of air against her fingers.

Butayna nodded. "The passage runs the length of the hillside. Crawl down it and you will emerge within the home of a family of secret Jews, whose forbearers have lived in Gharnatah for as long as my Jewish relations have. The family at the end of this tunnel will help you."

"To do what?"

"Survive." Then Butayna offered Jazirah her full regard. "Think what you will of Maryam, but know, she shall not allow Muhammad's punishment of her sons to go unanswered. When she strikes against us, take Yusuf through this tunnel or into the foothills above the *Jannat al-'Arif*. Go across the *Hadarro* River to the House of Myrtles in the Jewish quarter. Tell whoever answers at the gate Esperanza Peralta sent you. Such words will be enough to gain you admittance and ensure life for you and Yusuf."

"But Maryam would never hurt my son...." Jazirah trailed off when she realized how foolish she sounded. She had allowed Maryam to inveigle upon her, but what could Jazirah know of her true intentions. Faced with a choice of one of her own sons on the throne versus the claims of Muhammad or his little heir, Maryam would not prefer Yusuf to his uncles. For their sakes, she could harm a defenseless child.

Butayna patted Jazirah's shaking fingertips and held them. "I have shared much with you this day because I believe the knowledge might protect you and my grandson. Both lives are precious to me. You know a mother's love. It has no limits. Save Yusuf. Save yourself."

***

Fleet-footed, Jazirah scrambled up the steps of the summer palace's southern pavilion. The breath hitched in her chest as she raced north for Muhammad's quarters, filled with longing to hold her boy. His wails echoed from the second level of the tower where her husband resided. She bypassed the ever-present guards, took the stairs two at a time, and came to the open-air gallery between Muhammad's bedchamber and his dining space. She had last stood in the place on the evening when he hurled his terrible accusations at her.

Lubna waited at the top of the steps. She whirled at Jazirah's arrival. "My Sultana! I just arrived to fetch Prince Yusuf for his afternoon feeding. You were not in your chambers when I checked a moment ago."

"I walked today," Jazirah replied, glancing past Lubna's shoulder.

"In this heat?"

Jazirah never answered, enflamed by the sight before her.

As on the horrible night where he accused her of infidelity, Muhammad had the company of his *kadin*. He reclined at his leisure, a crystal goblet brimming with red-dyed *sharbah* in his hand. Beside him, Haziyya balanced not only her squalling infant, a honey-skinned girl named Leila, born three months after Yusuf's arrival. Muhammad's favorite also held a red-faced Yusuf, his pudgy arms extended for Lubna. When Jazirah drew closer, he screamed louder, this time for his mother.

Without any preliminaries, Jazirah snatched Yusuf from Haziyya. A sharp cry issued from the favored concubine, as she pressed her daughter against her rounded belly lest the girl slip away.

Jazirah expelled a ragged breath and kissed her son's curls and his face. He whimpered in her arms, his reddened cheeks unusually warm against her lips.

189

"Do not coddle him so," Muhammad advised. "The boy has a little fever, naught more to concern you—"

"He is my son! I understand his needs well enough." She handed Yusuf over to Lubna. "Take him to my chamber and give him a cooling bath. Go now."

"At once, my Sultana," Lubna mumbled before she hastened away.

Then Jazirah faced Haziyya. "Leave us. Take your daughter with you. I wish to speak with my husband alone."

Muhammad chortled and sat up a little. "You cannot dismiss my favorite—"

Jazirah turned her focus to him. "I am your wife, a Sultana of Gharnatah by virtue of our marriage. Does the title alone not guarantee me more respect than your lover?" She did not await his answer. Instead, she crossed her arms beneath her breasts and stared down Haziyya. "I will not ask you again to withdraw."

The golden base of Muhammad's goblet clanged against the flooring and some of the ice in the *sharbah* spilled. He glanced at his companion. "Please, Haziyya, bring our daughter to dinner tonight. Mayhap the day's heat is too much for her and she should be indoors."

"As my Sultan wishes." She rose with nimble grace despite her slightly rounded belly. Muhammad's third child grew within her. A babe conceived in spring, a future playmate for her ten-month old daughter. Haziyya balanced her fussy child on her hip and nodded to Muhammad. She repeated the same gesture before Jazirah, who turned away and closed her eyes. Haziyya's leather slippers slapped against the wood as she went down the narrow steps.

When Jazirah stood alone before her husband, she lowered her arms and faced him again. She began, "I respect you, my Sultan, as lord of Gharnatah, my husband, and father to the royal prince, but you must also acknowledge my status as his mother. I never want to see him in Haziyya's arms again. I would not entrust your concubine with my son."

A lazy grin stretched across Muhammad's lips. "He is my heir and she would never harm him for love of me. You do realize Yusuf and Haziyya's daughter are siblings. I love my children equally and wish them to grow in each other's company. Leila shall come to rely upon her brother."

"Yusuf had no fever this morning. If Haziyya's child is ill, then they should not be together at all. My son is barely a year old. He is susceptible to all manner of illness. I will not have him endangered."

He shook his head and reclined on his side against the cushions at his back.

She drew closer until she stood at his feet. "You will not gainsay my wishes. I am the boy's mother—"

"And I am his father!"

"A fact you are happiest to assert whenever you wish to frustrate me! I will not relent. Return Yusuf to my care at any time your concubine and her child are with you. I do not doubt your love for our son."

Muhammad had proved an excellent father, indulgent and always desirous to spend time with Yusuf. Shortly after the birth, he had pestered the midwife for proper instruction on how to swaddle and hold his child. He had even carved the ornate crib in Jazirah's room, along with its twin now placed in a corner of the sunlit gallery.

Now he yawned. "You are depriving our son of a proper upbringing beside his sister, but you may have your preference. When they are older, they might...." He trailed off and cradled his head on an upraised hand.

She inhaled, startled by his acquiescence. She had expected to argue with him long into the evening hours. When would their quarrels ever end?

She mumbled, "Th-thank you. I won't trouble you further."

As she turned to leave, his fingers closed on her wrist. She gasped, startled to find him upright and alert when he had appeared so indolent a moment before. He tugged her arm until she had little choice except to crouch before him.

"Why do you always flee from me?" He cocked his head, his stare intent.

She swallowed. "There seemed no reason to stay."

"For four months, since the imprisonment of my brothers for their treason, you have avoided me." His hold tightened. "Is the sight of your husband so disagreeable to you?"

When she hesitated, his grasp became an iron band, tighter than the manacles she had worn as a child of six in the dungeons of the citadel.

"Don't lie to me, Jazirah. At court, you wept for my brother, for Ismail, as my chief minister led him away."

"I wept for your kingdom, for Gharnatah!" A heavy lump in her throat turned her tone mournful, yet her response was forceful. "Strife between siblings ruined my father's life and destroyed the bond between brothers. Now in my generation, it's happening again. You once said our marriage would unite our family. There are still divisions between brothers. I fear for our son's future."

She longed to share her conversation of the earlier afternoon with Muhammad's mother, but the discussion would reveal more than Butayna intended for her son to know. Foolish hope for an easy rapport with her husband lingered in Jazirah's heart, which should have resented Muhammad for his neglect and favoritism toward a mere concubine whom he preferred over his wife. So long as he looked at her with doubt reflected in his gaze, they would never know the peace she desired. Still, she craved the impossible.

He slipped his hand beneath her billowy hair and stroked her nape. Her body betrayed her, for she shivered where his fingertips stroked tender skin. How was it possible for a man's touch to soothe and stimulate at the same time?

"I did not mean for you to shed such lovely tears." With his free hand, he skimmed a thumb beneath her eye, gliding over moisture she had not known dwelled there.

"You... you could rescind your order and restore harmony with your brothers," she whispered.

He gave a slow shake of his head. "You know why I cannot."

She did. Nothing else remained for her to say. Then why did she linger?

"Muhammad, I...."

He withdrew his hands. "Our son needs you. You should go to him."

She nodded. "You are right."

After she stood and plodded to the steps, he called out, "Jazirah, a Sultan, a man, is oft burdened by many regrets. I am sorry for my behavior in the months before Yusuf's birth, when I accused you of faithlessness. I have tried to be a good husband to you, but it seems I do not know how. I hope one day the past will no longer burden us."

She stifled a sob, barely trusting herself to speak before she whispered, "I carry the same hope. It must be enough for now."

Jazirah rushed down the steps, tears almost blinding her. She went to her summer quarters, pulling in the outer door behind her until dimness enveloped her.

From around the corner, voices came.

"What a pair we would make. A barren servant and a eunuch guard."

"I do not care. I have loved you from the first. When we met, Sultana Jazirah asked if I was more than my sword. I did not know I could be, until I loved you."

A soft sigh filled the hallway. "Oh Alfonso, what you ask is still impossible."

"Love is never impossible. I want more than your sweet kisses in darkened corners. I would have your heart, Lubna, as you have held mine."

"Don't you know? It is already yours. Still, I cannot forsake my duty. My Sultana and her son, they need me."

Jazirah had heard enough. She rounded the corner and found Butayna's captain and Lubna locked in an embrace. They drew apart, both with stricken, flustered expressions. Jazirah approached and nodded to the guardsman. "You will wait here."

She tugged Lubna behind her and closed the door on the captain's reddened face.

"My Sultana, I was not neglecting Prince Yusuf," Lubna pleaded even as Jazirah dragged her over to the crib, where Yusuf slept in sweet contentment. His mother kissed his soft brow, still somewhat feverish.

Then she straightened and regarded Lubna. "Did you think you could not love and do your duty by me? Tell me the truth now. Do you want to marry Alfonso Ruiz?"

Lubna pressed her hands to her chest and sank on the carpeted floor. "I would be his wife if I could." Tears slid over the pomegranate-colored blotch on her face.

Jazirah shook her head. "Who is here to stop you? Certainly not me. Get up and go to Muhammad's steward Mufawwiz. Tell him I need vellum. Bring me the ink and a reed pen from my stores. I am freeing you. Only a manumitted, former slave may wed. There is no reason you cannot remain my stewardess and be someone's wife."

As Lubna sat stupefied, Jazirah bent and hugged her thin shoulders. "I do need you, I always will, but so does the man who loves you. You each deserve happiness."

When Jazirah drew back, Lubna asked, "What of your own?"

Jazirah sighed and pressed her forehead to Lubna. "It may come." For the first time in many long months, Jazirah allowed herself to believe in the possibility.

Chapter 15
Ramadan

Sultan Muhammad V

Gharnatah, Al-Andalus or Granada, Andalusia
Ramadan 760 AH or August A.D. 1359 or Av 5119

At nightfall, Muhammad huddled with Ridwan beneath the gallery at the *Jannat al-'Arif*. The men stood together with their heads bowed, at a discreet distance from members of Muhammad's household. Seated around the low table of inlaid wood, Butayna and Aisha joked with the doctor Al-Shaquri and Faraj ibn Ridwan. Haziyya joined them, although she did not have to perform the fast, being a woman who nursed one child and carried another. She pressed kisses all over Leila's stomach. Lubna pointed out myriad stars to Yusuf, who nestled in her arms. Her husband, Butayna's captain, stood silent and watchful beside his elder brother, Pero.

On the twenty-seventh day in the month of holy fasting, the company had reveled in the ritual *iftar* feast and ended their daytime deprivation. They shared a lavish meal of which only slivers of tender, spit-roasted kid remained alongside remnants of beef and lentil soup, and a few *dafair* loaves. While Butayna did not observe Islam's sacred requirements, she could not resist the company of her daughter, whose morose moods had subsided of late.

Ridwan said, "Since the victorious return of Ali ibn Musa last month, the people of Aragón must wonder where Gharnatah shall strike next on behalf of Pedro of Castilla-León." Then he sipped from a cup of lemon-flavored, ice-cold *sharbah*.

Muhammad chuckled at his old teacher who puckered his lips as the mixture of snow and sour citrus hit his tongue. "Only the people of Aragón? I have determined Murcia shall feel the wrath of our mounted warriors under the command of your son Faraj." The chief minister's yellowed grin followed. Muhammad added, "No incursions into the Moorish quarter. I would not have the people of the true faith harmed. We shall discuss the matter when I meet with the *Diwan* tomorrow after public audience. Even Ibn al-Khatib must take some pleasure in my decision."

"He does not contravene your every decree, master."

"Only the ones he did not sponsor. Ibn al-Khatib takes liberties no other personal secretary would dare."

"Oh, there have been men like him before throughout your family's history."

"All of them lost their heads beneath the executioner's blade."

"Is this to be Ibn al-Khatib's fate?" Ridwan peered over the rim of his goblet.

"Allah chooses thus, not me."

With a nod to Ridwan, Muhammad strolled across the gallery until he stood beside his son. Yusuf wriggled and fussed in Lubna's arms.

Muhammad took the boy and kissed his dark curls, so like his mother's own. The full bloom of moonlight fell on his apple-round cheeks. He had many years before he might fully acquire the physical traits of his ancestors, but to his father, Yusuf seemed a perfect blend of his parents. He had his father's moods coupled with his mother's hair and pale skin. The child displayed his fine temper now, as he blubbered and wrenched at the gold-braided neckline of his white tunic.

Lubna reached for him again. "If the great Sultan wishes, I could take the royal heir to his mother. Prince Yusuf is not accustomed to the late hours the court adopts during Ramadan. It is well past his bedtime."

Although Muhammad could not dispute her reasoning, for the time was at least two hours past midnight, he hesitated to part with his son until Yusuf's screams rose to a crescendo. "Jazirah is breaking the fast with her father. I would hate to interrupt her."

Lubna ducked her head. "My great Sultan, I doubt my Sultana would view the arrival of your son as an inconvenience. She adores him as much as you do, master. Please, let me take him. A prince needs his rest. He sleeps best in his mother's arms."

"Do not carry him to her just yet. Walk with him a little through the gardens here. Mayhap a nighttime stroll would subdue him. Do not stray too far."

"I will not, master. Prince Yusuf shall be safe with me."

Although reluctant, nonetheless he gave his son over. Lubna held him on her hip, curtsied, and made for the stairs where her husband met her. They shared a brief exchange with Lubna shaking her head at the conclusion before she departed.

Who might have ever thought the fierce captain would have found a wife? They made a suitable pairing, though in Muhammad's view, few other prospects were open to either of them given his disfigurement and her distinctive birthmark.

Despite physical imperfections, Lubna proved a devoted servant and Muhammad better understood Jazirah's trust in the woman. Her soft crooning reached him as she stepped out beyond the north portico and headed to the gardens in the south, Yusuf's head resting on her shoulder. His watchful father kept an eye on them until Lubna descended the stairs again and disappeared into the shadows.

Her husband appeared beside Muhammad, his gaze intent on the path Lubna had taken. Muhammad clapped the captain's shoulder and rejoined those seated at the table. Ridwan had found a place beside Haziyya. Cradled in her mother's lap, Leila burrowed her face between Haziyya's breasts whenever the old minister smiled at her, only to giggle and peek at him whenever he pretended to turn away.

Muhammad held much gratitude for Ridwan's presence in his life, but none more so than the day the old man had presented him with Haziyya. On the morrow, he intended to raise a delicate matter with his council of ministers. If Haziyya gave birth to a son, Muhammad planned to wed her and raise her to the rank of Sultana.

The prospect raised another concern. What should he say to Jazirah of his aim? As his wife, she deserved to know first. Instinct warned she would not welcome the pronouncement. Despite her vow to the contrary, jealousy of Haziyya dwelled in his Sultana's heart. The certainty of it thrilled him, for her envy resonated with him. After their last meeting, suspicions about her disposition toward his brother Ismail lingered. Had Ismail been in sight, Muhammad would have run him through with their father's sword, kept in the adjacent bedchamber. Whatever Muhammad and Jazirah felt for each other remained uncertain, and while it was not love, he would never call it indifference.

"Brother?" Aisha drew him from reverie, while she offered him a chilled cup of *sekanjabin* and her gentle smile. He knew the source of her happiness upon the arrival of Ali ibn Musa in Gharnatah. Likely Aisha still held the hope Muhammad might reconsider her marital fate. For his part, he acknowledged the decision must come soon. It would be the first time in some years where a Nasrid princess remained unwed at the age of nineteen. He would not condemn a beloved sister to spinsterhood.

He accepted the drink of vinegar, sugar, and rosewater, and saluted her with the goblet. She nodded and turned from him, giving her full attention to their mother, who spoke with a yawning Al-Shaquri.

Butayna said, "It took me several years to grow accustomed to sleep in the day and this wakefulness at night during Ramadan."

The doctor replied, "The fast is a joy for the soul, but wreaks havoc on the body."

Behind them, Ridwan added, "I remember the first time I undertook the duty upon my conversion. As you say, a trial and a blessing, much like other aspects of life—"

"Great Sultan! Torches in the distance," Alfonso Ruiz called out.

Muhammad sipped the *sekanjabin*. "Why should such matter? More than half of Gharnatah is awake, feasting in expectancy of dawn and another day's fast."

"No, master! He is right. There are many torches, more than may be accounted for at this late hour." Pero rushed to his brother's side and gazed out into the dimness.

Those gathered with Muhammad gaped as he did at *Al-Qal'at al-Hamra*. With so many flames clustered, at first Muhammad thought the palace of his ancestors burned. Then the torchlights fanned out. Some to the south along the walls of the *Bab al-Sharia*, apart from others, which moved north along the street outside the harem, just as high-pitched screams echoed. Muhammad's heart thrummed as another group splintered from the second. The lights came from the west, their bearers approaching the summer palace. Shouts accompanied them.

Butayna cried, "My lion! What shall we do?"

Incapable of speech, he glanced at his mother, who appeared wide-eyed and ashen. She had never adopted such a shrill tone before, not even when he had misbehaved as a little boy. She covered her mouth, but her fearful gasp reached him still. He had to collect his thoughts and reach an immediate decision or none of them would survive the night.

Aisha draped her arm over Butayna's shoulder. "Muhammad, we must wait—"

"No, sister," Muhammad pronounced. "This is no time for delay. Come, all of you! The Ruiz brothers will lead us. Faraj, protect us at the back. Down the stairs. Move! Now!"

As his guests and family scrambled, Muhammad ushered the women he loved best before him. Haziyya gaped at him while he grabbed their daughter.

He said, "Love, we must hurry. I would do better to carry our child than you might on the steps. Go, swiftly, but have a care for yourself and the babe within you."

She cried, "*Amanar....*"

A momentary lapse, in which she called him by the name reserved for their private moments, revealed the depths of her worry for him. He pressed her on. "I shall keep you and our children safe."

Although Leila whimpered, he did not reassure his daughter. Instead, he bolted into his bedchamber and drew his father's sword. With it, he urged Ridwan and Al-Shaquri down the steps. Muhammad and Ridwan's son descended last.

On the landing, the captains had roused the men in their command. Moonlight glinted off Damascene steel and the large iron blades of sharp lances. Muhammad gave Leila over to her mother.

Aisha pleaded, "Brother, let us return to our rooms and bar the doors until we know the nature of this threat."

The acrid odor of fires filled Muhammad's nostrils. "Believe me, Aisha, we are in danger. We go as one body to the storerooms near the entryway. You will hide there with our mother, Haziyya, and my daughter. Al-Shaquri and Ridwan shall make their way to their homes and safety, I hope. The brothers Ruiz, Faraj, and I shall confront this peril with my loyal bodyguard."

"But the torches are coming up!" Butayna rushed to him and threw her arms around his neck. "Please, we must flee across the *Hadarro*. This is Maryam's revenge. I will not lose you!"

He tugged her fingers away and kissed them instead. "*Ummi*, I understand. You know why I cannot leave. My son is somewhere out in the night, defenseless—"

Butayna's captain shouted, "I'll find him and my wife, by your leave, my Sultan!"

Both Muhammad and Butayna turned to him at the same time. The tendons stood out along the captain's neck. Butayna withdrew from her son's hold and reached for her faithful protector's hand instead. A desperate cry escaped her. "Alfonso...."

"Do not fear. I shall return with Prince Yusuf and my wife." His fingers closed on Butayna's own. "I promise we shall see each other again, my Sultana. *Alteza.*"

Tears flooded her gaze, but she nodded. "Then go! Go with God, Alfonso, and may our Lord Jesus protect you forever."

She had never referred to her captain so informally. The man bowed before Muhammad and then clasped arms with his brother.

Pero said, "Do not fear, Alfonso, I shall guard those who remain here with my life. Be valiant in your service and come again to us."

"By God's grace, *mi hermano.*"

While he led his company out to the entrance beyond the storerooms and stables, Muhammad shared the kiss of peace with his doctor and chief minister. Ridwan also blessed his son Faraj before scrambling to keep up with Al-Shaquri and the warriors.

Only the family, Ridwan's son, and Pero with his warriors remained at Muhammad's side. Haziyya pleaded for silence from their child, while he proceeded to the steps of the southern pavilion. He turned and placed a finger over his lips. The women nodded. Faraj scanned their surroundings, ever watchful.

Then Muhammad signaled for Pero, who joined him. Both men held their swords aloft as they crept down the marble staircase.

"Stop!" Mufawwiz's plump features came into view. "Master, please! It is only your loyal steward. We are under siege! Conspirators, my Sultan. A eunuch brought word to me. Men have scaled the walls of the citadel, at least one hundred by his count."

The chief steward peered around Muhammad. "We must get the women of your household to safety across the *Hadarro* River and to the House of Myrtles with my old master, Juan Manuel Gomero. But, but where... where is Prince Yusuf? What of Sultana Jazirah and her father?"

Muhammad swallowed. "I have not seen them this night. As for my son, he... he is with Lubna. She took him for a walk in the summer gardens. I will not leave my wife and child behind."

Mufawwiz slapped a pale hand over his fleshy mouth. Then he glanced behind him. The torches shone through the woodland.

Muhammad grasped the chief steward's shoulders. "Listen to me! Hide my family in your storerooms and stay with them. My mother's captain is searching the grounds for my son and Alfonso Ruiz will know to bring Yusuf there. Do you understand?"

"I do, master! Where will you go?"

With a sharp glance at his family, Muhammad said, "I cannot abandon my home, my kingdom. Hurry now, take the women to safety."

The chief steward nodded. While he led the others away to the southern storerooms, Muhammad went in search of the palace guards with Pero, Faraj, and the rest in tow.

Already alert to the threat, sentries huddled along the ground at the entrance to the summer palace. Why hadn't they closed the gateway? Muhammad shook his head. What did it matter? This was the only direct path away from the summer palace, the sole route to reclaiming his throne.

Dense canopies of trees and bushes shadowed the grounds. The unidentified conspirators had doused their torches and concealed their location. Muhammad moaned, and his heart cried out for his son, trapped in the midst of peril.

He whispered, "Most Merciful, Most Compassionate Allah, please! Keep Yusuf safe."

One man at the forefront pointed. "Out there in the dark, my Sultan. I think—"

His words ended with a heavy thud. He fell against the companions behind him. Two bolts protruded, one from his throat and the other embedded in his chest. Blood pooled and spread in a slow circle across his tunic.

"Close the gate! Now!" Despite Muhammad's order, three more men died before they could accomplish his demand, blackened arrows jutting from their bodies. Even if the captain had found Yusuf and Lubna, they could not return by the same path without grave risk. Muhammad's enemies blocked the course to retaking the complex. How could he subdue them now?

"My Sultan!" Mufawwiz's high-pitched tone preceded his reemergence. He wheezed and bent as much as his high belly would allow.

"Why are you at my side? I told you to protect my family!"

Mufawwiz clutched his chest and sagged on his knees. "They... they are safe! More men... they came up the western tower overlooking the orchards and groves. The guards there must have admitted them. They may be here to help."

Muhammad prayed the man was not so naïve. These arrivals could have easily slain those who once guarded the fortification. His stomach fluttered. "Who leads them?"

"It is Prince Yahya, master."

Muhammad exhaled a huge breath. "Allah be praised! Faraj and Pero, you and my bodyguards are with me. You others, guard the door for the sake of your Sultan!"

Mufawwiz got to his feet with effort. Then he led Muhammad back beyond the storage area. Just before the stairs of the south portico, a score of men awaited from the Volunteers of the Faith, nine less than the fighters Pero commanded. Although Yahya had drawn his sword, his arms hung limp at his sides. He sketched a bow despite the heavy chainmail he wore.

Muhammad ran up the stairway with his breathless chief steward on his heels. "Yahya! I have never been so glad to see a Marinid prince in all my life. Do you know what has happened this night?"

Beneath half-lidded eyes, Yahya stared down the steps. "Treachery."

With a sharp cry, he raised his arm and flung his curved blade.

"My Sultan! No!" The scimitar plunged deep into Mufawwiz's thick belly, even as he shoved Muhammad against the adjoining wall and out of danger. Blood sprayed the stairs. The chief steward flopped backward. His limbs flailed and his neck snapped.

"*Rey de mi reino!*" Pero hauled Muhammad from the fray. Faraj led the royal bodyguards up the staircase and they clashed with Yahya's Marinid warriors. The white marble ran red.

Animalistic howls from dying men filled the air. When the brawl ended, two of Muhammad's defenders were among those who no longer lived. All of Yahya's men had perished, but their commander's body was absent, as were another pair of Pero's men.

Pero helped Muhammad to his feet. "My men must have given chase down the tower steps and out into the night. They would not have betrayed you and fled with the whoreson! Do you want me to find Yahya?"

"No!" Muhammad staggered to his feet. "Tell me your brother would have known the way north of the foothills as Yahya did, to come up through the tower. He would have taken another route if he could not reach us via the main gate, right?"

"He was always cleverer than me."

"Let us hope he remains so this night. Send some of your men to hold the entryway to the tower." He waved a hand to his chief steward's prone form. "I need a cloak to cover Mufawwiz. Have others take him to an empty storeroom. He deserved better than this end. Bring my family up."

Behind him, a deep pounding reverberated. He said, "Hurry, before they enter."

Pero did as commanded. Muhammad ignored the throbbing in his shoulder where he had slammed against the wall. He crouched beside Mufawwiz and closed the sightless eyes. "Loyal to the end. There shall be vengeance for your death."

By the time the women arrived, Faraj had covered the body with his own blue cloak. A stiff night breeze blew aside a fold in the cloth and exposed Mufawwiz's pallid face. Butayna wailed and fell to her knees beside the body.

Muhammad dragged her up and bore her pain-filled fury. Tiny fists battered his back, but he held her. "*Ummi*, Maryam and her accomplices shall pay for this night's perfidy."

Butayna sobbed, "Not Mufawwiz! He showed me kindness when I came to the *Jannat al-'Arif*. He risked so much in arranging for safe passage tonight."

"Then let us honor his sacrifice by living as he intended. Come, we must leave."

Muhammad tugged her across the blood-streaked floor. Aisha and Haziyya with Leila followed down the staircase within the western tower. At its base, Faraj joined Pero, who huddled with half of his men just outside the exit. When Pero signaled, Muhammad scuttled across the grounds to squat beside them.

Pero said, "We have discovered the two missing bodyguards, great Sultan. Both stabbed to death. Yahya has fled. We have hidden his victims in the underbrush, so the women would not see. The sentries assigned to this area met their ends by the treachery of the Volunteers, for we found those bodies as well.

Why did Yahya bring such a small number? He could have overwhelmed us with more."

Muhammad replied, "Mayhap they were his most trusted men. Ali ibn Musa took a sizable portion of the *Ghuzat* with him to Al-Jazirah al-Khadra and they have since returned to Wadi-Ash."

"Do you think the young prince knew of his kinsman's intent to betray you?"

"I do not know."

Muhammad shook his head. He must decide to flee or fight. He peered over his shoulder, to those whom he loved, huddled in the darkness. The rest of his protectors had joined them. The right choice would determine whether they all lived or perished.

He said, "By the hammering we can hear, the enemy is still barred at the entrance. How can we get away without mounts?"

Pero's grin showed gaps between his teeth. "We have had some help."

Just when Muhammad imagined he heard the snorts of horses, two pairs of them came into view, led by his mother's maidservants Jawla and Hafsa. The latter kept the animals quiet, while Jawla crept through the bushes toward the men.

"My Sultan. Hafsa and I realized what was happening. We went to the stables and brought these four strong mounts out, unable to manage more. We could not find Mufawwiz to tell him what we were doing." Her voice fell and she looked beyond Muhammad's shoulder. "Where is Mufawwiz?"

He replied, "He's dead."

Jawla swallowed and averted her stare. After a few rapid blinks, she said in a throaty tone, "The guards at the bridge across the river remain loyal. We must ride double if we are to reach the House of Myrtles. Juan Manuel Gomero sold us into the harem for a sole purpose. To protect this family." She studied the rapt faces of the bodyguards. "I do not know how we can ensure the survival of so many."

Pero said, "My Sultan, we are ready to make the ultimate sacrifice of our lives."

Muhammad replied, "I want you with me. Take Faraj upon the back of a horse. My mother and Aisha may ride double. I shall take Haziyya and our daughter. If your brother can make it, with my son...."

His voice trailed off and he bowed his head. He no longer spoke in childish absolutes. He could not save everyone, but to abandon his child or Jazirah seemed an impossible choice. Was she safe within her father's house? The ramifications of her closeness to Maryam bedeviled his thoughts. Still, he had to believe Jazirah would not have betrayed him. She could not have spoken to him of her hopes for a conclusion to their bitter past yet have secreted Maryam's plot. Or did he simply wish to believe so?

Something crashed through the woodland, banishing his morose concerns. He gripped his weapon, as did the warriors around him. Lubna burst through the tree line, a child clad in white clutched in her arms. Branches raked at her face and her unbound hair streamed behind her. When Muhammad would have whooped and waved her in their direction, Pero hushed him and pointed. His brother ran behind Lubna, a tattered, short cape billowing in his wake. He preceded half a score of others who wielded swords and spears, the latter hurled wildly at him. He evaded the weapons and pelted across the landscape. Where were the rest of the men he had commanded?

"My Sultan. Stay here," Pero whispered. He stood and roused his forces, "For Muhammad and Gharnatah!"

They echoed his rallying cry. "For Muhammad and Gharnatah!"

As his defenders sprinted across the ground, Muhammad kept his gaze trained on Lubna as she carried his dear son. Tingling suffused his body and the hilt of his father's sword slipped in his grasp. Perspiration stung his eyes. He couldn't wait anymore. He spurted to his feet and waved. "Over here! Over here, Lubna!"

She stumbled to a halt. Yusuf's cries filled his father's ears. Muhammad broke into a run while Lubna scrambled up the rock slope toward the source of his voice. Pero's men, discernible by their short mantles, countered the enemy. Shrieks echoed into the night. The earth rumbled beneath Muhammad's feet. Mounted archers, at least a dozen, appeared at the edge of the tree line. Several aimed at Pero's men and fired with deadly accuracy. Two horsemen broke away from their companions and urged their mounts after Lubna, bows fixed on her. She and Yusuf were so close.

"Run! They're coming for you," Muhammad screamed.

His warning did not help. With a jarring cry, Lubna sprawled across the dirt, an arrow shaft buried in her back. The bundle in her arms rolled away among the rocks. More arrows whizzed through the gloom and found their marks.

***

Sultana Jazirah

Jazirah applauded as the lithe dancer her father had hired finished her presentation, accompanied by the final strains of an *oud*. Red hair fell over the performer's thin shoulders as she bowed and exposed her full bosom. Jazirah's father tossed a purse filled with *dirhams* into her eager clutches. The coins jangled.

"Tell your mistress I am well pleased. I would enjoy seeing more of you."

Jazirah rolled her eyes at the woman as her impish smile revealed an understanding of his innuendo. While she departed the dining hall in the company of the musicians he had hired, he craned his neck for a last, fleeting ogle at the seductive sway of her wide hips. A slow smile curved his lips.

Jazirah giggled at his antics and sipped from her cup before she said, "I see your appetite for women has not altered with age."

Her father grinned at her. "Nor has my ability to enjoy them."

"You're irredeemable, Father."

"I am a Nasrid."

Jyoti sauntered into the room, followed by her son Dhanu who bore a platter of steaming delights. Jazirah peeked at the thick date and almond cookies, served alongside slices of sesame cake drizzled in honey. She groaned.

"Jyoti, you have to stop feeding me." She patted her lower abdomen, no longer maiden-flat after the birth of Yusuf. "I'm going to become fat."

The cook rubbed her own rounded belly. "Fat people are happy, my Sultana." She took the gilt tray from Dhanu and placed it between Jazirah and her father. He rose up on one elbow, grabbed Jyoti's thick wrist, and pulled her down for a quick kiss on the mouth. Dhanu giggled, but Jazirah stared at her father, aghast. Jyoti left with reddened cheeks, summoning her son after her.

Beatriz and Gonzalo, each of whom had knelt unobtrusively beside their respective owners throughout the *iftar* feast, offered the cakes and cookies on small ceramic plates. Jazirah recovered from her shock in time to accept the dish, although she did not eat straightaway.

"Father, have you taken Jyoti into your bed?"

He paused in the midst of chewing and then swallowed before he said, "An impertinent question to ask a parent."

She frowned at him. "I am also a parent, hardly a child unaccustomed to relations between men and women as a result."

"Would you care if I admitted to such?"

"Not in truth, if it is what Jyoti prefers as well. I never thought she would stop grieving for her husband."

"Since when did you worry for the plight of slaves?"

"I have always cared—"

"For Lubna alone. I date your interest in others from the time you freed her. This marriage business of hers. She can have no children. Her captain cannot sire any. What purpose did their union serve?"

"Does love and the heart's desire require a reason? Why should her marriage be a bother? She no longer pines for you. She is devoted to Alfonso Ruiz, as he is to her."

"I have seen them together. Forgive me, daughter, but you were never so sentimental about the lives of slaves. It's not as if they are a traditional couple."

"Well, look at you and Jyoti! Bedding your cook would be shocking behavior for you. You would not take Lubna as a lover, no matter how she made her interest clear."

He shook his head. "She always belonged to you in truth, never me. After she met the captain, her heart desired only him. Jyoti's love for her son does not interfere with our relations. We have both lost those whom we loved best in this world. She is a comfort to me as I am for her."

His choice still mystified Jazirah. "She doesn't even have red hair, Father!"

His loud guffaw rose to the rafters. She shook her head and ate a cookie, staring at the blood-red carpet. Then a piercing scream on the night wind jerked her from her stupor. She peered around the room. "Did anyone else hear the noise?"

Beside her, Beatriz said, "I did not."

"Nor did I, daughter."

"I could have sworn...."

"I'm sure it's just your imagination." Beatriz offered a soothing pat on her shoulder. Jazirah frowned at the woman, who removed her hand. Her cheeks glowed under the scrutiny. Lubna would have offered a gentle touch, borne out of the lifelong bond between them, but Beatriz had no such privilege of a long acquaintance.

Jazirah's father summoned her attention with, "You should have brought Yusuf."

"Muhammad wished to have him. I could not reasonably object to the request."

"Does the Sultan make requests or demands?" His sharp tone caused her to gape at him askance, but he continued, "There is no bitterness in your voice when you speak his name these days."

She cleared her throat and sat up. "Would you prefer if enmity soured my speech?"

"You know I would not. You have a sharp temper and woe betide the fool who trifles with you after you have argued with your husband. I am no such fool."

He sniggered, but she found no reason for amusement. "My husband is the most difficult, prideful, stubborn man I have ever known, but he is the best father in the world." At his frown, she added, "Besides you, of course. I would never deny Yusuf a chance to be with his father. Lubna will bring my son to me if necessary. You may see him at any time, but duty and the prevailing demands of the Castillan king beleaguer my husband."

"You understand the burdens he bears."

"I would not claim to know each one, but I perceive some of the difficulties."

Her abstinence from the rigors of the fast, due to Yusuf's continued suckling, allowed her to observe details about her husband's life. The *iftar* meal and evenings with his family had become Muhammad's refuge this month. An endless parade of ministers and courtiers sought him out during the morning. He gave over his afternoons to Ridwan and presumably matters of state in the early afternoon. While most slept away the deprivations of the fast, he did his duty.

"Mayhap, you have even grown to care for him a little?" Her father observed her over the rim of his cup.

She set down her plate and cleared her throat. "Would it be so incredible if I did?"

"I did not think you could care when he treated you so terribly before Yusuf's birth."

She glanced up and found her father's gaze still watchful. "Mayhap it is conceivable to forgive even if one cannot forget."

Once she could not have imagined such implausibility. The knowledge of Muhammad's wishes, akin to her own, gave her courage and hope. She would have chided herself even two months ago for permitting foolish dreams to flourish, but a duty to keep the secrets about him stirred an unexpected protectiveness of her husband. Given time, they could find a common path toward each other. Mutual devotion to their son had laid the groundwork. Could love grow from such feelings?

"Jazirah, you're lost in your thoughts. A common occurrence these days whenever conversation revolves around your husband."

She blinked and stared at her father. "It is late. I should go to the *Jannat al-'Arif.*"

"At this hour, my Sultana?" Beatriz retrieved Jazirah's empty plate. "It's so dark."

Jazirah glared at her maidservant. She had begged an indulgence earlier in the evening, asking to linger. Now she did not want to leave at all. Coupled with her attempts at familiarity, she stirred Jazirah's ire.

"Are my father's doors not guarded by Zabala and his men? Will they not see us to the safety of our home?"

Just then, a heavy pounding on the entryway filled the room. Beatriz rose quickly. "I shall see who it is."

As she scrambled to the door, Jazirah's frown returned. She asked her father, "Wouldn't Zabala have informed us of an arrival?"

He shrugged and motioned to Gonzalo for another slice of cake.

The heady scent of *ghaliya* wafted through the archway before Maryam entered the room, flanked by her guards and Beatriz. Maryam's blue *jubba* shot through with silver thread glittered like a thousand stars. She wore a diaphanous, shiny veil on her head.

Her smile dazzled. "A perfect night for a celebration, is it not?"

Chapter 16
Traitors

Sultana Jazirah

Gharnatah, Al-Andalus or Granada, Andalusia
Ramadan 760 AH or August A.D. 1359 or Av 5119

"Maryam! Why are you here at this hour?" Jazirah could not subdue the annoyance in her voice. While Maryam remained welcome in the house, she should have sent word of her intention to visit.

With a smile, Maryam replied, "What a poor greeting, Jazirah. This is no way for friends to meet. We are friends, are we not?"

She did not await a reply. "As it is, I had hoped to find you here." Then she glanced behind her as Beatriz peeked around her shoulder. "You did well, slave."

Beatriz mumbled, "Thank you, my Sultana."

A prickling sensation crept up Jazirah's spine. To her knowledge, Maryam and Beatriz had never spoken before.

Jazirah's father abandoned his relaxed pose. "Maryam, you cannot have come here in all your finery for this banal exchange."

She replied, "I came to proclaim the good news. My sons are free from the citadel."

Jazirah gasped and pressed her fingers to her parted lips. Maryam's pronouncement chased away all concern about her earlier words to Beatriz. Muhammad had refused the suggestion to free his brothers, only to pursue his own course. Their liberation was an unexpected choice for him, but the thoughtful man whom Jazirah had met in his gallery a month before could be capable of such a worthy gesture. The tiny flame of hope Jazirah had nurtured now burst into a bright fire. If Muhammad could learn forgiveness, surely her own path toward it lay ahead.

Then doubt intruded. Should she go to him? Would he view her excitement as she intended, based upon admiration of his decision? Instead, he might believe she rejoiced only for the freedom Ismail and Qays had regained.

Her father asked, "How did this event occur?"

Maryam answered, "By the sole means it could."

While her father nodded, Jazirah mused on the cryptic reply, not likely to derive from the happy conditions she had assumed. Still, she asked, "Where are your sons?"

Maryam's gaze darted back to her. "Oh, you shall greet them again in due time."

Behind her, Beatriz scowled and placed a hand on her hip. With the other, she pecked at Maryam's robe and drew attention again. "You see, my Sultana. I did my duty. Now I ask, remember your promise to me."

Jazirah scrambled to her feet. "What promise?" Her voice echoed to the rafters. A pit of unease settled in her stomach. Her mouth went dry.

Both women ignored her as Maryam replied, "I have made many vows of late. Remind me of what I said to you."

"You guaranteed freedom!" Beatriz exclaimed. "You told me if I did my part, you would let me go with my husband. We want to go home."

Jazirah staggered. Her limbs were so heavy. Their weight threatened to drag her down. She held her stance with her father's aid as he stood and placed his hand on her back. She glanced at him, but he shook his head slowly. Beatriz and Gonzalo's disloyalty had caught him unawares as well.

Maryam inquired of Beatriz, "Where is this husband of yours?"

Beatriz beckoned him. "Come, Gonzalo! At last, we can leave this place!"

Gonzalo peeked at Jazirah and her father before rising from the floor. He shuffled beside his wife, limp hair hanging over his eyes. Beatriz grasped his hand.

Jazirah cried out. "Traitors! How could you have betrayed the trust my father and I placed in you?" She shook her head. "Beatriz, I thought you were happy with me."

The hardened gaze shot her way reflected a hatred Jazirah had never known before.

"Happy? How could I ever have been while you bound me by a slave's collar in servitude? Your people stole me away and kept me from my husband. Moors like you gelded him! Now we will never know the joy of children! I vowed I would have the lives you stole from us. I secured a chance with Sultana Maryam, by revealing to her every detail of your household. She knew when you confessed your pregnancy with your pampered prince before the rest of the harem did. Whenever you argued with your husband, she had the circumstances from me first!"

"You spied for her?" Jazirah recalled how Maryam always offered comfort and knowledgeable advice in every situation. Was it only because she had obtained whispered words to guide her counsel?

Beatriz gave an ugly laugh. "I would have done anything to be free of you." She pleaded with Maryam, "Free us! You swore!"

"Indeed, I did." A wide smile upturned Maryam's mouth. She nodded to the men who protected her. "Free them."

Time slowed as the mercenaries dragged Gonzalo and Beatriz into their midst. Steel appeared in the hands of their captors, a blinding flash.

The doomed couple's screams rose to a crescendo. "No! No!"

The curved tips of daggers plunged repeatedly. Blood spewed from Gonzalo's mouth even as it ran red from the tunic plastered to his torso. Beatriz slumped on the floor, a crimson pool spreading beneath her prone body. A tiny gasp escaped her lips, as did trickles of blood. Then silence fell.

Jazirah clasped her hands to her chest, aware of her sluggish heartbeat. How could she have been so foolish to align herself with Maryam? Where she had once feared Butayna might have exercised undue influence over her father's household, Maryam had done so instead. Jazirah recalled Butayna's advice upon their first meeting. *'There is never a warning before the executioner arrives.'*

Now as Beatriz and Gonzalo met their deserved ends, Jazirah could not help but feel some sorrow for them. They had trusted Maryam so blindly, only to die at her hands. She had destroyed everything, but Jazirah swore she would never again fall prey to Maryam's schemes.

Maryam sneered and stepped away from her victims. "You will thank me for killing them, Jazirah. Loyal slaves are so difficult to secure. Traitors abound in your husband's former kingdom."

Jazirah swallowed past the dull ache in the back of her throat. In a low monotone, she asked, "His former kingdom?"

"He has fled Gharnatah without a fight like the coward he is. He has abandoned the Sultanate and you. My Ismail is master of Gharnatah now and he shall ascend the throne, as he should have when Yusuf died. Our people will acclaim him as Sultan Abu'l-Walid Ismail, the second of his name. They will forget your husband. We are free forever from Muhammad's tyranny."

He no longer held the throne. The idea seemed inconceivable. Muhammad loved Gharnatah. He believed in his birthright. He would not have discarded it unless Maryam's forces had overwhelmed him. "How have you done this?"

"The events of tonight were ordained long ago, Jazirah, when Ridwan and Ibn al-Khatib interfered to put Muhammad on the throne in Ismail's place. At least, I shall never have to concern myself with Ridwan again. He died upon the threshold of his house, a mewling weakling, who begged for his life and those of his wife, daughters, and their husbands. Muhammad's folly occurred when he imprisoned my sons on a whim. He set the course of his failure and flight in motion. His actions allowed those who remained uncertain of the future to cast their lots with his enemies. For if he could have consigned his brothers to jail, could anyone else ever be safe?"

Jazirah ran a hand over her face. Poor Muhammad. He had done his best as Sultan, as a man, but Maryam's treachery had ruined him. If in truth he had fled, Jazirah could not blame him for the choice to leave her behind. Mayhap, in the end, no other alternative had existed. Where was he now? She prayed for his well-being.

Maryam intruded on her thoughts, demanding, "Will you weep for him? Is he not the same man who refused to offer your father a governorship? Who humiliated you on your wedding night by spending the rest of it with his lover? The one who once accused you of faithlessness."

He was also the husband who had sired a most precious life within her, their son.

Jazirah lifted her gaze. "Where is Yusuf? He was with his father tonight. Where is my son?"

Her father drew closer to Maryam. "Indeed. Where is my grandson? You have not spoken of him, yet you swore he would not suffer in this coup!"

A sharp pain lanced Jazirah's side beneath her breast. All her reserves of energy dissipated and she slid to the ground in a quivering heap. Tears blinded her as she attempted to focus her watery gaze on her father. "You knew? You knew they would do this to my husband. They have stolen his throne and our son's heritage!"

His shoulders set firm, he refused to meet her regard. "Jazirah, it was only a matter of time! You know the sort of ruler Muhammad had become. His disdain of even the most loyal among courtiers did not endear him to anyone. Is it a wonder his governors waned in their support and joined this conspiracy against him?"

She slapped her hand against the floor. "Damn you for a traitor and a liar, Father! The least you will do is look at me. You knew! You've known of Maryam's purpose long before this night. All those meetings and dinners with the provincial governors! How could you scheme with them to take Muhammad's throne and rob your own grandson of his inheritance?"

Then she remembered the past and a conversation in his cell at Shalabuniya. "By the Prophet's beard, this is not the first time you have betrayed your own family, is it? What about our imprisonment? Did you consign your own family to hell because you betrayed your brother? You once said I had never asked if the rumors were true. But they were." Tears stung her eyes and she shuddered in horrified revulsion. "What sort of man are you to destroy your own family?"

With a heavy sigh, he turned to her at last. "I knew little of Maryam's scheme. Never the particulars of when or how it would occur. I wanted no part of it. No matter how her co-conspirators entreated, I refused all of their attempts to bribe and cajole."

He swung his stare to Maryam. "The best I may say for this viper is she forestalled any attempt to force my hand through threats of violence against you. She protected you for her self-interests."

Jazirah wiped her tears away. She rose once more and glared at him. "Why should I ever believe a word from your lips again? You're a traitor, just as my husband has always known." She brushed past him and advanced on Maryam, halting when less than an arm's span separated them. "You have not told me of my son. Where is Yusuf? Did Muhammad take him? Yusuf is his heir. I want my son here in my arms. Now."

Maryam laughed. "When I first knew you, the role of Muhammad's wife seemed undesirable. Now, you are a Sultana for true. Indeed —"

Jazirah cut her off. "Where is my son, Maryam?" She crossed her arms beneath her breasts and pressed her lips together.

Maryam stiffened and her cool smile slid away. "After dawn, you shall see Yusuf again. I promise."

***

Sultan Muhammad V

Gray clouds against a veil of stars obscured the new moon briefly, enshrouding the landscape in bleakness. Despite the wooden interior door swinging on its hinges with each wind gust, Muhammad could not see beyond the iron gateway of the residence his mother had indicated as the House of Myrtles. No lights shone from the whitewashed structure behind a stout wall. Somewhere in the blackness, a dog barked. Leila whimpered in her mother's arms. Muhammad cocked his head and whispered for Haziyya to quiet the child.

"She's hungry and frightened, my Sultan."

He replied, "She is not alone, but you must hush her for a time."

Haziyya said nothing further. Then came the rustling of silk followed by loud smacks and gurgles as Leila suckled at her mother's breast. At any other occasion, Muhammad would have shown some concern for how Haziyya exposed herself before other men. Such trivial matters no longer affected him. So long as Leila drew no attention to them with her cries, they might gain a respite.

Having escaped the carnage at the summer palace, Muhammad had led his bedraggled companions down toward the ravine through which the *Hadarro* River rushed. With the aid of guardsmen who remained loyal and withheld the questions evident in their confused expressions, the small band had crossed the footbridge into the neighborhood of Al-Bayazin. Now they hid with their horses along a slope bounded by bushes and myrtle trees across the paved route.

Muhammad asked, "*Ummi,* does it appear safe?"

He had little choice except to defer to Butayna, as she joined him in the lead of their company, leaving her maidservants Jawla and Hafsa at the rear. Moonlight peeked from behind the clouds and cascaded over the trees. In their hasty retreat, his mother had lost her veil. Coppery hair hung in a thick braid over her right shoulder. She assessed the two-storied building and their environs.

"We cannot stay here. Our wounded are too many. For their sakes, I shall call at the house." She glanced behind her. "All of you must wait here."

Aisha pleaded, "*Ummi,* let Faraj go with you!"

Muhammad and his mother peered at Ridwan's son, who crouched beside his master. Faraj still pressed a hand to the jagged tear in his tunic where a sword had sliced him open from waist to hip.

He grunted with a nod. "I am ready, my Sultana."

"You are not," Butayna stated. When Muhammad would have protested, she silenced him with a severe glance. "Nor are you, my lion. With an arrow in your leg, it is a wonder you can stand at all. I will go alone to the House of Myrtles."

Muhammad trembled as pain caused by the shaft embedded in his thigh ran the entirety of his injured limb. His mother rose and brushed aside leaves from the detritus clinging to her *jubba.* He could have smiled at her fastidiousness with her robe if his leg throbbed a little less.

She crept across the cobblestones. Her fingers traced the edges of a rust-covered doorknocker carved in the shape of a lion's head before she rattled the gate.

Muhammad held his breath and scanned the other façades for the appearance of lights in windows or faces peeking into the night. Two further tries from Butayna produced another solitary bark in the quarter along with a faint speck of light, which shone through the iron grille of the entrance.

A gruff voice echoed in the darkness. "Who calls at this grave hour?"

"Esperanza Peralta," Butayna answered.

"Who?"

"Binta, I don't have time for your foolishness! You know my name and my purpose at such a dreadful hour. Open the damnable gate and be quick about it!"

The flicker of light drew closer. The interior door banged against the wall and the gate creaked. A portly woman stood behind the grille. A lantern held up by a meaty hand revealed her bulbous nose and fleshy lips set within a broad face. Mouth drawn in a firm line, she glared into the gloom, and a frown appeared as she focused on the shapes among the trees.

"Who's with you in the shadows?"

Butayna glanced over her shoulder. "The remainder of my son's household. Where is your master?"

"In his bed."

"Then wake him!"

The charcoal-skinned woman scratched her double chin and fixed her glare on Butayna. "In whose name? Your son's own?"

Butayna tilted her head. "Mine. I am the mother of the Sultan, the rightful ruler of Gharnatah. Your master will awaken for me."

Then, the iron gate slammed shut in her face. Muhammad did not know what to think as she flipped her braid behind her and returned. She crouched before him.

"How does your leg fare? Do you suffer overmuch?"

The strain of the last year and a half between them had ebbed away, swept aside by the tragedies of this night. When he regarded her, he saw the woman whom he had trusted as a boy. The mother who had long loved him without reserve had not shrunk from his side in fear tonight. She was not a Nasrid by birth, but at every moment, she embodied the strength of generations of women born into his family. Had his father been alive to see her, he would have been proud.

"It is a minor ache." The lie revealed itself in an intense twinge, which spiked across his leg. He bore the spasm and ground his teeth together.

Butayna's sigh filled the air. "I am your mother. I will always worry for you and your sister. You have never needed to pretend for my sake and it is useless to try now. Truth has always served us better than lies," she said, reaching for her daughter's chin. As she patted the skin, Aisha's eyes swam with unshed tears. Butayna added, "We have lost too much."

Some losses were beyond measure. Muhammad swallowed and blinked, and his stare slid away. Butayna touched his chin and drew his gaze. Despite his efforts, tears glided down his cheek. She raked her thumb across coarse stubble.

"There will be opportunity for regret, grief, and vengeance. We need rest now."

He sniffled. "And afterward? Where do we go from here?"

"You are still the lord of Gharnatah and our lives. Only you can decide what we will do, where we will go, my lion."

He splayed his hands. "And if I don't know the path to the future?"

"You don't have to find all of the answers tonight."

Yet, somehow, he must discover them for those whom he loved, for all who remained at his side. Otherwise, his followers would perish and the sacrifices of others for their benefit would have been meaningless. The pleasures of his life as a Sultan lost all relevance, compared to the welfare of those who depended on him.

Behind them, the gate swung open with a clang. Butayna stood and held out her hand for him. He accepted her aid and forced himself to rise. She slipped an arm around his waist. "Lean upon me now."

"*Ummi,* you can hardly expect to bear my weight," he protested.

"If this night, this life in Gharnatah has taught me anything, I have learned I can bear many things. Now come," she instructed.

At her side, he hobbled across the narrow street. The others he led, many of them muddied and bloodstained, followed in a slow amble beneath the horseshoe archway and into the courtyard. The surly woman who had greeted Butayna turned on her heels, headed for the house. Except for a marble bench set under a lone myrtle tree, the courtyard stood bare.

In the doorway, a crook-backed man awaited them. His rheumy stare wandered over the faces of his guests. When he saw Butayna, recognition lit up his careworn features.

In a hoarsened voice, he said, "My honored Sultana. The hour is grave."

She replied, "My need is dire, Juan Manuel."

Here stood the Jewish merchant whose house she had frequented each month. Muhammad looked from her to the stooped man. The wind disturbed wisps of thin hair atop his head. He shuffled toward them with heavy grunts, supported by a walking stick. A strong gust would have likely toppled him at any moment. He made as if to bow before Muhammad and Butayna, but she laid a hand on his spindly arm. The gap-toothed smile on his speckled face caused the lined features to retreat and gave a hint of the young man Juan Manuel had once been.

Butayna's familiar gesture toward him roused some discomfort within Muhammad. What intimacies had she shared with this merchant?

Juan Manuel cleared his throat. "Ask what you would of me. It shall be done."

Butayna said, "We have wounded. Will you send for a physician to attend them? A doctor who can be discreet."

"Assuredly. You and yours must come inside. I have no chamber large enough where all of you might gather. It would be best to go to the inner courtyard. My servant Binta will show you the way."

"I remember the route," Butayna said. "Come, all of you."

She led their family and retainers toward the door. Up close, something familiar in the jutting lower lip of Juan Manuel's servant stirred Muhammad's memories. Then he halted beside her. "Ifrit. You could be none other than a close relation to my Aunt Leila's favored slave, who perished after the great pestilence struck Gharnatah."

Binta nodded. "I was her mother. Ifrit is dead because of her loyalty to your aunt."

Butayna added, "Ifrit gave her life and service for all of Yusuf's family. We remain grateful. You should be proud of your daughter, Binta."

"I always am." Binta stared down at her hands.

Muhammad walked with his mother through the shadows of an antechamber. Shoes and cloaks clustered along its southern wall. A central staircase dominated the space. Binta took the steps, while Butayna went through a doorway and out into a garden of marble and shrubbery. She guided Muhammad to the closest stone bench, where he sank down and struggled to keep his wounded leg outstretched. The discomfort of the rough and sharp arrowhead beneath the skin paled in contrast to the anguish he held at bay.

Butayna's lips brushed against his brow. She whispered, "I need you to be strong a moment longer."

Their family and retainers lined the wall opposite Muhammad's seat. Haziyya took a bench for herself, still nursing their daughter. Butayna joined the bedraggled band. She knelt at the left of Aisha, who wept beside two prone bodies laid next to each other on the tiled footpath. Pero still drew shallow breaths, the rise and fall of his chest barely visible. Yusuf's eyes remained closed since Muhammad had retrieved him from the carnage below the summer palace. The child had not stirred for an hour.

Juan Manuel did not appear again. Instead, a retinue of boys dispersed throughout the garden and ignited pairs of freestanding candelabras stationed at each corner. Light illuminated the fatigued faces of Butayna and Aisha as they wept. Then mother and daughter embraced, offering each other comfort.

Muhammad's chin dipped to his chest. He closed his eyes, unable to bear the sight. Self-recriminations filled his mind. A steady throb began at his temple. He bore the blame for the ignominy and fatalities his household had suffered, scattered from their palace like frightened mice. If he had behaved differently, if he had dealt effectively with Maryam and her sons long ago, this night might have never occurred. How his enemies must have gloated when they knew he had abandoned *Al-Qal'at al-Hamra*. At least his father had not lived to witness the dishonor.

He bowed his head and gritted his teeth against another shard of pain digging deep into the flesh.

"My eunuch summons medical help," Juan Manuel said. His unexpected appearance jolted Muhammad to an awareness of his surroundings again. Along with the servant boys, girls and young women offered water-filled cups and bowls of sliced figs, pitted olives, and crushed dates and almonds. Muhammad dismissed a yellow-haired girl with widened eyes who quivered before him. Her lower lip trembled as she glanced at Juan Manuel, who patted her head and sent her off.

Then he said, "You should eat something, my Sultan, especially if you have undergone the month of fasting."

Muhammad muttered, "What would you know of my needs?" He turned his face away and glared at the boy closest to him, huddled beside the candelabra. Far from being cowed, the child eyed him in return.

Uninvited, Juan Manuel took the meager space beside Muhammad on the bench. Had any of the wounded among the royal guard been capable, they would have shoved the presumptuous slave seller to the ground with the base of their lances. Five of Pero's company remained with the living. Five, from a band of forty! They had borne their listless commander, pierced by two arrows still lodged in his chest and abdomen, into the House of Myrtles. If the breath of life lingered within Pero, it might not last much longer.

Muhammad shook his head. The Ruiz brothers merited better than this fate, having served him so faithfully for almost ten years.

With a hard thump of his walking stick on the ground, Juan Manuel said, "I know more than you would believe possible, my Sultan. I pay well to keep informed of events within and outside of Gharnatah."

Muhammad faced him. "Then if you discern so much, why didn't you send a warning to us before conspirators clambered over the walls of my palace?"

Juan Manuel lifted his unkempt eyebrows. "Did the bitter fruit of this night ripen suddenly? The seeds of it took root over many years, long before the death of your honored father, *El Dio* preserve his memory."

He paused and looked to Butayna as she hovered over the figures on the ground. "Did your mother ever tell you of the day we first met? She was proud even then. A bright girl, so sure of her destiny and the people at her side. She judged Maryam for a friend, whereas I required just one glance at the woman to ascertain the trouble she might cause. Maryam created this calamity. No warning from me could have prevented its occurrence. Maryam knew the truth your honored mother would not accept. They were destined to be rivals, even before both entered the harem of your great father."

A deep scowl sent a throbbing ache through Muhammad's forehead. "You think you understand my mother so well."

The grin Juan Manuel offered did not help. "I comprehend her better than most do, even you, great Sultan."

How dare this arrogant wretch hold such aspiration? If Muhammad still clutched his father's sword, he would have thrust it between this vile merchant's teeth.

"What is your relationship with my mother? What power have you cast over her?"

Butayna looked up, a glance over her shoulder directed at them. Muhammad ignored the question in her gaze.

"Is this what you believe, my Sultan? She is indebted to me. Oh, no, no, no! Far from it." Juan Manuel's look turned wistful. "She has granted me a glimpse of a bright future, more than I have ever deserved."

Heat, fierier than the brightest candelabra, flushed through Muhammad's body. He hauled the slave merchant up by the neckline of his tunic, tearing the fragile silk.

"Stop speaking in riddles, man!"

Butayna rose and shook her head, her mouth falling open. "No! Don't hurt him, Muhammad! What do you think you're doing?"

Just then, the servant Binta ushered two men in hooded, black cloaks with yellow stars sewn on their left sleeves into the garden. As both pulled back their cowls, Muhammad released Juan Manuel.

Binta bowed. "The doctors ben Zarzar."

The father, Pharez, bowed toward Muhammad. Pharez's son, Abraham repeated the gesture before both men straightened. Muhammad pinched the bridge of his nose and shook his head. He recognized them. Of all the physicians Juan Manuel could have bidden, he had summoned these two, the eldest of whom served Jazirah's father.

Butayna clasped her hands. "Doctors, thank you for coming to our aid. I do not doubt we may rely upon your talents and assistance, as well as your silence." She waved to her family. "The wounded are many and they need your help if we are to leave this place alive."

The elder of them nodded. "You may trust in both of us, my Sultana."

He moved toward Muhammad, who waved him off and pointed to the two bodies aligned on the floor. "No! You will see to them first!"

Pharez bowed. "As you wish, my Sultan."

Juan Manuel rose and gave a stiff bow. Muhammad sucked his teeth and ignored him. The moon became a waning crescent when Muhammad's turn for medical aid arrived. He focused on the eastern sky rather than the rippling pain as Pharez twirled the shaft. Then he sliced a narrow slit up the leg and enlarged the arrow injury. Viscous warmth trailed down Muhammad's limb and soaked his *sarawil* until the trouser leg clung to the flesh. The old doctor probed with a fingertip before he heaved a weary sigh.

"Hmmm, good, good. It did not strike the bone. While I can remove the arrow, my Sultan, you must rest afterward for it shall cause grievous pain."

Muhammad had rested enough. He gritted his teeth. "Just take it out!"

Butayna hovered beside him. He might have found her sighs an irritant on any other occasion. Instead, he derived strength from her closeness and her slim fingers upon his shoulder. When Pharez retrieved the bloodied shaft and arrowhead intact, Muhammad shuddered and Butayna patted him.

She whispered, "The worst of the long night is over. The doctors ben Zarzar have done us a kind service."

"I will require further duties from father and son," Muhammad stated.

Her nails indented his tunic and Pharez glanced up from his work as he cleaned the wound. The doctor's throat bobbed. "Ah, what would you have of me, my Sultan?"

Muhammad looked to Abraham, who had just finished sewing up the gash in Faraj's side. "Does your son ride well?"

The physician nodded. "Hmmm. Abraham is a fair rider, great Sultan."

"And you?"

Pharez made a squeaking noise in the back of his throat before he coughed. "Ah... I... ah... I manage well enough, my Sultan."

With a stifled groan, Muhammad bent and clapped the old doctor's arm. "Good."

***

Muhammad summoned Juan Manuel, just as shimmery pink gave way to radiant orange bands along the horizon. The old man shuffled into the garden, his head bowed. Only Butayna remained with her son. Their household had gone out to the courtyard, where fresh mounts awaited all who could ride. Those

219

with grave injuries would travel in a covered cart, protected by the men on horseback.

Abraham ben Zarzar had left at Muhammad's order, bound for Castilla-León and the court of King Pedro. Pharez would await word from his son before the elder doctor made an even more perilous trek up the Sabika hill to *Al-Qal'at al-Hamra.*

When Juan Manuel would have bowed, Muhammad shook his head. "No time." He glanced over his shoulder, where Butayna stood a few paces behind him. "Leave us, *Ummi.* I wish to speak to this man alone."

She protested, "My lion, please allow—"

He lifted his hand and she lapsed into silence. He said, "*Ummi,* henceforth I will rely upon you with faith. But you must understand there are decisions I have to make now as Sultan, choices I cannot defer to anyone, even you."

Butayna nodded and bowed with a smile on her lips. "I hear and obey, my Sultan."

She touched Juan Manuel's shoulder briefly before she departed.

Alone with the slave merchant, Muhammad rose with the aid of a walking stick Juan Manuel had lent him. Gingerly, he tested the strength of his damaged leg. Satisfied the limb could bear his weight with the help of the wooden rod beneath his arm, he made a tentative step and then another. Although his muscles throbbed in fiery protest, he continued toward the door. Juan Manuel fell into step beside him.

"I require truth between us, Jew. Why are you so obligated to my mother?"

"She should inform you of the reason, great Sultan."

Muhammad bit the inside of his cheek. "I am asking you."

"What will you do if I refuse? Shall you have your men arrest me and throw me into the dungeons of *Al-Quasaba*?" Despite the low growl in Muhammad's throat, Juan Manuel added, "Forgive my obstinacy. It is a tale only Sultana Butayna may tell you when she is ready, though I believe if you inquire, she will offer the truth at any time."

Muhammad shook his head. As soon as his companions were safe, he would seek answers from his mother.

For now, he asked, "You have concluded all of the arrangements?"

"I have, my Sultan. Guards loyal to you still protect the northern city gate of *Bab Fayy al-Lawsa.* From there, you shall go east to Wadi-Ash."

Rooted to the tiles just outside the doorway, Muhammad glared at him. "The *Ghuzat* control the city. Their commander Yahya betrayed me tonight."

"His relation, Ali ibn Musa, has nominal power over the Volunteers of the Faith, since he returned to the city after rendering assistance to King Pedro against Aragón." While Juan Manuel endured the frigid stare focused on him, a little chuckle escaped his lips. "As I have said, I pay well for knowledge. You should go to Wadi-Ash. Only you can give Ali ibn Musa his true desire. Or do you believe his interests do not extend beyond a marriage to your sister Sultana Aisha?"

"What else does Ali want?"

"Have you never wondered why the Marinids honored Yahya with a post in Al-Andalus? His clan shares blood ties with the Marinids and Yahya is a worthy candidate to claim power in Al-Maghrib al-Aksa. The Marinids sent him here to serve you, but his clan's ambitions have not faded. Young Ali ibn Musa is a warrior in the spirit of his kinsman. Mayhap his relations shall realize their ambitions of a legitimate claim to the mastery of Al-Maghrib al-Aksa, especially with the support and recognition of the Sultan of Gharnatah."

As Muhammad laughed, the rich, throaty sound bolstered him after a night of cruel death and heartbreak. "If you perceive so much, then you also know I cannot wed my sister to Ali. Not unless the alliance would be fortuitous for both Gharnatah and Al-Maghrib al-Aksa."

"The promise of the future holds great appeal. It can blind the foolhardy to reality."

"Humph. You should have served on my council of ministers. You are almost as devious as they are."

"Why would I have sought service on a council where most of your ministers might call me 'the clever Jew' behind my back? Here, in this place, I know who and what I am, my Sultan. Your people would deem me as little more than a pawn in their schemes. I am no one's instrument."

Muhammad looked at him squarely. "Then why are you doing this? Why do you help me? Do not tell me it is only a debt repaid to my mother. Speak the truth. What do you want from me?"

A deep sigh filled Juan Manuel. "In the Christian and Moorish kingdoms, my people toil at the mercy of masters who revile us, even as they encourage our usefulness as traders and our talents with gold and silver. My people have no home they may call their own. It is my hope Gharnatah might become a haven for them. I shall help you reclaim what is yours, if you will swear to grant my people the freedom to worship, to exist without persecution, to live as Jews. Give me your pledge and you shall have my support until the end of my days."

Leaning heavily on the walking stick, Muhammad cupped his hands. Juan Manuel placed his fingers within Muhammad's hold. The pair shared a nod.

"You have my oath, Juan Manuel Gomero."
"And you have my aid, great Sultan."

Chapter 17
Losses

Sultana Jazirah

Gharnatah, Al-Andalus or Granada, Andalusia
Ramadan 760 AH or August A.D. 1359 or Av 5119

The glare of sunlight pierced the lattice and the curtains hung over two windows in the dining hall. Jazirah raised her head from the low table and her swollen eyelids lifted, taking in the grim evidence of Maryam's duplicity. A trail of bloodied streaks extended into the next room. Maryam's men had dragged the bodies of Beatriz and Gonzalo behind them as they left the house. Jazirah's father had not summoned his servants to cleanse the room. Now the remnants of the *iftar* meal attracted flies. Small, black pellets had appeared next to crumbled cookies.

Jazirah blinked and rubbed at her eyes. An ache ran the length of her body as she stretched. She shook her head, unable to banish the fog enmeshed in her mind.

"It is dawn. Maryam will come soon."

She turned toward the sound of her father's voice. He sat between the windows, which fronted the indoor courtyard. When he looked at her, shadows haunted his gaze. His lips parted as if he intended to say more, but no sound came out. Just as well. She no longer wished to hear anything he might say.

Two desires prevailed upon her, to hold Yusuf again and to know Muhammad's whereabouts. The bitter tears she had shed during the night were as much for him as for worry over their son. Whatever destination Muhammad had chosen, she prayed he might be safe with Yusuf at his side. She wanted her little boy, but she could not protect him from Maryam here. How might she get away and follow Butayna's instructions to reach this House of Myrtles in Al-Bayazin?

The door at the entrance of the house slammed, but Jazirah did not allow fear of an intruder to overtake her. Instead, she reached for some leftover pomegranate juice, swished it around her mouth, and spat the sour liquid back into the cup. Then she stood, just at the moment when Maryam entered the room alone, dressed in radiant, yellow silk. A smile of satisfaction still etched on her lips, she surveyed the room. When Maryam saw she stood upon a point where blood ingrained the wood flooring, her grin ebbed and she drew back a pace.

Jazirah eyed her in silence before Maryam said, "Have you forgotten your courtesies? Does custom not require you to bow before me? I am the mother of the new Sultan after all."

"Muhammad remains the ruler of Gharnatah, the only one I shall acknowledge," Jazirah replied. "For as long as he is Sultan in my mind, then Butayna remains the *Umm al-Walad*. I shall never honor you as I would my husband and his mother."

"Child," her father warned.

She shot him a withering glance over her shoulder. "You may bow before this vile bitch if you wish, like a lowly dog at the feet of its master. I will never submit. Mine is the blood of Sultans. She will forever be little more than a slave raised up to be my uncle's wife. If he had lived to see her now, I do not doubt he would regret the choice."

Maryam flushed a bright hue of red. "Do not speak as if you knew my husband or my love for him!"

"My husband should have killed you long ago!"

"Maryam holds your son's fate in her hands," Jazirah's father admonished as he joined her next to the table. "Think of little Yusuf's life before you speak."

She ignored his advice, even if she judged it sound. "Now you suggest prudence, when you were so willing to throw away my son's birthright for the sake of her sons. You disgust me!" To Maryam, she said, "You swore to show me Yusuf. Where is he?"

Maryam cast a careless wave of her hand. "Come and see him." She turned on her heels and Jazirah followed.

Although her father walked beside her with a hitch in his gait and rubbed his hip at intervals, she refused him any assistance and kept her gaze on Maryam's back while they entered the lush courtyard. Aromatic juniper swayed above the shrubbery in the early morning chill. Maryam trailed her fingertips casually through the water in the central fountain.

Jazirah looked away for a moment, reminded of when she had made a similar carefree gesture upon her arrival in Gharnatah. Three years had passed since the day in the month of Safar, when she had viewed her new home with nonchalant disdain. Now its environs were as familiar to her as her son's sweet smile and his dimples. The prospect of seeing him again drove her onward, despite the bloodied trail beneath her feet, which extended through the doorway up ahead. She would burn the soiled shoes after today.

Outdoors, she looked for signs of Zabala and his cohort, but found none. Only splotches of red dotted the steps, set apart from where the crimson streaks thinned.

Jazirah demanded, "Where is my captain, Maryam? What has befallen him and his companions? Have your men killed them as well?"

Maryam reproached her with an impish smile. "Such assumptions you make! We have not killed everyone. There are some, like your captain Zabala and his men, who judged surrender as the wiser choice. They are in the dungeons of the citadel, where they will remain. You'll have new... protectors soon enough from among these men."

She indicated a cadre of her guards, who stood just outside the fence. Their number had doubled to twenty, where just a few hours earlier there had been ten. If Maryam required such protection, mayhap her circumstances were more tenuous than she wished for Jazirah to believe.

A steady breeze blew crisp leaves into marble fountains and along tiled pathways. As they strode the cobblestone streets between two rows of Maryam's sentries, Jazirah looked for some sign of acknowledgment, even sympathy, in the faces of collared slaves who swept and cleaned. Butayna had told her those persons loyal to this Juan Manuel Gomero would seek out Jazirah at the right time. Her need had never been so great. Yet, everyone she encountered stared at the ground or shuffled away.

Jazirah glared at Maryam a few paces ahead of her. Muhammad had demanded signs of respect from his people to be sure, but such emotion did not shine in these turbulent gazes before they slid away. No displays of deference, but of naked fear, as if a glance from Maryam or her guards would seal a person's fate as a prisoner in the citadel, or worse. What sights had these slaves endured in the night?

Maryam led them toward the gate, which bordered the court and the citadel. Jazirah expected to pass beneath the archway and into *Al-Quasaba* itself. Where was Yusuf, imprisoned in the rooms of the watchtower, or worse, in a cell? If so, could she break free with him and make for any of the hidden exits beneath the ramparts? He must have survived a bitter night, but mayhap not alone. He would not have been so frightened if Lubna remained with him.

Instead, Maryam detoured to the north and strolled beside the stone balustrade, which bordered a narrow gorge. Those who had inhabited *Al-Qal'at al-Hamra* before Jazirah's family constructed a brick footpath, which linked the citadel and royal court across the ravine. Maryam palmed the abraded surface of the packed earth wall, which rose to the height of her thigh, before she turned to Jazirah. "You wanted to see your son. He is here."

Jazirah's father issued a sharp cry, barely stifled behind his hand, while she drew back and looked around her. "What are you saying?"

Maryam shook her head. "You asked for Muhammad's heir. I have brought you to the place where you might find him." She pointed down into the ravine.

The wind died. All sounds faded, except the rush of each ragged breath torn from Jazirah's body. Only when the silence became overwhelming did she speak. "You cannot... he... where is he? Please, I just want Yusuf...."

A heavy ache swelled in her throat. She crossed her arms over her abdomen, where not so long ago, she had carried her dear child, loved him even before she ever saw his sweet face. He could not be.... Maryam could not mean.... Jazirah bumped her thigh against the thick, uneven barrier and the material scraped at the skin under thin cloth. She pushed away from the wall and steadied herself.

Maryam's hand fell to her side and she clasped her fingers, as she looked over the balustrade. "I did not want this to happen, Jazirah. I swear it as a mother. I would have kept the boy locked up, but the others, they were overzealous in their pursuit of Muhammad." She raised her head. "You must believe me for I have lost children as well. I did not wish the death of your son, but like the coup against Muhammad, I suppose the loss was inevitable. You must accept this outcome...."

Jazirah refused to listen further. She stumbled along the walkway and rounded Maryam. Peering down into the chasm, the number of bodies left her staggered. She began to count them in her mind. One, two, three, four.... Then the first recognizable face came into view, Beatriz, with the wind rustling her long, yellow hair. Her husband Gonzalo sprawled beside her. Others soon followed. The chief minister Ridwan, along with a little girl's figure nestled against his form, and his wife, whom Jazirah had barely known. Nearby, a body facedown, clad in dove-gray robes, with a crimson stain spread across the back. Thin fingers wore the white gloves favored by the chief eunuch Hisham. Jazirah had never liked him, but he did not deserve this cruel fate. Muhammad's prized doctor Al-Shaquri lay among the dead, an ugly, red line across his throat with his head bent at an odd angle. Then Mufawwiz. A hand, which would never rise again, rested on his bloated belly. No, none of them had earned their brutal deaths, their bodies discarded like litter.

After Jazirah had tallied almost forty clustered bodies, she stopped the count. Beneath a thin willow tree, which demarcated the midpoint of the wall, she paused at the sight of a tattered red cape, its strings still tied around the neck of Alfonso Ruiz. Strewn around him were the corpses of other royal bodyguards, but he stayed distinct, even at such a depth, for the deep scar crisscrossing the hard lines of his face.

Then a streak of dark brown hair drew Jazirah's gaze. She covered her trembling lips with shaky hands. Lubna sprawled atop others, her arms and legs splayed out at unnatural angles. Her body had landed beside a tiny form clad in a torn, bloodied tunic, which had once been immaculate white. Gold braid sewn to the neckline hung loose, almost ripped away. Where there should have been a child's head beneath a mop of black curls, only the lower half of a cherubic face with puckered lips remained.

Behind Jazirah, Maryam said, "My guards told me Prince Yusuf was trampled by a horse in a field below the summer palace. His life would have ended quickly."

In Jazirah's blurred gaze, the landscape undulated. The top of the wall rushed up to meet her. The unexpected strength of arms about her, which dragged her back from the precipice, left her stunned for a moment. Then she fought against the embrace those limbs offered. "Get off me! Let me be with my son!"

"No, daughter! I will not lose you as well!"

She railed and struck out at her father. "Let me go! Let me go to him."

"Jazirah!" Her father rocked her in a firm embrace, as if his hold could assuage all the evils she had endured. "Yusuf is gone, sweet child. You cannot be with him."

"But I want to be." She shuddered and swallowed a bitter taste in her mouth. Her lips slackened, but no words issued. Only a guttural scream before the tears fell. Her nails raked the stone beneath her feet until her fingertips bled. Her father gripped her tighter as a torrent ran down her cheeks. Her sobs washed away all sights, the wall bordering the ravine where her child's body and the citadel where she had suffered as a six-year old girl, frightened in the dark. She wept for the tender babe stolen away.

All the while, her father sought to comfort her. When her tears subsided to deep shudders, which wracked her body, he lifted his chin from atop her head.

"You're a treacherous bitch, Maryam! Jazirah is right. Muhammad should have had you killed years ago. Now your eldest son has claimed the throne by treachery. Your men have chased Muhammad from Gharnatah. His son, my grandchild is dead! What more do you intend for us? Or have you had your fill of blood and betrayal?"

Footfalls shuffled across the pavement and halted at Jazirah's feet. Maryam cautioned, "Careful, Prince Ismail. Bitterness does not become you. Let your daughter have her cry now. The pain of loss will fade with time. I know from harsh experience. You'll both learn soon enough of the roles you shall play in my son's Sultanate."

***

In Exile
Sultan Muhammad V

Wadi-Ash, Al-Andalus or Guadix, Andalusia
Ramadan – Shawwal 760 AH or August – September A.D. 1359
or Av – Elul 5119

Muhammad raised a hand to his hood and pulled the dark material slightly back. He sat his horse beneath the austere walls of Wadi-Ash. The city rose up in the shadows of giant shards of sandstone, which ranged as far as the mountains. The nearby river gave Wadi-Ash its name. Mid-morning light glinted off brass helmets and exposed the craggy faces of sentries posted atop the wall. They scrubbed at bleary-eyed gazes and peered down at him beneath the standards of the Nasrids, emblazoned with a red shield bearing crosswise white letters above a gold fringe. Interspersed on thin poles were the olive green and gold banners of the *Ghuzat*. What did the insignias denote? Were the Volunteers of the Faith loyal to Muhammad?

He called out, "Open the gate in the name of Abu Abdullah Muhammad, the Sultan of Gharnatah!"

Crossbows appeared in the hands of the watchmen, one of whom glowered at him from the height of the ramparts. "What gives you the right to make such a demand? I take no orders from hooded strangers! Leave before you regret your arrival."

Muhammad cursed under his breath. This would be harder than he had expected.

Beside him, Faraj leaned forward in his saddle, fingers shielding his eyes from the sun's glare. "The warriors of the *Ghuzat* were always too bold for my tastes."

Muhammad ordered, "Put your hand down, Faraj." He maneuvered his bay stallion closer to the base of the wall, where the stout city gate remained closed to him. "I am Muhammad ibn Yusuf, the Sultan of Gharnatah! I demand entry into Wadi-Ash by my own authority."

The man who had challenged him spat over the wall. "Bah! The Sultan! Why would he be here?"

Then one of his companions spoke to him and pointed, presumably at the guards and women. A torrent of whispers filled the air. The insolent guardsman wiped his crinkled, olive-skinned brow before he turned away. Another took his place. Others lowered their crossbows.

Muhammad dug his heels into his mount's side and urged the horse back to his company. He slowed his mount beside his

228

mother at the forefront. Behind her on another horse, Haziyya gazed at him as she cradled Leila close. Halted beside Haziyya, Aisha's turbulent gape revealed her uncertainty. Her mare nickered and flicked her tail restlessly. Butayna's servants, Jawla and Hafsa, drew long knives.

Muffled behind her veil, Butayna asked, "How long will we have to wait, my lion?"

He answered, "For as long as it takes Ali ibn Musa to get out of bed. Let us pray he does not have his men fire on us with their crossbows. I want you and the others of my family out of range. Ride to the last rock knoll we passed and wait there. If there is trouble, you must flee."

"Where might we go without you?"

"Anywhere, except Gharnatah. We cannot return there, not yet." Then he reached for the child snuggled in her arms.

Wrapped in just a cloak retrieved from one of the Christian guards killed the previous night, Yusuf whimpered and crinkled up his reddened face, his fat lips pursed. Muhammad patted the dark hair and reached for his treasured son, his firstborn whom he had almost lost. When the arrow had gone through Yusuf's foot, the boy had squealed louder than he did now. Muhammad rescued him, but the wound would still leave a permanent scar. Muhammad had almost failed his son and he continued to do so, uncertain how to offer comfort as Yusuf turned away, burrowing against the folds of his grandmother's robe.

She rubbed his back and kissed the crown of his tiny head. "You must give him time. Yusuf has known dangers no child of his age ever should, what with the fall, the arrow through his foot, and the doctor's efforts to remove it. Pharez said only a miracle will prevent Yusuf from suffering pain for the rest of his life, but at least, your son will walk again. For now, he craves a female touch to comfort him. Likely, he clings to me because he misses Jazirah."

Muhammad did not say he missed her as well. What would be the point? His wishes to the contrary would not summon her to his side, nor eliminate the possibility she had known of the night's events beforehand. Despite his misgivings, he sent a silent prayer heavenward for her. Jazirah had survived the deprivations of Shalabuniya. She had to live through this trial.

His mired thoughts did little to ease the shame swirling in his gut. He had abandoned her to fate. She should have been at his side. He should have protected her, safeguarded his loved ones from Maryam. His failure had nearly cost him the life of his son.

Butayna reached for his hand. "I told Jazirah of the House of Myrtles a month ago. She will know where to go for help."

"If she can get away," Muhammad mumbled. In his mind, the words were different. *If she chooses to get away.* Old doubts concerning her always gnawed at him at the wrong time. Then he raised his head and focused on the present. "Do as I have said, *Ummi*. Withdraw from the reach of the arbalesters."

She looked beyond him. "It seems I do not need to, my lion."

He looked over his shoulder, as Ali ibn Musa arrived on the wall and shouted orders down below. "Hurry! Open the gate for the mighty Sultan and his family now! Damn you, camel-eating sots! I'll kill you myself if you don't draw back those bars quickly enough." In a huff of annoyance, he disappeared.

Muhammad heaved a weary sigh and rubbed his palm over his face. Caution kept him nervous, for Ali could still invite them into the city, only to arrest them. Mayhap Yahya had fled here. Muhammad chided himself for an earnest fool. He might have made another mistake. He should have kept his family and the wounded back beyond the reach of the crossbows aligned on the wall. Had he brought his family and retainers here upon the advice of Juan Manuel only to expose them to greater peril?

Faraj and the remaining men of the royal guard closed ranks around Muhammad, the women, and children. As it was, the men could not shield everyone, for the wounded in the cart had no defense at the rear of the cortege.

The heavy wooden doors inlaid with metal spikes croaked. Ali hurtled through the opening in bare feet, his tunic unlaced.

"Oh!" Aisha dismounted before Muhammad could stop her. She rushed into the arms of the Marinid prince and embraced him. For his part, Ali looked beyond her to Muhammad, before he tugged her arms from around his neck and bowed before her.

When he straightened, he inquired, "My Sultana, are you well? Why are you here? What has happened in the capital?"

She drew back, as if she suddenly recalled the proper decorum. "I am well, thank you, commander, but we need your help."

Muhammad demanded Ali's attention. "You mean you don't know anything about what happened during the night in Gharnatah?"

Ali left Aisha's side and fell to his knees in the dirt between Muhammad and Faraj's horses. "Mighty Sultan, I do not, but it must have been something awful, if you have arrived at Wadi-Ash with your women and children." He raised his gaze. "And so few guards. Where are the rest of your protectors?"

Muhammad ignored the question. "Where is Yahya?"

Faraj brought his scimitar down on the back of Ali's neck. At the slightest command from Muhammad, the warrior would slice the prince's head from his shoulders. Faraj could accomplish the grim task before the bolts from the arbalesters felled him in retaliation. He glanced at Muhammad, who nodded. None of them had reason to trust the *Ghuzat*. Up on the wall, some of the lowered crossbows came into view again.

Aisha cried out, "Muhammad, no!"

He did not lift his head, his stare fixed on Ali. "You will be silent, sister."

Ali held himself rigid for the space of several breaths before he raised his open palms. "I have not merited your mistrust, mighty Sultan, but if Yahya has, then he acted alone. I am loyal. I have not seen my kinsman since departing Gharnatah a month ago upon your orders, taking the majority of the *Ghuzat* with me. You sent me here to hold this city and kept Yahya at court. I have done my duty, unaware of his activities in the capital. If this must be my final hour, then I would give a last command to the *Ghuzat*. They shall not strike you and yours down or seek vengeance for my unworthy death."

Muhammad ground his teeth together. Then he asked, "Can I truly rely upon you?"

Before Ali answered, he flicked a quick glance at Aisha. "I vow you may believe me, my Sultan."

At a gesture from Muhammad, Faraj sheathed his sword again. Ali rose and Aisha rushed to his side. She gazed up at him with adoring eyes. They shared an intense regard, while he waved to the men on the wall, who lowered their weapons.

Then Ali turned to Muhammad. "Wadi-Ash is yours."

Ali and Aisha walked beside Muhammad's mount as he entered the city, followed by his weary companions. Faraj led Aisha's horse behind his own. The animals trotted over the worn cobblestones of the old city and came to a halt near a square, set with a large fountain. Five boys suddenly appeared with buckets and rushed to water the horses. Another five drew bowls of water for the new arrivals to drink.

Muhammad dismounted with a groan and rubbed his injured leg, stiffened by the journey. Faraj brought him the walking stick. Pride might not have let him accept the rod in the past, but he leaned heavily upon it now as he accepted some water. He drank greedily before he raised his gaze to the distant citadel. Its square towers perched on the flat summit of a sloping hill at the center of Wadi-Ash.

"As soon as you are ready, my Sultan, we may ride on." Ali approached, still with Aisha at his side. "Yesterday, I received an important guest from Al-Maghrib al-Aksa, one whom I know shall be pleased to see you again."

***

A loud groan escaped Muhammad as his chief judge and the ambassador to the Marinid court, Abu'l-Qasim Sharif al-Sabti, embraced him and clapped his back. Built like a bear with a

231

flabby belly, Al-Sabti released his hold and shook his grizzled head.

"When I returned to Al-Andalus for my son's wedding this week, I had imagined I would greet you, my noble Sultan, at Gharnatah. Yet, I find you at Wadi-Ash, with your household." Al-Sabti stroked his long, gray beard and cast a wary glance over those who followed Muhammad. "Though unaccompanied by any of your courtiers. What of my friend Ridwan and the prideful fool Ibn al-Khatib, where are they?"

"I shall speak of them in a moment. It has been many years, too long since we last met in my council chamber."

"Indeed, four years since you named me as your envoy to Al-Maghrib al-Aksa."

"Much has happened," Muhammad added. Al-Sabti had served as a *qadi* in Gharnatah for over four decades and swiftly ascended to his rank as head of the judiciary. In the abrupt transition to the reign of Muhammad, there seemed no reason not to keep Al-Sabti in the role and expand his duties.

Ali bowed beside the men and straightened. "Mighty Sultan, I sent ahead for food and the comfort of you and your household. If you will follow me." He indicated the paved walkway and the double doors studded with iron rivets beneath an archway.

"You may escort my family," Muhammad replied. "My children are hungry and tired. Is there a physician here as well?"

"Ibn Khatima al-Ansari is a fine doctor, with a house in the city below the citadel's walls. I will send a eunuch to fetch him."

"Thank you. In the interim, Al-Sabti will walk with me through the gardens." Muhammad glanced at Faraj and shared a nod with him. He would protect the family if Ali had been less than forthright.

Muhammad left them in Faraj's care, leading the ambassador down a slight slope and through the hedgerows of a nearby eastern garden. Each footfall pained Muhammad, but he refused to submit before adversities. Never again.

He said, "Your return to Al-Andalus is fortuitous. You are a devoted servant and a trusted lawgiver, a boon to the reigns of my grandfather, his sons, and to me. May I call upon your aid now?"

Al-Sabti fell into step at his side. "Ask what you will, noble Sultan. It shall be done."

"Then to do so, you must know the events of last night. The account is fresh in my mind, but still difficult to examine."

By the time the men had circumnavigated the four quadrants of the garden, Muhammad concluded his story. Al-Sabti displayed varying reactions throughout the tale, veering between an incredulous look beneath a wrinkled brow, coupled with a heavy-footed gait or at times, a frozen stance in which he neither blinked nor released a pent-up breath. His face had gone from hues of angry red to pallid gray as Muhammad revealed the night's horror.

Together, they paused beneath the scant shade of a poplar tree. Muhammad leaned against the trunk. "You will go to Gharnatah. As a respected judge, you may travel with impunity. None would dare attack you. I want you to discover three things. One involves the fates of my courtiers, especially Ridwan and Al-Shaquri. Maryam despised them both, chiefly Ridwan for naming me as Sultan when she had presumed her eldest son would inherit the throne. Her dislike of my doctor seemed more... personal. I have never discovered what he did to offend her. Then there is Ibn al-Khatib. Has he survived or is he among the dead? If he lives, is it because he joined the conspirators?"

Al-Sabti patted his rounded belly. "If I discover the latter is true?"

"Then, he must receive an end befitting his treachery." Muhammad straightened and admired the towers of the citadel, burnished by mid-morning sun. "I will have my revenge against all who had connived against me. Everyone."

"Well, as you know, there is little goodwill between Ibn al-Khatib and me. He envied my rapport with your noble father and believed I imposed my will unduly. How could I have done so when the Sultan's personal secretary has always enjoyed intimacy with the sovereign, which no chief judge could ever achieve? Preposterous fool of a man! Still, I shall do all as you ask. Your second charge?"

"Learn the identities of the governors still loyal to me. I do not doubt Muhammad the Red of Malaka has aligned himself with Maryam and her sons against me. What may I expect from the masters of Lawsa, Madinah Antaqirah, and Al-Hamma? Will they declare for Maryam's son and close their gates to me?"

"I understand. And the third order?"

Muhammad's gaze returned to Al-Sabti's own. "I need to know about my wife, Jazirah, the daughter of my uncle Ismail, who once governed this city until his treason. I do not doubt he sided with those who colluded against me as well. What I need to know is how my wife perceived the night's events. Did she have a role in them or knowledge beforehand? What has she done since my... leave-taking?"

Al-Sabti looked away. "Er, indeed. When I heard of your union in the courts of Fés el-Jedid, it seemed a... remarkable choice. A traitor's daughter for your bride, hmmm."

"I want to know the truth about her. Did Jazirah betray me, too?"

***

Ten days later beneath a blistering noonday sun, Al-Sabti knelt before Muhammad in the courtyard surrounding a shimmering pool. Fish with scales in shades of orange, bright blue, and black darted through the water. Muhammad stood beside the marbled edge and threw crumbs of flatbread into the water. Behind him, his mother and Faraj sat on a Persian carpet. Aisha and Haziyya remained indoors and played with Muhammad's children. Pero stood grim-faced, stationed against a column. The captain had resumed his duties with the blessing of the doctor Ali had recommended, though Ibn Khatima had also warned the Christian warrior the wounds in his chest and abdomen would reopen if Pero did not exercise due care. Muhammad knew only gratitude for the return of his most capable fighter. Pero grieved the loss of his brother Alfonso in private, never allowing his sorrow to interfere with his duties.

Muhammad listened while Al-Sabti relayed information. "My noble Sultan, you charged me with three tasks. The guards at *Al-Qal'at al-Hamra* admitted me after I revealed my identity and purpose as the marriage feast of my son. No one questioned me further. First, I ensured my son and the family of his bride-to-be were safe. In view of the... changed circumstances within the capital, they have delayed the wedding in favor of a more auspicious time."

When his ambassador paused and turned aside, Muhammad followed the direction of his stare. "Al-Sabti, be assured my mother and Faraj are welcome at my side. You may speak in full candor as if you addressed me alone."

With an audible swallow, Al-Sabti gave a grave nod. "As you wish, master."

Muhammad threw the rest of the bread into the pool. His thigh twitched, not entirely the lingering effect of the wound. An empty feeling settled in the pit of his stomach and he licked his dried lips. "What is it? What did you learn?"

"Many of your courtiers are dead, their bodies thrown into the ravine between *Al-Quasaba* and the courtyard of the council chamber." Al-Sabti shook his head. "A shameful display."

Faraj demanded, "What of my father? Was my father among them?"

At Al-Sabti's nod, Faraj turned his head away. Despite trembling lips, he asked, "My mother? My sisters and their families? We were to celebrate the marriage of my youngest sibling in three days' time."

Al-Sabti replied, "You are the only survivor among your household."

A tiny sob from Butayna drew her son's regard. She covered her mouth and wept. Muhammad clasped his hands behind his back. Ridwan dead. The possibility once seemed incomprehensible, when he had been such a vibrant and vital man.

The heavy sigh from Al-Sabti echoed across the courtyard. "Muhammad al-Shaquri was also among the dead. The slaves I spoke with say they cut his throat through the bone, almost severed his head from his body. Ibn al-Khatib remains a prisoner in *Al-Quasaba*. His sister has written from their birthplace in Lawsa with an exceedingly generous offer of ransom. It would seem your stepmother is in favor of the claim, my master. She expended much of her resources to finance this coup."

Muhammad nodded. "Money my father had provisioned for her in his will. I am surprised Ibn al-Khatib is still alive, but Maryam's greed does not astonish me. Ah, Al-Shaquri. I loved him as my father did. Have they anointed the false Sultan yet?"

"No. Maryam awaits the arrival of Muhammad the Red from Malaka. The governors of Al-Hamma, Lawsa, and Madinah Antaqirah are already in Gharnatah. They have declared for Abu'l-Walid Ismail as the heir of Yusuf, may Allah preserve his memory."

"What?" Butayna raised her head. "They cannot take the throne from you!"

A hand raked across his face, Muhammad muttered, "They can and they have. In my cities, I had one hundred ninety-five thousand infantry, including sixty thousand bowmen and thirty-seven thousand cavalry. Will no one except these foreigners here support me?"

Butayna scrambled to his side and framed his face in her hands. "Your enemies and their collaborators will die a thousand deaths for this treachery!"

He loosened her hold. "How? How am I to avenge my losses and reclaim my throne? Will two thousand *Ghuzat* perish for my sake? No. There must be another way. I must have a majority of support within Al-Andalus."

Then he said, "Al-Sabti, in the time of my father, he sheltered a pair of rebel Marinid princes, Abu'l-Fadl and Abu Salim, the sons of Yusuf's old ally. The two were brothers and rivals of the old Marinid ruler, Abu Inan Faris, before my ascension."

A smile relaxed Al-Sabti's severe visage. "And now, Abu Salim sits upon the throne of the Marinids. He would remember your father's aid."

"Good. Now, I also asked you to ascertain the well-being and state of my wife."

"Fear is rampant in Gharnatah, my Sultan. The few slaves who would speak to me did so in darkened corners, when they could be certain Maryam's spies were not watchful. They told me no one has seen Sultana Jazirah since the morning after the coup. She, her father, and Maryam went to the gorge then. Sultana Jazirah wept."

Muhammad explained, "Her stewardess Lubna died protecting our son. The conspirators must have flung Lubna's body over the wall as well."

Relief flooded him. Maryam had not killed Jazirah, but uncertainties overcame even this respite. Did Jazirah live only because of her devotion to Maryam? His wife must have despaired after Yusuf. Even if she did not love Muhammad, he held no doubts of her feelings about their son. Yet, Muhammad still did not know of her disposition. He vowed he would, one day. He would have her back in his arms and discover the truth reflected in her eyes. He would know whether he had chosen a loyal wife or a traitor like her father.

Chapter 18
An Unlawful Union

Sultana Jazirah

Gharnatah, Al-Andalus or Granada, Andalusia
Shawwal 760 AH or September A.D. 1359 or Elul 5119

A heavy thud on the door did not rouse Jazirah. She ignored the rattling of the handle. The Persian cat Thalj, curled up beside her since the second call to prayer, now scrambled to the adjacent room in a haze of white fur. Jazirah clasped the *khamsa* worn on a necklace, but the talisman had not ensured prosperity, as she had hoped for on her nuptial night. Even locked inside her chamber within *Al-Qal'at al-Hamra's* harem, with the crossbar drawn across the door, she could not escape Maryam.

"Jazirah! Jazirah, open this door." Maryam's shrill words echoed through the wood. "This is the behavior of a child! You are nineteen years old. Dearest, don't do this! You are making matters worse for yourself. My children would be so disappointed in you if they saw this spectacle now, especially Ismail."

All true. Yet, Jazirah marveled at Maryam's ability to couple seeming concern with her relentless demands. Maryam loved two aspects of life, power and her children, especially Ismail, for his ascendancy had paved the path to her glory. With her continued manipulations, she bent him to her will. She thought to exert her influence over everyone's lives, but Jazirah would not let Maryam rule her destiny.

Jazirah refused to submit to the farce Maryam and Ismail tried to perpetrate even as they forced her to attend mealtimes beside mother and son each day within Muhammad's former rooms. They were not a happy family enjoying communal food and conversation. Jazirah ignored both of them and never asked how Ismail had survived his time in the citadel. She no longer cared. For his part, he always appeared discomfited and bewildered by her refusal to speak, as if he and his mother had not ruined all Jazirah's hopes.

"Jazirah! Talk to me."

Why, when Jazirah only wished for silence and solitude? Better not to say anything at all. Words would not avail her now. Tearful pleas in the wake of Yusuf's murder had not granted her a reprieve from the loss of her son.

Gone forever, just as her father said. When Yusuf had met his death beneath careless hooves, shouldn't she, as his mother, instinctively have known? Although she had seen the body, Yusuf lived on in her heart and mind.

More than three weeks later, she still berated herself for the tragedy. No better than a blind fool, no wiser than Beatriz and Gonzalo, she had fallen prey to Maryam's machinations and ignored Muhammad's instincts about his stepmother. Other regrets overtook her. She should have never let Muhammad keep their son on the final night. She did not want to believe her husband had deliberately fled without Yusuf. Just as she never envisioned he might have abandoned his home. Or his wife. Had he spared one thought for her during his escape?

Gossip and whispers followed her through windswept corridors. Muhammad had fled into the night, securing only the lives of those women most important to him, his mother and sister, along with Haziyya. He had not even attempted to fight. A slave had found his father's sword abandoned beneath the hedges bordering the summer palace. Ismail had claimed the weapon for his own, which Maryam swore her husband had intended for his favorite child and heir, not his eldest son.

Muhammad the coward. Muhammad the deposed. Jazirah no longer cared how his detractors condemned and reviled him. If she ever saw him again, she would seek an answer to the sole question occupying her wounded heart and fraught mind. *Why hadn't he saved Yusuf?*

Fresh tears gathered and she drew up her knees to her chest. A ripple and ache tore across her stomach. She sat on the floor of her antechamber, a copy of *Al-Qur'an* at her feet held shut by the book's iron clasp. She had slept on the ground every night upon returning to her room in *Al-Qal'at al-Hamra*. Her private chamber, dominated by the bed where she and Muhammad had conceived their son, offered no comfort.

The door to her rooms shook on its hinges and the wood splintered. A gleam of silver appeared in the wide gash left behind. An axe. Maryam's men had brought an axe to bear against her door. Why couldn't they just leave her alone and let her die? She closed her eyes while the blade's heavy thuds continued. Even when they stopped, she did not look toward the shattered entryway.

Then Maryam said, "Stand aside!" A soft creak of the iron joints preceded footsteps. Slippers smacked the flooring. A heavy sigh preceded a tense silence.

"What happened here? Barred her door against you, did she?" A gruff voice filled Jazirah's ears. Her bladder loosened and she pressed her thighs tightly together before she humiliated herself in front of her tormentors. "I told you to remove the lock!"

A huff of exasperation followed. "You may be my son's principal advisor, Muhammad the Red, but Ismail is Sultan! Not you!" A feather-light touch swept over Jazirah's arm. Even as she recoiled, the hand groped her flesh. "Besides, this one is still an important part of Ismail's family. I would not strip away all the trappings of a royal life."

Heavy boots crisscrossed the floor. "But you would suffer her silly behavior." A brawny hand closed on Jazirah's arm without mercy. She opened her eyes and stared into the red-rimmed, unrepentant glower of the governor of Malaka. He hauled her up. She braced her palms against his hefty chest and pushed at him, even as his grip tightened until she could not bite back the scream deep in her throat.

"Would you see her bruised before the ceremony?" Maryam demanded, her hands knuckled against her hips. "Release Jazirah at once!" When Muhammad the Red swung his heavy-browed glare to her, she stepped back a pace. "You must listen to me. I want her unharmed. Now, let her go."

His blunt fingers twitched as he swept thick auburn hair back from his forehead, before he propelled Jazirah away. She landed on the velvety cushions lining the wall. Her mouth agape, she stared at him while her heart thumped in her throat. His uncontrolled movements of the head returned, as he peered between Maryam and Jazirah repeatedly. She would not give him the satisfaction of the sight of her hand soothing her arm. A mark would be evident by the next day.

He closed a hand on Maryam's wrist. "You will not give me orders again. Never forget who I am and who you are."

She tossed her shimmering, black curls, although the teeth indenting her lower lip told of the discomfort his callous touch evoked. "I am the *Umm al-Sultan*."

He sniggered. "Did you choose this title yourself? Is the *Umm al-Walad* no longer good enough for you?"

"Too oft, the slave mothers of Sultans have used it. Yusuf freed me before we wed. I refuse to accept a title, which affords me no dignity. I am a Sultana."

With a shake of his head, he released her and sauntered away. "Call yourself whatever you would like, just so long as you do not forget my role in your son's rise to power. His pampered posterior would not be so comfortable on the throne if I had not put him there. You will remember this fact."

Once he had left the room, Maryam uttered an audible sigh and wrapped thin fingers around her wrist. Then she glanced at Jazirah. "See how you have vexed him? You must be cautious! We need Muhammad the Red."

Jazirah muttered, "You need him."

"No, no, no, all of us here rely upon him, even my sons. Muhammad the Red secured the support of the other governors. Would you endanger our lives? We cannot anger him." Maryam took to the adjacent cushion. "Why must you behave as a recalcitrant child in his presence?" She scanned the room with a frown, her lips thinned. "I shall summon my slaves and have them whipped for the state of this chamber. Dust everywhere!"

"You killed my servants."

Maryam gave a dismissive wave of her hand and rose from the seat. "And look at you, wearing last night's clothes from dinner when it is nearly time for tonight's meal." She crinkled her nose. "Have you washed for the day? Likely not. You must come with me to the bath."

When Maryam held out her fingers, Jazirah whispered, "No."

Maryam cocked her head. "What did you just say to me?"

"Are you deaf now? I said no."

"You seem to believe you have choices! Why do you continue with this assumption?"

Jazirah shook her head and slumped against the pillow at her back. "Leave me be, Maryam. Your son has the throne. My son is lost to me forever. Are you so foolish, so prideful, you cannot see when you have won? All you have wished for is now yours. Just go away. Leave me here to die."

Rich laughter from Maryam floated to the inlaid ceiling. "You think death is still an option for you? I control your fate! I decide if you live or die."

She walked away and gestured behind her to her men. "Take her."

When the guards' hands closed on Jazirah, something inside her broke. After the loss of her son, the flight of her husband, and the betrayal of her father, she had no reason to live. Blood pounded in her ears. Muscles strained beneath her skin. She raged against her captors, swinging and kicking wildly. Her foot connected with one man's groin and he crumpled in agony. The death stroke might come quickly, Damascene steel laid against her neck. At least, she would see Yusuf in Paradise.

Maryam screamed, "Hold her! If she wants to make a fool of herself, then so be it. Come, it's time for her bath!"

Allah had forsaken Jazirah. No swift demise, only further misery. Six men hauled her bodily out of the room and down the stairs in Maryam's wake. Despite the screams and the fists, which bashed against their bodies, they did not relent. The guards bore Jazirah out into the afternoon sunlight, its full glare striking her in the face. She closed her eyes, but not before she noted how curious onlookers took in the sight. Slaves and guards alike lined the walls and witnessed her shame as Maryam's men bore her across the garden, along corridors and down two flights of stairs to the changing room. The bath superintendent looked up from a corner opposite the entryway, where he stood in a circle of attendants.

While the guards set Jazirah on a stone slab and forced her to remain seated, Maryam strode back and forth with her fingers pressed to her temple. Then she stopped pacing. "Well, what are you men waiting for? Strip her!"

The overseer offered, "My honored Sultana, let us...."

Maryam screeched, "Get back, you ugly toad!" She pointed at those in her command. "They will take off her clothes."

Jazirah slapped at rough hands, which ripped her robe from her shoulders. Bared to the waist, she covered her breasts as the men heaved her to her feet and dragged the tattered material down her hips. As a little blood seeped between her thighs and trickled down her leg, the guards drew back.

"It is no more than a first show of woman's blood for the month. A good sign!" Maryam snapped. "Now take her inside." When they wavered, she yelled, "Do as I say!"

Again, Jazirah endured the humiliation as she crossed the tiles. Her captors took her straight into the hot water. Attendants followed and ministered to her. The skin Muhammad the Red had clamped his hand on flushed pink at first, but in the heat became a fiery blemish.

Maryam stood at the edge of the bathing pool, her robe clinging to her. She pressed a hand to her breastbone. "We could have avoided this unpleasant evening if you had only cooperated. What did you think your fit of temper would gain you? Naught but your disgrace!"

Jazirah hunched forward as an attendant washed her back. "I pray to live long enough to see your end."

***

Bathed, dressed, and in a clean robe Jazirah plodded behind Maryam, past whitewashed houses aligned along the wall from the gate of *Bab al-Sharia*. Lights glowed in windows, but no laughter or music echoed from within. At a dip in the path, Maryam stopped before a two-storied house, the lattice unfurled over apertures. The massive gate was open. A marble walkway lined with horseshoe archways and flowerpots interspersed between them led to double doors of cedar wood. Under the lintel, Jyoti's son Dhanu stood with a lit torch in his hand.

Jazirah studied the frontage of the residence. A new coat of lime wash covered the bricks. Curtains sewn with gold thread blew inward on the light breeze.

She turned to Maryam. "This is Ibn al-Khatib's house. You said I would see my father this evening."

"My son intends to grant your father a governorship. Should he not also have a fine house here? Why not the property once held by an exiled minister?"

Would Maryam's son, for Jazirah refused to name him the Sultan in her mind or on her lips, have been so generous? After all, he must have heard how his uncle reviled Maryam for the murder of Yusuf. Was this gesture no more than a poor attempt to soothe the loss of a beloved babe with the balm of a governorship?

Jazirah lifted her chin. "Your son is almost as much a fool as you are!"

Maryam's nails closed on Jazirah's chin and dug into the flesh. "My son lives! Yours is dead because you trusted Muhammad to protect him! Who is the fool here?"

Although tears sprang to her eyes and an ache filled her throat, Jazirah managed, "I should never have let you influence me!"

Maryam released her. "I'm so sorry you feel this way since we are to be closer than ever now." She waved Jazirah through the gate. "Get inside."

Jazirah had no choice. She stepped beneath the marble arch and turned just as Maryam pulled in the iron postern. She stared at Jazirah before she said, "Do wish your father well for me. I know this has been a difficult period for him, but we must grow accustomed to the changes under my son's regime. You most of all."

"I am to live here now?"

"For a time. Until the wedding." Maryam crossed her arms underneath ample breasts. Her deep sigh of gratification filled the air.

Jazirah pressed her fingers to her belly. Her stomach roiled, but she did not believe her womanly time caused the stir. She swallowed past a sour taste in her mouth. "Whose wedding?"

"Yours, my dear. My son summoned the *ulamas* to his court and the judges have agreed. Since Muhammad the deposed is no longer Sultan, you are not a Sultana of Gharnatah. My son can change your status. There is royal blood in you, which my cohorts and I have never overlooked. Equally important, you have proven fertile and already birthed one heir. There is no reason why you cannot have another."

Even as Jazirah shook her head, a scream of denial trapped in her throat, Maryam affirmed, "You will marry my son."

***

Two Thrones
Sultan Muhammad V

Wadi-Ash, Al-Andalus or Guadix, Andalusia

Dhu al-Hijja 760 AH or November A.D. 1359 or Marcheshvan 5120

Ibn al-Khatib knelt before Muhammad in the forecourt of Wadi-Ash's citadel. Shadowed by Faraj and Al-Sabti, Muhammad leaned forward in his seat and waved to Pero, who stood aside with his sword leveled at Ibn al-Khatib's chin.

Muhammad scratched his beard. "Why are you here?"

Ibn al-Khatib bowed his head and sobbed. "Please, honored master, I have always been loyal. Do not judge me for past disagreements between us! I always meant to ensure Gharnatah's future—"

"Stop!" Muhammad held his palm up in a bid for silence. "Whose future are you securing now? Of all my high ministers left behind in Gharnatah, you are the only person still alive. Al-Sabti tells me your sister's husband personally delivered a fine ransom two days ago into my treacherous brother's hands. You could have gone home to Lawsa, yet you sought me out. Tell me why. I will know the truth from the lie upon your lips. If your answer annoys me, my captain shall cut off your head. Speak."

When Ibn al-Khatib raised his chin a notch, Pero slid the blade under his jaw and edged close to his neck. The old man swallowed and reached with shaking fingers inside the cloth satchel slung over his shoulder. He held the vellum out. The red wax seal of the Sultans of Gharnatah remained unbroken.

Muhammad swallowed at the sight and then waved his hand. "Pray, read it to us. In my council chamber, you were always most enamored of the sound of your voice."

Ibn al-Khatib read, "From the Sultan Abu'l-Walid Ismail, of the Nasrids. The prince of the faithful and the lord of Al-Andalus—"

With a rueful chuckle, Muhammad turned to Al-Sabti. "The lord of Al-Andalus, when the territory my ancestors claimed has not extended beyond the banks of the *Wadi al-Kabir* in over one hundred and twenty years?"

The supreme judge nodded. "The usurper is ambitious, my master."

Since Ibn al-Khatib had lapsed into silence during their exchange, Muhammad urged him on. "Do continue, but if you refer to the traitor as anything but Ismail while you read his words, Pero will take your head before you can finish the letter!"

"Ahem." Ibn al-Khatib cleared his throat. "Before I continue, may I have some water? I'm so parched. No food, no drink, even though I begged. Even a man's enemies may have water."

Muhammad smirked at the ragged robe and Ibn al-Khatib's unkempt, unshaven features. A thick mustache and beard could not hide the crusted blood at the corner of his lips. Dark bruises shadowed his reddened eyes.

"No, you may not have water. I have yet to determine whether you are a foe or an ally. I do not waste precious resources on fools who may be wasting my time. Read on," Muhammad demanded.

Ibn al-Khatib began again. "From... Ismail ibn Yusuf to Muhammad ibn Yusuf. I do not greet you in the name of peace, brother, for I have long known harmony could never flourish between us. I have righted the grievous wrong you did, when you claimed our father's throne in my stead. My honored mother and Muhammad the Red of Malaka tell me you are a, ahem... er, coward, and I believe it must be so, for you have fled our birthplace without your wife and child and left our father's sword in the field to rust. You have no sword and no land. My spies tell me you have taken refuge with the rebels among the *Ghuzat* at Wadi-Ash. I vow this will not continue. Within seven days, you and all your compatriots must withdraw from Al-Andalus. Leave, Muhammad, or by the eighth day, the host from Malaka, Lawsa, Madinah Antaqirah, and Al-Hamma, in the company of the *Shaykh al-Ghuzat* with his reinforcements from Runda shall be at the gates of Wadi-Ash. Withdraw and you may live. Remain and you will die, but not just you. Every man and woman in the city will share your fate. Bowstrings shall encircle the throat of every child. Go, while you still can, Muhammad, for if I must send the host to Wadi-Ash, you shall not live long enough to regret their appearance. Respect this."

Muhammad stared at the cobblestones. His forefinger dug concentric circles at his temple. Leave Al-Andalus. Wasn't exile from Gharnatah enough? How could he ever leave his home? He had hoped in vain that territories like Qumarich or Naricha, which had not yet declared for his traitor brother, might have granted him sanctuary. Either those governors were too afraid of Ismail's co-conspirators, or others appointed by Ismail had replaced the former leaders.

He glanced at Al-Sabti, who averted his gaze. Muhammad asked, "What of your letter to Abu Salim in Fés el-Jedid?"

Al-Sabti replied, "The Marinid Sultan has not sent a reply, my master. Mayhap my messenger has not even arrived yet."

Muhammad pounded his fist against the chair's wooden arm. "But he must! He must or my family will die!"

"You cannot let this occur, my Sultan," Ibn al-Khatib interjected. "If you do, the great legacy of Sultan Muhammad *al-Fakih*, of his noble daughter Sultana Fatima, and of her grandson, your blessed father Sultan Yusuf, may Allah preserve their memories forever, their proud heritage will fade with you and yours."

He was right. Muhammad could not let such a fate occur.

Ibn al-Khatib continued, "Even if you believe I am a pompous fool, great Sultan, you have never overlooked my skills as an orator. Allow me to write to the Marinid court on your behalf. Let me convince their sovereign of our urgent need. Let me serve you."

At a nod from Muhammad, Pero sheathed his sword again. Muhammad stood and beckoned his minister. "You may have your water."

As the men withdrew into the complex, Faraj at Muhammad's side, the commander paused at the edge of the courtyard. Squeals of laughter from the children echoed beyond the dividing wall.

Muhammad asked, "What is it, Faraj?"

"Something puzzles me about the damnable letter. Your traitor brother was never as bold as the author of the missive. If Ismail composed it, he spoke of Sultana Jazirah and Prince Yusuf, of your having left them both behind. Not just your wife, but your son as well."

In his shock at Ismail's demand, Muhammad had not considered the import of such words. Their significance lingered as he preceded the others into the sunlit courtyard where Butayna held Yusuf and Aisha carried Leila as they twirled the siblings around the width of the pool. A watchful Haziyya nestled beside a column.

"By the Prophet's beard!" Ibn al-Khatib's exclamation drew everyone's attention. He clutched at his chest and staggered against the masonry. "Prince Yusuf is alive!"

Muhammad demanded, "Tell me why you are surprised. Why did you and Ismail think my son was not at my side?"

Ibn al-Khatib coughed. Muhammad bellowed, "Someone, get him some water."

Haziyya clambered to her feet, despite being eight months with child, and poured a glass from the pitcher atop an adjacent table. She moved to Muhammad, who handed the water to Ibn al-Khatib. The minister drank eagerly and wiped his hand over his mouth. Butayna and Aisha drew near, open-mouthed at the sight of him.

He said, "Before I left Gharnatah, the soldiers showed me the bodies of everyone who had been killed and thrown into the ravine. I recognized Ridwan's robes and those of the chief eunuch, Hisham. There were also... children in the gorge. One was little, like Prince Yusuf, dressed in a tattered tunic with gold braid. Just like the garments I had grown accustomed to seeing the prince wear."

Clothing Lubna had sewn for the boy. Muhammad lifted a hand to his lips before he turned to Al-Sabti. "After you returned from your visit to Gharnatah, you told us Jazirah had gone to the gulley with Maryam, where my wife wept."

Butayna clutched Yusuf tighter to her chest, although the boy squirmed. "*Madre de Dios!* Jazirah believes her son is dead?"

Muhammad nodded. "Maryam must have told her so." He rounded on Ibn al-Khatib again. "Who was the child in the ravine? Why did Jazirah think he was Yusuf?"

Ibn al-Khatib looked away. "The child's body... was mangled. The head crushed." He shook his head. "But why did they gain hold of the prince's tunics? Would someone have taken the trouble to go into the summer palace and retrieve one of the garments, ripped and bloodied it to wrap an innocent child's body within?"

"They did not have to," Muhammad whispered. "Yusuf was with Lubna. He fell after an arrow pierced her back. One hit him too, straight through his foot. I tore his tunic to bind it around the injury, but I couldn't stop the bleeding with such thin material. He fainted. I grabbed a dead officer's cloak and left Yusuf's garment behind, alongside my father's sword—"

"Where Maryam's men found both," Ibn al-Khatib finished for him. "She had all the proof she needed to convince Sultana Jazirah of her son's demise. But to what end?"

No one could answer him.

***

Off the coast of Sabta, Al-Maghrib al-Aksa or Ceuta, Morocco
Dhu al-Hijja – Muharram, 760 AH or November A.D. 1359 or
Marcheshvan – Kislev 5120

As Muhammad expected, his household accepted the news from Gharnatah with resignation. Butayna immediately ordered Jawla and Hafsa to begin packing the few garments they had bought while in Wadi-Ash. The family's destination remained unclear. On the next day, Abu Salim's offer of a haven inside Al-Maghrib al-Aksa arrived via an exhausted messenger on horseback. The Marinid Sultan promised Muhammad would find others loyal to him in the one place Jazirah would not have appreciated. The captains of ships at Shalabuniya had agreed to Abu Salim's request to transport Muhammad and his entire entourage across the White Sea to Sabta, a city on the coast of Al-Maghrib al-Aksa. Muhammad rejoiced with his family and Muslim retainers in the mosque of Wadi-Ash. Then on the last day of the week, his household prepared to ride out. Although he had not needed Ibn al-Khatib's letter, he required the minister's services for the future.

Six hundred warriors of the *Ghuzat,* just under a third of the Marinid forces loyal to Ali ibn Musa accompanied Muhammad, leaving behind their compatriots who adhered to Yahya's leadership. The denizens of the city lined the streets and threw petals at the feet of horses clambering down the sloped hill from the citadel.

Muhammad led his company from Wadi-Ash south to the coast. Along the journey, he contemplated Jazirah's state of mind. If she believed Yusuf had died on Maryam's orders, there could be no reason for his wife to have cast her lot with one who had countenanced the death of a beloved son. Mayhap Jazirah remained blameless in the events of the prior month. Shame swept over Muhammad for having considered the opposite possibility. If only he could have sent word of the truth to her, but he would not risk more lives. Pharez ben Zarzar had attempted to visit Jazirah's father in the guise of his personal physician, but the guards assaulted Pharez, broke up his medicine chest, and called him a filthy Jew.

The vessels cast off from Shalabuniya in the early afternoon with the promise of reaching Sabta before nightfall. As the last galley rowed away with Muhammad, his family and closest companions aboard, he looked out on the waters lapping at the shore and vowed he would return. Then within an hour of *Salat al-Asr*, Haziyya's labor began. The old midwife had predicted the child would come in the next month of Safar, but mayhap she had miscalculated.

While Haziyya labored below deck, aided by Butayna and Ibn Khatima, who had decided to accompany the émigrés, the anxious would-be father awaited news. By the next prayer time, rain lashed the ships. As white-capped waves tossed the galleys about the slate-gray sea, Muhammad, his royal guard, and Faraj heaved the contents of their stomachs over the railing. Only Ali, Al-Sabti, and Ibn al-Khatib seemed unaffected. The captains sought refuge from the storm, along with the payment Muhammad had vowed they would receive in Fés el-Jedid. He depended on Ibn al-Khatib's wit to influence Abu Salim's generosity. The debt demanded restitution. How could he repay?

Lost in his thoughts, Aisha stunned him when she appeared at his side. Sodden robes clung to her. Precipitation had plastered her hair and veil to her head.

Muhammad grasped her shoulders. "How does Haziyya fare? Is the child here?"

Aisha shook her head. "Your favorite does her best, as does *Ummi* and Ibn Khatima."

"I'm still uncertain he can aid us, but without a midwife, we have no choice."

"There is something you must know." Aisha swallowed. "Haziyya's baby is turned the wrong way. Ibn Khatima says the head should present first, but it does not."

"What will happen to Haziyya?"

"I don't know! Ibn Khatima is going to try to turn the baby, but as you say, he is not a midwife and has never done this before."

When he stared at her, rendered mute by a temporary constriction of his throat, she kissed both of his cheeks. She did not seem to mind the stench of vomit on his waterlogged cloak. "I must look in on the children again, but I believe they are still sleeping. I shall pray for Haziyya, brother, for us all."

She descended from sight again. Muhammad lifted his head. Rainwater like the fine points of needles pricked his face. Then as quickly as the fierce gale had arisen, the wind abated. Clouds parted and revealed the murky sky. Lights on the horizon beckoned.

"Land!" The word passed among the galley crews.

The vessels closed in on docks where other ships had berthed for the night by the time Aisha returned. She was not alone. Butayna stood with her, a gray bundle balanced in her arms. Muhammad approached, his heart hammering in his chest. She pushed aside the folds of cloth around the scrunched-up, reddened face and revealed the lower half of the tiny babe's body.

"I have another son?" Muhammad gaped at her. She nodded through her tears.

He claimed the boy and lifted him high. "A second son!" The entire ship cheered him on. Pero and Faraj jostled each other to see the newborn, but Butayna squeezed between them and laid her hand on Muhammad's forearm.

She said, "Ibn Khatima has done his best for Haziyya. She wants to see you."

Muhammad took in his mother's trembling lips and sucked in a harsh breath before he expelled it again. "No!"

The noise on the deck died down. Bewildered, he looked at Aisha, who turned away with a sob. Ali emerged from the crowd and drew her within the lean-to tucked near the stern, where she cried against his shoulder. The assembly parted for Muhammad, who descended the stairs with his child nestled in his arms.

Below in the murky hold, Ibn Khatima stood beside his patient, laid out on a blanket. The lack of proper lamplight did not alter Muhammad's awareness of the blood. Its cloying, metallic odor saturated the dank air. He slumped to his knees beside Haziyya. She had never looked so pale, her eyes heavy-lidded.

At the sight of him, she whispered, "*Amanar*, I'm so sorry—"

"Hush, rest, love. We have arrived at your homeland—"

"I... love you, Muhammad ibn Yusuf." Her head lolled. "I always will. I grieved for your trials... but, but I was glad to be at your side while you... endured them."

Tears cascaded down his cheeks. He bent and pressed their child into the crook of her arm. "Haziyya, please don't leave him! He needs you. I need you!"

She breathed, "You have each other...."

A last, faltering sigh followed and then Haziyya spoke no more.

***

In the shade of a pale pink morning, Muhammad dug the burial place along the sandy coast of Sabta. He refused any help, even from his guardsmen. They stood as silent sentinels while he hefted Haziyya's body, wrapped in white linen procured from a kindly draper in the city. Only then did Muhammad accept aid as he handed Haziyya down into the grave where Faraj and Ali received her body and laid it out. Muhammad's men assisted their climb, but he alone covered the site. Butayna held his newborn son and wept, while Aisha balanced Yusuf and Leila on her hips.

With the sand heaped again, Muhammad whispered, "I knew you as Haziyya al-Riyad, but you came from the mountains of Al-Arif in this land with another name. Now I have returned you to the shores of your ancestors. In their mighty company, may you watch over Al-Maghrib al-Aksa forever."

He closed a tight fist around her blue beaded necklace with its four-pointed silver pendant. Then he draped it around his neck. The ornament hung above his heart. He went to his mother. A light kiss on the baby's head did not stir him.

Butayna sniffled. "What will you call him?"

Muhammad answered, "Saad. His name is Saad ibn Muhammad."

"But the name means felicity or good fortune in Arabic."

He rested his forehead against his mother's brow. "Mayhap with our arrival here, we have left the worst behind us. Prosperity shall reign from now on."

***

Fés el-Jedid, Al-Maghrib al-Aksa or Fez, Morocco
Muharram 761 AH or December A.D. 1359 or Kislev 5120

Ten days passed with Muhammad still ensconced at Sabta in cramped quarters. Ibn al-Khatib had gone south to the capital at Fés el-Jedid the day after their arrival, with a promise he would secure a swift welcome. When his letter came, offering final fulfillment of his vow, Muhammad's doleful mood dissipated. He packed up his family and they traveled by camel caravan. After the first day's soreness, of which all complained, Muhammad learned to sway with the movement of his mount across long stretches of arid desert. Tuareg guides spoke to him of the benefits jujube and tamarisk trees offered lost travelers. The yips of foxes echoed at night. Muhammad recalled how his great-grandmother Fatima once spoke of her husband Faraj's sojourn in old Fés and his disgust with the camel meat.

To the northeast, the broad Wadi Fés separated the city from its jumbled predecessor. Sunlight glistened on the water in early afternoon. The caravan, now bedecked in leather canopies painted turquoise and gold, passed through a city gate. Bright blue swirls at the top of the postern contrasted with the sand-colored columns and arches. People thronged alongside the roads for a glimpse of Muhammad and his entourage. The *Ghuzat* marched before him, their gold and green banners billowing on the breeze. If Muhammad's great-grandfather Faraj had found Fés el-Bali chaotic, Fés el-Jedid followed an orderly plan. A riot of color led the travelers to their destination. Sweet-scented jasmine, red rose petals, and blue flowers the guides named jacaranda littered the palatine route. Cedar trees shaded the road.

The *Ghuzat* headed for their barracks after entering the gate, but Faraj remained with the stated intention of speaking to his master about Yahya's betrayal of Muhammad. In the shade of the palace's austere walls, Muhammad sighted Ibn al-Khatib next to a man so slender, a slight desert wind might have blown him away. On stout wooden poles, the red and gold flag of the Marinids fluttered above their heads. Camel boys lowered their animals with slow and steady hands, but Muhammad still gripped the forked horn of the saddle. On the first day of the journey, Faraj had provided the lesson of how quickly anyone could tumble forward on the dismount. As Muhammad removed his foot from the stirrup, his dromedary snorted foam. Avoiding a spray of white lather all over his silk garments, Muhammad found himself surrounded by little slave girls with silver collars and damask roses tucked in their hair. They offered warm bowls of rosewater, glasses of almond milk flavored with orange rind, and dates.

Muhammad headed for his minister who bowed and introduced his bronze-skinned, blue-robed companion. "My Sultan, I present the honorable vizier Umar ibn Abdallah."

Up close, Umar reminded Muhammad of a weasel perched on its back legs. Thin, sharp features beneath shorn hair, coupled with large ears, gave him a distinct look. With little fanfare, he escorted Muhammad and his entourage through winding corridors into a large, columned hall. Guests lined the northern and southern walls. Identical thrones, one empty, occupied opposite sides of the room. Sultan Abu Salim Ibrahim ibn Abu'l-Hasan Ali of the Marinids smiled at his guests.

Chapter 19
The Marriage Bargain

Sultan Muhammad V

Fés el-Jedid, Al-Maghrib al-Aksa or Fez, Morocco
Muharram 761 AH or December A.D. 1359 or Kislev 5120

Abu Salim presented a fuller face than Muhammad recalled from his boyhood. The puffed-up cheeks of the Marinid ruler glowed above a thick beard with a few sprigs of gray. The rounded belly jutting from beneath a golden robe suggested a rich diet. Muhammad took these signs as confirmation of his host's prosperity.

From his gilded seat, Abu Salim leaned forward and waved to the identical throne at the opposite end of the reception hall. With a slight nod, Muhammad took the offer and crossed a honeycomb of vivid tiles in blue, green, and yellow pigments. Abu Salim sat in the midst of a full assembly, which included women who wore light veils over their hair and displayed their faces. Naked curiosity lit their bright gazes as Butayna and Aisha took positions next to Muhammad while he relaxed against a silk cushion sewn to the throne. His guards, along with Faraj, Al-Sabti, and Ali gathered on his left side. The fine attire of Muhammad and his companions matched the styles of the Marinid courtiers, thanks to clever bartering by Faraj at Sabta. Jawla and Hafsa knelt at Butayna's feet and drew more interest than any other arrival, likely for their russet-colored hair. Each servant held one of Haziyya and Muhammad's children, but Muhammad's commander Faraj handed Yusuf to Aisha.

At a signal from the Marinid Sultan, the court herald thumped a silver-capped rod against the ground. The droning buzz of conversations among at least one hundred spectators faded away in the cavernous room, lit by windows of multicolored glass. When Abu Salim clapped his hands, a baldpated man approached the center of the four-columned chamber. He bowed three times before his sovereign and once to Muhammad, each of whom acknowledged him with a nod.

Faraj whispered in Muhammad's ear. "This is the grand vizier Ibn Marzuq. He is well-liked among the Marinids, but also has his enemies within the ministerial body."

Muhammad nodded. He studied Umar, whose visage had darkened at the sight of Ibn Marzuq. The Marinid court did not differ from its Nasrid counterpart, with rivalries between powerful families. A conflict existed between these two ministers, yet Ibn al-Khatib had aligned himself upon arrival with the lesser man. Muhammad gave his councilor a sidelong glance and resolved to speak with Ibn al-Khatib later, then turned his attention to Ibn Marzuq's speech.

"In the name of Allah, the Compassionate, the Merciful, the *Amir al-Muminin*, commander of the believers, Abu Salim Ibrahim ibn Abu'l-Hasan Ali welcomes his guest Abu Abdallah Muhammad ibn Yusuf to Fés el-Jedid." He bowed again in acknowledgement of his leader. "Great master, your splendid generosity is beyond compare. Like a loving father who has bestowed gifts upon your children, so have you cared for the people of Al-Maghrib al-Aksa. Who has not seen the truth of your benevolence or witnessed your acts of compassion? The proof lies within the city's walls, its *madrasas* established for the education of all citizens and its hospitals, which benefit rich and poor alike."

He turned and waved to Muhammad. "Now comes this supplicant before you, this rightful Sultan of Gharnatah, overwhelmed by deceit in his own land. He entered this court with all due humbleness. You, mighty lord, have welcomed him. You have granted him audience here among this fine assembly. You gave him food and drink in traditions long derived from our ancestors in the desert. Praise be to God for your hospitality to your guest. May he and all those whom he cherishes know the blessing of your charity." He pressed a deep-veined hand to his heart and bowed to Muhammad. "May Allah bless our guest and his household and grant them peace."

As applause filled the room, Muhammad displayed appreciation with polite nods, although he seethed inside. While Ibn Marzuq withdrew and stood beside his master, Muhammad considered the terms the Marinid minister had chosen. Supplicant! Humility! Yet, none could deny the dishonorable events, which had led Muhammad to appear at the court of his ally as little more than a beggar king.

With a nod from him, Ibn al-Khatib came to the center of the room. He bowed and said, "In the name of Allah, the Compassionate, the Merciful, the *Amir al-Muslimin*, the prince of the faithful, Abu Abdallah Muhammad ibn Yusuf honors and affirms his friendship with his generous host Sultan Abu Salim Ibrahim ibn Abu'l-Hasan Ali. My worthy counterpart has stated the truth. Treachery drove my great master from his throne in Gharnatah and out of the land of Al-Andalus."

Murmurs filled the court, especially from among the women who exchanged dismayed whispers. Ibn al-Khatib raised his hands. The herald thumped his stick on the tiles until the room's occupants quieted again.

Ibn al-Khatib continued, "My noble lord appealed to the grand commander of the believers and relied upon his largesse. Tales of Sultan Abu Salim's bounty have reached us even in the mountains of Al-Andalus. While there may be variances between our courts, common beliefs unite us."

After a brief pause, he turned to Abu Salim. "It is our faith and reliance upon the tenets of Islam, which binds us. The five principles guide us in our duties before God and other men, with charitable acts chief among our responsibilities. Bound by faith, we are the righteous believers. We perform good works under the watchful gaze of Allah, the Compassionate, the Merciful, who sees all. Who may stand against those united by faith?"

Mirrored smiles on their faces, both rulers rose at the same time and applauded Ibn al-Khatib. All the onlookers joined in. The Marinids valued honor above all else and the outward symbols of a man's decency included his generosity, but Ibn al-Khatib reminded the court of the foundation of charity, in the precepts of Islam. If Ibn Marzuq had meant to bolster his master's reputation by degrading Muhammad, Ibn al-Khatib had succeeded in reminding the observers about the humility and sacrifice required of all Muslims, even Sultans. Umar did not attempt to hide his sneer as he offered an oblique glance to Ibn Marzuq. For his part, the chief minister stared straight ahead and clapped his hands along with others.

Servants dispersed through the room with bowls of warm rosewater and food on tiny, ceramic dishes. Muhammad relied upon Faraj to identify unfamiliar dishes. Among Muhammad's family, each person chose a clear favorite. His mother liked the couscous drizzled in peppery argan oil best. His sister preferred Faraj's favorite, a *kufta* of minced lamb rolled into lemon-sized balls and served with a zesty saffron sauce. Muhammad chose the skewers of roasted lamb, which left the taste of garlic and lemon juice on the tongue. None of the courtiers appeared perturbed by having to eat with their hands at such a large assembly, as long as the slaves with rosewater remained nearby.

When Ibn al-Khatib drew near, Muhammad asked, "When may I meet in private with my kind host?"

"On the morrow, two hours before *Salat al-Zuhr*. It is Abu Salim's custom when the noonday prayer is finished to hear petitions from the public, starting with the complaints of women. Then after the prayers of *Salat al-Asr* in the afternoon, he attends to the men."

"You have ingratiated yourself with this minister, Umar ibn Abdallah, yet also neglect the grand vizier Ibn Marzuq. Why?"

Ibn al-Khatib bent with his head close to Muhammad. "Great Sultan, when I look to the future of this country, I foresee it is wiser to be Umar's friend than his enemy. These people are sycophants, whom the Marinids have placed here. Even those who acclaimed you in the streets are from elsewhere. The people of Fés el-Jedid have never favored Marinid rule. Why do you think Ali ibn Musa returned with you, if not to ferret out discontent among the populace and test their amenability to the interests of his clan? Why should the people honor Abu Salim with their full trust, when almost everyone he has appointed was born outside of this city? The grand vizier Ibn Marzuq hails from the city of Tilimsan. He spent some years in Gharnatah during your father's reign after Sultan Abu Inan exiled him, returning in the year before Sultan Yusuf's death. The public treasurer is from Chella, and the chief of police, and Abu Salim's chamberlain were born at Sabta. None of these men can match Umar's ambition or vie with his heritage. His family hails from Fés el-Jedid."

Muhammad would have argued for temperance in relations with Umar. Instead, he clamped his jaws shut as a woman attired in silvery-blue silk approached him with two guards at her back. Before she spoke, Muhammad noted her ice-blue eyes between the slits of the double veil she wore. She dipped into a deep curtsey and held the pose. He gave permission for her to rise.

She began, "The peace of God be with you, most gracious and blessed sovereign of Gharnatah. Forgive the intrusion of one who is so insignificant within this court—"

The lilt of her voice made Muhammad look at his mother's servants, for their dulcet tones matched this woman's own. The cup of savory mint in Butayna's hand almost slipped from her grasp. A few droplets of tea sprinkled the floor. Immediately, a eunuch rushed into their midst and cleaned up the liquid.

Butayna handed the vessel to Jawla and moved toward the stranger. "Shams ed-Duna? Is it really you? It's been nearly nineteen years."

"Sultana Butayna honors me with her remembrance." Shams ed-Duna lifted a slim, pale hand decorated with henna dots. She removed her face veil to reveal fine-boned features, coupled with a thin nose, pallid cheeks, and a pointed chin. While she remained beautiful, there were delicate, crinkled lines at the corners of her eyes and creases around her lush mouth.

With a shake of her head, Butayna whispered, "I never thought I would see you again. We separated after the Christian marauders attacked the joint Marinid and Gharnati encampment near the waters of the Salado. I thought you were dead." Her eyes watered. "But you're not. You survived the battle."

The two women embraced as friends of old while Muhammad pondered the extent of their closeness. What might it mean for their sojourn in Al-Maghrib al-Aksa if his mother had an acquaintance among the Marinid courtiers? Their reunion drew stark stares. Even Abu Salim lifted his gaze from a bowl of dates and observed the interaction. When Butayna and Shams ed-Duna drew apart, tears glistened on both of their cheeks.

Butayna patted her friend's arm. "We have much to discuss."

Shams ed-Duna clutched her fingers. "Not here, I pray. Too many watchful eyes and listening ears." She pitched her voice lower. "Abu Salim intends for all of you to reside within the palace grounds in a *riad*, a house with a garden courtyard of your own. He has charged me with the escort of the women of your household there. We may talk upon our arrival."

Butayna smiled. "I hope it will be the first of many opportunities."

"There is also a Christian priest at the palace whom I have relied upon in my darkest hours. He is available to hear your confession."

"Thank you. I and others among my Sultan's guards would be glad to meet him."

***

Beneath an evening sky bathed in red, Muhammad walked with his mother, who clung to his right arm while his sister leaned on his left. The trio meandered through an avenue of aromatic bay laurels, returning to the large estate Abu Salim had assigned to them. A mild temperature had descended. At the midpoint from the house, Aisha paused and tugged one of the bay leaves before she sniffed the greenery.

She said, "Faraj told me the leaf makes a wonderful tea."

Butayna replied, "I shall have Hafsa brew us some cups later. Mayhap by the time of our return, she and Jawla will have prepared the children for bed. Faraj said this month begins the olive-picking season. It is also a period of festivals lasting long into the night."

Muhammad took in the scenery. "The evenings are so long here. Not like home."

Butayna squeezed his forearm. "No other place could be Al-Andalus. We have come from afar, but I do not believe the journey was a mistake."

He said, "We had little choice." They resumed the stroll to the house. "*Ummi,* what did Shams ed-Duna say when you both left the reception hall before me?"

"Abu Salim is genuine in his favor and grace. There are others, including the chief minister Umar whom Ibn al-Khatib favors, who hold unknown motives for having counseled the offer of asylum for us. Shams ed-Duna was the favorite of two Sultans

255

before Abu Salim. He would not shame himself by claiming her as well, but he admires the Englishwoman greatly as his relations did. She shares in his secrets."

"I understand how a favored concubine can hold a man in her spell."

Aisha rose on tiptoe and kissed his cheek. "Dear brother. You will always love Haziyya, but Allah ordained her time."

"Life does not always grant us our heart's desire. I should have married her years ago, rather than permitting the customs of the harem to dictate our futures."

He halted this time and looked squarely at Aisha. "I wish to speak of the future with you, dear sister."

She swallowed and nodded.

He continued, "The debt I have incurred on our behalf is enormous. I have considered all methods and possibilities of recompense throughout the day and have arrived at a conclusion. I have no means to repay Abu Salim, except one."

Aisha said, "A royal marriage, an alliance between our kingdoms."

He leaned forward and nuzzled her brow, which she permitted. He whispered, "I know this is not what you would wish. Your love for Ali is as clear as sunrise over the desert dunes. I do not doubt he will long for you until the end of his days. I take no pleasure in denying either of you a most fervent wish."

She drew back and gave him a sad, little smile. "The Marinid Sultan seems kind as his chief minister affirmed. I do not doubt Abu Salim would be a worthy husband."

Muhammad shook his head. "According to Ibn al-Khatib, Abu Salim has the four requisite wives to whom he remains devoted. There are those among his brothers who might make a suitable spouse. I shall learn of each one and choose the best candidate to ensure your happiness."

"Only Ali could have granted me such. I do not doubt you will provide a suitable husband." She twirled the thin bay leaf stem between her thumb and forefinger. "Permit me one boon. Before you make the announcement of such a union, allow me to tell Ali first. I would not want him to learn the truth as the Marinid courtiers will. I love you not only as my brother, but also as lord of my life. I would never disgrace you or attempt to thwart your plans. Ali deserves to hear of them from me."

He draped his arm around her shoulders and drew her into a tight embrace. "I believe you are right. You may speak with Ali alone, but know my intent will be the same. Duty is a burden no Sultan can evade."

"Nor a Sultana," she whispered, her words muffled against his silken tunic. He rested his brow against hers for a final time before he released her. She turned on her heels and strode to the whitewashed residence.

He breathed a ragged sigh and bowed his head.

Butayna said, "Let your sister be. She must reconcile herself to this fate. Come. Time for truth-telling between us."

She drew him to the stone steps of the house and they sat together. There she released his hand. "When we were at the House of Myrtles, I overheard your questions to Juan Manuel before the doctors ben Zarzar arrived. You wanted to know of the connection I shared with Juan Manuel. It is a kinship bond, which stretches to the time of the Jews in Toledo."

Although the word 'kinship' sent Muhammad's mind reeling, he listened in silence.

"The Ben Esra family of Toledo supported the king of Castilla-León because of his love for their beauteous Rahel, a bond ravaged in a day of carnage by jealous Christian courtiers. They almost annihilated her family. Only two young boys, her nephews Simeon and Naphtali, survived the massacre. Simeon took the family name of Peralta and became my great-great grandfather. Naphtali claimed the name Gomero and became Juan Manuel's great-grandfather. My Jewish roots are even closer. My own mother was Jewish. She converted to wed my father, a prominent physician in the court of Castilla-León. Through me, you and Aisha have a Jewish grandmother and a Jewish heritage stretching back to centuries ago."

Her words evoked a memory in Muhammad. The arrival of Jazirah and her father, the praise Al-Shaquri had offered Pharez ben Zarzar, only for Muhammad to dismiss the doctor as a Jew. His mother had bristled at his derisive tone. At last, he understood her reaction.

"Now, you know everything, my lion. No secrets remain between us. Speak to me. What do you think and feel?"

He sputtered, "How can I ever compose sensible words to convey thoughts and feelings? My Christian mother has Jewish blood through her mother. By Jewish laws, you are a Jew even if you began life as a Christian. My father taught me the Muslim faith, but the same Jewish law applies to me. Who am I, *Ummi?*"

"Tell me, is the Muhammad who ruled Gharnatah as the son of Christian and Muslim parents any different from the Muhammad who knows his full heritage?"

When he could not answer, she captured his face between her fingers. "You are my son, but you also represent the best of the three sister faiths of Christianity, Judaism, and Islam. After you have regained the Sultanate, and you will, you must ensure the fair treatment of all within your realm regardless of their faiths."

He said, "Juan Manuel made me promise I would provide safe haven for the Jews in Gharnatah after I reclaimed my throne."

"Will you do this because of what I have told you of your legacy?"

"No. I will do so because it is right."

***

Sultana Jazirah

Gharnatah, Al-Andalus or Granada, Andalusia
Muharram 761 AH or December A.D. 1359 or Kislev 5120

During late evening, Jazirah opened her eyes to the sight of Maryam beside the bed, with the dwarf Nazhun at her side and three young black women wearing slave collars, one whom Jazirah believed she might have seen before. Maryam's grimace deepened the age lines already dug into her forehead.

"Do you intend to stay abed all this while when you are to wed the Sultan? I have ordered the public bath near the mosque closed on your behalf. There has been feasting all week and now you must be married on the seventh evening." When Jazirah did not move, Maryam muttered. "The least you may do is show gratitude for the arrangements I have made. Do I have to call my guards to remove you?"

"No. You may remove yourself. You are standing so close to the bed frame, your knees press against it and I cannot throw back the coverlet."

Maryam's dark gaze narrowed, but she and Nazhun stepped away so Jazirah could rise. Maryam and her slave led the way from the room in haste and grudgingly allowed Jazirah scant opportunity to tie the strings of a mantle around her neck and shove her feet into fur-lined, leather boots. The black slave women followed her out of the chamber. Maryam greeted them at the bottom of the second landing with an exasperated huff.

"Can't you do anything right these days, Jazirah? You will need a hooded mantle and gloves. It is freezing. I will not have your coughs and sneezes tonight during the wedding ceremony." She grabbed Jazirah's hands, inspecting them. "And the henna is smudged across your palm. How is it possible?"

With a wearied sigh, she turned to Nazhun. "Await her and come to the bathhouse when she has the proper attire. I shall ensure all is in readiness and meet you there. You know there will be consequences if there is any delay, Nazhun."

The rounded face of the slave blanched before she bowed her head. "I won't make you wait, my Sultana."

"Good." With a curt nod to the attendants behind Jazirah, Maryam led the trio down the next flight.

Nazhun waved Jazirah to the second floor. "Please, my Sultana! You must hurry. Sultana Maryam will be vexed if we are late."

"You are terrified of her," Jazirah observed.

The dwarf looked away. "You should be scared, too. If she thinks you have disobeyed her, she can have her men beat you about the soles of your feet with a stick, so the bruises will not show. She is powerful."

Jazirah shook her head. "Power can be little more than a sorcerer's illusion. Maryam and her foolish son possess no authority, except in their minds. Muhammad the Red controls Gharnatah now."

"Please, don't make her angry with me! She may not hurt you, but...."

Nazhun's plight weighed upon Jazirah, until in a huff she retreated up the stairs and retrieved one of her hooded mantles and her gloves. She rejoined the slave, who breathed a palpable sigh of relief.

As they went down the stairs, Jazirah asked, "Why are you beholden to Maryam? She told me a tale once of how you had saved her from being poisoned by Butayna, which must be a lie, as all else Maryam said."

Nazhun peeked around her while they emerged in the central chamber with cushions stacked along the walls. "It is true. Butayna poisoned Sultan Yusuf's mother and would have poisoned Sultana—"

Jazirah snagged Nazhun's red cape. The slave squealed and attempted to whirl away, but Jazirah's grip tightened. She fell to her knees before the dwarf. "Stop fighting against me and lying for her. I want to know the truth! Only you can tell me."

Nazhun's façade crumbled and her expression contorted before she hid her face behind her hands. "You know the truth, my Sultana! You know Sultana Maryam!"

"I do, but I want to hear you say the words. In fact, just one is required. Tell me, did Maryam order the murder of my uncle Yusuf's mother and arrange matters so Sultana Butayna would appear guilty?"

"Yes!" Nazhun cried. She huddled on the ground and sobbed, while Jazirah released the cape and rose to stand over the miserable woman. Poor Nazhun. She had carried this burden for so long. Jazirah did not doubt Maryam must have manipulated the slave into helping her kill Sultan Yusuf's mother. After all, Maryam had confided Nazhun's former role in service to the murdered queen.

"Arise and wipe your tears. You know Maryam. She has no sympathy."

It took several breaths before Nazhun sat up. Jazirah hauled her to her feet. "Come, we must reach the bathhouse."

As they went, Nazhun said, "My people are Christians from a land called Eire. We believe in hellfire. I am damned in the hereafter for all I have done in this life."

Jazirah replied, "If God, whom Christians, Jews, and Muslims worship, is just and merciful, mayhap He will see your suffering now and grant you peace in Paradise."

They arrived at the redbrick frontage of the *hammam*, where Maryam waited. With an impatient wave, she ushered Jazirah inside. Then she snapped, "We must go, Nazhun! Why is your face so red?"

The slave waddled behind her with her head bowed and hands clasped behind her back. "I do not know, my Sultana."

"Well, there must be a reason...." Maryam's voice faded as she rounded the corner with her long-suffering servant in tow.

Within the bath's rooms, the three black slaves tended Jazirah in silence, coating her face in almond paste before escorting her into the pool of warm water, where one of the women disrobed and joined Jazirah. With a mixture of cucumber juice, honey, and rosewater, the slave washed away the almond scrub applied to Jazirah's cheeks and brow. As the fragrant liquid sluiced over her face, Jazirah began to weep. Even a glimpse of Thalj would have cheered her, but the cat and her offspring seemed to have disappeared. Most of all, Jazirah missed Muhammad, her son, and Butayna.

She had done grievous wrongs to Muhammad's mother, valuing Maryam's words over the truths Butayna had spoken. How could Jazirah ever beg Butayna's forgiveness, without the knowledge of where Muhammad and his mother resided or even if they lived?

"Oh, my Sultana, do not cry! All *Al-Qal'at al-Hamra* knows you wed the false ruler Ismail by force. He might be a prince of the Nasrids, but he could never compare to our noble master, Sultan Muhammad."

At the voice in her ear, Jazirah lifted her head and turned to regard the slave. "Are you loyal to Muhammad?"

"We were the personal attendants of our noble master until Muhammad the Red and Sultana Maryam conspired to steal the throne for Ismail. I am Bahar and these others are my companions Qamar and Suna."

"I did not believe any of Muhammad's close retainers survived the purge. How have you done so?" Jazirah surveyed the women's faces, while they giggled.

Bahar said, "For Sultana Maryam, one Nubian looks no different from another. After we knew of the revolt against our master, we asked the bath superintendent to help and he assigned us to his staff, where we have served for the last four months."

Jazirah pleaded, "Tell me, do you know anything of my husband? Where is he?"

Bahar shook her head, as did her fellow bondswomen. "We have not received word of the Sultan's whereabouts after he departed *Al-Qal'at al-Hamra*. We know he is alive. In the aftermath, our former master, Juan Manuel Gomero at the House of Myrtles sent word to everyone among the slaves who serve him here."

As Jazirah scraped her back against the tiled wall with a wince, water sloshed over the edge of the tub.

Jazirah gripped Bahar's fingers. "Please, tell me true. Did I hear you speak of Juan Manuel Gomero? You are one of the slaves he assigned to help Muhammad's family?"

Behind her, Qamar placed a light hand on her shoulder. "We all are."

"Then you must help me leave! I cannot wed Ismail." Her words became a litany. "I cannot! I cannot!"

Qamar rubbed her shoulders. "You must. When there is a better opportunity, we shall help you escape, but the plans must be flawless. You are a Sultana of Gharnatah. You can do all things."

***

Slaves escorted Jazirah to Maryam's quarters where others arrayed the reluctant bride in red and silver silk. Rubies adorned her hair, her throat and wrists, and her earlobes, which Maryam had ordered pierced a month ago against Jazirah's protests. A silver veil went over her head and shiny, red boots of the finest Córdovan leather covered her feet. Maryam affixed a flowing mantle in alternating bands of black and silver around her shoulders. Then Maryam reached for the *khamsa* and ruby worn on Jazirah's necklaces.

Jazirah warned, "Touch my jewels or even attempt to remove them, and I swear you shall die before this evening's end."

Maryam lowered her hands and cast a glare around the room. None of her attendants would meet her gaze. She eyed Jazirah again and snapped, "Impudent wretch! Why my son should desire you for a wife, I shall never understand. Turn. Let me have a full look at you."

Jazirah did turn, only a slight movement of her head to see her betrayer better. "I am not your plaything, to twist and fashion as one would a child's doll."

Maryam struck her hard across the face, yet Jazirah did not reel. Although a warm trickle ran from her nose and her eyes stung, she stayed upright. The slaves around her veered away, their gazes fastened to the carpeted floor.

"I have had enough of your bad temper today, Jazirah! You are still alive because Muhammad the Red demanded it! If I had my way, you would have joined your spoiled son in the ravine! You think you are better than me but cut us both and your royal blood would be the same color as mine!" Maryam paced the floor and wrung her hands. "Now, what am I to do with you? If there's a mark on your face, if my Ismail questions it in the presence of Muhammad the Red...." She halted and raised her forefinger. "None of you will speak of this! Leave! Do you hear me? Get out now!"

As the women scrambled for the doorway, Jazirah wiped a bloodied smear with two fingers. Maryam grabbed an embroidered handkerchief. "Let me do it."

Jazirah warded her off with a shove. "No! Don't touch me with your filthy hands, stained with the blood of innocents! You killed my son, just as surely as if you had been atop the horse to trample him."

She snatched the cloth and blotted her flesh.

Maryam demanded, "Will you tell my son of my... lapse?"

Jazirah cocked her head. "Don't you mean will I inform Muhammad the Red of your abuse? Why should he care? Shall I next expect him to defend me against you? Of course not, nor do I need his help." She offered Maryam her full regard. "Your son is no more than a pawn. His master counseled this marriage to bind a pretender—"

"Ismail has no master. He is the rightful ruler!"

Jazirah continued as if no interruption had occurred. "To Muhammad's queen and legitimize a false claim. No matter how you may compel me, I shall never be your son's wife for true. I'll remain the wife of Muhammad until death."

"I can arrange your demise soon if you would like."

"Do you believe your intimidations concern me? You have taken from me all whom I have ever cared about and I will have my vengeance! When you breathe your last, I shall stand beside your body and rejoice at your ending."

Maryam closed in on her, their faces a hand span apart. "If I die, I promise to take you with me. You will not escape fate!"

"Neither will you," Jazirah vowed.

***

The wedding ceremony between Jazirah and Ismail occurred in the heart of the harem's courtyard. Seated beside her in red, black, and gold brocaded clothing, Ismail's fingers shook as they closed around Jazirah's hand. Four red and gold bolts of transparent cloth tied to poles cordoned off the space. Torchlight revealed the gold threads in the silk. Before the *imam* of Gharnatah, with Muhammad the Red, Jazirah's father, and Ismail's younger brother Qays for witnesses, her father pledged her consent to the marriage. The *imam*'s upraised stare flicked to Jazirah, but she kept her lips clamped together, always aware of

Muhammad the Red's presence just at her back. He carried his sword, and while she did not know whether he would have used the weapon against her if she had refused the union, the possibility of her father's death remained.

She blamed herself for a fool's love of a traitor. She should not have cared if her father lived or died. He had not concerned himself with the consequences of the coup for her or his grandson. Had four months passed without him?

As the *imam* blessed their united hands and recited verses from Al-*Qur'an* over their heads, she noted how Ismail peered at her. His fingers shook. Likely, he believed this wedding would fulfill those lustful imaginings oft reflected in his lingering looks. At the conclusion, Jazirah pulled away from him.

Maryam pushed the edge of the curtain aside and held out her hand. Jazirah refused the touch and rose of her own accord. Her father mumbled something, which she ignored. Twin tents of gold at the boundaries of the eastern and western pavilions encircled sections of the garden. The silk canvases served as separate reception areas for the male and female guests. Jazirah sat on a large cushion in the center. She recognized none among the bright faces of women who wished her felicitations, offered marital advice, and presented their gifts.

The *khamsa* and the ruby were cold between Jazirah's breasts. She had kept the vow made on her bridal night to Muhammad. She would wear the jewels forever, reminders of her heritage and all she might have had with her rightful husband.

Raucous laughter came from the opposite tent before a eunuch appeared and bowed several times beside Maryam. She made an impatient wave. He knelt and spoke with her. She looked up, her stare flitting to Jazirah. Maryam's eyes widened, before she stood and clasped her fingers. "It would seem my son is eager for the bedding!"

The guests shared nervous laughs.

Maryam added, "Although it is not the usual occurrence for a bride to go to her husband's bed before she has received his marital gifts, I suppose they are less important than the getting of heirs."

Jazirah did not doubt the order came from Muhammad the Red. He had dictated every course leading to this night.

Maryam cleared her throat, licked her lips, and commanded, "You shall come with me, Jazirah, to the Sultan's chamber."

Maryam and her cohorts intended to sully the bed of the rightful ruler with the mimicry of a night of passion between Ismail and Jazirah, but she would not permit his hands upon her.

Maryam blinked rapidly and her gaze darted around the tent. She bit her lower lip before a little giggle escaped her. "Come now, Jazirah! It is not as if you are a virgin...."

She broke off the line of speech before veering too close to the truth. A silent battle of wills ensued. Then Maryam said, "Do not keep my son waiting! What would your father say if he knew of your reticence?"

The implicit threat of Muhammad the Red gaining an awareness of the tension in the women's tent would not bode well for Jazirah's father. She held fast to the promise of aid from Muhammad's former attendants as she rose. She trod the marble walkway without truly seeing it, her focus inward while she imagined a means of escape.

Distracted, she let Maryam's slaves surround her and remove her garments, except for the *qamis* worn against her skin. The women withdrew, Maryam the last among them. Alone, Jazirah strolled through the rooms and admired Muhammad's collection of books still along the walls. Little else remained of his personal trappings. She fingered the sword hung on a bracket in the dining area. Ripples of steel shimmered along the blade's length. She had seen the weapon on the night where she and Muhammad first dined together.

"Do you contemplate murder?"

She whirled at the sound of Ismail's voice and found him leaning against the archway shared with the bedchamber. Clad in a tunic like hers, his long hair flowed to his waist. Such an effeminate fashion for a man. At least, he had not braided the length of his black locks with silk ribbons. She sneered and turned from him again.

"Jazirah, you must talk with me at some point. This silence cannot continue."

She folded her arms beneath her breasts. "Do you wish to speak of the murder of my little son at eighteen months' old? Your theft of your brother's throne? The deaths of guiltless people whose only crime was service to Muhammad? This farce of a marriage between us? How Muhammad the Red views you as little more than a pawn on his chessboard, which he may move when needed? I shall have no more of lies! Tell truths to me or do not speak at all."

"I did not order any of the acts you have—"

She rounded on him. "Then you are a fool who lets others use you for their purpose! Muhammad was many things, but never a fool. I will not accept you as husband or my Sultan."

Lisa J. Yarde

Chapter 20
The Judges

Sultan Muhammad V

Fés el-Jedid, Al-Maghrib al-Aksa or Fez, Morocco
Rabi al-Awwal 761 AH or February A.D. 1360 or Shevat 5120

Three days of festivities preceded the marriage of Muhammad's sister to Prince Abd al-Aziz, younger half-brother to Sultan Abu Salim. Both monarchs had agreed upon the choice and Muhammad gained Aisha's assent. Undoubtedly, she lamented the decision, but did so in the privacy of her room. In her outward appearance, she offered little except smiles at the feasts arranged in honor of the wedding. Her union reflected the desert-dwelling traditions of the Marinids' ancestors. Since the fathers of both bride and groom were deceased, Muhammad and Abu Salim served in respective roles.

Abu Salim arrived at the *riad* on the first morning of revels to submit the formal proposal and marital contract to Muhammad. Ensconced for several hours in a second-floor antechamber until the evening, he and Abu Salim argued the terms of the contract, with Muhammad looking to secure several concessions from Abd al-Aziz, including the right for Aisha to sue for unilateral divorce if he abused her, as well as the preservation of her dower in the event of separation.

By the second day, Abu Salim and Muhammad had agreed on the terms, including the promises the latter desired. He even won a third compromise securing Aisha's rights to raise her future children without interference or supervision from the court, if the prince should die while their heirs were young. By Maghribi law, the father held power over the family and without him, control of the children reverted to his relatives.

From Abu Salim on Abd al-Aziz's behalf, Muhammad received and presented Aisha with a trousseau of gold coins in strongboxes totaling twelve thousand *dinars*, gemstone jewelry set in silver and gold, rugs, and a new copy of *Al-Qur'an* with gold lettering. Her personal property for life would be on display during the marital feast. Muhammad delivered to Abd al-Aziz bolts of silks and woolen textiles, copper utensils and bowls, blankets, and bedding, and via Juan Manuel's connections to Jewish bankers throughout the city, completed his sister's dower with an offer of a hundred thousand *dinars*. He would have large obligations to fulfill in the future, already indebted to the Jews for sums, which had bought slaves and fixtures for the *riad.*

At Abu Salim's insistence, Muhammad also pledged the city of Runda as part the dowry for when he acquired rule over Al-Andalus again. Dowers rarely contained bequests of property, but the requirement hinted at the Marinid Sultan's plans. If the *Ghuzat* remained in Al-Andalus for the future, Abd al-Aziz would become their leader and have his base at Runda. Abu Salim either trusted his brother or wanted him away from the court. Muhammad tasked Ibn al-Khatib with discovery of the truth.

The third day arrived and hastened the departure of Ali, who took the small number of *Ghuzat* as had returned with him from Al-Andalus into Marrakech, where rabble-rousers protested Marinid rule. Abu Salim could have sent any of his detachments, but Muhammad assumed Ali had volunteered.

The marriage occurred at night beneath the stars in the courtyard of the *riad.* Braziers warmed the guests, the men and women seated separately by custom, while Aisha and Abd al-Aziz sat next to each other on a dais. He flicked nervous glances in her direction, but each look became increasingly admiring. Her dainty hands picked at slices of square-shaped *msemen,* the soft layers of dough stuffed with savory vegetables. Soon, Abd al-Aziz fed her from their shared bowl of lamb tagine with dried apricots. She held him enthralled each time she lifted her veil while revealing her face to him, not their guests.

Seated near Abd al-Aziz and Abu Salim in a place of honor, Muhammad turned from the sight of the couple. Ibn al-Khatib approached with a black-bearded man. A thin nose and thick brows gave him a handsome appearance. He was twenty-eight years old, nineteen years younger than Ibn al-Khatib, who introduced him to Muhammad. "Great Sultan, the honorable Ibn Khaldun al-Hadhrami."

Since their arrival in Fés el-Jedid, Ibn al-Khatib had spoken well of the former secretary of Abu Salim who now served the judiciary. Something glinted in Ibn Khaldun's dark-eyed gaze before he lowered his lashes and bent his head. Muhammad overheard Abu Salim's muttered curse. When he snapped at a nearby servant for more lamb tagine, the subtle dismissal of Ibn Khaldun did not surprise Muhammad.

Still, he said to Ibn Khaldun, "Upon my arrival in the great hall, your name reached my ears, spoken by almost everyone in admiration. I am told your poetry is sublime."

In a smooth voice, Ibn Khaldun replied, "You're too kind to me, mighty Sultan."

"Shall you recite for us tonight?"

Ibn Khaldun looked beyond both monarchs to the groom, thoroughly absorbed with his bride. "Prince Abd al-Aziz did not ask me."

"If I asked you?"

Ibn Khaldun averted his stare. "I would have to comply, although again, if the prince did not ask me to recite at his wedding, it would seem... strange to his guests."

"Ibn al-Khatib tells me you are from Al-Tunisiyah but descended from an Andalusi family. Your *nisbah* Al-Hadhrami indicates no town of Al-Andalus or Al-Tunisiyah."

"The familial name connotes the origin of my tribe in the city of Hadramut in Yemen, before we came to Al-Andalus after Tarik's conquest of Christian Spain six centuries ago."

"What made your family leave Al-Andalus?"

"The Christian advance. The last of my Andalusi ancestors left when the third King Fernando of Castilla-León arrived, renamed our homeland as Sevilla, and ordered every Muslim in the city to flee or fall under the sword."

Muhammad did not comment straightaway. His ancestor, the first Muhammad of Gharnatah had played a key role in the Christian monarch's conquest of Sevilla. Besides, Muhammad had already known the answers to every query he made. Ibn al-Khatib had provided them, and so stood by in silence with a puzzled expression.

Muhammad said, "My mother is a Christian, though she is not from Sevilla. Were you aware of my full heritage?"

Ibn Khaldun mumbled as his gaze slid away, "I was not." His muted tone suggested the truth coupled with some curiosity.

"Have you ever traveled to Al-Andalus?"

"I have not, mighty Sultan. I planned a visit twelve years ago when I was sixteen, but a beardless boy. My father gave his permission to my chief tutor, whom I was to accompany. Then the black plague descended. More than one thousand people died each day. I lost my father, mother, and many of our relations in Al-Tunisiyah. Allah punished us for our excesses, sparing only me, my elder brother Muhammad, and my younger brother Yahya."

The hitch in Ibn Khaldun's voice and a quiver across his chin spoke of the pain those memories inspired. Muhammad had lost as well during the pestilence, his aunt Leila, who had raised him. He sensed some self-castigation in Ibn Khaldun's tone, as if a survivor's regrets burdened the man. Muhammad's father had held a different opinion of the sickness responsible for so many deaths, a belief in contagion, which required containment before it spread between people. However, the occasion of Aisha's wedding would not be an opportune time for a discussion of dissimilar beliefs.

"I am sorry for your losses. Mayhap one day, you will see Al-Andalus, Ibn Khaldun."

The way Ibn Khaldun's eyebrows flared while his gaze flew to Muhammad suggested intent to follow the barely disguised suggestion. Ibn Khaldun had ingratiated himself with Ibn al-Khatib as a means of escape from a court where Abu Salim no longer held him in favor. Would it be wise for Muhammad to aid his flight? How might he do so if no loyal kingdom awaited him at home?

Muhammad nodded. "I hope you both enjoy the rest of the feast."

Ibn al-Khatib recognized the dismissal. He bowed and Ibn Khaldun mimicked him.

For the rest of the night, Muhammad pondered the introduction he had made, at least until his sister prepared to retire to the palace with her new husband.

At the entrance to the house in the shade of the bay laurels, Aisha knelt before her brother and pressed her lips to the hem of his state robe. He raised her up and kissed her forehead. In the slit between her veils, her eyes shone like the stars.

He whispered to her, "Remember, you are a Sultana of the Nasrids, always."

"I recall my duties, brother, and my promise to be a good wife."

In the subsequent silence, he accepted how such vows would never let her forget Ali, but she would not shame her new husband. Muhammad helped her onto the back of a garlanded camel. She grasped the saddle's horn and held on as the dromedary rose. Surrounded by her husband's family with Abu Salim in the lead, her mount lumbered across the ground and took Aisha to her new home.

Soon afterward, the guests dispersed. Muhammad received the congratulations of many among them before their departure. The sight of Umar huddled with Ibn al-Khatib gave him some displeasure, especially when Ibn al-Khatib turned and spied Muhammad. The grave expression on the old minister's face did not bode well.

He bowed beside Umar, who made the same gesture to him and repeated it for Muhammad, before leaving the courtyard.

Ibn al-Khatib came up the steps. "My Sultan, Umar has brought word from Al-Andalus. You will not like it."

***

At the center of the *riad*'s antechamber, where Muhammad oft wrote his correspondence to King Pedro each month to ascertain news of Gharnatah, Ibn al-Khatib sat with Muhammad on his left and Butayna on the right.

"Tell us the news," Muhammad ordered.

Ibn al-Khatib's stare dipped to the wooden floor. "The traitor Ismail, averring his claim to rule Gharnatah and disavowing your own, approached the *ulamas* of Gharnatah demanding dissolution to your marriage with Sultana Jazirah. The adjudicators have issued their *faskh,* a judicial decree of divorce. Jazirah is no longer your wife. She has married your brother."

A steady pulse thumped at Muhammad's temple and filled his ears, almost drowning out Butayna's horrified gasp. "How could the judges do this? We must awaken Al-Sabti and hear what he has to say."

"He will have little to offer, *Ummi.* He has been here with us, unaware of the actions of his fellow members in Gharnatah's judiciary."

"He is still the chief judge, my lion. Ismail has not appointed another or stripped Al-Sabti of his position. These judges made such a ruling without him. This is not a simple case of theft, but a serious matter! They have granted a unilateral divorce. How? Jazirah would not have pressed for it."

"Wouldn't she?"

Muhammad recalled the interaction between Jazirah and Ismail before little Yusuf's birth, where she had placed Ismail's hand on her belly. Muhammad's brother had dined in Jazirah's company and shared pleasant interludes with her several times, according to Muhammad's spies. Now she believed their son had died. For her, no further ties to Muhammad existed. Would marriage to Ismail have been such a difficult choice?

With a wave, Muhammad dismissed Ibn al-Khatib for the night. Beneath the archway, the old minister sagged against the wall and gripped the post. "Master, I am sorrier than I may be able to express. While I was among those who questioned the choice of Sultana Jazirah as your bride, I do not doubt this is a hard loss for you. I grieve for the blow to your pride."

"Thank you."

While Ibn al-Khatib shuffled down the stairs and off to his modest *riad,* Muhammad rose and pushed open the lattice doorway adjoining the antechamber, which led out to a balcony perched over the entrance. He gripped the wooden balustrade until the thuya wood creaked. Passing below, Ibn al-Khatib bowed again to Muhammad, who lifted his stare to the stars. Somewhere in his palace, Jazirah slept beneath the same constellations beside her new husband. The brother who had stolen Muhammad's throne had also claimed his wife.

His fist hit the wood with terrifying force. The shock reverberated through his hand. Butayna rushed on to the verandah and grasped his fingers, pressing light kisses to them. "Oh, my lion, do not think this way."

He glared at her. "Do you claim to know the workings of my mind now?"

"Jazirah did not betray you with Ismail! This wedding cannot have happened with her consent. Maryam or Muhammad the Red, someone forced her."

"You hold this belief because you shared such a close connection with my wife?" He wrenched his hand away. "You understand her motives and behaviors almost as well as you do my thoughts."

"I do know your mind and heart, your Nasrid heart, which swells with such pride when you look upon the son you created with Jazirah. The boy is her image, but he has your fierce temperament. The perfect union of his father and mother. She would not have soon forgotten the child Maryam forced her to believe is dead. Could Jazirah have witnessed such a sight, yet chosen the man whose theft of your throne seemingly cost her this precious life? She loves your son—"

He snarled, "She never loved me!"

"Did you ever give her a chance?" When he turned his head away, she grasped his chin and forced him to meet her intent stare. "Did either of you ever truly give the other an opportunity to know love? Before the wedding, you spent months apart. After Yusuf's conception, even more time passed in which you were hardly ever together. Among his duties as chief eunuch, Hisham kept records of all the harem women with whom you had coupled. You bedded Jazirah once in three years of marriage. Once. How could attachment, intimacies, or love form between two people who could not come together?" She released him and looked out on the avenue of bay laurels swaying in the night's cool air. "You never let yourselves love each other."

Unable to refute her words, Muhammad swallowed his bitterness, where it churned in a sour stomach. How could Jazirah have married Ismail? Had she longed for the day? Had the coup given her the chance to get rid of the husband she despised? For every query burgeoning in his mind, a counter question challenged him. Had no other choice existed? How could she have ever wanted Ismail, yet looked at Muhammad with such ardor in her gaze every time they saw each other? Would a woman devoted to her son have wed the man whose reign presumably caused the child's death?

Muhammad sank to the ground and cradled his head in his hands. He should have been a better husband and Sultan. Now he had lost his kingdom and his wife.

***

The next morning, when he awoke to break the previous night's fast, Muhammad found guests awaiting him in his writing room. Al-Sabti bowed, while the turbaned man beside him mimicked the gesture before he rose with a grunt. He swept a wrinkled, spotted hand over sagging jowls.

Al-Sabti said, "Sultana Butayna summoned me at dawn. I have brought my companion Ibn Battuta, whom you may recall from his journeys throughout Al-Andalus during the reign of your father."

"Join me in this repast." Muhammad gestured both men to the carpeted floor where the trio sat at a table laden with fruits, boiled eggs and cheese, flatbread and a steaming pitcher on a tray surrounded by small cups for the *nakhwa* in the vessel.

While slaves poured the hot drink, Muhammad said, "I recognize the great traveler Ibn Battuta." At the elder man's nod, Muhammad continued, "We never met when you visited Gharnatah in the time of plague. My father's duties had kept him from offering a personal welcome and my tutelage at the Madrasa Yusufiyya ensured an absence, but I do recall seeing your caravan leave the city."

In a gravelly tone, Ibn Battuta replied, "You honor me, great Sultan, as did your pious grandmother. She greeted me in the name of Sultan Yusuf, Allah preserve his memory, and funded the duration of my stay, for which I was most grateful."

Al-Sabti said, "Abu Salim's predecessors appointed Ibn Battuta as a judge. When your honored mother summoned me to the *riad* with terrible tidings, I requested my fellow arbiter to join us. This is grave news, the marriage of your treacherous brother to your wife."

Muhammad sipped the bitter *nakhwa* before he asked, "Is their union lawful?"

Al-Sabti deferred to Ibn Battuta, who said, "My brothers of the high courts have ruled upon the basis of the facts presented to them. You no longer possess lordship of Gharnatah. Another sits the throne in your place. It does not matter how he acquired his position in the view of the law. Since his rule invalidates your own, you have lost your claim to all you once held, including your wife."

Al-Sabti concurred with a nod, but Muhammad pounded the table and rattled the silver pitcher and cups. "I do not accept the judges' decree! Somehow, Ismail must have bribed or pressured them."

While Ibn Battuta gasped, Al-Sabti shook his head. "A grim accusation, my Sultan."

Muhammad railed, "I care not how the claim would seem! I know the law from you, Al-Sabti. You tutored me in its concepts from boyhood. Our laws allow a man's brother to wed his former sister-in-law if the husband died or divorced from the woman. My marital contract, which Jazirah's wretched father signed, banned separation even if she proved barren. No judge can alter such intent. I claimed Jazirah's maidenhead on our wedding night. She gave me an heir. She's mine! I will not give her up."

***

The Marriage Bed
Sultana Jazirah

Gharnatah, Al-Andalus or Granada, Andalusia
Jumada al-Ula 761 AH or April 1360 AD or Nissan 5120

The crack of Maryam's palm against Jazirah's cheek stirred a swell of screams, which resounded within the walls of the royal bath. Attendants and the eunuchs Maryam had assigned to Jazirah cringed in horror, as Maryam dragged Jazirah by her curls from the marble slab on which she had lain naked beneath a masseur's hands. Hair pulled from the roots set Jazirah's scalp afire. She fought against the violent hold.

Maryam backhanded Jazirah three times, screaming all the while, "Where is my son's heir? Each night, Ismail calls you to his bed! After four months of marriage, you should have enough of his seed for many sons. You refuse to give him even one!"

A shove sent Jazirah sprawling across the tiles. She wiped at trickles of blood from her mouth and nose, while Maryam vented her rage.

"I have questioned the concubines he has bedded, but none of them can explain their failures. I should have them all sold from the slave pens in *Al-Qaysariyya*! My son says you have lain with him each night, but how have you failed to quicken with his heir? You are certainly not barren. The birth of your wretched child with Muhammad is sufficient proof. Tonight, you will come to your husband. I shall ensure he beds you well." Maryam's bloodshot gaze swept over the room's occupants. "Prepare her for the Sultan!"

When she left in a swirl of silk, Suna rushed to Jazirah's side and offered a warm, wet cloth. "Oh, my Sultana! For your face."

Jazirah took the linen and whispered, "Don't let Maryam's eunuchs see your concern for me. If they alert her, she will question you." She waved the slave off.

Suna swallowed, rose, and backed away with her hands clasped before her. Jazirah stood and stumbled back to the marble slab. She stretched out, her head pillowed by her hair. "Finish," she instructed the masseur.

The eunuchs brought Jazirah from the *hammam* an hour before *Salat al-Maghrib*. She enjoyed some solitude during the evening prayer before they escorted her to Ismail's apartment.

When she entered, the low table in the central chamber held no dinner as customary. Maryam and Muhammad the Red stood on either side of the wood.

272

He glowered at Jazirah. "Your husband awaits you. Go to him if you don't want to see your father's head mounted on a spear!"

Jazirah squeezed past a screen beneath the archway, which opened on to the bedroom. On opposite sides of the bed, two slave girls stood. Ismail hovered in a corner next to the window. He turned and looked at Jazirah, wide-eyed with his gaze reddened like his mother.

Behind the screen, Muhammad the Red's voice boomed. "Undress them!"

Jazirah rubbed her wet hands on her robe before she crossed the carpet. Myriad questions darted through her mind. All revolved around one dilemma. Could she do this, submit to Ismail's touch while the pair behind the screen spied upon them? The servant closest to her hesitated in the approach, while the other girl went to Ismail.

Soon divested of a plain, white robe, Jazirah shivered in the coolness of the room despite the presence of braziers. Ismail cupped his hands over his groin area.

A chuckle rumbled from Muhammad the Red's chest, followed by a whisper from Maryam. "Hush! Would you disturb them? Isn't it enough for you to insist on my son's... performance when bedding should be a private affair?"

The slaves pulled back the coverlet and Jazirah stumbled to the mattress. She reclined, her hands fisted next to her. Ismail joined her, resting on his side with his head propped up on his hand. Maryam ordered the slaves to leave the room.

Ismail had lied in part to his mother. Jazirah had slept with him each night in the bed, like brother and sister. His ragged breaths warned of fear and excitement.

When he slid a hand across her belly, she stifled an urge to roll away from him. He said, "Just pretend they are not here."

She snapped, "How can I? They are both behind the screen."

He made no reply, only continued to caress her with feather-light touches across her abdomen. The smoothness of her skin seemed incapable of arousing him, in contrast to Muhammad. Ismail's flaccid manhood rested against her leg. She closed her eyes and blotted out the sight of him.

If her lawful husband had touched her, she would have been unable to withhold a response. She squeezed her eyelids shut and summoned his image in her mind. Until these long months of his absence, she had never imagined how much she would have missed the sight of him. She had begged Bahar to send word to her former master Juan Manuel, a plea for more information about Muhammad, but Bahar explained communications always came from the House of Myrtles to her. How difficult might it be to send one via reverse means?

Ismail's cold fingers on her breast chilled her and she quivered. He must have taken the movement as a sign of enjoyment, for he rolled atop her. His fondling intensified, as did her disgust. When he pressed his fleshy lips against hers, she squirmed and turned her head away.

He insisted, "You have to kiss me. We must behave as a true man and wife. Don't you understand how important this night must be for both of us?"

For him and his mother, most likely. Jazirah muttered, "I may have to bear your careless fumbling, but I shall never grant you the intimacy of a kiss."

The memory of one night with Muhammad had shown her how stirs of desire could burst into a bright flame between lovers. Her heart cried out for her true husband and she lolled on the pillow, letting tears seep into the silk.

Ismail brushed her cheek. "I'm sorry, I know how difficult this must be for you, but we must both try. Jazirah, I could make you happy, I could please you if you would let me or told me how."

She had not had to show Muhammad. He had instinctively perceived her passionate nature, which responded to him alone.

Ismail demanded her attention again. "I am your husband! Why won't you listen?"

"Because I am wed to another! Don't you see? How can I ever accept you, when I belong to Muhammad in my mind and soul? I joined with him for necessity's sake, but the vow I made at our wedding remains sacred to me. The decrees of men, of those judges who sided with your claim, cannot absolve my duty or loyalty as his wife."

Ismail reared up and searched her gaze. "You love him? After how my brother ignored you in favor of his concubine and fled Gharnatah with her? Do you think he cared for your fate when he left you behind? How can you love him after his neglect?"

Jazirah could not deem the turbulent emotions swirling around her thoughts of Muhammad as love. The feeling had come upon her so gradually from the moment Butayna revealed her son's hidden heritage. Affection for Muhammad had blossomed within Jazirah, only to have him wrenched away from her in a night of blood and death. Before she had told him of her caring, of how much she thanked God for the blessing of motherhood, which their marriage had granted her. Even with Yusuf gone, she clung to the all-too brief time she had known with him, and his father. Now she would never have the chance to speak with Muhammad again.

Behind them, Muhammad the Red muttered, "Enough talk from you two!"

Maryam retorted, "Be quiet! How can a man concentrate on lovemaking when you interrupt him?"

"Is he a man or an ignorant boy? Has she even moved once or spread her legs for him? Do you need my help, boy? Do you know how to mount a woman?"

"Don't use such despicable speech and a condescending tone with my son! He is Sultan and you are the husband of my daughter, father to my new granddaughter. Ismail is growing stronger. Even the Castillan king must respect him, for he has agreed to a yearlong peace with my son's kingdom. One day, Ismail will not need you."

Ignoring the argument, Ismail stroked the side of Jazirah's face. "I love you." In horror, she stared up at him. He continued, "You may not believe me, but I have loved you from our first meeting, although I knew I could not have you. Muhammad did not deserve you for a wife. He never understood your value, which extends beyond your royal blood or your beauty. You are resilient, stronger than any woman I know, even my mother. You are faithful to those whom you care for, and if it takes me the rest of my life, I vow to earn your trust and loyalty. With Muhammad gone, you and I have a chance to know love. My reign has changed everything for both of us."

She dismissed his words as she rejected his affection. "Your rule is unlawful! This union is a mockery of marriage. Love another, for I shall never return your feelings."

He touched her cheek again. "You don't mean those words. Why are you here with me if you haven't considered the possibilities of our future together?"

She shied away from him. "You know why! For the same reason I let you take my hand before the *imam* of Gharnatah. Now you want to claim what you believe is your due. Get on with it. The sooner you are done, you may leave me be! I have no wish to endure your mother and Muhammad the Red's scrutiny all night."

Each time Ismail attempted to kiss her, she shoved at his face. Soon, he ceased all attempts. Instead, he reached down between them and attempted to arouse her with his fingers. She winced, her body unresponsive.

In spite of his efforts, Ismail's own flesh betrayed him as well. His manhood had not hardened despite her proximity. Even anger had never abated Muhammad's arousal.

She stared at Ismail, watched the furrows creep across his brow, his teeth tugging at his lower lip, the moisture seeping beneath his lashes. Then his lower half sagged against hers and he lifted his head, looking behind him.

"I can't do this with you two staring at me!"

Muhammad the Red stomped around the screen's width and stood beside the bed. "Listen well to me, boy. I am not leaving this room until you have claimed this woman as a real man takes his wife!"

In the end, he did withdraw sometime after moonlight flooded the chamber. Rumbles of laughter mingled with his heavy-booted footfalls. Ismail rolled away from Jazirah and she turned her back on him as well. Cruel fate had claimed her young son and allowed her union with an impotent fool.

Chapter 21
The Final Coup

Sultana Jazirah

Gharnatah, Al-Andalus or Granada, Andalusia
Sha`ban 761 AH or July A.D. 1360 or Tammuz 5120

A shadow fell over Jazirah. She stirred from fitful sleep with a groan but refused to acknowledge the presence of another person in her bedchamber. It could not be Maryam, for her cloying fragrance would have warned of her arrival. Muhammad the Red's heavy footsteps preceded his entry into any room, so not him either. Ismail had proved too timid to dare visit Jazirah in her quarters.

"Sultana Maryam calls for you. Now."

When Jazirah did not answer, a nameless eunuch gripped her shoulder and shook her. Only then did she raise her head. She glared at his olive-skinned hand until he withdrew his touch and backed away from the bed.

In the mid-afternoon heat of another summer, Jazirah did not bother to don a robe over her light tunic. She slipped her feet into leather sandals and swept hair from her shoulders before she followed the eunuch.

They stepped out into a dazzling haze of light as it radiated over the *Jannat al-'Arif.* The sun's glare alone did not cause her to avert her gaze. Since Maryam had forced her to retire to the summer palace as was customary during the season, Jazirah could not look anywhere without recalling her son and husband as she had last seen them almost a year ago. If only she could reconcile herself to the loss. She had tried in vain through eleven tortured months.

Worse than the absence of Muhammad had been a strange sensation of Yusuf's nearness. Consigned to the same room she had occupied as in previous years at the residence, every inhalation stirred the scent of her son. The evening wind at times brought with it a child's cry and her ears pricked, certain she had heard Yusuf. He had learned a few words in the summer before his death. His memory haunted her, but she had to accept the truth. She would never see him or his father again.

She mounted the stairs the eunuch gestured to within the base of the southern pavilion. Maryam, with her self-bestowed title of *Umm al-Sultan* had claimed the section of the summer palace, which belonged by tradition to the Sultan's mother. Jazirah found her seated alone on the second floor just inside the doorway, which led out to the shaded balcony. For once, not even Nazhun stood by her side. Maryam looked up from the dish of sliced pomegranates set on the carpet. Red juice stained her fingertips, which she wiped on a linen square.

"You certainly took your time in coming to me, Jazirah. Still rebellious this morning, hmmm? One day, your stubborn pride must fade."

"When will such a day arrive, Maryam? Imprisonment at Shalabuniya did not break me. Not even the loss of my darling boy has destroyed me. My pride endures because I am a Nasrid. Humility is against our nature."

Maryam waved away the response. "Sit! You are making my neck hurt. I have no wish to repeat the same tireless arguments with you. Instead, let us speak of tonight and what will happen between you and my son in his chamber."

As Jazirah sat on the carpet across from Maryam, she sighed. "Why do you still believe your son can perform in bed? He is impotent, Maryam, you must accept this. Surely, among our learned Moorish doctors, must be someone who can treat him."

"Shut your mouth! My son does not suffer from impotency! I have questioned the slaves he has bedded. All deny this claim."

"They lie. Why would any among them admit their master's failings in bed and risk his ire, or mayhap, your own for making such a declaration? Thrice now, you have watched Ismail and me abed. Have you also stood behind lattice screens to view him with his concubines?"

"The problem lies with you, Jazirah, not them. You have caused Ismail's troubles. You do not know how to excite my son. His father was a passionate man. His vigor matched mine and we were well suited. As for you? Instead of touching your husband, you are as a cold, dead fish with him. This stops now! His father preferred his women astride. Tonight, you shall do the same with Ismail."

Jazirah shook her head. "The sexual positions we adopt will make no difference."

"If you want your father to remain among the living, you shall do as I command! I have a good incentive for you. On my orders, this morning Muhammad the Red removed your father to a cell in *Al-Quasaba*. He shall remain there until you have given my son the heir he needs."

A moment's panic ensued, before Jazirah drew even breaths. "You made the choice or Muhammad the Red did?"

"He does not control me!"

Jazirah yawned and rested her head along the stair banister behind her. "Doesn't he? I tire of your old threats, Maryam, always the same to compel my obedience. I pity you for all your supposed power is but a shadow to Butayna's own. She commanded without coercion. Only the strongest of Sultanas can. I have learned from them, the lessons from Butayna's life, the history of my aunt Leila, and of my great-grandmother Fatima. To be a Sultana of Gharnatah is to claim power and exercise it with confidence in the rightness of your actions. You think ordering about pitiful slave girls and eunuchs in the harem grants you the superiority Butayna held. You will never be like her, no matter how hard you try."

"Be quiet!"

"If your Ismail were a true man, the rightful sovereign of Gharnatah, he would have learned to withstand your dictates years ago, and mayhap, he might have resisted Muhammad the Red's influence over both of your lives. Ismail's flaws are not of his own making. You have raised little more than a weak-willed, impotent wretch—"

Maryam lunged at her, but Jazirah readied herself for the assault, and shoved Maryam back. "Not again! You will never lay your bloodstained hands upon me."

Ragged breaths filled the room as Maryam righted herself and rubbed the back of her head where she had struck the wall. "I'll have you killed for these insults!"

"You will not for so long as you need an heir to legitimize your son's rule. Isn't this the reason you advocated the marriage? Your power extends no further than making my life miserable. Even such circumstances must end. After today, you will never forget who I am and who you are. You're a Sultana by fortunate birth of a son alone. I needed no royal marriage to bolster my status. I was born a princess of Nasrid blood."

Maryam's spiteful gaze narrowed, but her lips trembled. Jazirah rose. "I feel sorry for Ismail most of all, burdened by you for a mother, and bedeviled by Muhammad the Red's authority. I shall speak with your son tonight of my concerns. Mayhap he shall be willing to seek a doctor's help for his troubles. Otherwise, I cannot aid him. Now, where is your chamber pot? I need to make water before I visit the great mosque for *Salat al-Asr*."

With a weak wave, Maryam gestured to the next room with her bed at its center. Jazirah rose and went behind the lattice screen. She raised her dress up and squatted over the ceramic pot. When the last droplets of urine fell, she wiped herself with one of the linen pieces stacked nearby.

Before she rose, the thud of heavy boots echoed from the adjoining room, followed by Maryam's voice. "Fatima, dearest daughter! I did not expect.... Ah, I see you've brought

Muhammad the Red. Sweet child, I had not known you came to the capital. Is my namesake with you?"

"I did not bring your granddaughter, *Ummi.*"

"You traveled from Malaka without her? How could you have left such a dear babe behind...? Muhammad, what are you doing? Take your hands off me!"

Hints of a ferocious struggle ensued. A sharp thump along a wall followed by strangled, rasping gasps. Jazirah clapped her hand over her mouth and prayed no one would hear her breathing. All too soon, an eerie silence filled the southern pavilion.

Then the second female's voice sounded again. "Is it over? Is she dead? Praise be to Allah! I don't know how much longer I could have borne her criticisms in letters from the capital about the importance of bearing you a son. She was the vilest creature I have ever known. A horrible mother. My siblings and I shall be better off without her. Leave everything to me. I shall convince Ismail of the necessity of her death. She ruined him, too. Now she is gone, and you and I may have peace. Mayhap, we shall try again tonight for the son you crave."

A heavy rumble filled Muhammad the Red's throat. "We don't need to try."

"You revealed your plans for my mother and summoned me to the capital. I thought you meant for us to try for a son this time. You have been long absent from my bed."

"You've given me a weak daughter. Maryam birthed five daughters compared to two sons for her husband. I won't suffer his fate. You may join your wretched mother!"

"Husband, no...." A pitiful scream sent shudders through Jazirah's body. She scrabbled at the wall and gripped it with clenched fingers, lest she fall and alert the murderer to her presence. Tremors coursed through her agonized limbs.

Muhammad the Red muttered, "I don't need you, Fatima, or any female within your family to legitimate my rule. I shall claim the throne of Gharnatah! Your brothers Ismail and Qays will not survive the night."

Clattering and rolling sounds preceded a sickening thud. Then the footfalls fell again, booming on the stairs. Jazirah waited for the space of several hitched breaths before she crept out from behind the screen.

Maryam stretched out on the floor, her arms splayed from her body, her robe wet and clinging to her inner thighs with the stink of urine rising from the cloth. Red spots dotted her opened eyes and her lips remained slightly parted, but no breath issued between them. Jazirah stared at Maryam's chest, still surprised when it no longer rose and fell. Whereas Jazirah had once imagined she would experience triumph at such a moment, the violent death left her numbed and cold.

A peek over the railing revealed the body of Maryam's daughter, black hair sprawled at the base of the steps. Her neck at an unnatural angle and her feet resting on the third step revealed how Muhammad the Red must have thrown her over the banister.

Jazirah would have to take those same stairs to escape. She did not doubt Muhammad the Red intended her death as well. Mayhap he had already gone to her room. She had to flee the summer palace and get across the *Hadarro* River. Somehow, she must find this House of Myrtles on her own and then.... What then?

She shook her head and scrambled down the first flight. Near the third step, she slowed and clambered around Fatima's body. At the base of the stairs, a burly hand closed on her arm.

She stifled the scream in her throat as Nazhun hushed her and pulled her behind a column. "My Sultana! Please be quiet. Guards have taken Sultan Ismail and Prince Qays to the citadel. I saw Muhammad the Red come from my mistress' chambers, while I waited in the shadows. I was bringing her *sharbah* to drink. Is Maryam dead along with her daughter?"

"She is. Muhammad the Red will kill me. Can you help me get away?"

With a widened stare, Nazhun looked at the body at the foot of the stairs. Then she nodded. "I will try. Come, you will be safest if you go through the trees and brush down to the river."

Nazhun tugged her, but Jazirah halted when they crossed the garden courtyard. "No! I cannot go to the river, not yet. Take me to the quarters of the bath attendants. From there I must reach the citadel."

"What? Why?"

"Don't question me, Nazhun! Now, come."

Jazirah pulled her hand and they fled through the upper gardens, and bypassed the entrance to the water staircase, which flowed from a fountain just outside the family oratory. They crashed through woodland and emerged at the base of a thick wall.

Nazhun said, "Muhammad the Red dismissed many of the guards patrolling *Al-Qal'at al-Hamra* in the last few days. Most of the men are his from Malaka. Everyone who has ever lived here knows I have served Sultana Maryam. Muhammad the Red's guards will want to take me...."

Jazirah's hold tightened on Nazhun's hand. "No! There can be another life for you."

Tears trickled down Nazhun's cheeks. "After all I have done, suffered, and allowed? I no longer deserve life. I don't want it. I will run for the gate...."

"No, Nazhun!"

"When I do so, you had best use your only chance to sneak past the guards and get to your destination. God be with you always, my Sultana!"

"No!" Jazirah's heated whisper could not halt Nazhun, who sprinted across the grounds and through the opened gate as fast as her short legs could take her.

She shouted, "Murder! Muhammad the Red has done murder at the *Jannat al-'Arif.*"

Horrified screams followed as did the shouts of guards. Jazirah used their distraction as Nazhun had intended for her. She slipped through the gatehouse unnoticed by the men, one of who knelt and aimed his arrow at Nazhun's retreating form. When a screech pierced the air, Jazirah did not look behind her. She swiped at tears shed for Nazhun's loss and scrambled behind brick houses dotting the complex. She climbed over the wall of one residence, which abutted the first palaces built in the reign of her great-great grandfather Muhammad *al-Fakih.* Through his gardens and past the final home of her great-grandmother Fatima, Jazirah ran until she reached the redbrick quarters assigned to the bath attendants. One eunuch dropped a bundle of linen he carried on his way to the storeroom of the baths.

Jazirah cried, "You there! Fetch the slaves Bahar, Suna, and Qamar at once!"

He bowed and left the cloths on the ground. Jazirah bent against a wall, clutched her sides, and swallowed harsh breaths. She gripped the *khamsa* and her wedding pendant, both necklaces hanging to the ground. Once she had straightened, the slave women arrived and bowed at her side.

She did not bother to explain her arrival, only said, "You must come with me to *Al-Quasaba.* You must help me rescue Prince Ismail."

Bahar frowned. "You mean the false Sultan? Why would anyone, especially you, need to save him?"

"I do not mean him. I speak of my father."

***

Jazirah tugged the veil over her mouth closer and whispered, "Bahar, are you certain this plan will work?"

At the forefront of a score of female bath attendants, some of whom carried jugs with stoppers, Bahar replied, "Of course, it will. The men of the citadel have never been able to resist us or our wine."

"Wine? How did you get wine?" Jazirah asked.

Her companions giggled as they passed through the gate separating the palace environs from *Al-Quasaba*. When they emerged beneath the shadows cast by its stout walls, Jazirah dared not look behind her to the gorge. She proceeded with the other women to the next barrier. The gate master eyed them beneath knitted brows.

"Ah, women. Whores. It's not even sunset. Are you so bold to ply your trade now?"

Bahar approached him. "As if the hour of love mattered to those of you who spend coin and those of us who wish to have it." She caressed his olive-brown arm and pressed her breasts to his chest. "Don't you want me? Shall the others and I leave? With our wine as well?"

When Bahar drew back a little, he snagged her arm and pulled her close. "I'll call for someone else to keep watch in my place."

Her hands were already unlacing his leather tunic. "Do so."

He waved the other women along the footpath. Bahar flashed Jazirah a grin before she pushed the gate master into the shadow of a secluded corner. The bath attendants dispersed, boldly approaching men where they found them. Some of the hapless fools eagerly held out cups when offered wine.

Suna and Qamar led Jazirah through a series of turns until they emerged at the start of the sole street leading through the barracks. Light shone from opened windows and doors.

Qamar whispered, "If your father is here, my Sultana, he will be in the dungeon. There is a trap door down to it from the second floor. We will need rope for him to climb. There are guards stationed outside the entrance to the second floor."

Jazirah asked, "How can we get to my father with so many men around?"

Qamar looked at Suna, who nodded and said, "We shall have no trouble."

When both women sauntered down the street, drawing whistles and chuckles from guardsmen idling in their doorways, Jazirah mimicked them, although her heart hammered in her chest. A few men pulled at her garments, but she slapped their hands away as the women who led her did.

"They're probably hunting for officers tonight," one gap-toothed man growled.

"To be sure, they don't want you, pig-nosed son of a donkey! Smell their perfume! These are costly women by the look of them. Save your *dirhams* for the smelly ones. They'll cost you less. Truth be told, they're all an ugly wretch like you can afford!"

While laughter boomed in the wake of the insults, Jazirah hastened to keep pace with Qamar and Suna. They reached the doorway of the watchtower, guarded by two men.

Suna whispered over her shoulder, "Remember, at least two more patrols inside," before she approached the guards. Both grinned at each other and her as she caressed each man's cheek. "Are you lonely? Shall I warm you?"

One sentry guffawed. "Can you warm us, as you say, at the same time?"

She rose on tiptoe and pressed her wide mouth to his before she did the same to his companion. "Let's find out." She led them away with a wink at Qamar and Jazirah, who ducked inside the opened doorway at the southeast corner of the tower. When Jazirah pushed in the portal slightly, the wood creaked. They might have some warning if any of the sentries approached. A staircase of narrow carved steps led to upper floors. Water dripped steadily in some unseen place. Around a sharp corner, two men peered down the corridor from their stations beside a door.

One shouted, "Stop! Why are you two here?"

Qamar replied, "For the same reason women always come to the citadel."

Her veil fluttered to the ground and she approached the shortest of the pair. Her arms snaked around his neck and she pressed her lean body against his. "The life of a tower guard offers little diversion. Would you prefer a few pleasant hours away from duty and the stench of prisoners? Mayhap a little time with me?"

He smirked at his companion. "I would enjoy it."

The other man at the left of the entryway looked over Jazirah. "Who's this?"

Qamar raised her head from pressing kisses to her chosen victim's throat. "Just another nameless prostitute. Why care about her when you have me? Wait your turn and see what I can do."

Jazirah quaked as the tallest of the pair seized her hand. Then she swallowed and stepped closer. He yanked her hard against him, pawed at her veil, and delved his fingers through her hair. "I prefer bashful women."

Qamar caressed the guard whom she held enthralled. "Isn't there a more private place we could go? What's beyond this door?"

"We can't go in," he murmured against her throat as he fumbled with his waistband. "We keep important prisoners there. I locked two more up myself just today. No one will check on them until the morning. Now, no more talking."

"If you insist." She pushed down the guardsman's trousers over his hips and maneuvered him against the adjoining wall. She raised her leg and his hand swept over her buttocks, lifting and supporting her with his forearm. He grunted and bit her neck and shoulders.

Jazirah swallowed and placed one hand around the waist of the man who held her. "Please, be gentle. I've never done this before."

He chuckled. "All the whores say the same!"

He mashed his mouth against hers. She clamped her lips closed, refused to let his tongue between her teeth. He pulled hard on her curls, setting her scalp afire. The moans of his companion made Jazirah turn her head slightly. Qamar's hand had slipped to the man's waist as he thrust inside her. The slave's fingers closed on his dagger. Jazirah opened her mouth, gave her target the desire he craved, and with one hand slid her fingers to his nape. He rubbed his hardness against her belly, just as she pulled his knife from its sheath and drove the blade repeatedly into his side. She swallowed his gurgled cry. A similar shriek followed from his counterpart. Anyone who overheard would assume sounds of passion echoed from the tower.

Jazirah stepped back and blood dripped from the weapon. The sentry slumped to the floor, pressing his fingers to his waist. Qamar drew apart from the other man, still holding the hilt of the blade she had rammed at the base of his neck. Froth and spittle seeped through his gaping mouth. His wounded fellow guard issued one scream before Qamar took the blade in her hand, came to him, and drew it across his throat.

A look passed between the women. They had done murder. Even if for the sake of Jazirah's father, would Allah forgive?

"First time killing a man?" Qamar wiped the dead soldier's blood on his tunic.

Jazirah swallowed and shook her head. "The second."

Qamar stood. "Why did you do it before?"

"To save myself."

"And now to save your father?"

"Yes."

"Then we cannot delay. Consider your purpose, my Sultana. Think of your father, not these fools here. They are beyond your concern now."

With both men dead, Jazirah retrieved the key from an iron hook along the wall and opened the door. She stepped inside a white-columned room lit by two northern windows, which narrowed as the openings reached the perimeter wall. Her father and Zabala looked up from their positions, seated on dank straw scattered at the base of the wall. Both wore manacles around their wrists, chaining them.

Qamar came in, looked at the pair, and held up another set of keys. "These must be for the chains."

She handed the keys to Jazirah, who crouched and unlocked her father's manacles first. "We must leave. Now!"

He asked, "Have they not consigned you here, too? I came this morning to the dungeon below and found Zabala." He indicated the trap door at the center of the square chamber. "Then later, they hauled us out and made Maryam's sons go down via hand ladders. I have not heard them since then."

Jazirah looked at the trap door. How easy would it be to pull on the iron rung and lift the wood? Then she shook her head. Her father's rescue presented enough dangers. She could not save Maryam's sons from their fate. *Could not or would not?* An inner voice nagged at her, but she chose to ignore it.

She said, "Muhammad the Red sent them here. He strangled their mother and murdered his own wife. He'll kill me as well."

"Why didn't you escape instead of coming here?"

"I would not leave you behind."

He swallowed and lowered his gaze. She turned to Zabala and unlocked his chains. "You are well enough to leave this place, captain?"

He nodded. "Although I hate to go without my men."

She replied, "We cannot worry for them now. If they have survived the dungeons thus far, mayhap one day...."

Her voice trailed off. She could not know how the future might unfold, but the next few moments were critical to their survival. She said, "Come, you must put on the cloaks of the guards, they are long enough to cover your garments."

Outside the door, Qamar stood between the two bodies. She had placed the weapons in each man's hand, smeared blood on their fingers, and removed their red capes. She tossed them on the ground and then said to Jazirah, "Come, my Sultana. I found the well where we may wash our hands of the stains."

When they returned, the men still stood thunderstruck at the sight of the dead. Jazirah ordered, "Put the cloaks on! The helmets, too. There, in the far corner under the stairs."

She went for the keys and handed both sets to Qamar, who returned one ring to the iron hook on the wall and the other to her victim's sword belt.

Then Jazirah's father asked, "How did you manage to kill these men, daughter?"

"You underestimate the wiles of determined women. Allah will forgive Qamar and me for our sins today if we succeed in saving your life." At his frown, she stood with her arms akimbo. "You dare not judge me after the things you've done!"

She turned to Qamar. "I wish you, Bahar, and Suna could come with us."

"You know we cannot. The other guards will want to know how two of their fellows died. You must leave before Muhammad the Red discovers your ploy."

"And when he learns two of his prisoners are missing?"

Qamar shrugged. "Sentries who allowed themselves the distraction of women and drink while Muhammad the Red ordered Maryam's sons held here will be his chief concern. These fools will not recall our faces, only a night's pleasure and drunkenness. Even if I should lose my head, I would have endured any risk to honor my master, Sultan Muhammad."

Jazirah retrieved her veil. She led her father and Zabala outdoors. She linked arms with both men and told them to keep their heads down. She strolled up the avenue between them. Chuckles greeted her.

"Ah, this one is greedy! She takes two at a time!"

"Mayhap, I'll return for more." Her voice came muffled behind the veil. "It takes a lot of effort to satisfy a woman like me."

Ignoring her father's shocked gasp, she propelled him with Zabala up the cobblestone street. Just as they rounded a bend and headed for the exit, Qamar's wails filled the air. "Oh, help! Two of these fools here fought over me. Now they've killed each other!"

All the shiftless soldiers now ran for the watchtower. Jazirah prayed Qamar would also use the chance to get away before the men surrounded her, asked questions, and opened the door to find one set of their prisoners gone. If any among them remembered how Jazirah had led away two men dressed as guards, they would know a woman masquerading as a prostitute had freed them.

At the height of the commotion, Jazirah took her father and Zabala to the dilapidated portion of the wall Butayna had shown her in the previous summer. The men pried back the metal grate. Jazirah's father crawled down the muck-covered tunnel first. She followed with Zabala, who closed the opening behind them.

He whispered, "I pulled the ivy across, tried to make the hole in the wall appear undisturbed to any passerby. Where does this lead?"

"We shall discover together. Go," Jazirah urged her father.

Her palms slid across unimaginable grime. She could not fathom how disgusting her appearance would be. The ground was loamy and foul. The stink of fetid water invaded her nostrils. She bowed her head and kept crawling.

Zabala exclaimed, "How deep in the earth are we?"

Since none of them knew, no one answered. As the tunnel leveled out, heat baked them and perspiration coated Jazirah's brow. She wiped the sweat away, knowing she also smeared dirt on her face.

Her father said, "I see a little light up ahead. I can hear children's laughter."

Jazirah heard them, too. She hastened her companions along, until they reached a shaft long enough for a man to stand within. Air filtered through circular holes in a metal cover at the top of the shaft and an argument between children reached them.

"Faraj, give me back my doll, or I'm getting Father."

"He's asleep, Fatima. Here's your foolish doll back."

"I'm telling *Ummi*."

"Wait!" Jazirah's father called out. "Don't go, children."

Something blotted out the light before a little girl screamed. "There's someone down there! Let's get *Ummi*."

Footfalls returned later and metal creaked before candlelight flooded the shaft. Jazirah's father groaned and covered his eyes. A hemp fiber rope tumbled down to him. He gripped it and climbed up the wall. Then he held the cord for Jazirah and urged her to do the same. Zabala aided her, his hands on the back of her thighs, for which he mumbled an apology. The trio soon stood in a storeroom lined with satchels, crates, broken furniture, and rusted old pots. A woman with faint white streaks in ebony hair trailing to her hips bowed before them and gestured for the children to do the same.

Jazirah's father said, "Please, Asiya, stand, you and your children. We are within your home."

She did so, resting her honey-colored hands, creased and speckled, on her children's heads.

He turned to Jazirah. "This is Asiya, who was the faithful maidservant of more than forty years to your great-grandmother Fatima until her death. Afterward, Asiya married at Shalabuniya."

Something in the woman's warm smile stirred Jazirah's childhood memories, but before she could speak, Asiya turned aside to her son, who hugged her waist. "Go, Faraj. Wake your father and tell him to come to the storeroom." To her daughter, she said, "Bring water and soap for the washing of hands. Then heat water over the fire. Prince Ismail and his companions will want to remove the muck from their bodies."

Shuffling footsteps preceded the entry of a grizzled man with a bent back. Jazirah stifled a cry as she recognized him and finally recalled why the woman at his side seemed familiar.

She cried, "Samir, our old jailor! My God, you're here in Gharnatah."

He bowed and a groan escaped him. Samir had to be at least eighty years old, yet he had sired two children in the last decade on a woman likely in her early fifties, if her appearance betrayed the truth of her age. Asiya helped him stand and she rubbed his back, while he said, "Princess Jazirah, you honor me. You have grown into a tall, fine woman, but I would recognize you anywhere even after long years. As I would know your noble father, Prince Ismail."

Asiya said, "I must remind you, she is a queen of Gharnatah now, dear husband. She wed Sultan Muhammad, Sultana Fatima's great-grandson."

Jazirah replied, "Muhammad's mother had shown me the hidden exit from the citadel, which she said would lead to the home of secret Jews."

Samir nodded. "Before his death, my father told me of how my mother named me Shimon at birth and placed this six-pointed, gold star on a chain around my neck." He reached an aged hand beneath his tunic and drew out the pendant. "I have never removed it. Nor have I shunned my Jewish heritage."

Asiya added, "I converted for love of my husband after we were married at Shalabuniya. Our children arrived a year later. They know the truth of our religion, but they also know it must remain a secret for our safety."

"Send our boy, Asiya," Samir ordered, "to the House of Myrtles. Juan Manuel Gomero will want to know of our guests."

***

Juan Manuel arrived just as Asiya finished setting the table for a meager meal of flatbread, lamb stew, and roasted eggplant. Her children, whom she had named for her former mistress and Jazirah's great-grandfather, aided her. Darkness fell over Al-Andalus, so the children brought candles sputtering to life. Jazirah and her companions had washed and received fresh clothing.

Young Faraj led Juan Manuel, who leaned on a walking stick, into the small dining room. Samir greeted him with a kiss on each cheek. "*Shalom.*"

"*Shalom*, my friend, and joy to your house." Juan Manuel looked past Samir's shoulder unabashedly at Jazirah. She blinked and turned away, made uncomfortable by his scrutiny. Samir introduced her, her father, and Zabala to the man, identified only as the owner of the House of Myrtles.

Juan Manuel laughed. "My friend here does not approve of my livelihood. He chooses to forget I am a slave merchant, one of the best in Gharnatah. I am also a loyal subject of its just ruler Sultan Muhammad, may *El Dio* restore him to his rightful throne." He cocked his head and eyed Jazirah's father. "The Sultan believes you have betrayed him. Why have you fled *Al-Qal'at al-Hamra*?"

"I have been guarded in its watchtower since dawn. Muhammad the Red revealed his true nature. He has imprisoned his cousins Ismail and Qays. He will have them killed, I do not doubt, just as he murdered their mother."

"Maryam is dead? I wish I might say Gharnatah is better without her, but if Muhammad the Red has claimed the throne, the city, the Sultanate may be in danger." Juan Manuel slapped his thigh and then cursed. Asiya's children giggled even as she hushed them.

Juan Manuel continued, "Forgive me, my prince. The fate of Gharnatah is no longer a concern for you and your daughter. Eat and rest well tonight. Tomorrow you shall come to the House of Myrtles at dawn and then leave its walls with the priest."

"A Christian priest?" Jazirah questioned.

"Yes, my Sultana, one of the Trinitarian Order. For more than five years, Sultana Butayna has given of her wealth attained at her husband's death so Christian captives could return to their families. As it happens, Fray Antonio will lead a group of captives back to Murcia at dawn. You will join them. The city guards will ignore a bedraggled group of captives so long as the Trinitarians pay the toll. It should be easy for you to go from there down to the coast and hire a ship with some of the money I shall provide, to take you to Al-Maghrib al-Aksa."

Jazirah repeated, "Al-Maghrib al-Aksa?"

A grin splayed across Juan Manuel's wizened features. "Yes, my Sultana, for there you shall find Sultan Muhammad at the royal court of Fés el-Jedid, the Marinid capital city."

Chapter 22
The Riad

Sultana Jazirah

Fés el-Jedid, Al-Maghrib al-Aksa or Fez, Morocco
Shawwal 761 AH or August – September A.D. 1360 or Tishri 5121

The first sight of blue and whitewashed houses atop the hills of Fés el-Jedid brought swift tears to Jazirah's eyes. As her horse approached the city gate, the moment where she would meet Muhammad again drew closer. Did he know of her coming? On the morning when she had parted with Juan Manuel before the doorway of the House of Myrtles, he had promised to send word to Muhammad of her intended arrival with her father and Zabala.

However, her travels to Al-Maghrib al-Aksa had not gone smoothly as Juan Manuel predicted. During the previous month's fast of Ramadan, boat captains idled on the docks at the Andalusi city of Marballa with little eagerness to venture across the waves, no matter how many satchels of coin Zabala jangled in their faces.

Now, six weeks after she had left Gharnatah, so many emotions filled Jazirah's heart. What would be the first words she and Muhammad exchanged with each other? Would recriminations or sadness at the loss of their son overshadow the reunion? Would Muhammad embrace or shun her? What did the future hold for them, since Gharnatah's high judges had decided Muhammad could no longer call her wife?

When she spied short scarlet capes fluttering on the breeze, she had an answer about the extent of Muhammad's knowledge. Double rows of ten guards on horseback lined the street, scanning the crowd. Many of the men bore features she did not recognize, but one among them she identified as Pero Ruiz. She urged her mount toward him. Her father and Zabala's horses followed.

At the gate, she slowed her mare and tugged aside the veil over the lower half of her face. "Captain Pero."

He inclined his head and a little smile tugged at his lips. "My Sultana. It pleases me greatly to see you again. We have anticipated your arrival."

He peered behind her and the grin ebbed. "Prince Ismail." Then he laughed. "Zabala, you old dog!"

The men maneuvered their mounts beside each other and clasped arms.

Zabala said, "Those whoresons didn't kill you! Good. When last we saw each other, we left a game of chess unfinished. We play again tonight in the desert."

Pero threw back his head with a loud snort. "I look forward to winning against you as I have oft done." Then he patted Zabala's arm. "They didn't kill me, *amigo*, but many of us died defending our Sultan and his family, including my brother."

Zabala sighed. "I gave up hope for Alfonso long ago, after praying he would have joined me in the watchtower. They separated officers from their men, sent mine to the *corrals*. I thought I was the only captain who had survived."

Then the men reached for each other and shared a hearty embrace. Jazirah looked away, her eyes welling again.

As they drew apart, Zabala asked his fellow captain, "Who are your new *amigos*?"

Pero nodded to his company. "The Sultan has reconstituted the royal guards. Five of mine survived, so he promoted them to officers' ranks and gave them command over others assigned to his honored mother and sister, and to his children. Our Sultan purchased Spanish Christians captured and taken to the slave markets of this city. Men like us." Then he sent one of the men ahead with curt instructions, "Tell Sultana Butayna we are returning with her family from Gharnatah."

He turned to Jazirah. "We go to the *riad*, which is the house the Marinids provided for the Sultan."

She rode beside him through the enchanting, colorful city. "What day is it, captain? We have lost track of time after traveling from Chella at the coast with our Tuareg guides."

Pero answered, "In your calendar, my Sultana, it would be the fifteenth day of Shawwal in the year seven hundred and sixty-one, while for me it is the twenty-ninth day of August in the year of one thousand, three hundred and sixty. Exactly twelve months since the coup happened."

When she made no reply, her father asked, "The hour?"

Pero gave a curt glance over his shoulder. "Your *Salat al-Zuhr* occurred some time ago."

They bypassed an enormous gate topped with blue swirling designs and then turned eastward, rounding the whitewashed wall. A footpath in grassy fields gave way to a street bordered by aromatic trees. At the end of the road, a two-storey house arose. At the base of its steps, Sultana Butayna awaited, flanked by a yellow-haired man in a scarlet cape. The wind rustled her orange and blue garments. A gauzy veil revealed her hairline. Thin brown braids adorned with blue and silver beads trailed beneath the cloth.

Jazirah dismounted without accepting her captain's offer of help. She approached Butayna and bowed before her. As tears threatened again, she swallowed.

Butayna said, "Arise. I once told you one queen does not bow before another."

Jazirah straightened. Her father joined her and made his obeisance, which Butayna accepted with a brusque nod. Then she looked beyond them. "Captain Pero, my son still attends public audience at Abu Salim's court. Will you return with your fellow guardsmen to await Muhammad?"

Jazirah's heart thudded. She would have to wait a little longer for her reunion, but now, the impending moment terrified her. She rubbed at her chest and expelled an uneven breath.

Butayna looked to her. "Are you unwell, Jazirah?"

"It must be the arid air. I have not grown accustomed."

"You shall." Butayna dismissed the men on horseback. Only Zabala remained. He fell to his knees on the ground before her. She bent and touched his shoulder. "Stand, Zabala. I am pleased to see you again. Are you the sole survivor among your men?"

"My men are in the *corrals* of the citadel, my Sultana. I have not seen them, although I have heard their cries from the cells."

She shook her head. "My brave countrymen. Some of them must have survived the corrals. They did in the months before I rescued you. We must believe in the power of Christ to save their lives. In the meantime, you will not remain idle. You shall gain command of others here." She gestured to her companion. "This is Garcia, a fellow captain who serves me in the... absence of my Ruiz. Garcia belonged to the Hospitaller Order in Castilla-León, until pirates from Al-Maghrib al-Aksa attacked the galley on which he sailed."

Zabala and Garcia took measure of each other and shared a nod. Butayna led them indoors through an opulent room covered in rugs with silk cushions along the walls, gold-coated sconces, and flowering plants in brightly painted pots.

Butayna ordered, "Captain Garcia, take Prince Ismail with Zabala to the dining area. I need to speak with Sultana Jazirah alone."

She sat on a cushion and patted the space beside her. Jazirah settled next to Butayna and rested her hands in her lap. Both women were silent until the men dispersed. Then Butayna placed her fingers atop Jazirah's own.

A simple touch summoned the sadness, heartbreak, and regret Jazirah had kept inside for so long. She sobbed, crying even harder when Butayna nestled against her and patted her back.

"You are safe at last. Hush. Maryam and Muhammad the Red, they can never hurt you again. No one will harm you here. You must believe me. Sweet Jazirah, weep no more."

When Jazirah's tears had subsided, Butayna offered her a square of linen from a bowl of cloths set on a table beside her.

Jazirah began, "So much has happened. I don't know where to start."

"At the beginning. Tell me all you have suffered."

Jazirah wept again as she spoke of the night of the coup and its aftermath. She could not ponder the sight of Yusuf's battered body in the gorge, but she told of her father's acquiescence to the coup, her forced marriage to Ismail, and Maryam's attempts to get a grandchild. Then Jazirah spoke of Maryam's death.

When she finished, she looked at Butayna, whose eyes had reddened also. Butayna wiped at her wet cheeks and clenched her own piece of sodden linen.

Jazirah shook her head. "After all I have told you, after everything Muhammad and you suffered by her will, how can you cry for her?"

Butayna sniffled. "I do not weep for Sultana Maryam. My tears are for Miriam Alubel, the girl who was once my friend at Talavera de la Reina. I never knew coming to the land of the Moors would have changed both of us so much." She patted her face for the last time and then said, "Dearest, you have not spoken of your son...."

"I can't talk about him!" Jazirah rose from the cushion. "Please do not make me."

Butayna stood as well and grasped Jazirah's shoulders. "I wanted to prepare you before you suffered a great fright. There is something you must know of Yusuf...."

Just then, the bubbling laughter of a child drifted from the inner courtyard. Jazirah peered intently through the archway leading outdoors. "Muhammad's children with Haziyya are here. I want to see them. Did Haziyya have a son or another girl?"

She rushed outside with Butayna on her heels. "Jazirah! Wait."

A little girl with long, beaded plaits skirted the flowerbeds. Butayna's red-haired servant Hafsa chased her. "Sultana Leila! What would your grandmother say if she knew you were outdoors in this heat? Come here now!"

She carried a dark-haired baby on her hip, but the boy who raced after Hafsa made Jazirah stumble to a halt at the top of the stairs. She gripped the column at her side before she fell backward.

Black curls spilled around the child's bright face, one she had seen in her dreams of twelve months past. Eyes so like hers sparkled in the sunshine. From his puckered lips, a soft, lisping voice mimicked the servant. "Come back, Leila! Come back."

Jazirah cried out, "Yusuf!"

She raced down the stairs to the center of the garden and hoisted him into her arms, holding him close as she sobbed anew. "Yusuf! Oh, my son! You're here! You're alive."

Several moments passed before his wails penetrated her awareness. He reared back, wriggled, and slapped her face. "Let me go! Grandmother! Help me."

Butayna came down the steps and patted Jazirah's arm. "Release him, please."

Jazirah blinked against the harsh daylight and shook her head. "You don't understand. I thought he was dead...."

"I know, I know." Despite Jazirah's protests, she wrested Yusuf away and hugged him, kissing his head.

Jazirah sank to her knees. "Why? Why are you taking him away from me again?"

Butayna summoned Hafsa, who had taken hold of Leila. "Get the children above stairs again, please. I wanted to delay this reunion in such circumstances until I had told Jazirah the truth, prepared her somehow."

Hafsa mumbled, "I'm sorry, my Sultana. Forgive me."

"Oh, my loyal one, I don't think the truth would have made the meeting any less of a surprise. Please, take them now."

As Hafsa led the three children up the steps and down a corridor, Butayna knelt beside Jazirah in the dirt. "You have not seen Yusuf in a year, since he was eighteen months old. A child who had just started walking three months before and learned his first words. Now he is two and a half years old, and he can run, jump, and sing. He does not remember you, Jazirah. You'll need to give him time."

"But he's my son!"

"Dearest, he will always be your son. He needs time to remember you are his mother."

As a fresh round of tears overwhelmed Jazirah, Butayna rested her forehead against hers. "So much has happened. So much for you, for Muhammad with Haziyya's children, for Yusuf, but at last you are together again. Let time wend its course and lead each of you along the path where you may find yourselves together in trust and love, as a family."

Despite her sorrow, Jazirah agreed not to pressure Yusuf to return her long-absent affections. For now, her knowledge of his good health and proximity had to suffice. Her father also wept once he heard the news in the dining hall where Jazirah and Butayna retired.

Overwhelmed by his sentiments, he asked Butayna if he might withdraw from their company. "If your captain would show me to the nearest inn, I can arrange for my own comfort. I would not expect Sultan Muhammad to have made provision for me. I promise I shall not leave Fés el-Jedid until he summons me. I... should like to see my grandson again, if his mother and father will permit it."

Butayna nodded. "You are correct. Muhammad does not want you under this roof. An inn will be unnecessary. The high judge Ibn Battuta has offered you rooms in his home near the palace. Garcia can convey you to the property now if you wish it."

"I do."

"Then leave us."

Jazirah's father glanced at her. She avoided his stare. Just because Yusuf lived did not mean she had to forgive her father. Not yet.

Before he withdrew, Butayna called to him. "Jazirah told me of what you did, or rather, failed to do in the months before the coup. You are aware Nasrids do not absolve guilt easily, least of all my son who inherited my pride coupled with the arrogance of his forbearers. Muhammad will consider a sin of omission the same as any overt action against him. If he asks my opinion, I will not plead for leniency on behalf of my beloved husband's brother. When you face Muhammad's justice, he shall be the sole arbiter of your fate."

"I understand, Sultana Butayna."

Zabala cleared his throat. "Sultana Jazirah, shall I accompany your father?"

"You may if you wish, captain."

When the men departed, Jazirah said, "Although I struggle with my father's decisions still, at least, I may be assured he will not come to harm with Zabala for his protector."

Butayna reached across the table and patted her hand. "Eat. You'll soon grow accustomed to the texture of couscous. Chicken tagine is delicious beside it."

Jazirah shook her head. "I'm not hungry. I cannot help but think of what you said to my father. If Muhammad cannot forgive easily, how will he behave with me? Can he accept the presence of a wife absent from him for so long, forced to marry the brother he despised, a prince who betrayed him and stole his throne?"

Butayna could not answer. Instead, she asked, "Do you know the fates of Ismail and Qays?"

"Before we sailed, we heard the talk. Muhammad the Red ordered their executions, along with everyone else in their households."

***

Muhammad slowed his strides as he crossed the palace courtyard at sunset. The sight of Pero and his men just outside the doorway of Abu Salim's audience chamber held one meaning.

Jazirah had come at last, for Pero once vowed he would remain at the city gate during daylight hours awaiting her arrival. Muhammad had imagined the moment of their meeting for three weeks since he first received word of her intent.

He acknowledged the obeisance of his men with a nod and ordered them to stand. "Where is she, Pero?"

"Sultana Jazirah is with your honored mother at the *riad*, my Sultan."

"When did she come?"

"Almost three hours have passed by the count of the water clock in the audience chamber. Shall we return to the residence, master? I have brought a horse for you."

"We ride now."

Muhammad mounted a dapple-coated Arabian. The short distance between the palace and the residence did not allow much opportunity to consider all he would say, yet he had rehearsed varying words many times over the intervening weeks. He would demand to know the role Jazirah and her father had played in the events leading up to the coup. Then he wished to hear her reasons for marrying his brother. Lastly, he would require her to explain her purpose. Why had she come to him?

At the entrance to the *riad*, he leapt from his horse and tossed his reins to Pero, who snatched the leather from the air with a deft hand. Muhammad took the short stairs two at a time and crossed the threshold. His children's laughter echoed from the garden. He paused just inside the archway. Hafsa held Saad, while Yusuf and Haziyya chased each other through the shrubs. Beneath the shade of a tamarisk tree, Jazirah stood alone.

Her temple pressed against the trunk. Long arms hung at her sides and her shoulders drooped. The wind lifted her thick hair and revealed her bowed back.

Muhammad dragged moist palms over the sides of his tunic before he smoothed his hair. Should he go to her or wait for some sign of acknowledgment? He found himself unable to move. Huddled in the corner, he gazed at her profile. Had it been so long since he last saw her? Had she always been so beautiful? He recalled the dust-covered, tattered sixteen-year-old who had arrived at his palace four years ago, recriminations and dissatisfaction in her frigid gaze. The woman before him now at twenty years of age displayed the same quiet resilience, her rapt gaze on the children.

They realized he stood among them first. "Father!"

Leila and Yusuf competed to reach him. As he bent and enveloped them in his arms, he peeked over their tiny, dark heads. Jazirah held his regard. His heartbeat turned heavy and sluggish. Even time seemed to slow for a moment until Yusuf's voice and persistent tugs on his father's neckline penetrated Muhammad's awareness.

"Presents, Father?"

"No, my greedy son." Yusuf would not understand the return of his mother was a gift beyond measure.

Muhammad hoisted the children on his hips. He stepped out on the gallery bounding the garden. Jazirah made tentative, slow steps in his direction and then halted. Hafsa brought Saad to him and he kissed his son's forehead, while never breaking eye contact with Jazirah. When the maidservant stepped back, Muhammad eliminated most of the distance between he and Jazirah.

Yusuf wrenched Muhammad's neckline again. "Who is this?" He pointed a fat finger at his mother, who bit her lower lip. Her action stirred a shiver in Muhammad's body.

He said, "You would not remember her, my son, but she oft held and kissed you at night. When you were little, you called her *Ummi*, one of your first words. She is your blessed mother."

Her regard left Muhammad and alighted on her son again. She stepped forward, her lips parted. Such longing reflected in her eyes.

Muhammad nuzzled Yusuf's head. "Would you like to call her *Ummi* now?"

"No!" Yusuf wriggled until his father set him down. Soon, Leila demanded to join him and they frolicked again. Muhammad acknowledged it would be a difficult transition for the boy who had lived too long without a mother.

Jazirah bowed her head and sniffled. She stepped back a pace and stared at the dark brown earth.

Muhammad reached out and tipped her chin up, found her gaze watery as he expected. He would have pulled her into his embrace and comforted her, except she mumbled, "My Sultan."

He gave a slight shake of his head at her formal tone and removed his hand. "You are well?" Polite banter seemed a safe choice.

"I am. So is my father. He came with me to Al-Maghrib al-Aksa as we intended and is now at the home of...."

"...Ibn Battuta," he finished for her. He had not known what to expect for the course of their first conversation, but if she preferred to speak of the past without delay or evasion, he welcomed the approach. "I made the arrangement. I could not be certain of my actions once your father came into my presence again. I do not doubt he betrayed me in the conspiracy of Muhammad the Red and Maryam."

She admitted, "My father was a traitor. He was aware of the plans and told no one."

Muhammad gritted his teeth. Once she had begun their discussion in this manner, he would not shy away from seeking hard truths. "And you? What did you know before they took my throne from me?"

An unnatural stillness overcame her. Her chin trembled and when she made to open her mouth, a broken sigh whistled through her lips.

He shook his head as his scalp prickled. "I had hoped lies and half-truths would no longer bedevil us, Jazirah."

"I did not have foreknowledge of what they intended to do! I discovered the plot and my father's complicity on the morning afterward. Maryam made me think you had abandoned me and left Yusuf behind. I have believed him dead all this time."

Evening clouds drifted over Muhammad's head, pale orange puffs against a blue-gray sky. He lifted his gaze to them. "Yet, you married my brother four months afterward. You knew of my abhorrence for him and his mother, and still you wed him."

"Should I have killed myself?" When he could not answer, she breathed a heavy sigh. "I wanted to die on the day Maryam showed me a body she wished me to believe was our son, murdered and tossed into a ravine. I almost leapt to join him, but my father stopped me. He saved me. Would you have preferred my death over marriage to your brother? Would you?"

He regarded her again. "I have never desired your death. You had no other choice than marriage to my traitor brother?"

"Do you have to ask if I would have wed Ismail of my own volition?"

"You let him put his hands on you! Do you forget I saw you with him before your father's house?"

"This is the source of your anger? Will you next insist on knowing whether I enjoyed his attentions when we were abed?"

His fists tightened, but then he turned from her. "Are you carrying his child?"

"Would I be here if I perceived such a calamity?"

"I am no heartless beast to murder a babe, no matter what you may believe."

"You threatened Yusuf with death when you believed he was sired by another man. Why should I have expected otherwise if I carried Ismail's heir? As it was, your brother could not... perform as a man. He tried three times to claim me, but impotence afflicted him. I am certain I carry no child of his."

Relief flooded him, but he swallowed his sigh. "I wanted you and our son with me."

"Then why did you leave me?" Her shrill tone shattered the joyful mood of Yusuf and Leila as their play ceased. Little Saad wailed and burrowed his face on his nurse's shoulder.

Muhammad waved them away. "Take them inside, Hafsa. Now."

"Of course, my Sultan," she whispered, grabbing Leila and Yusuf's hands to lead them out of the garden.

"Why I have to go?" Yusuf demanded.

Hafsa hushed him. "Come, my sweet prince. You can play above stairs."

"Why, Muhammad?" Jazirah insisted as the children retired. "Why did you take Haziyya and leave me behind to face our enemies alone?"

He clapped a hand to his head and stared at her anew, incredulous. "Our enemies? Didn't Maryam wear the guise of a friend? I warned you, Jazirah, I warned you about her wiles before we married, but you would not listen! You had to learn of her deceit on your own."

"A harsh lesson when I thought our son had died for my folly." She clasped her fingers and turned from him slightly. Again, a powerful urge swept over him to drag her into his arms and reassure her of their safety. Yet, he kept his distance.

Instead, he answered, "I wanted to rescue you. I tried, but the conspirators were at the gate of the summer palace. I could not get to you."

"Where is Haziyya? Why haven't I seen her with the children?"

He frowned at her. "Didn't my mother tell you? On the night of our arrival along the coast, Haziyya died in childbirth with our son. The doctor Ibn Khatima saved Saad."

A dazed look came over Jazirah's face as she gaped at him. "I'm sorry. You loved her greatly."

"You despised her for loving me, for giving me children. Don't pretend otherwise."

"I did not wish her dead! Never wished harm to her or her children. You could not have expected me to take joy in her presence. I was your wife, but you valued her."

He muttered, "I did not think my sentiments ever counted with you."

She lowered her gaze. "They have always mattered, even when I wished otherwise."

Jazirah returned to the tamarisk tree, her arms around the trunk. "You received word of my plans from Juan Manuel Gomero. You knew my intention to come here. Why did you allow it? What shall our future be? Do we even have one?"

"Why are you asking me now? How can I know? We are seeing each other for the first in long months."

"I told you last summer, we shared the same hope of prospects where the past no longer weighs upon us. I still hold this expectation. Finding my son here alive and thriving has rekindled my faith. What do you want from me, Muhammad?"

How could he answer? He once thought he might have prepared for her arrival, but so much remained uncertain between them. If he questioned her father about his failures and executed the man, what would the act mean for Muhammad's life with Jazirah? As she had asked, could they share an existence after all they had endured whilst separated?

"I don't know what I want any more, Jazirah." Unable to look at her further, he left the garden. With each footfall, the emotional divide between them lengthened.

***

A full week passed in which Jazirah attempted to adjust to life in Al-Maghrib al-Aksa. The people of Fés el-Jedid amused her with their lyrical speech, brightly painted houses, and spicy foods. They displayed little interest in her beyond her coin at the marketplace. She purchased her own slave rather than taking one Butayna had offered, which summoned a surprising nod of assent from Muhammad's mother.

The young eunuch Kissenga, a Nubian Christian, took to his duties well. Mayhap too well. He dressed Jazirah and tidied her chamber each day, but also protected her in the bath even when she did not require defense. The attendants approached her with hesitant steps and halted whenever her slave's glare fell on them. While Jazirah insisted he did not have to inspect and sniff all foods brought to her room, he did so nonetheless. At least he refrained from the practice when she dined with Butayna. He carried a long staff of acacia always and held the wood with the precision of a soldier bearing a spear. He tapped it on the ground whenever he escorted her through the streets, so all knew of her coming.

Today, he stood silent beside her in the garden while she sat on the steps. Kissenga had braided her hair in the style Butayna favored of late. A girlish giggle echoed, but Jazirah pretended to ignore it. Leila peeked out from behind a bush, where she had attempted to hide for most of the hour, while Jazirah behaved as if she did not notice the child. Jazirah plucked a damask rose and twirled it between her fingertips. Her nose buried in its pink petals, she inhaled and sighed.

Leila emerged and when Jazirah looked at her directly, the girl did not dart behind another shrub. Instead, she ambled across the ground and paused halfway. Even when Jazirah beckoned or offered the rose, Leila would not move.

"Kissenga, stop frowning. You're scaring the child." Indeed, once Jazirah looked up at him, his usual glower faded while he attempted a smile. More like a pained grimace.

Leila came to her and Jazirah offered the flower. "It's pretty. Just like you."

With her honey-brown skin and black hair in tiny plaits, little of Leila's features marked her as a Nasrid child. Whereas her brother Saad resembled his father's family, Leila would have blended well among the Tuareg tribes, distinguished only by her lack of blue-stained skin.

Leila touched the rosebud. "Pretty." Then she patted Jazirah's cheek and repeated, "Pretty." She drew closer and leaned upon Jazirah's knee, fingering one of the long coils of hair decorated with silver beads. "*Ummi.*"

Jazirah stared at the child. Mayhap Leila only remembered how Haziyya had worn her hair, but the word she whispered stimulated such a longing within Jazirah to hear her son, any child call her 'my mother' again.

She tucked the late-blooming rose behind Leila's ear. Then she raised her head and found Muhammad watching her from the opposite side of the gallery. Dressed in sand-colored robes, his hair and mustache oiled, he stood in a circle of his guards. He had avoided her since their tense reunion. Neither seemed to know the means to leave their impasse behind and walk the path to forgiveness together. His sun-bronzed face revealed nothing, but within the eyes, some hint of desire for her burned brighter with each passing day. He might not know what he truly wanted of her, but he still desired her.

Jazirah's muscles quivered, but she did not look away. Lubna had once told her love could flow from desire. Jazirah intended to discover the truth of those words.

Chapter 23
The White Mountains

Sultan Muhammad V

Al-Arif Mountains, Al-Maghrib al-Aksa or Rif Mountains, Morocco
Muharram 762 AH or December A.D. 1360 or Kislev 5121

At the invitation of his brother by marriage, Abd al-Aziz, Muhammad took his family and retainers on a trek with Aisha and her husband through the limestone peaks of Al-Arif before winter descended in full. Aisha had been forlorn for over six weeks, having suffered the disappointing loss of what should have been her first babe. Muhammad felt some reassurance in the choice of Abd al-Aziz, who remained as gentle and attentive to his wife as he had been at their wedding feast. He kissed her brow or her hand, even in close company with others. Aisha accepted his kindness, but dark circles still shadowed her reddened eyes each morning of their journey. Muhammad suspected the sadness had as much to do with her loss as her unhappiness in the union. In private with him, she had asked for news of Ali ibn Musa, but Muhammad knew nothing of the Berber commander's whereabouts. Despite her husband's devotion, Ali's claim on her heart endured. For respect of Abd al-Aziz and the alliance Muhammad had fostered with the Marinids, he would not make inquiries on Aisha's behalf.

The riders stopped at villages on their westward expedition and enjoyed the hospitality shown at every meager residence. To the collective amazement of all, they found gazelles, which Muhammad had heard of upon his arrival, but never seen. Abd al-Aziz pointed out a *fanak*, which he said appeared most oft at night in the desert. The sand-colored fox with large ears led her litter of three kits into a burrow. Another larger fox with a huge lizard in its jaws scuttled behind them and disappeared into the hole.

Abd al-Aziz leaned toward Aisha on her mount. "They mate for life."

She offered him a slight smile but made no reply.

Jazirah delighted in the trip most of all. She seemed more relaxed these days, mayhap in the knowledge of Muhammad's meeting with her father last month. It had been brief and occurred in the privacy of Ibn Battuta's home. Jazirah's father acknowledged his sins and begged for forgiveness. Muhammad still had to decide regarding the man's fate, but the future with Jazirah proved more of a preoccupation.

She spent much time as had become her custom with Yusuf, Leila, and Saad. She pointed out many features of the craggy landscape and compared them to the home none of the children remembered. Saad preferred to be in her arms rather than with Hafsa. The first time his wife had held Haziyya's son, a tremor jolted Muhammad's body before he chided himself over foolish fears. Jazirah reveled in Saad's closeness and he took his first steps at just over a year old with her aid across a weathered rock face. Leila had quickly warmed to Jazirah as well, calling her *Ummi,* to which she oft responded with a warm smile or embrace for the child. Only Yusuf remained reticent, but Muhammad believed with more time, their stubborn son would recall and accept his mother.

Jazirah's attentive nature to all of Muhammad's children reminded him of how much he admired her role as a parent. She had been devoted to Yusuf, their boy who had thrived in her care. Where he might have feared she could not demonstrate the same measure of love for children she had not borne, she proved him wrong. Mayhap he had been wrong in many of his assumptions about her. Before their first meeting, he had dismissed her as little more than a traitor's daughter. Yet, of her own free will, she had come to him in Al-Maghrib al-Aksa at her father's side. Braving the possibility of Muhammad's anger and rejection, and uncertain of her fate. Only a faithful and courageous woman would have undertaken the risk. Only a true Nasrid princess.

Muhammad considered his future as the company set out again at mid-morning. They left behind a small community at the base of the semiarid lowlands and rode through woodlands of juniper, cedar, fir, and oak trees, which hid a steep ascent through sheered rocks. When their footing became unsteady, everyone dismounted and led their horses by hand. They ascended to the higher elevations and stopped at midday beneath a tree canopy. Abd al-Aziz's porters retrieved satchels and crates carried by mules. All except the Christians in their company settled down for prayers. Then the meal followed, in which they listened while Abd al-Aziz and Al-Sabti reflected on the beauty of the mountains.

Jazirah placed Saad on her lap and fed him with mashed chickpeas. Muhammad smiled as his little son squished pulp between his fingers and smeared most of the food all over his mouth. Jazirah laughed at him and kissed his hair before she shared a long look with Muhammad over the boy's head. Afterward she turned away and cleaned Saad up, snuggling him close to her. Leila nestled against her grandmother and listened to Butayna's soft crooning. Despite restless eagerness to explore more of the countryside, Yusuf remained at his father's side. Muhammad settled him on his lap and told him stories of *djinn* who haunted mountaintops, which delighted the boy. When the children finally slept, Jawla and Hafsa carried them beneath the shade of a large tent.

Muhammad left the encampment and strolled to the height of another ridge, partly covered by a patch of snow. He circled the crag and marveled at the white-capped mountains around him. Having grown up beneath the shadows of other mist-enshrouded peaks, the majestic beauty of the terrain evoked terrible longing within him. He had to return home.

In recent weeks, he had exchanged terse letters with King Pedro of Castilla-León, demanding to know why he had forgone their friendship in favor of tribute from the new pretender called Muhammad the Sixth. If Muhammad the Red thought a Sultan's title and the payment of homage in gold coins to the Christians would ensure his reign, he would learn his mistake. With or without Pedro's aid, Muhammad intended to recover Gharnatah. He had to win the support of his people. When he achieved his aim, no one would ever take his throne again.

He stopped his musings as the clouds parted and a dark shape became visible on a cliff in the distance. He gasped as a lion with a thick, black mane settled on its hindquarters atop the bluff. The beast stared out across the mountain peaks. Wind rustled his fur.

"Magnificent," Jazirah whispered as she joined Muhammad.

"I never imagined we would see the like," Butayna said at his left shoulder.

Together the trio stood in silence and watched the lion, which soon rose and dipped below the height of the rock.

Butayna patted Muhammad's arm and turned away. She sought out Abd al-Aziz, who shared her excitement at the sighting of such a dangerous creature.

Jazirah turned to Muhammad. "The lion is your emblem, your mother believes so."

He nodded. "Persian rulers have associated lions with kingship for ages, as long depicted on their coats of arms. Mayhap the spotting of one today is a sign of my rule."

Afterward, he offered her his forearm and they descended from the heights together.

***

Sultana Jazirah

Fés el-Jedid, Al-Maghrib al-Aksa or Fez, Morocco

Muharram – Safar 762 AH or December A.D. 1360 or Kislev – Tebeth 5121

Dusk blanketed the city and a new moon shimmered through sparse cloud cover while Jazirah returned to Fés el-Jedid at the end of the month, riding beside Muhammad. At the entrance to the *riad*, she alighted and took a sleeping Saad up the stairs. She paused in the doorway and looked back at his father. He kissed Yusuf who had snuggled in Jawla's strong arms. Muhammad had been pensive on their return. Jazirah did not doubt thoughts of Gharnatah occupied his mind.

With Butayna's servants, Jazirah placed the children on their pallets in a room between hers and Butayna's own. She closed the doors to the small balcony adjoining the bedchamber lest insects disturbed the little ones. She dismissed Jawla and Hafsa, who promised they would look in on the princes and princess during the night. Two of the children's guards took positions on either side of the door. Saad awoke just as Jazirah laid him beneath the blanket, so she picked him up and walked with him, crooning softly. Soon his deep, even breaths returned.

She nuzzled his brow and whispered, "Sleep well, sweet child."

Love for all of Muhammad's brood burgeoned in her heart. Although her own son by him still regarded her with suspicion, Leila and Saad clung to her as children who desperately needed a mother, as much as she needed them. She placed Saad under his blanket and kissed his hair.

When she looked up, Muhammad leaned against the doorframe. She swallowed and brushed a thick lock of her tresses away from her face.

Once she rose, he entered the room and took her hand. He drew her out to the terrace, where both of them gripped the balustrade. They were silent for some time before Muhammad cleared his throat.

"You are good to them. I thank you for it. Thank you for loving my children."

"They are children. What else might you expect?"

"Resentment and bitterness. You did not give birth to two of them."

"They need a mother. You and your family have cared for them, but they require a mother's love and patience. I am glad I am here for them."

Muhammad placed his hand atop hers. "I need you, too."

Her skin tingled where he touched and her belly fluttered. "You need me?" Her voice warbled and giddiness almost overwhelmed her.

"I must have your support of my plans. I have decided to enlist the aid of Ibn al-Khatib and his friend Ibn Khaldun. Their letters must persuade Pedro of Castilla-León to aid me in the recapture of Gharnatah."

Jazirah swayed. Only his touch kept her upright. He had not meant a more personal wish, as she had anticipated. The truth should not have shocked her, but his quest meant an end to their almost idyllic time in Al-Maghrib al-Aksa as a family. "You want to return to Al-Andalus? To fight Muhammad the Red for the throne?"

"Has there ever been another choice?"

She pulled her fingers from beneath his. "There are always other alternatives. Muhammad, we were so happy during the last days in the mountains of Al-Arif. Gharnatah will always be our home, but you do not have to return there now. You have a life here with your children... with me if you wish it. Isn't this enough for you?"

He shook his head. "I wish you and our children could satisfy all my desires. Gharnatah called to me, a pull homeward, stronger than I have ever felt just before I saw the lion. You were right. You said the beast was my symbol. A sign of the future and the path I must pursue to reclaim my throne."

She stepped back. "Then you would abandon us for a gilded chair."

"The throne means more to me than this. You know why."

"I don't care!" When Yusuf coughed behind them, she lowered her voice. "Please, Muhammad. It has been four months since my arrival here and just when we are finally together, you and me with our children, you want to leave us again. I beg you do not. I don't want you to go."

"Jazirah, I have to return. My brother Ismail and Muhammad the Red, they stole not only my throne, but also my children's heritage! I cannot abandon it for their sakes or mine."

"Does a throne matter more than the love of Yusuf, Leila, and Saad? Than their worry for you? They won't understand! They will only see you are leaving them."

"You shall be here. You and my mother will care for them—"

"No! They need their father and mother. You see how Yusuf still shuns me."

"The boy is stubborn, a trait for which we share equal blame. Give him time."

"And what of me and my hopes for our future? What will happen to me in your absence? How do you expect me to bear your departure? What if you should die or suffer grave injury? How shall I live in uncertainty apart from you again, not knowing if you are dead or alive?"

He grabbed her arms and pulled her against him. His lips hovered just beyond her reach, his eyes dark and unfathomable despite the light of the moon. "Why do you care, Jazirah? Hmmm? Tell me why you care so much."

"You know why!" Weak-kneed, she clung first to his forearms and then draped her hands around his neck. The silky hair at his nape brushed her fingertips. "Can't you see the proof of my feelings in my eyes? You are the father of my beloved son. You are the only lover who has ever called me your own. Yours was the touch I desired each time Ismail laid his hands on me. Yours were the kisses for which I yearned. I never wish to be apart from you again."

His sharp intake of breath gave her some satisfaction, but not the full measure she truly craved. Silence swelled and dragged on between them. She took the course he would not, bent her head, and pressed her lips against his. She closed her eyes and kissed him as she had longed to for months, telling him by touch all she had not said since the moment of their reunion where she knew at long last of her true feelings for him. For in the midst of her shame and regret at her behavior during their union, as well as the forced marriage to Ismail, the hope she carried for a life with Muhammad had compelled her to confront the bitter truths, to speak in utter candor with him. Because she adored him and would never have secrets from him again.

She almost cried when at last he responded, his hands roving her back, her hips, and up her spine. He cradled her nape and then held her face between his hands. He touched her so lightly, his fingertips barely grazing her cheeks. His lips were softer than in her memory, his kisses slow and protracted. He smelled and tasted of cinnamon, cardamom, and ginger from the meal they had last enjoyed. She opened her eyes and found his gaze in the darkness. Tenderness and longing filled her.

"*Ummi?*"

They pulled apart as Leila's voice sounded. She stood in the doorway leading to the balcony, rubbing her eyes. "*Ummi*, I want water."

Muhammad groaned, but Jazirah nodded and ushered the girl back to her bed. "Rest, I'll get a cup for you."

By the time she returned from the cistern near the kitchen, Muhammad knelt beside Leila. Jazirah gave her the glass. Leila drank and closed her eyes again.

Jazirah whispered, "I beg you for her benefit, for the sake of your sons, stay."

Muhammad did not reply.

***

Seated with Butayna and Aisha after the evening meal three weeks later, Jazirah sighed and cradled her chin on her palm.

308

Her fingertips tapped her cheek idly. She gazed out of a north-facing window as sheets of rain pelted the *riad*, but the water and accompanying wind obscured her view. Aisha had joined them for dinner, so she could not return home just yet. No one, but a fool would have ventured outdoors into the downpour.

Muhammad's sister sipped her bay leaf tea and set it down on the table inlaid with mother-of-pearl. "*Ummi*, may I ask about a matter between husbands and wives?"

Butayna answered, "My sweet, naught is forbidden in conversation between a mother and daughter, even one who is married."

Aisha cleared her throat. "It concerns my husband. He came to me last night. Something he did in my bed has left me... troubled."

At the words, Jazirah raised her head and regarded her companions. Butayna's eyebrows lifted and a fire lit her gaze, as oft happened whenever she suspected anyone had mistreated those whom she loved. "Was he ungentle with you?"

"Oh no, never. Abd al-Aziz is a generous and affectionate lover, which is the reason I feel so terrible for having caused his disappointment."

"You shared in the loss of your babe with him, Aisha. I once suffered the same self-recriminations after similar circumstances. Do not permit such feelings to overwhelm you. Allow time, healing, and mutual regard to provide you the peace you need. Did you have any discomfort when he sheathed himself inside you?"

Aisha replied, "My husband's manhood is not large to begin with, so no."

"Have you ever experienced a large manhood with which to compare Abd al-Aziz?"

As Jazirah's mouth fell open, the pair at the table shared a laugh.

"*Ummi*, for shame! You know I went to my husband's bed as a virgin. I never gave myself to Ali, although I permitted him to kiss me."

"Daughter, you did not!"

"Why should I have gone to my husband's bed frightened of his embraces? Besides, I sought the kisses from Ali."

"I don't suppose he objected to them?"

"He was not to blame! I am a Nasrid. I am accustomed to getting what I want."

"You were always too bold for my liking."

"I'm your daughter. Where do you suppose I acquired the audacity? Ali never compelled me. When I kissed him sometimes, I could feel his desire for me against my belly. He and Abd al-Aziz differ in such... respects."

Butayna shook her head, while Aisha continued, "Last night, my husband did not seek his pleasure. He undressed me and when I wished to do the same to him, he stilled my hands. Instead, he just kissed me everywhere, even... down there."

"Did you enjoy his attentions?"

"Oh, indeed! I have never felt the like as when he used... his mouth... on me."

"Then, my dear, I don't understand your concern."

"Is such a thing permitted between husband and wife?"

"So long as there is mutual enjoyment, a husband and wife may share all forms of pleasure in their marital bed. Your father and I certainly did."

"Would you have allowed him to do as Abd al-Aziz did to me?"

"I never stopped my Yusuf! Your father was a most ardent lover and I believed he liked to astonish me when we were abed. In time, I learned there could be as much joy in the giving and receiving of those... kisses as Abd al-Aziz bestowed upon you."

"*Ummi!* You didn't do the same to Father with your...."

Butayna rolled her eyes. "Oh, please, don't look so surprised! I discovered all facets of my passionate nature in your father's arms. I gained and received equal delight in our lovemaking. My devotion to him only increased the pleasure. Even now for many nights, I have longed for his hands upon my body and his voice in my ear again. He taught me love, but he also showed me desire."

Aisha reached for her mother's fingers. "I know how much you cherish him still."

In the corner, Jazirah reflected on Butayna's words. Lovemaking had strengthened their bond. Even six years after her husband's death, she had not forgotten his touch.

When the rain stopped some time later, Aisha rose with Butayna. The women embraced and Butayna blessed her child.

Then she said, "Do not await your husband's summons tonight. Seek him out. Show him your gratitude in kind for the pleasures you have received. Your initiative will enchant him, and mayhap, you shall find joy in pleasing him."

"Thank you, *Ummi*. Just when I believed there were no more lessons to learn, you have taught me once again."

"You are a woman wed, daughter. You didn't need my aid. Let instinct guide you."

Afterward, Butayna sat beside Jazirah and talked of her wish to visit the marketplace on the next day. "Mayhap you and your Kissenga could come with me and my servants. It is better for you than staying in this *riad* where you argue with Muhammad over his decision. Yes, I know of his wish to return home and your objections. Your daily quarrels are no secret as neither of you take trouble to lower your voices, so don't frown as if I had spied upon both of you. Tomorrow, I want to see the spice merchant first because—"

Jazirah stood. "Forgive me, Butayna. I just remembered I wished to speak with Muhammad tonight."

"Only speak to my son?"

Heat swept up Jazirah's cheeks, but Butayna laughed, grasped her hand, and kissed her fingertips. "Go to him and bed him well, daughter. Bed him well."

***

As the call of sentries at the palace proclaimed the hour of midnight, Jazirah left her room clad in a mantle and walked down a long hallway to the opposite end. Kissenga had undone and re-braided her hair again with silver beads at each end, which clinked against each other as she moved. Outside Muhammad's room, Pero stood on duty beside the door. Stiff-backed, he bowed as she approached.

"I am dismissing you for the night, captain."

He straightened and mumbled, "Forgive me, my Sultana, but my master alone may discharge me."

"Go find Garcia or any of the other men! I don't want you listening at the door while I... talk to Muhammad."

Pero nodded. "As you wish, my Sultana."

She waited until his footsteps faded before she knocked.

"Enter." Muhammad's voice echoed through the cedar.

She pushed open the door and found him seated at a dinner table. Two corked inkpots and four rolled parchments with unbroken, red wax seals littered the surface, in the center of a large room of plants and braziers interspersed in each corner. Incense dispersed in a white haze through holes in the heaters. Green drapery hung around a large bed occupying the corner, while at the opposite end, a lattice screen partly obscured alcoves stuffed with textiles and shoes. Sparse quarters compared to Muhammad's at home in *Al-Qal'at al-Hamra*.

A reed pen in hand, he scratched the tip of it across the surface of the fine vellum. Seated cross-legged, he lifted his head from his writing briefly to regard her. "Jazirah, I told you earlier this morn, I don't wish to battle with you each day. Tomorrow my personal appeal to King Pedro must accompany letters written by Ibn al-Khatib, Ibn Khaldun, Al-Sabti, and Ibn Battuta, all of whom are learned men who shall champion my cause before this faithless Christian king. The hour is late. You should be in bed."

Her stare flicked to his mattress. "I have not come to argue with you."

He groaned, put his pen down, and gave her his full attention. "Then why are you here? What do you want?"

Jazirah approached. When she stood at his side, she tugged at the mantle's strings and pushed the wool off her shoulders.

311

The breath hissed between Muhammad's lips as she revealed her nakedness. Except for the *khamsa* and ruby pendant draped around her neck and the silver beads, she wore no other adornment.

She said, "I want you. Not the Sultan of Gharnatah who fights for his throne or the *Amir al-Muslimin* who defends the faith of Islam. Just the father of children whom I love, even if I did not give birth to all of them. The man who has pleasured me as no one else can."

As she threaded her fingers through his hair, he grabbed her wrist, none too gently. "Do you truly want this? Want me?"

"Why do you doubt? You knew from our wedding night how I desired you—"

"Will you turn from me again? You sent me from your bed when I would have reassured and comforted you."

She reached for him once more and smoothed her fingertips over his furrowed brow. "I had been plagued with nightmares of the jailor Harun in the weeks before we married. On our first night together, I envisaged his face."

"Why didn't you tell me?"

"I was afraid you wouldn't understand or forgive. I was foolish, but I'm not fearful any more. You are not like Harun. You would take no pleasure in harming me."

A wide swipe of his arm scattered all the contents of the table. He appeared unconcerned as to whether the ink spilled, as he tugged her down and seated her on the table. Then he released his hold, pushed her thighs apart, and rose between them. Her nipples tightened and a bolt of lust pierced her belly.

She did not wait for his caresses. Instead, she untied the laces of his tunic. He lifted his arms and she dragged the garment by its hem up and over his head. She smoothed her palms over his shoulder, across the fine hairs on his chest, where a silver pendant hung from a necklace of beads. Her hands strayed to his belly until she reached the band of his trousers. Anticipation surged through her, set her blood boiling as her fingertips dipped below the band. She pushed the cloth over his hips and scooted closer to him.

"Jazirah," he groaned softly between gritted teeth. "I don't wish to hurt you, but I don't know if there can be tenderness at this time."

She leaned toward him, kissed his crinkled brow. "Take me. I am yours, forever."

He looked down between their bodies. His turbulent gaze roamed over her form, almost reverent in his regard. She burned at every spot where his eyes lingered, her breasts and belly, the apex of her thighs. With skin so hot, how did she manage not to burst into flames? The small, strangled sound at the back of his throat hinted at the war raging inside him, as if he fought for control over his desires. When he raised his head, her breath caught. For the first time, she became aware of an emotion she had never seen before in his expression. Fear. Was he scared she had not spoken true and would reject him? If it took her until the end of her days, she would convince him. She tugged his face to hers, seeking his lips.

Muhammad's restraint broke. His fingers delved in her hair, a fistful tangled in his hands as he yanked her tresses and pulled her down. His mouth opened and she swallowed his impatient moan. Her hands swept down his neck, around his shoulders, and across the muscles of his back bunched beneath her touch. She pulled him closer, hitched her thighs against his hips, and locked her ankles behind him. When he broke their kiss, she bit his lower lip. His mouth took a heated path down her neck, tongue licking at the hollow of her throat, teeth nipping across her collarbone and to her breasts. She arched her back as his warm lips closed on the tip of her breast, while he probed the underside. As he took her nipple between his teeth, she gripped his head, and kept him there.

His hardness brushed her inner thigh. She angled her hips and reached down between them, guiding him within her. The first thrust turned their moans to mutual gasps of pleasure. He pulled back and slid inside her so furiously, tears sprang to her eyes, as joy and pain coupled. His hands slipped down to her waist and held her in place. She buried her face in his neck, opened her mouth, and tasted the salt of his skin. The wood beneath her creaked and banged against the floor, but she did not care. Soon a fine sheen of sweat covered both of their bodies, slick wherever they touched. The sound of skin against skin mingled with sighs and groans. As she sought his mouth again, she vowed never to let him go.

***

Neither stirred from the cold ground where they lay atop Jazirah's mantle as sunlight filtered through the lattice over windows. Wrapped in each other's arms, her leg thrown over his hip, she sighed and pressed her lips to his brow. The squeals of children echoed from down the hall.

Muhammad murmured, "They are such early risers. Hafsa will tend to them."

Jazirah said, "You have not slept. Each time I stirred in the night, you were awake."

"I'm not tired."

"Then I have not done well by you."

He laughed and drew circles along her hip. "Believe me, you have. My muscles will be sore later and those scratches on my back still burn. You are most demanding."

She fingered his beaded necklace. "We have not shared such joys since our wedding night. Why is this ornament familiar? Have I seen it here on Tuareg people?"

He ceased the movement of his hand. "You may have. This one belonged to Haziyya. When she died, I could not bury it with her."

Jazirah raised her chin and rested it atop his head. She blinked back tears and cleared her throat. "It's beautiful. Just as she was. Leila will be like her mother."

Muhammad rolled and took her with him. His hands tightened on her hips even before she attempted to sit up. She lifted her head and looked down at him.

Her necklaces hung between them. He grasped the ruby. "You kept your vow."

"I swore I would never take them off. Maryam tried to remove the jewels on the day she forced me to wed her son. I promised she would be dead before evening."

He palmed her cheek. "So fierce, so lovely." With a sigh, he added, "You deserve only the truth. Haziyya loved me as I loved her, not only as my companion, but also as mother to two of my children. She was a good parent to Leila and would have been equally devoted to Saad. I would have married her. For the life we shared in too brief a time and the children, I shall never forget or cease to love her. I never thought I could be twice blessed with an equal in my passions, until you came into my life."

A dull ache spread within Jazirah's heart. Confirmation of his lingering attachment after Haziyya's death stirred deep-rooted fears. Was Jazirah to live with the shadow of her husband's lost love forever?

He grasped her chin. "From the moment you entered my rooms with your head held aloft, and your gaze wide and assessing, I wanted you. I had never desired another woman so much in my life, not even Haziyya. After the wedding, I assumed my sentiments would change once those initial desires found fulfillment in the marriage bed. One night with you was not enough, but I never dared hope for more after you had dismissed me. Instead of resentment, my longing increased. Not just for your body, but knowledge of the workings of your mind and the pathways of your heart. There is room in my heart to love you, Jazirah. Will you let me?"

She brushed her hand against his bearded cheek, then lowered her mouth to his, and kissed him at her leisure. The kisses became demanding in the next breath. Atop him, she joined their bodies again. Would the love he offered be enough?

Chapter 24
The Ministers

Sultan Muhammad V

Chella, Al-Maghrib al-Aksa or Salé, Morocco
Jumada al-Ula 762 AH or March A.D. 1361 or Nissan 5121

At Chella on the northwestern coast, Muhammad dismounted from his horse in front of a blue house beside the *Bou Regreg* River. Jacaranda petals bordered the cobblestone path through a garden, which abutted the columned frontage.

Muhammad murmured, "Ibn al-Khatib has done well for himself here."

On her mount, Jazirah replied, "Your sister spoke to me of his stipend of five hundred *dinars* a month from Abu Salim. With the benefit of such generosity, it is no wonder Ibn al-Khatib did not wish to leave Chella and insisted upon your arrival here."

He wagged his finger at her. "Jazirah. Be sweet. He commanded no such thing. Ibn al-Khatib tends to his wife. She only joined him last spring and now she is ill."

She sneered and looked away, while he chuckled and shook his head. Ibn al-Khatib had removed to Chella just after the arrival of Jazirah and her father on a pretext of touring Al-Maghrib al-Aksa. She had questioned his departure and in recent weeks, Muhammad admitted the truth. Before her appearance in Fés el-Jedid, he and Ibn al-Khatib had quarreled over her return. Ibn al-Khatib recommended banishment for her and death for her father. When Muhammad refused, his minister stayed away.

Muhammad came around the horses and lifted her down. His hands lingered at her thickened waist and he kissed away her frown until she rewarded him with a wide smile. He did not fear she would be rude to Ibn al-Khatib, but there had been some trepidation over her wish to partake in the visit to Chella. Jazirah bore slights like none other. Seven months after their arrival and her reunion with Yusuf, she still had not forgiven her father and refused to let him see the boy, although Muhammad would have permitted it. He had not forgiven her father either, but he could not harm the man.

Three among the thirty guards in their wake carried their children. One handed down Saad to Jazirah, who accepted the squealing boy's kisses and returned them with equal joy.

Muhammad took Leila and balanced her on his hip, while Pero alighted with Yusuf, who wriggled and demanded, "Down! Down now!"

Muhammad and Jazirah shared an intent look. She warned him, "If we do not take the trouble to correct him, our son will become unruly."

"He's just a boy, Jazirah. He'll outgrow his childish temperament."

As her brows arched and her frown deepened, he sighed and said to his eldest son, "What have I taught you? Learn politeness even to those who serve you. Say 'please' if you wish Pero to put you down."

Yusuf gave Muhammad a fierce scowl and received another scolding. "Don't you dare look at me in such a manner! I am your father and you will obey."

With a pout on his lips, Yusuf looked at Pero. "Down now. Please."

Jazirah turned away, but her shoulders shook, and a snort escaped her. Muhammad nodded to Pero, who shrugged and placed the prince on the ground.

A eunuch came out of the house and rushed to greet them. He bowed profusely and Muhammad had to stop him after the fifth prostration. "Take us to your master!"

"He is with his wife this morning, mighty Sultan. She does not fare well."

Muhammad preceded the others into the house, where a small repast awaited them. Jazirah encouraged the children and their protectors to eat, but she refrained along with Muhammad. For all the opulence outside the house, the wooden floors were dusty and bare of carpeting. Frayed cushions lined the walls. In the wake of his wife's illness, had Ibn al-Khatib lost interest in his domicile?

Muhammad paced several times and then withdrew to the doorway leading to an enclosed garden. Jazirah stood and rubbed his shoulders.

She asked, "Do you believe Ibn al-Khatib will be too preoccupied to help you?"

He answered, "I don't know. The timing of the letter he wrote to King Pedro, along with the missives from Al-Sabti, Ibn Battuta, and Ibn Khaldun could not have been better. Muhammad the Red is grumbling about tribute without treaty for Castilla-León. Pedro wants the coin from Gharnatah to fend off Aragón's interests in the peninsula and his half-brother Count Enrique de Trastámara's attempts to procure favor with the Castillan nobles while he endures exile. If Muhammad the Red insists on intractability for long, mayhap I won't need another appeal from my minister to make Pedro see he should offer me his full support."

He gasped as Ibn al-Khatib crossed the garden. The downcast features and shadows beneath his eyes conveyed the strain he faced. He had never appeared so haggard before in such coarse woolen garments.

He bowed stiffly and mumbled, "Great Sultan, my Sultana, the peace of Allah be with you and yours."

Jazirah ignored his greeting and kissed Muhammad's brow. "Let me take the children to the river. You have much to speak of with Ibn al-Khatib."

As she left them and herded the children with their guards outdoors, Muhammad admired the sway of her hips. Then he turned and found Ibn al-Khatib gaping at him.

"You have reconciled with Sultana Jazirah, master?"

Muhammad grunted. "Our relations are not your concern!" When Ibn al-Khatib blanched, Muhammad softened his tone. "Tell me instead of your wife. How does she fare?"

A heavy sigh followed. "She is not long for this world."

"I grieve for your suffering. Your love for her remains evident."

"You did not come all the way from the capital to learn of her well-being."

"I did not."

Ibn al-Khatib indicated the garden. "Shall we take a stroll? Good air from the seaside will warm us."

Outdoors, Muhammad summarized the state of affairs between Gharnatah and Castilla-León for Ibn al-Khatib, as Al-Sabti had reported them two weeks ago. An odd role reversal when Muhammad had long depended on his minister for news.

Ibn al-Khatib said, "So, you believe Muhammad the Red may refuse to send tribute until the terms of a new peace treaty are in place? Would he rouse King Pedro's ire? The Castillan monarch does not have a reputation as a forgiving man."

"An understatement by any estimation. I hope Muhammad the Red is so foolish as to withhold the coin he's stolen from my treasury." Halting beneath an argan tree, Muhammad leaned against the bark. "I hate to ask, when all your concern must be for a beloved wife, but I need you to influence King Pedro again."

"I shall write a letter on your behalf, my Sultan."

"Thank you. Will you return to the capital when matters... conclude here?"

"I intend to. Abu Salim's minister Umar would like to see me return."

"You have heard his most audacious proposal of late?"

"Word reached me, my Sultan, even here. With the death of Abu Salim's fourth wife in childbirth, Umar proposes his youngest sister as a bride for the grieving widower. I assume Abu Salim has accepted?"

"When I dined with my sister and her husband, Abd al-Aziz told me his brother Abu Salim will accept. Umar aims high with the match."

Ibn al-Khatib gave a rueful chuckle. "He always has. He wants a grand vizier's position and will not settle for less."

"The current grand vizier, Ibn Marzuq, doesn't hasten toward his death."

"Mayhap his rival Umar will speed the journey."

When Muhammad whistled, Ibn al-Khatib nodded. "Ibn Marzuq called upon the services of your good doctor Ibn Khatima, who told me privately of his suspicions regarding poison. He warned the grand vizier to replace his entire household, especially the staff in the kitchens."

Muhammad sighed. "This place is more dangerous than Gharnatah."

"Surely, your household is not in peril. Abu Salim respects Sultana Aisha and extends his admiration for his sister by marriage to your family."

"I'm not worried about Abu Salim's regard."

The men retreated indoors, where both sat in chairs and savored cups of mint tea. Muhammad soon placed his empty vessel next to a gilded book, opened to a page.

His gaze narrowed as he read the words in silence. Then he fingered the gold lettering of the last verse and quoted, "There is naught but Allah."

Ibn al-Khatib responded, "*Tawhid*. Whatever is of this earth, you and your children, this house, this earth, all pales in significance where Allah exists. His divine presence bursts forth from the setting sun as it melts and plunges into the lap of twilight, in the silvery rivers and streams—"

Muhammad waved his hand. "Less of your poetic verses, I pray! Let us speak of this book. These lines are elements of Sufism. I was unaware of your interest in Sufi mysticism. When did you begin the study? Moreover, under whose influence?"

"You would not know this, master, but during your father's early reign, he encouraged compromise between the orthodox views of Islam and the doctrines of Sufism. Before my father and brother died in the service of your father at Salado, both explored the mysteries. Under their direction, I began visiting the lodges of Sufi orders throughout Al-Andalus and Al-Maghrib al-Aksa. The masters of each order have welcomed my exploration."

"Are you telling me you've become a Sufi disciple now? Is this the true reason for your withdrawal to Chella and your residence here?"

With a chuckle, Ibn al-Khatib shook his head. "I am not set upon the path. My concerns are of this world. I am sympathetic to the principles alone, not an adherent."

Muhammad wished to believe, but he wiped a hand across his warm brow. How could his father Yusuf have encouraged reconciliation with heretical dogma and allowed Ibn al-Khatib's family to dabble in such beliefs, which favored austere asceticism like monkish Christians in their cells, and validated all other religions rather than recognizing the supremacy of Islam? Even the veneration of Sufi masters in the same manner as Christians worshipping saints denied the very principles of the true faith.

Ibn al-Khatib interrupted his brooding. "Does mysticism trouble you? Sufism does not question the oneness of Allah. It is the journey of a true heart."

"I've heard enough of Sufi doctrine for today! I ask you not to speak of it again, for your sake and my own. You are well aware you have enemies even in Al-Maghrib al-Aksa, like the grand vizier Ibn Marzuq, who has grown jealous of his master's patronage of your writings. I don't count myself among your detractors from Gharnatah, but you must know Al-Sabti may never forgive your offense against him during my father's reign. He is still the nominal head of Gharnatah's judiciary, which looks upon Sufism as heresy. You must remain... guarded in your speech and writings. Focus on your duties to me. There are grave matters for the future of my Sultanate requiring your attention."

Ibn al-Khatib nodded. "I remember them, my Sultan."

***

The bed frame groaned and rattled as Muhammad's body banged against the wood. With one hand, he reached for Jazirah's fingers at the edge of the mattress. She gazed at him in full admiration as he held one slender ankle with his other hand and bent his head slightly to bestow a soft kiss.

"More," she moaned dazedly. He smiled at her demand and increased the tempo. When her teeth bit her lower lip and her stare became heavy-lidded, he almost came undone. Her lean legs draped against his chest and her other fingers twisted in the folds of the bedclothes. Every cry she gave tormented and delighted him. He did not doubt whether anyone who remained awake after midnight in Ibn al-Khatib's household heard every sound emanating from the bedchamber. While he pleasured her, propriety held no meaning. He had made love with Jazirah every day and night of the last four months, both never tiring of each other.

When he slammed his hips against her a final time, his groan echoed to the rafters as did her laughter. Once his heart stopped

319

pounding, he released her legs and draped them over the foot of the bed before he staggered to her side. He rested his head on her sleek thighs, which still trembled beneath him. His fingers palmed her belly, no longer flat, as he remembered from their wedding night.

He said, "We have lain together for several weeks, during which you have not bled."

She rolled her flushed face toward him, a satiated grin on her lips. "I have not had my woman's blood since the night before we returned from the mountains."

He raised his head and then pressed his ear to her belly, while she stroked his hair idly. "Jazirah, would you have told me of our child if I had not noted the width of your waist earlier today, or if I had not asked now?"

"Our customs do not encourage lovemaking between a man and his pregnant wife. I suppose I did not wish to stop sharing a bed with you."

He held her wrist. "As if I could keep from you. We must be cautious in the coming months. Speak to the royal midwife when we return to Fés el-Jedid." He pressed a kiss to her flushed skin. "A daughter with your hair and smile this time."

She giggled. "I shall give you only sons, Muhammad, I am certain."

He gazed at her. "Grant me children as proud and lovely as their mother." Their stares locked together. "I would count myself truly blessed."

***

Fés el-Jedid, Al-Maghrib al-Aksa or Fez, Morocco
Shawwal 762 AH or August A.D. 1361 or Elul 5121

On a bright summer morning at the end of a week, Muhammad emerged from the *riad* and found his household awaiting him. They lined the courtyard of the house, servants mingling with his councilors Al-Sabti, Ibn Battuta, Ibn al-Khatib, and Ibn Khaldun on the left. Faraj held the reins of Muhammad's gold-bridled horse at the forefront of two hundred royal guards, all Spanish and Portuguese Christians captured by the Marinids. A handful of them would remain behind, including Zabala and Butayna's captain Garcia. Pero stood on the other side of Muhammad's mount. He stroked the black Arabian's forelock. On the right, Aisha awaited Muhammad with a hand resting on her husband's forearm. Butayna gazed at her son from beside Abd al-Aziz. Jazirah swallowed and looked aside to where Yusuf, Leila, and Saad fidgeted in front of Jawla and Hafsa.

Yusuf whined, "I'm hot!"

Hafsa patted his head. "Say your farewells to your father and then you may go into the house, little prince."

320

Muhammad crouched, the metal rings of his thigh-length coat of mail scraping the ground. He beckoned his children who ran to him, each jostling the other to be first to reach him. He kissed their dark heads and blessed them from the eldest to the youngest in turn.

"I don't want to receive reports of your pride and stubbornness. Listen to your mother while I am gone," he admonished. He looked up at Jazirah. "She shall care for you, but you must care for her as well and the babe inside her."

Leila fingered the blackened links across his chest. "Where are you going, Father?"

"Home to Gharnatah, my sweet girl, and soon you shall be with me." He reached up and drew Haziyya's necklace over his head. He placed it on Leila instead. "This once belonged to someone whom you may not remember. It should be yours now."

She examined the silver pendant before embracing him again and kissing his cheek. "Thank you, Father."

Yusuf demanded, "Will you have a present for me in Gharnatah?"

Muhammad chuckled and kissed his forehead. "The best present of all. The kingdom you will rule when I am gone."

Yusuf stamped his foot. "I want a real present!"

Muhammad shook his head, stood, and called to his mother's servants. Each bowed before him and wished him well before escorting the children inside.

Then Muhammad came to his sister and Abd al-Aziz, the latter whom he clasped arms with before saying, "Honor my sister always."

Abd al-Aziz nodded. "Aisha is a priceless pearl. I shall treasure her."

"Dearest brother!" She threw her arms around Muhammad and clutched at his neck. Then he felt the hard protuberance beneath her robe. When he drew back and gaped at her, she nodded. "I did not say anything although it is almost the fifth month of my second pregnancy. The last disappointment happened at such an interval."

He kissed her brow. "Trust in Allah and you shall soon hold your child."

Next, he took his helmet from Butayna. She grazed his cheek. "Go, my lion, and reclaim your kingdom. Wherever you may travel, know my love remains with you."

"I have never doubted, *Ummi*. Protect our family."

She looked to Aisha and Jazirah. "They are daughters of my body and spirit. I shall keep them and your children safe."

He held his hand out for Jazirah. "Walk with me."

She blinked and laced her fingers with his. They ambled to where Faraj and Pero stood. Both men withdrew and mounted their horses.

Jazirah said, "Muhammad, this plan of yours to secure King Pedro's commitment still concerns me."

"Is this why you were so restless in the night? I should have made love to you again and soothed you to sleep."

"As only you can, but know, even your tender touch would not have calmed my reservations. Your strategy is audacious."

He chuckled. "One way to describe it."

"Have you considered the consequences if Pedro accepts your offer of Andalusi cities in exchange for his assistance?"

"I have. If he can hold the cities his men capture, he may have them. If."

She shook her head. "Your tactic hinges on possibilities you cannot control. What did Ibn al-Khatib say of this offer? What did your mother recommend?"

"Neither of them knows of my intent. I only shared it with you."

Her eyes widened. "Muhammad, you honor me with your trust, but...."

"You may believe in me, Jazirah."

"I do. I love you."

Not the first time she had said so, but each time he heard her words, contentment overwhelmed him. He reached for and caressed the jutting belly beneath her mantle. He knelt and pressed a kiss there. A little sob escaped her.

When he stood again, he wiped away the tears trickling down her cheeks. "Be well and send me word of our child. I shall be at Sevilla for some weeks."

"I will write to you when our son is born."

He chuckled. "How can you be so certain we shall have another boy?"

"I know him. I have felt his powerful kicks for months now. Only a Nasrid prince would be so fierce."

His fingers lingered on her face. "I hate to leave you when his birth is so close at hand."

"I pray you may reclaim your kingdom and we may come to you in Gharnatah, where you shall hold this son of ours and bless him."

"I have a wish for us, too. Someday soon, I pray you may look upon me, call me your husband again, and know I am yours. You have never ceased to be my wife, but our laws say I am no longer your husband. I would be so again, not because familial duty or necessity required vows from either of us, but because you have longed for me as I have longed for you."

He took her in his arms, kissing her with all the love in his heart. As she clung to him and sniggers or gasps followed, neither of them cared whether their embrace caused anyone else embarrassment. When she released him, he grasped her hands and raised them to his lips.

"You and our children are my life. After this moment, we shall never be apart."

He let her go, placed his foot into the stirrup, and swung into the saddle. He put the helmet on his head and looked down at her, memorizing the curves of her lips, the roundness of her cheeks, the shimmer of unspent tears in her eyes. Then he dipped his head and she tiptoed to kiss him again.

He whispered against her lush lips, "I love you, Jazirah. I will always love you."

She stepped back, hands resting on her belly.

He drew his sword, turned the horse around, and addressed his men with one word. "Gharnatah!"

They echoed his cry and drew their weapons, thrusting them toward the golden sky. "For Gharnatah and Sultan Muhammad!"

With a nod to the four ministers who had helped him secure promises of aid from King Pedro, Muhammad trotted his mount through a path the men cleared for him. When he reached the end of the column, Jazirah's father inclined his head, dark eyes visible on either side of the nose guard projecting from his silver helmet. He wore an old mail shirt with too many dented metal loops.

Muhammad asked, "Are you prepared?"

"To prove my loyalty to you, my love for my daughter and grandson, and my faith in Gharnatah's future under your reign. I am ready."

"You have asked me to trust you, a difficult task given our histories. Still, I have never doubted your love for Jazirah or our birthplace. You do this to win your daughter's forgiveness, not mine."

"What is greater? A father's love for his child or a husband for his wife? There can be no comparison. Yet, you and I share such love for my daughter and Gharnatah."

Muhammad nodded. "Then let us reclaim our homeland. Together."

***

The Vizier

Sultana Jazirah

Fés el-Jedid, Al-Maghrib al-Aksa or Fez, Morocco
Shawwal 762 AH or September A.D. 1361 or Elul 5121

On the morning after Abu Salim's marriage to the sister of his minister Umar, Jazirah remained at the palace in the company of Aisha. Mutual concern and love for Muhammad had brought the two women together, but when Aisha confided the news of her pregnancy, Jazirah stayed at her side to offer comfort and reassurance.

At mid-morning, the pair strolled through the palace gardens offering polite nods to the courtiers whom they passed. Zabala and Kissenga trailed at a discreet distance. Both men appeared resentful of the other's role in Jazirah's life while she dismissed their rivalry over her protection as foolish behavior.

Aisha asked, "How do you fare? Your time must be close."

Jazirah patted her engorged belly. "The royal midwife says so each day."

"You have been fortunate, blessed with trouble-free pregnancies twice over."

"Fortune shall favor you as well, Aisha. You have the devotion of your prince and soon, you will have his child to hold."

Jazirah and Aisha admired a sunken garden of roses, violets, and jasmine, before the latter said, "You love my brother. I don't love Abd Al-Aziz. He is gentle and so kind to me, but my heart longs for another. I wish I carried the child of Ali ibn Musa. He has not come to Fés el-Jedid since my marriage more than a year and a half ago. Do you think he remembers me?"

When Jazirah would have answered, a blood-curdling scream shattered the tranquility of the garden and sent tremors through her body. Zabala and Kissenga raced to her side. The terrified courtiers dashed between rows of bushes, only to have their throats or bellies cut by blue-robed warriors who emerged from the palace. They slashed at everyone in their path indiscriminately, men and women, old and young.

Kissenga brandished his staff and growled over his shoulder. "Go home. Now!"

Zabala thumped Kissenga's shoulder with the pommel of his sword. "What do you think to do with your stupid stick, man?"

Aisha screamed as one of the assailants barreled toward them. His bloodied dagger brandished in the air, he uttered a stream of curses. Kissenga smacked his arm and leg with the acacia wood, felling him. For good measure, the eunuch bashed him over his head and cracked his skull.

Zabala closed his mouth, sheathed his weapon, and hoisted Jazirah in his arms. "Forgive me, my Sultana."

Kissenga hefted Aisha and both men ran from the carnage unfolding in the palace. They darted behind tall bushes and hedgerows to make their way to the northern gate, where Aisha demanded passage. Free from the palace, they ran to the *riad*, never stopping until Zabala set Jazirah on the steps. Then he collapsed in exhaustion.

Butayna emerged from the house. "I saw you running here. What happened?"

Between ragged breaths, Aisha explained the violence they had witnessed. "Oh *Ummi*, it was terrible!"

Butayna said, "Come in and let us bar the doors."

Jazirah swayed and rubbed a dull ache across her back. "I think I need my bed. Help me."

Kissenga and Zabala grabbed both of her arms, looked at each other, and nodded. She mumbled about the folly of men while they ushered her into the house.

***

The hour of midnight arrived and brought with it Jazirah's second son, who entered the world with Butayna's aid. Despite the concerns she expressed to Jazirah, they could not risk opening the door for anyone, so no summons went to the royal midwife or even Ibn Khatima. Zabala and Kissenga served as protectors, for the few Christian guards Muhammad left behind had not appeared. Jazirah put aside concern for their absence while she cradled her child and kissed his brow still spattered with mucus and blood. Butayna awaited the appearance of the afterbirth.

Jazirah said to her, "For all your fears about your ability to aid me, I think the old midwife in Gharnatah would be proud of you."

Afterward, Butayna brought water and washed her grandson, while Jazirah cleaned herself up as best as she could. The children had refused sleep after the cries came from the birthing room. They rushed in at Butayna's summons, ahead of Aisha, Jawla, and Hafsa. The excited brood crowded around the bed for a look at their new brother.

Leila asked, "What's his name, *Ummi*?"

"Fool!" Yusuf snapped. "Fathers give the babies the names."

Jazirah wagged her finger at him. "You must be kinder to your sister, my stubborn son." He frowned at her before she turned to Leila. "Your brother is right and your father would give the name if he were here. As it is, we talked before he left, and we agreed to call your brother Nasr. It means 'helper' in our language."

Her gaze swung back to Yusuf. "Friendship between brothers is important. When you are Sultan, you must have aid to govern Al-Andalus. Your brothers shall be your strength."

Within moments, Kissenga appeared in the doorway. "Prince Abd al-Aziz has come."

Aisha came around the bed. "My husband is here?" She whirled toward her mother. "Should we let him in, *Ummi*?"

325

Butayna sighed. "He loves you, I have no doubt. I do not think he will harm us." When Aisha rushed to the exit, Butayna followed. "I won't let you face him alone!"

Another hour passed before Jazirah insisted the children should sleep. She permitted their united demand to stay with her and allowed them to recline on pallets in her chamber, while Kissenga guarded the door.

Jazirah rocked Nasr, who had fallen asleep at her breast. Then Butayna and Aisha returned. Both of them stood pale at the foot of the bed.

Jazirah looked up. "What is it? What happened?"

Aisha murmured, "The minister Umar ordered the arrest of Abu Salim. Umar's supporters have killed the Sultan and all his followers. His brother Abu Tashufin rules in Abu Salim's place."

Butayna sank down on the bed, her fingers clasped. "They killed my friend Shams ed-Duna as well, because she shared Abu Salim's counsel. She only wanted to see her English home again. Now, she never will."

Aisha added, "Even worse, it appears some of the guards Muhammad assigned here knew of the plot and aided Umar. The captain Garcia leads them. He shared in Umar's treachery. My husband believes we are safe. He has pledged loyalty to Abu Tashufin to secure our lives."

Jazirah clutched her new son closer and looked at her children curled up on pallets beneath her window. "What will become of us?"

Silence answered her.

Chapter 25
The Cortes

Sultan Muhammad V

Ishbiliya, Al-Andalus or Sevilla, Kingdom of Castilla-León
Dhu al-Qa`da 762 AH or September A.D. 1361 or Tishri 5122

Two kings strolled arm-in-arm through the gardens of the palace at Sevilla, each accompanied by one trusted guardsman. Although Muhammad and Pedro of Castilla-León were close in age at twenty-three and twenty-seven years old respectively, they could not have been more different in appearance. Pedro stood taller than Muhammad, whose sun-bronzed complexion contrasted with Pedro's sallow features. Blue eyes regarded Muhammad, oft with curiosity, beneath pale-yellow eyebrows.

"You are not the sole person ever betrayed by a brother. *Madre de Dios*, what I wouldn't give to kill that *bastardo* Enrique, the *conde* de Trastámara, whom Leonor de Guzman claimed as the son of my father. Enrique still holds me responsible for the deaths of his mother and our brother Fadrique."

Muhammad knew better than to question his fellow monarch's guilt. Besides, he had not arrived in Sevilla to listen to Pedro's family troubles.

He said, "While I shall revile Ismail forever for his betrayal, he did not plan the coup against me alone."

"Ah, then we must speak of this Muhammad *el Bermejo*."

"*Si!* The people of Andalusia grow tired of him. The governors only need a little encouragement from me to throw off his yoke."

"Hmmm, encouragement. By this word, you mean bribes." Pedro halted, his hold on Muhammad's arm jerking him to a stop as well. "What shall I gain in return for the... inducement I may provide the Granadine nobles?"

Muhammad looked at him squarely. "Any city of Andalusia which your men can capture and hold may be yours, except where the citizens would do me homage at Granada, Malaga, Ronda, Alhama, Antequera, Loja, and Almería."

"Each of those cities remains so valuable to you?"

"With the exception of Granada, I mean to punish the masters, not the denizens, of those territories for their betrayal of me."

Pedro raised those fair brows again and tugged at his earlobe. He ran his hand over his yellow hair and gave Muhammad a tight smile. His pallid countenance reminded Muhammad of the stark visage Jazirah had shown him on the morning of his departure when they spoke of his intent to offer Pedro cities in exchange for aid. As they had first talked of it during the previous night, she had reasoned Pedro would never believe him. Who would?

Pedro repeated, "Any other city my men can capture?"

"And hold," Muhammad added, though he doubted his Christian counterpart heard. Pedro released Muhammad, turned away, and bounced on his tiptoes for a moment. When he spun around, the gleam in his eyes and the ruddiness of his cheeks conveyed his assent.

He said, "You understand I must meet with the *Cortés* to discuss your request. My principal advisors will have questions about you and your promises. Already, some among them wonder at your presence here." He spread his arms wide, showing off the embroidered sleeves of the *jubba* from Fés el-Jedid, the fine robe one among many of Muhammad's gifts to the Christian king. "My detractors believe I am even fonder of Moors than Jews."

Each group likely had their uses in Pedro's opinion, but Muhammad kept such thoughts in his head. "You do not rule by the consent of such men. God granted you this kingdom of Castilla-León. By God's grace alone, you shall rule it as I shall govern Granada again."

Pedro gave an approving nod and they continued their tour of the gardens across a patio of ochre and sage-colored tiles, bounded by hedges. Pedro's ancestor Alfonso, whom his people called the Wise, had constructed a palace incorporating little except a patio and the retaining wall of the Moorish castle Al-Muwarak, built in the days of Al-Muwahhidun rule over the peninsula.

As they strolled beyond a large central fountain and headed for a grove of orange trees, Muhammad added, "If you prefer, I would be happy to attend the *Cortés* and address any inquiries."

"Your attendance may sway my council." Pedro rubbed his hands together. "This exercise is just what I needed. You may not have heard, but I lost my Maria de Padilla just two months ago. She left me with an heir and three daughters to raise. One shall be for the Church, but I consider other possibilities for the younger two girls."

Muhammad had learned of the death of Pedro's official mistress from Ibn al-Khatib while in Fés el-Jedid. Even an official marital union when he was fifteen had not kept Pedro from his true love. Now both women had died, Pedro's queen in mysterious conditions. Muhammad did not know what to think of these circumstances, except the Castillan king might prove the most unpredictable ally Gharnatah ever sought.

Muhammad said, "I grieve for your loss."

"You have never spoken of your own marital state. I know you have children."

"Three, soon to be four. It seemed impolite in view of your grief to mention my happiness, but my wife awaits the birth of our next child in Morocco."

Muhammad smiled as Jazirah's image came to mind. He sighed deeply, as the pain of her absence struck him. After he won his capital again, he would send Pero for her and their children. Afterward, Muhammad would never leave Jazirah's side.

Pedro intruded on his thoughts. "Your wife? I had some strange news from my councilors of a woman who was your wife before she wed your brother. Do you speak of the same woman?"

Muhammad grunted. How had the Christians gained access to such intimate details of his life? In the months after their reunion, Jazirah had often spoken with him about her forced marriage. Although he would forever despise his enemies for what they had done to her, mostly he marveled at her resilience. She might be the strongest woman he had ever known, rivaling his mother. By the grace of God, Jazirah would be his forever.

He told Pedro much the same. "She shall always be mine."

Pedro nodded. "I understand." Then he cleared his throat. "Where shall we attack first?"

Muhammad smiled at the forgone conclusion of acquiescence from the Castillan councilors. "I'll tell you a little of what the pirates of Morocco taught me. The coasts of the peninsula are always ripe for an attack at this time of year. I have nominal command of six galleys, a gift from Abu Salim."

"Excellent. To this number, I shall join five of my galleys to strike out against the coastal cities. Would my admirals enjoy the sea breezes around Malaga?"

"They might find them fair and pleasant."

***

The *Cortés* or parliament of Castilla-León met at the command of King Pedro in Sevilla on a morning exactly two weeks later. Among them were all the bishops of the kingdom, from Burgos and León even, and the grand masters of every knightly order, including Don Diego Garcia de Padilla of Calatrava, brother to the king's deceased mistress. Among the courtiers gathered to witness the unfolding of the proceedings, Muhammad found a familiar face in Abraham ben Zarzar, whom Pedro had employed after the days of the coup in Gharnatah. For some reason, the Jew avoided Muhammad, but he could not allow Abraham's strange behavior to concern him. Yet, he also considered the

329

possibility Abraham might have conveyed the circumstances surrounding Jazirah's forced union with Ismail. How else might the Castillans have known?

Muhammad dismissed such concerns as he stood at the center of the assembly dressed in fine robes he had acquired in Fés el-Jedid with a long, sand-colored turban wrapped around his head. The cold regard of most of the men in the room did not worry him. Pedro would browbeat them into submission. A single attendee embodied the concerns of those who wished to dismiss Muhammad.

Pero López de Ayala stroked his oiled, black beard and continued his soliloquy, which had begun an hour ago. The man reminded Muhammad of Ibn al-Khatib, yet another fine orator enamored with his own voice.

"Now comes this Muhammad, this beggar king of Granada, seeking coin and horse to regain a lost kingdom. Why should we aid such a man? If he was fool enough to permit the loss of his throne to his brother, who in turn let this Muhammad *el Bermejo* take it from him, why should we bear the burden?"

Muhammad had oft chided himself with the same arguments. If he had failed to hold his land against his enemies, he might not deserve to rule.

Ayala continued, "This fight for the lordship of Granada does not concern us. The *Reconquista*, the reclamation of lands for Christians should be our interest! If this Mohammedan wishes to do battle for his kingdom, let him beg elsewhere."

Murmurs of assent rose to thunderous shouts of approval. Pedro's councilor basked in the acclaim of those surrounding him. Pedro allowed the approbation for some time before he waved away Ayala and nodded to Muhammad. The court herald demanded silence in the name of the king.

Muhammad laced his fingers together behind him and turned in a slow circle as he spoke. "Honored nobles of Castilla-León, I have not the grace and wit of the esteemed Pero López de Ayala, who speaks as he should for the benefit of his country and its king. Yet, I consider the past and the future of us all as I press my claim. Almost one hundred years ago, my ancestor the first Muhammad of Granada aided King Fernando in the conquest of Sevilla from its Muslim rulers. Since then, Granada's kings have fought beside and against the kings of Castilla-León. Where there were... variances between us, my ancestors battled for the preservation of their religion and culture, the rights any man—"

Ayala demanded, "Why should we support any among the heathen Mohammedans in their quarrels over a throne? Let them kill each other for it!"

More supporters joined him, but Pedro demanded quiet again.

Muhammad continued as if no interruption had occurred. "My ancestors fought for rights any man desires and deserves, but despite the differences between our religions, our peoples have shared concerns. In Portugal, Castilla-León, and Aragón, there is common interest with Granada. We would each keep our borders intact, hold this peninsula for ourselves, and thwart the effort of outsiders to take this land for their own. Surely, you fine men are aware of the ambitions of the Marinids to emulate the conquests attained under Almohade and Almoravid interlopers. I was a guest of the Moroccan king for some time and privy to his council meetings. Believe me when I say Abu Salim would conquer this land and rule from Morocco. Andalusia is my birthplace, but my mother, an honored queen of Granada hails from this country at Talavera de la Reina."

The evident shock on the faces of the assembly amused Muhammad, which he hid behind a tight-lipped smile. Some might have fallen into an apoplexy if he had also mentioned his Jewish heritage, but the claim would not bolster his cause.

He added, "My loyalty is to this land of my birth, as fierce a devotion as yours. Granada has played its part in keeping the Moroccans at bay. We are all that stands in the way of another wave of invasions from across the Mediterranean Sea. Infighting will occupy Granada while I campaign against the pretender who sits my throne. Who will look to the defenses on the southern coast of this land?"

He peered at Ayala, whose eyes had widened, and at Pedro, who gave him a nod.

Then Muhammad said, "Ayala says I should beg elsewhere. Where shall I go? To the king of Aragón, a persistent enemy of Castilla-León? The struggle with your opponent has abated for now with your latest treaty and you have surrendered custody of some castles you had claimed, but how long shall the terms of truce hold? If I should seek Aragón's support, will its sovereign remember your treaty then?" He paused and reviewed the blanched faces. Many among the *Cortés* looked to Pedro, whose expression remained unaltered except for pale, thinned lips.

Muhammad halted in the center of the room. "Among the Saracens of the Holy Land, there is a proverb now centuries old. The enemy of my enemy is my friend. Would Castilla-León prefer to keep Granada as an ally? I invite you erudite men to consider the future of this kingdom if Aragón should prefer amity with Granada instead."

He bowed before Pedro, who waved him away. He turned on his heels to rejoin the trio who awaited him at the door.

"My Sultan," said his uncle, Faraj, and Pero, each saluting him. Muhammad acknowledged their mutual gestures and preceded them out of the noiseless chamber.

***

Three hours later, a red-faced Pedro stomped outdoors to the garden where Muhammad's men had erected a tent. Muhammad sat beneath it in the company of his uncle and Faraj while they ate sesame and anise cakes. Pero noted the king's presence first and alerted his master.

Muhammad wiped his fingers on a linen cloth while the king berated him. "Not well done, not well done at all! You may have achieved your aim, but you made me appear the fool. My men spent hours talking of how the threat of invasion from the Moroccans will become reality while you and your traitor cousin fight for the crown. They berated me for having made peace with this upstart Muhammad *el Bermejo* and accepting his offers of tribute!"

Muhammad did not say how he had oft pondered the same action as disloyalty. After all, Pedro had pledged him friendship at the start of his reign only to betray him and extend peace to Muhammad the Red.

Instead, he asked, "What has your council said of my request for aid?"

"Oh, you may have your money and horses. Thirty thousand of our *maravedies* and the best warriors to help you in the *Reconquista* of your kingdom. Even the masters of Calatrava and Santiago have pledged some of their knights."

"I do not want them." Muhammad would not allow the Castillans to claim all the glory or Andalusi townships, despite his promises to Pedro.

"You have no choice! You will accept them. Be on your way by morning. You will go south to Ronda."

The men beside Muhammad gasped, while he glared at Pedro. "Ronda? The bastion of the Moroccan host? Shall they open their gates to me, so their commander Yahya can cleave me from neck to navel as he would have done two years ago?"

Pedro's frown faded. He bent over and laughed, clapping his hands to his knees. "You were never so poorly informed as now. Ronda will welcome you, for the garrison is under the command of Yahya's son Uthman, who cursed and berated his father after the coup for his betrayal of you. Uthman held the city against his father and refused to give him command of the warriors behind the walls. Yahya is at Guadix. In Ronda, you shall establish a new government and plan your enemy's end."

***

Runda, Al-Andalus or Ronda, Andalusia
Dhu al-Qa`da 762 AH or September A.D. 1361 or Tishri 5122

Five days afterward, the citizens of Runda thronged the cobblestone street leading from the *Bab al-Maqabir* at midday and welcomed Muhammad within the walls. He had skirted the city and entered via the southernmost gate at its commander's behest. Foremost among the delegation which greeted him was Uthman ibn Yahya ibn Rahhu in the midst of his men, who flew the banners of the *Ghuzat* and Gharnatah. Uthman dismounted from his horse and knelt beside Muhammad, pledging the loyalty of his warriors and the city.

He said, "Mighty Sultan, I pray, do not judge me by my father's actions. He is unworthy to remain *Shaykh*. I have written letters to my master Abu Salim regarding this matter and can only pray for the removal of my father from his post."

Muhammad ordered Uthman to rise. "Prove your loyalty to me and mayhap we shall oust your father from Wadi-Ash before long. Get on your horse and escort me to the citadel. We rode hard and my men are tired, in need of food and rest."

As Uthman led the arrivals over uneven terrain, women pelted them with oleander flowers and laid palm branches in the road upon which their horses trod.

Muhammad turned aside to Pero. "I wrote to Jazirah upon my arrival at Sevilla, yet I have had no word from her. Even my mother and Ibn al-Khatib have not sent letters. Tomorrow, you will direct one of the best captains of the old guard, whose loyalty is beyond question, to visit Al-Maghrib al-Aksa with missives for my wife, mother, and Ibn al-Khatib. In truth, I simply wish to know how Jazirah and our children fare, whether she has given me a new son or daughter. Are she and all our children safe?"

Pero nodded. "My man shall discover the truth. It shall be as you command."

***

Fés el-Jedid, Al-Maghrib al-Aksa or Fez, Morocco
Dhu al-Qa`da 762 AH or September A.D. 1361 or Tishri 5122

Jazirah lifted Nasr from her breast and cradled him against her chest, stroking his back. He wriggled in his blanket, his tiny head tucked beneath her chin. By candlelight, they sat in the dining area of the *riad* with Butayna three hours after the evening meal. Although slaves had cleared the table of dishes and cleaned the room, the women lingered. Butayna had dismissed her servants to their pallets.

"Why has he not written to me?" Jazirah whispered.

"Muhammad may have done so, daughter. The Marinids might be keeping you from receiving his dispatches. No one has heard from him, not even his ministers. Ibn al-Khatib promised to get a letter out."

"If he can." Jazirah closed her eyes briefly, but the tears seeped beneath her lashes still. "You must think me so foolish, weeping like a weak-willed woman for Muhammad."

She sighed and regarded Muhammad's mother. Across the room, Butayna lifted her gaze from the leather-bound Bible in her lap. "I believe you are a woman who loves and misses my son, as much as I adore and miss him. There is no shame in tears shed for the ones whom we love. Many a night, I have wept for my husband and none could console me, for I shall never see him again."

"Don't you believe in a God who would allow a Christian and a Moor to find happiness in Paradise?"

"I do, but there may be some time before we see each other again. I have my family to live for now, Aisha and Muhammad, you and the children."

Jazirah swallowed. "Can you ever forgive me for my treatment of you in Gharnatah? I did not know whether to trust you or Maryam. I let myself be led astray by her lies."

"You may remember when I spoke with Aisha of my loss of a babe. A daughter who preceded Aisha's birth. The midwife assured me the child had formed enough to know the sex, but I never saw or held her. I wished for many blessings with my Yusuf, the joy of more children among them. Now, I have you for a daughter."

"I don't remember my mother, but Lubna loved me for many years. She is gone, but now there is you. Thank you for caring for me as a mother would, for loving my son when I thought him lost forever."

From above stairs, a child's whimper echoed. Both women said, "Yusuf," at the same time.

Butayna closed her Bible. "I'll see to him, Jazirah."

"You should rest. Besides, I need to put Nasr in his cradle."

In the end, they mounted the stairs together, and went into the children's room. Hafsa and Jawla snored steadily on either side of the door, unaware of how Yusuf thrashed and sweated in his sleep. Butayna held out her arms and took Nasr, while Jazirah rushed to her eldest son's side. She crouched beside him, wiped his wet brow and cheeks, and kissed him.

"Hush, my son, hush. You are having a bad dream, naught more."

He rolled toward her, his fingers brushing against hers. "*Ummi....*"

The breath caught in her throat for a moment. She looked to Butayna through unshed tears. Then she stretched out on the ground beside Yusuf and hugged him close, pressing kisses to the top of his head.

"Hush now. I'm here, I'll always be here."

When the moon intruded between slats in the door to the balcony, loud banging came from the first floor. Jazirah raised her head and looked across the room to Butayna, seated beside Nasr's crib on a wooden stool.

Butayna grumbled, "What does the snake Garcia want at such an hour? Is it not enough for him to keep us guarded in the *riad* day and night? You stay here, Jazirah, with the children. I'll go down and see what he wants."

When an interminable time had passed, Jazirah kissed a sleeping Yusuf again and rose, just before the door creaked. Butayna beckoned her with a wave.

Jazirah stepped out into the corridor, surprised to find Ibn al-Khatib awaiting her dressed in a black, hooded mantle. "How did you get past Garcia's men?"

He jangled a bag of coins. "We are lucky those on duty at the *riad* are greedier than Garcia, who is simply ruthless. I have had word from Sevilla of our Sultan."

Jazirah's heart leapt. "How is he? Is Muhammad well?"

Butayna patted Jazirah's forearm. "Calm yourself. He is well."

Ibn al-Khatib said, "The Castillan king summons a council meeting of his most important nobles and clerics in Sevilla to decide upon Sultan Muhammad's request for aid to retake Gharnatah. He reached Sevilla in safety, but we may not know the outcome of his appeal for several days."

Jazirah clasped her hands, bowed her head, and whispered a silent prayer for Muhammad's safety.

"There is more, my Sultanas. Muhammad the Red has learned of our Sultan's purpose and directed his agents to influence King Pedro against giving succor to my master. Muhammad the Red also sent men to demand our release into his custody."

Butayna tapped her lips with a fingertip. "Muhammad the Red means to use us as pawns to compel my son's withdrawal. What does Abu Tashufin intend?"

"My Sultana, Umar is the power behind the throne. He has not let his puppet Abu Tashufin perform a single act or make any decision. I have no doubt Umar will keep you here for ransom to Sultan Muhammad."

Jazirah sneered. "You would know. You have been Umar's friend since your arrival."

He nodded. "I counseled him against detaining your family here, my Sultanas, but Umar will not listen to me. He is drunk on power and my... disappointment in him is beyond measure. Still, I must play my part lest he grow suspicious."

Butayna asked, "The guards you have bribed tonight, can you persuade them to let us go?"

Ibn al-Khatib shook his head. "There is not enough gold in my coffers or this country. I did manage to send a reply to my source in Sevilla. I told him the words, 'All is not well.' I could not say more for fear the messenger might not remember it all. Mayhap my words will be enough to let Sultan Muhammad know we are all in danger. Before his departure, he charged me with a sacred duty. The protection of this family. I will not fail my master. Whatever you may believe of me, know my loyalty to your family shall never cease."

Jazirah and Butayna shared a look, but both maintained their silence.

Ibn al-Khatib drew up his hood. "I must return to my house in the city. When I have word of my master's fate, I shall try to come again."

He departed and the door downstairs closed with a click of the latch. Butayna embraced Jazirah, who returned the gesture. The pair held each other tightly in the encroaching darkness.

***

Malaka, Al-Andalus or Malaga, Andalusia
Muharram 763 AH or November A.D. 1361 or Kislev 5122

"What are you saying, Pero? My family must remain hostages in Al-Maghrib al-Aksa until I pay their ransom of two hundred thousand *dinars* to Umar. First, this enigmatic message from Ibn al-Khatib, 'All is not well.' This was his meaning?"

The red-faced captain knelt before his master in the center of the crimson tent erected far afield from the walls of Malaka, where Muhammad's men had besieged the city for just over two weeks. Faraj stood at Muhammad's right. Jazirah's father staggered against the canvas. Ibn Kumasha, a sprightly, gray-bearded man with a tongue to rival the smoothness of Ibn al-Khatib's own, served as Muhammad's personal secretary. He ordered his clerk, the young man Ibn Zamrak, to fetch water.

With knuckles pressed hard against the rough-hewn tabletop, Muhammad shook his head, scarce able to believe the words from his captain's mouth even though all had heard them. Jazirah. Their children. His mother. What could he do for them? He did not have even a tenth of their ransom. He had spent almost all the funds the Christian king provided him.

He demanded, "Is my household well? Was your man able to see my family at the *riad*? What of my sister in the palace compound?"

Pero answered, "The residence is under guard by some of the same Christians freed from the dungeons of Fés el-Jedid. The captain does not know of Sultana Aisha, but at times, he did observe Sultana Jazirah or Sultana Butayna, discernible by the color of their hair. At the last sighting, Sultana Jazirah walked

336

the avenue of bay laurels with a bundle tucked in the crook of her arm."

Muhammad's son or daughter. Relief flooded him but could not erase all his concerns. "Then the same sentries I trusted to protect my family are loyal to Umar?"

When Pero nodded, Muhammad sank into the chair behind him. The wood creaked as he bowed his head. Merciful Father, he had left his family in such peril! He had to withdraw from Malaka, abandon the siege immediately, and sail for Al-Maghrib al-Aksa to negotiate for their release. A bitter retreat where victory had once seemed so close, but his fears for his family overruled other interests. Gone were the days in which he would depend on others to secure their futures. Somehow, he would find the money to ensure their freedom.

A moment later, water sloshed on the table and splashed his elbow. He lifted his head and stared into the stark gaze of Ibn Zamrak, who backed away.

Ibn Kumasha pleaded, "Forgive him, mighty Sultan."

Muhammad dismissed the concern. "It's only water." He pointed to the gold-glazed pitcher. "Ibn Zamrak, pour some water for my uncle before he faints."

Then a sentry begged admission and bowed before Muhammad. "My Sultan, you must come and see. Malaka has surrendered."

"What?" Muhammad gripped the edge of the table. "After its nobles swore to hold out against me until reinforcements came from Muhammad the Red?"

In the midst of his words, Uthman rushed inside the tent. A grin splayed across his lips and he waved Ibn Zamrak over with the water pitcher. "Those reinforcements will never arrive. I have had word from loyal men in Wadi-Ash. Muhammad the Red is furious at King Pedro's avowed support of you. The usurper is amassing Gharnati forces and the *Ghuzat* under my father's command to attack Jaén. The *imam* of Malaka and the chief judge are prepared to do you homage and surrender this city without a fight."

Muhammad pushed back the chair and stood, crossing the ground in swift strides. He shoved the tent flap aside and emerged to the cheers and shouts of a thousand warriors loyal to him, two hundred of them royal guards and the rest a mix of Gharnati troops and Volunteers of the Faith from Runda. In the distance, the soldiers atop the walls of Malaka had raised white flags beside the red and gold banners of Gharnatah. More importantly, the gates swung open and a deputation led by two gray-robed men materialized beneath the battlements.

Muhammad closed his eyes and inhaled the scents of pine and eucalyptus trees swaying above the encampment. His father

Yusuf had added a curtain wall between the governor's castle and the citadel. His great-grandfather Faraj had governed Malaka for decades. Now the patrimony derived from Faraj's second son and passed to his descendant Muhammad the Red belonged with its rightful master again.

Chapter 26

Pawns

Sultana Jazirah

Fés el-Jedid, Al-Maghrib al-Aksa or Fez, Morocco
Rabi al-Awwal 763 AH or January A.D. 1362 or Shevat 5122

Jazirah clutched Nasr on her lap and gathered her children around her. Icy morning air filtered through thin seams in the lattice windows. Beside Jazirah and her brood, Butayna sat on a chair while Abd al-Aziz knelt before them and said, "Abu Tashufin is no longer Sultan of Al-Maghrib al-Aksa. A son of our brother Abu Inan Faris, Abu Zayyan, rules again at the minister Umar's behest. Abu Zayyan had held the throne just before Abu Salim ousted him."

The women looked at each other. Another regime change had occurred in less than six months.

Butayna asked, "Why did Umar rid himself of your brother Abu Tashufin?"

Abd al-Aziz shook his head. "Who can know the thoughts governing Umar the madman? I beg you for your safety not to visit the markets even with your Christian guards. They will never guarantee your safety. They are here only to ensure you do not attempt to escape Umar's clutches."

Jazirah asked, "Where could we go? I am a woman with a little babe and three small children. I would never leave my family behind. We are little more than pawns in this game Umar plays with my husband."

Butayna patted Jazirah's arm. "Tell us, how does Aisha fare?"

The instant smile on Abd al-Aziz's lips flushed his cheeks pink and chased away his stark pallor. "She and our daughter are well. I wish I might bring little Butayna to see you, but Umar will not permit my child or my wife to visit the *riad*. Aisha misses you terribly, my Sultana, but she is well. The presence of our daughter cheers her."

Jazirah asked, "Has Muhammad continued his demands for our release?"

Abd al-Aziz nodded. "Letters arrive from Malaka every few weeks at regular intervals, despite winter storms on the coast. I have heard Umar does not take trouble to read the entirety of the missives if the first few lines make no promises of ransom. Ibn al-Khatib has begged Umar to relent, but the minister will not."

Butayna replied, "My son will never cease his efforts to negotiate our return home."

Jazirah chafed inside. How much longer could they endure this confinement, cut off from Aisha in the palace and from Muhammad? When she had heard of his bloodless victory at Malaka and the surrender of Runda to him, her heart soared. Yet, she wept at night, her tears seeping into the dark curls atop Yusuf's head as her eldest son nestled beside her. She had missed Muhammad so much in half a year spent without him. When would he hold their Nasr or the other children again? When would he smile at her and tell her of his love?

Yusuf looked up at her. "*Ummi*, I want Father."

She bent and kissed his hair. He always made the same request. "Hush, my little love. Your father is well. We shall see him soon."

"You always say so!" Yusuf wriggled away from her hold and ran from the antechamber. His sister went after him. "Yusuf! Wait."

Butayna stood as if ready to go after them, but Jazirah insisted, "Please, stay. They will seek out Jawla and Hafsa for comfort. I'm not worried for them within the walls of the *riad*."

Saad hugged Jazirah and she patted his shoulder before she addressed Abd al-Aziz again. "If you can speak with Ibn al-Khatib in private, tell him to go to the Jewish quarter and seek out the money-lenders." She turned to Butayna. "Mayhap they would be willing to loan us funds for the ransom."

Butayna nodded and smiled at her. "Mayhap."

Abd al-Aziz frowned. "Why should the Jews of Al-Maghrib al-Aksa help you? Your husband has already incurred large debts for this household by begging for money from the Jews."

Butayna ordered, "Do not question her! The command of a Sultana should be enough for you. If you love my daughter, if you would see her family well and unharmed, please do as Jazirah asks. The Jews will understand the request even if you and Ibn al-Khatib remain puzzled."

***

The Gates of Wadi-Ash
Sultan Muhammad V

Wadi-Ash, Al-Andalus or Guadix, Andalusia
Rabi al-Awwal 763 AH or January A.D. 1362 or Shevat 5122

Muhammad's restless mount snorted, and white puffs of steam filled the air, while the beast's master patted and stroked the bay stallion's powerful neck. The Gharnati warriors, eleven men across in ranks of twenty deep, stood at Muhammad's back. Pero and Jazirah's father sat mounted on his left accompanied by

Uthman of the *Ghuzat*. Faraj commanded his own light cavalry units armed with javelins, swords, and shields. Even with so many warriors at his disposal, Muhammad eyed the walls of Wadi-Ash with unease. He had returned to the city, which had been his refuge in temporary exile twenty-seven months after a shameful departure. Now, he shaded his eyes against the glare of the sun at late afternoon and viewed the land with a conqueror's intent, although uncertainty plagued him.

From the vanguard, Don Diego signaled to him. With Pero alone, Muhammad urged his mount forward. A sour mood suffused the ranks of the Castillan men, bolstered by knights from the Orders of Santiago and Calatrava nominally under the command of the latter's Grand Master Diego. Together, they had taken eleven Andalusi towns in the last two months after Muhammad claimed Malaka. Pedro had requisitioned the captives and booty taken from each engagement. He promised repayment, but as far as Muhammad knew, the men sworn to follow him had yet to receive their coins.

A bridge over Wadi-Ash's river separated the men from their objective. Two thousand Castillan infantrymen eyed Muhammad, but he kept his gaze fixed on King Pedro. Bedecked in a silk *pellote* emblazoned with a quartered coat of arms, the golden castles of Castilla-León coupled with the red lion, Pedro also wore a gold crown fitted atop his helm. Muhammad had given some thought to his counterpart's stupidity. With the glittering crown, Pedro made himself an easy target, rather than a rallying point for his soldiers. Among them, he alone displayed a broad smile.

"A good day to give battle to Muhammad *el Bermejo*'s forces again," he pronounced. "They shall fall before Calatrava's *caballeros* and my infantry as they did at Jaén." When Muhammad made no reply, Pedro clapped his shoulder. "Be of good cheer! You're almost as dour as my confessor. He claimed ill omens preceded this fight. I believe we have enough men to claim the city."

Muhammad began, "You have one thousand cavalry, including six hundred *caballeros*, accompanied by two thousand infantry with bowmen, but you do not know—"

"How many of these Moroccan Volunteers of the Faith can Yahya still command? Less than a thousand? His son has amassed forces here, including those who have defected from Yahya each day."

"We have been in the *vega* of Granada for weeks. Don't you think Muhammad *el Bermejo* became aware of our intent after we swung north of Alhama? Why did you leave warriors near the township when we needed them here?"

Several among Pedro's councilors cursed at Muhammad, including the Grand Master of the Order of Santiago and even the bishop of Jaén, who instantly repented his blasphemy.

Don Diego hushed the men and sneered at Muhammad. "You do not have authority to question our king. You are little more than his vassal, even if you call yourself a king in your own land."

Pedro insisted, "We have enough men."

Shouts drowned out anything else he might have said as the city gate opened and the defenders rushed to the bridge. Pedro's laughter boomed as the enemy infantry lined up beneath a high arch at their end.

Muhammad did not smile, for he recognized no green and gold banners of the *Ghuzat* among their opponents. All carried the red and gold shield of Gharnatah in support of Muhammad the Red.

Pedro muttered, "It begins. Don Diego!"

The master of Calatrava ordered his men into battle just as the forces of Muhammad the Red marched six men abreast, their footsteps timed to the pounding of battle drums. When the two armies met in the center of the river overpass, ferocious fighting ensued, and steel weapons clanged. Muhammad pressed a fist against the spasms beneath his breastbone. The blood-spattered Castillan fighters cheered in triumph as they looted the bodies stretched before them.

Muhammad cried, "Fools!" as a second wave emerged from the city, in deeper ranks than the first. This time Don Diego committed his knights to the battle and they slaughtered their opponents to a man. With the third charge, Muhammad sent in his cavalry upon their light mounts under Faraj's command. Uthman joined with his men from the *Ghuzat.* Even Jazirah's father rode into the battle, his sword held high and a cry on his lips. "For Gharnatah and Muhammad ibn Yusuf!"

Only high-ranking members of the Nasrid royal guard remained at Muhammad's side. The forces within Wadi-Ash kept coming even as sunset cast an angry red glare over the stark walls of the city.

A harsh breath torn from Muhammad signaled the changing tide of the battle. More of the enemy poured through the city gate, trampling their fallen companions in their haste to reach the Castillans. Cavalry were among the defenders, but the majority included infantry, with men bearing crossbows. The arbalesters gave a volley. Thousands of black arrows darkened the sky and blotted out the dying sun. Calatrava's *caballeros* raised their shields too late.

With a reddened face, Pedro shouted at Don Diego and struck him with his riding crop. "Pull them back! Goddamn you! Get my men out of there!"

"They're my men!" Don Diego spurred his horse into the fray. Even he faded from sight, swallowed up by the enemy, who ran down the Castillan and Gharnati forces.

Pedro ordered a retreat. Muhammad glowered at him and cursed him for a fool but commanded the same. Faraj, Uthman, and a handful of men returned to Muhammad, flecks of red sprayed across their faces and mail coats.

He scanned their expressions. "Where is my uncle? Where is my wife's father?"

Uthman shook his head. "He was beside one of my warriors, mired in gore up to his arms. His sword slashed with the strength of a younger man. I have not seen him since then."

The bloodshed continued. Looting began again, this time executed by the defenders of Wadi-Ash.

"Master! We must leave," Faraj urged.

Muhammad looked back the way they had come. Pedro's gold crown gleamed in the distance as he whipped his mount and urged it across the plains away from the city.

***

Ishbiliya, Al-Andalus or Sevilla, Kingdom of Castilla-León
Jumada al-Ula 763 AH or March A.D. 1362 or Adar II 5122

Several weeks after the disaster at Wadi-Ash, Muhammad stood dressed in the green and black of mourning, within the recesses of Pedro's throne room. While the gardens just outside were lush, the interior needed repairs to cracked walls and chipped masonry. The palace of Pedro's ancestors showed its age.

In the center of the chamber, packed with stone-faced nobles whose visages rivaled the cold regard of their king, Don Diego knelt alone with his head bowed in disgrace. Blood stained his arm and his side despite a clean bandage around the limb. One other knight had returned. He stood among a cadre of Pedro's personal guard with his hands behind his back, unable or unwilling to lift his gaze. When his commander mumbled the last of his remarks, Pedro pounded the arms of the throne and charged the master of Calatrava to repeat himself.

Don Diego said, "Muhammad *el Bermejo* avows he will only ransom the remaining knights if you, *rey de mi reino*, abandon your support of Muhammad of Granada. Muhammad *el Bermejo* released me and one other of the Order, so we might bring you these words."

Pedro covered his frigid stare with a shaking hand. "Get out of my sight."

He spoke softly, yet Muhammad heard him.

343

When no one moved, Pedro bellowed, "Get out of my sight! All of you!"

Courtiers scrambled. Muhammad did not delay his departure. Pero and his royal guardsmen coalesced around him as they left the throne room.

"King Muhammad!"

Despite the utterance of his name, he did not turn around.

"King Muhammad! Please, wait."

"Master," Pero pleaded.

With a loud sigh, Muhammad turned and awaited the knight who had accompanied Don Diego back to Sevilla. The warrior bowed before him and held out a blackened coat of mail. Blood clung to the broken iron rings.

"Muhammad *el Bermejo* demanded the return of this to you. It belonged to a prince of your people."

The sharp gasp from Pero made Muhammad glare at him. Had his captain only just accepted the truth Muhammad had known since they fled the battlefield at Wadi-Ash? Muhammad took the armor and draped its heavy weight over his arm. Jazirah's father would never wear the battered chainmail again.

The *caballero* gave him a curt nod and departed.

Muhammad resumed his withdrawal, clutching the mail shirt against his chest. "Pero, find Faraj and Uthman. Tell them we must ready for our departure by tomorrow morning. I am done with this Christian king and his folly."

"Will you take your leave without a farewell to the king? What shall we do, master?"

"Meet the rest of the army. Our siege of Gharnatah will go forward as I have planned." He halted again and ran a thumb over his bearded cheek. "Before we leave this place, I must write the hardest letter I have ever had to compose to Ibn al-Khatib for my Jazirah. Send word by the swiftest means possible. She must know of her father's death. My mother must comfort her for I cannot."

***

Gharnatah, Al-Andalus or Granada, Andalusia
Jumada al-Ula 763 AH or March A.D. 1362 or Adar II 5122

A fine wintry mist enshrouded Gharnatah's redbrick walls and cast a gray pallor over the city at sunset. Movement and torchlight atop the battlements signaled the awareness of the defenders as Muhammad's army drew up north of the city. Over ten thousand strong, most of the troops had come from Muhammad the Red's birthplace at Malaka, a distinct pleasure.

Muhammad gazed upon the ramparts of his beloved city. Malaka, Lawsa, Al-Hamma, and Madinah Antaqirah had sworn fealty to him, their governors offering homage despite

Muhammad's promise of retribution. The sight of the last territory still under enemy control stirred a powerful urge in Muhammad to race down the slope right up to Gharnatah's main gate, the *Bab Ilbira*. At *Al-Qal'at al-Hamra,* the watchtower of the citadel overlooked the Sabika hill and stood strong. To the left the throne room, which Sultan Yusuf had rebuilt and redecorated some years after Muhammad's birth, had its familiar façade pierced by windows. Torchlight illuminated the whitewashed walls of the *Jannat al-'Arif,* the scene of so much carnage and death almost three summers ago.

For the rest of his life, Muhammad would devote himself to banishing those nightmarish memories. His palace would be a home for his children, where they might play in the gardens and skip through the water channels flowing from fountains. Where he and Jazirah might begin anew, their growing bond strengthened forever. Not by tribulations, but the love they had discovered for each other.

By the help of Allah, the Compassionate, the Merciful, he prayed to retake Gharnatah with little bloodshed and risk to his people, as at Malaka. Muhammad the Red would not surrender the city easily, after the likely blow to his pride when news of Malaka's capitulation had reached him. Agitation must have worsened his annoying tic and made him jerk his head from side to side uncontrollably.

Muhammad turned to Faraj and clapped his shoulder. The commander had lost too much on the terrible night that haunted them all years later.

Faraj said, "When this city is ours again and all the fighting is done, I shall find a beautiful woman of Gharnatah to wed. I pray she will give me handsome daughters and strong sons. I shall name my firstborn son for my father."

"Ridwan would have liked your choice," Muhammad replied. "He sees you from Paradise and will know how you have decided to honor him."

Then he nodded to Pero, who could not restrain the grin displaying his yellowed teeth. The dark gleam in his rapt gaze spoke of the desire for vengeance on behalf of his brother Alfonso.

Pero asked, "Shall we bring up the siege weapons, master? Show this pretender our intent to take this city?"

Muhammad shook his head. "I belong to this place. You know I would not shatter one brick within its walls. We will camp here for the night. In the morning, we make our demands."

Dawn came swiftly and Muhammad knew every waking hour before its arrival. Worry for Jazirah and his children consumed him, and he had surrendered to sleeplessness. Had she received his letter concerning the death of her father? She had not parted well with him, annoyed by his insistence upon accompanying Muhammad from Al-Maghrib al-Aksa. Would she hurtle blame for his death at Muhammad's feet?

He had accepted his uncle's sacrifice as atonement for the intervening years. Muhammad would remember the man as a doting father and a prince of Gharnatah. The battered mail shirt remained in Muhammad's possession and he intended to nail it to the wall of his bedchamber beneath his father's sword. It would serve as a reminder of how ultimate loyalty could come from those least expected to render it.

Sunrise brought the arrival of a delegation from the city, headed by its second highest judge Abu'l-Hasan al-Nubahi. He dressed in an austere black robe with a belt of green and gold stripes of silk tied around his thick waist. He preceded other members of the judiciary attired in the same manner. Muhammad welcomed them within the confines of his tent and offered them water and dates. They bowed and accepted his hospitality, the men taking to the floor where Muhammad joined them with Uthman, Ibn Kumasha, and Ibn Zamrak behind him. Pero hovered at the entrance of the tent. His fingers gripped the hilt of his sword. Al-Nubahi oft flicked glances in Pero's direction before scratching at his whitened beard or covering his cough. By the third hack, Muhammad gritted his teeth and glared at Al-Nubahi.

A slave brought bowls of rosewater and the men washed their hands. Then Muhammad asked, "Has Muhammad the Red sent you to negotiate? There shall be no bargains between us. The other provinces have yielded. I will have Gharnatah."

Al-Nubahi looked at his fellow judges. "We are aware of your intent, great Sultan. We have not arrived as the official representatives of Muhammad the Red—"

Muhammad slapped his thigh. "Then why in all the Christian hells are you here?"

Fraught glances met his stare. Al-Nubahi licked his lips. "Er... I... uh, well, we represent the *khassa*, the nobles of Gharnatah, who plead for mercy. They tolerated the rule of—"

"Wait!" Muhammad surged to his feet. "Why have they sent you to speak to me and why has the pretender allowed you out of the city for such a purpose?"

"Well, he is not here, my Sultan. Gharnatah is yours."

Muhammad would have staggered backward, but Uthman wrapped thick fingers around his master's calf.

Al-Nubahi continued, "Muhammad the Red fled the city as your warriors encamped on this bluff last night. We had at least three days' warning from trade caravans regarding your journey here. Before he left, I begged an audience with Muhammad the Red and cautioned him against a protracted fight with you.

Gharnatah is yours again, my Sultan, as it always should have been."

Muhammad knelt and bent his body double until his brow touched the floor. He doubted the men would fail to notice the tears trickling beneath his lashes, but no shame befell him. At last, the long struggle had ended, and he could walk the streets of his city again.

He did not do so until midday. At the *Bab Ilbira,* he dismounted. On either side of the postern, Pero and Faraj exchanged worried glances before they joined him. Uthman took the reins of their three horses and followed as Muhammad walked over cobblestones familiar to him from birth. He recalled the day when his mother had escaped *Al-Qal'at al-Hamra* with him and Aisha for a few hours, where he roamed Gharnatah as a casual observer. No one had shown concern for a boy and girl pelting through narrow streets, their mother on their heels, her trilling laughter chasing them.

The royal bodyguard fanned out with swords drawn and kept a surging crowd at bay. Many citizens fell to their knees, but most gaped at Muhammad. He gave no orders for any among his company to remind his people of the respect due to him. Instead, he trudged up the sloping knolls and admired the whitewashed facades clinging to the slopes. Some houses had pots of bright flowers stationed on either side of their doorways. Although his muscles cramped while he ascended the steep inclines of the Sabika hill and wove a path through its woodlands, he did not stop. Soon, he caught a faint glimpse of an image through the tree canopy. He raced ahead of his company. The clip-clops of hooves trailed him.

He halted in the shadow of the *Bab al-Sharia,* his father's great gate. Above it, the Hand of Fatima etched into the masonry appeared just as he remembered.

The gate master opened the southern entrance to the palatine city before falling to the ground where he bent and pressed his forehead to the earth. Muhammad entered his home to the cheers of courtiers thronging the courtyard. Again, his bodyguards hastened to keep the crowd back while he moved through their midst.

First, he headed to the *rawda,* where he stood alone within the cemetery's boundaries before his father's grave. His vision swam as he studied the white marble slab etched with the regal titles of Sultan Yusuf.

He whispered, "Noble and most beloved Father, I have returned to the land of our forbearers. I shall never leave it."

Next, Muhammad went to the bath attached to the mosque, where he performed the minor ablution with the aid of startled attendants. Then he went to the mosque where he spoke alone with the *imam* of Gharnatah, who received him well. Afterward, at his behest, the *imam* summoned all the believers inside, so they might observe prayers with their rightful ruler. Muhammad could barely speak his devotions, overcome by the return to his birthplace and the welcome of his people.

***

Late in the evening, Muhammad emerged from the royal bathhouse. His three attendants, Bahar, Qamar, and Suna tailed him with his personal implements provided by the bath superintendent. Servants along the corridors bowed low as Muhammad strolled past them, his hair slick and wet as the ends of it dripped water on to his robe. A flash of white fur darted across his path and he halted. The slaves brushed against his back with murmured apologies, but he dismissed their words.

He called, "Thalj?"

He bent and reached for the scrawny cat, which crouched and shivered at his feet. He lifted and cuddled her and stared into her eyes. "Oh, my Thalj. I'll won't ever leave you behind."

At the rear, Bahar said, "We had promised Sultana Jazirah we would care for her, but just after the queen escaped, Thalj disappeared with all her kittens, master."

Muhammad nuzzled the Persian's head with his chin. "She is home now, as I am."

In his robing room, Muhammad sat Thalj on a stool while his women dressed him. Qamar lingered at her task, smoothing her fingers over his trim stomach, hardened by months of battle preparation. She fitted his *jubba* and fastened the robe while offering her usual smile. His cat purred and looked up each time one of the women approached him.

Bahar smoothed her hands over Muhammad's dried hair and coated it with argan oil from Al-Maghrib al-Aksa before she retrieved a brush. He could not ignore the movement of her breasts beneath silk across his back. He had not bedded a woman since the previous summer, although some women of the Castillan court in Sevilla had beguiled him with their candid gazes of appreciation.

When Bahar finished, Suna asked, "Are you hungry, master?"

Somehow, he suspected she did not speak of food, but he replied, "I am not. I shall retire to my writing desk and compose letters announcing my return to my household in Al-Maghrib al-Aksa. Before I do so, I must complete one important task."

"Shall we leave you then?" Bahar asked, her lips a slight pout.

He laughed. "No, you may wait with me."

At the desk, he selected three of the finest sheets of vellum, stretched them out, and wrote almost identical language on each. He waited until the ink dried. Ibn Kumasha had found the great seal earlier and brought it to Muhammad. With red ink, he stamped the three documents.

Then he turned to the women. Poor Suna yawned behind her hands before she begged for forgiveness.

He waved away her concern. "I shall not keep you from your pallets much longer. These three sheets record your manumission. I am freeing each of you for your years of devoted service to me and your aid to my Jazirah."

The trio looked at each other. Then Bahar said, "As free women, we choose to stay and serve you."

When he shook his head, Suna burst into tears. "Please don't send us away!"

He left the stool and enfolded her in his arms, kissing her brow. He had never noticed the smoothness and fragrance of her skin before. After he released her, she still sniffled.

Qamar said, "Suna and Bahar are right. We do not wish to leave you. We have been here at your side since you became a prince of your own household. We choose to remain with you. We would never leave your side."

Why shouldn't he take the invitation reflected in their gazes? He had lain with each of them in his youth, years ago as a boy of thirteen. Still, the man he had become wanted one woman in his arms, the sole person he cherished as his lover and confidante. Soon, he would officially make her his wife again.

Bahar ducked her head and wiped at the corner of her eye, but not before a trembling lower lip evidenced her disappointment. Muhammad sighed. He would be no man to trifle with any woman's heart or give false hope. He belonged to Jazirah. Bahar and her counterparts would understand soon enough. He reached for Bahar's chin and lifted her gaze to his. She rewarded him with her usual smile.

As his hand fell away and she drew back, a sly smile curved her delectable lips. "Besides, master, it is only through service to you where I may admire your warrior's body with impunity."

Muhammad threw back his head and laughed, loud rumbles echoing to the ceiling.

***

Sultana Jazirah

Fés el-Jedid, Al-Maghrib al-Aksa or Fez, Morocco
Jumada al-Thani 763 AH or April A.D. 1362 or Nissan 5122

For a month after Jazirah learned of her father's death at Wadi-Ash, she withdrew into a melancholy from which none could stir her, not even little Leila with her sweet smiles for her mother. If Jazirah had thought to find solace in her family, a lingering sadness had proved her wrong. Her milk dried up and Butayna intervened through Ibn al-Khatib to provide a wet nurse for Nasr. Jazirah had failed her son. Even worse, she hardly cared.

Regrets ensnared her. She should have forgiven her father before his departure and demise. Now she would never have the chance to do so. She did not know what the enemy had done with his body. He would not know her children, whom she had spitefully kept away from him. She wished for one last chance to tell him how much she loved him, how the past and their lives at Shalabuniya would have been impossible to survive without the need to care for him as his health waned. His physical weakness had given her strength and purpose for both of them and the trials they faced together.

On the spring morning when Butayna's voice and knock came at her door, Jazirah rolled on her bed and pulled the coverlet over her head.

From the foot of the mattress, Kissenga asked, "Mistress, shall I let the Sultan's mother in?"

Beyond the entryway, Butayna called out, "You shall most certainly allow my entry, Kissenga. Jazirah! Stop this foolishness and unbar your door. We must talk. You cannot continue this way. The children miss you!"

Jazirah clapped her hands over her ears.

Heavy thumps against the wood caused her to bolt upright. She stared hard at the portal, unable to believe Butayna held the strength to kick it inward. As thuya planks splintered and gave way, Kissenga gripped his acacia rod crosswise. Jazirah scrambled and huddled behind him, taken back to Maryam's invasion of her room before the forced marriage to Muhammad's brother.

Jazirah cried out as Pero entered the room, his red cape swirling around him. He bowed and stepped aside, permitting Butayna's entry with Zabala behind her.

The smiles on the trio's faces told Jazirah all she needed to know, but she still asked, "We are leaving? We can go home?"

Pero nodded. "My Sultan secured backing from the Jews of Gharnatah for part of the ransom payment."

Butayna added, "Combined with the rest we were able to secure from the Jews of this country, Umar has little choice except to let us go."

Zabala observed, "He could always go back on his word and demand more coin." Everyone glared at him as if he had turned thoughtless.

Jazirah shook her head. "Please, my captain, don't give the vile Marinid minister any ideas." When she rose from the bed, Pero and Zabala averted their eyes from her thin tunic, which revealed her form beneath the gossamer silk. Kissenga brought her a *rida.* The folds of the robe enveloped her.

"Where are my children, Butayna?"

"At play beneath the bay laurels. Hafsa and Jawla took them for a walk. My servants grew tired of my grandchildren's cantankerous natures."

Jazirah frowned. "My children don't complain overmuch!" As Butayna giggled at her, Jazirah realized how foolish and overbearing she seemed. Her children might not be perfect, but in her view, she would not wish them to be any different.

She dashed from her room, bolted down the stairs, and out through the door to the avenue of trees. Saad and Leila skipped up the path, while Jawla balanced Nasr on her hip. Hafsa had hoisted Yusuf on her shoulders.

Jazirah called to them, "Children!"

Yusuf demanded Hafsa hand him down. When she did, he raced against his younger brother and sister to join their mother. Jazirah crouched, enfolded her brood in her arms, and kissed their heads.

Leila asked, "Are you better, *Ummi*?"

Jazirah tweaked her girl's thin braids. "So much better, my sweet child! Your father has rescued us. We're going home to Gharnatah."

Chapter 27
Union

Sultana Jazirah

Gharnatah, Al-Andalus or Granada, Andalusia
Sha`ban 763 AH or June A.D. 1362 or Sivan 5122

Jazirah's sandaled feet slapped the tiles of the courtyard as she dismounted from her mare and moved toward the harem's doors. She stared into the recesses of a familiar, but darkened hallway. After having dreamt of her return to *Al-Qal'at al-Hamra* for so long, she hesitated to cross the threshold. She had anticipated a joyous reunion with Muhammad, but why had he not greeted them at the port of Al-Mariyah, or just outside the *Bab al-Sharia* upon their arrival at the palace?

"*Ummi.*" Yusuf's wistful voice drew her attention. He had insisted on riding with her from the coast, taking to the mare well. She reached for him and set him down at her side. At the age of eighteen months, he had left Gharnatah with his father. Now at five years old, a curious and imperious child had returned to the birthplace he did not recall. He held on to Jazirah's hand and peered down the corridor, drawing close to her and clutching her leg.

"Don't fear," she whispered. "This is your home."

He buried his face against her knee and she patted his curls. She would ensure he learned to love Gharnatah as his parents did.

Butayna, her servants, and the rest of the children joined her with Yusuf. They had said a poignant farewell to Aisha and her family three days after Pero's arrival. He had brought them north to Chella, where Ibn al-Khatib returned to arrange the sale of his house before they all boarded a vessel under the command of the admiral of Al-Mariyah. The children took well to sailing, even Nasr. The other three could never have fathomed the dramatic events, which had brought them by ship before.

When Jazirah looked at Kissenga, he had completed a circular turn, his gaze assessing as he reviewed their surroundings. Zabala stared at the Nubian also with a bemused smirk on his lips before he dismounted. Kissenga's usual frown fell into place, before he acknowledged Jazirah's glance with a nod. She shook her head. One day, she would teach the Nubian to smile and take some enjoyment of life. As she had discovered, existence held more pleasures than pains. She vowed on the blood of her father and the sacrifice he had made of his life, she would never subside in melancholy again, no matter the difficulties she faced. She would thrive with her beloved children and Muhammad at her side.

Ibn al-Khatib addressed her and Butayna. "By your leave, my Sultanas, I must depart. I would seek out fellow members of the chancery and introduce myself as a counterpart."

Jazirah rolled her eyes. "You mean as the most likely candidate to be chief minister, no doubt." When he raised his eyebrows, she grinned at him. "My husband has spoken well of this Ibn Kumasha who serves as his *katib sirri-hi* now. I'm sure your first wish is to ensure the new personal secretary does not vie for the position you anticipate Muhammad shall award you."

"My Sultana, I would never presume!"

She giggled. "Oh yes, you would." Then she nodded to him. "And mayhap, you should. The role of *hajib* is too important for just anyone to accede to it. I do not doubt Muhammad shall favorably judge your years of service to him, especially in Al-Maghrib al-Aksa."

He tilted his head, as if observing her in full for the first time.

She added, "My son is the acknowledged heir. In your capacity as chief minister, you will influence the state of affairs my Yusuf inherits. I shall be mindful of your role, Ibn al-Khatib, as you guide the future of Gharnatah's government."

He smiled and made his obeisance again before he departed.

Pero bowed. "I sent word from Al-Mariyah of our safe arrival. The Sultan awaits us."

He ushered them indoors. At Butayna's insistence, Jazirah led the way with Yusuf at her side. When they reached the end of the vestibule, she stopped short. Every other member of the royal bodyguard lined the harem beside maidservants and eunuchs. Muhammad stood beneath the pavilion bordering his rooms. He held a fluffy, white cat flicking her tail in his arms. His attendants Bahar, Suna, and Qamar stood on the left.

A hitch in Jazirah's stride made Butayna inquire after her health. Jazirah looked over her shoulder. "I promise I'm well. More than well."

She led Yusuf and the others along the garden path, weaving between the orange trees. Muhammad stooped and put Thalj down before he flung his arms wide. The first three children rushed to their father, but Hafsa brought Nasr.

Then Yusuf bent and petted Thalj. "Father, you got me a cat! I knew you would remember my present."

Jazirah chuckled but could not bring herself to correct him. Leila and Saad mimicked Yusuf's interest, but no great length of time passed before Thalj tired of their attention and scrambled inside Muhammad's apartments. Being children, they gave chase. Something unseen crashed to the floor and Muhammad's attendants dashed inside behind the frightened cat and exuberant children.

In the meantime, Muhammad took Nasr in his arms. He reviewed his new son with such wonder in his eyes. Tears welled in Jazirah's gaze. Butayna clutched her fingers, while they stood idle. Then Muhammad returned Nasr to Hafsa's attentive care and held out his hands.

"Jazirah. *Ummi.*"

Both women stepped toward him. He kissed his mother's fingertips and welcomed her home.

Butayna said, "Aisha sends greetings and news of the second child she carries."

Muhammad nodded. "I wish I could have met my niece."

"You may. There will always be princes of Gharnatah in need of royal wives. Who better than a Marinid princess with a Gharnati mother?"

Butayna drew back as Muhammad tugged Jazirah into his arms. Her hands at his neck, she pressed herself to him, and kissed him as she had longed for during ten months. He gripped her robe and almost tore the silk. Pero and Zabala's mutual chuckles interrupted them.

Muhammad's knuckles grazed Jazirah's cheek. "Do you remember my wish for us?"

She nodded. "I do. I still carry the same hope and longing deep in my heart for us and a future untouched by the past."

"Then marry me and let us embrace a new future together."

***

Twenty days later, Jazirah sat beside Muhammad. They celebrated their marital feast with close family and retainers seated on either side of them, no divisions according to gender. While the chief minister Ibn al-Khatib seemed perplexed by the arrangement, he had not resisted when Butayna took the cushion next to him and began a debate on the mirrored principles of the Christian religion and Sufi doctrines. Whenever Muhammad sent a worried gaze in their direction, Jazirah drew her husband's attention to her with a light caress of his cheek. He never failed to bestow a warm smile or a gentle touch in kind.

He said, "When you agreed to wed me again, you declined my offer of a bridal trousseau. What shall I give you instead of gifts?"

She kissed him lightly. "Grant your wife one wish. Remove the heads of Muhammad the Red and his confederacy from atop the citadel's walls." When he frowned, she rushed on. "They had already been there for three weeks prior to our arrival, after King Pedro sent them to you. The Christian king denied you the honor of killing your foe but thought to appease you by sending the head here. All Pedro has done is to inspire the grim fascination of our eldest son. Yusuf is enthralled by the sight and always demanding Zabala or any of the royal guards take him to *Al-Quasaba* to look at the heads on the wall."

"You disagree with my treatment of our enemies?"

"I would shed all brutal reminders of the past." She nuzzled his cheek. "Take them down, please. For me."

He sighed. "Very well."

Pero had his most trusted captains of the old guard, including Zabala, along the walls of the harem's garden courtyard. Muhammad ordered them to relax and enjoy the feast. Zabala and Pero entertained the children with a display of their tactics with the sword. Yusuf grew bored and drifted to sit in his father's lap with Thalj firmly tucked against him. The Persian cat seemed resigned to the insistent demand of her new little master to hold her whenever he could. Her offspring from two other litters tussled and chased butterflies among the flowerbeds, but the eldest among her brood, Nawar, Hamza, and Usaamah nestled at Muhammad's feet and waited for tidbits he offered from his plate. Kissenga had stopped frowning long enough to engage in an animated conversation with Jawla in a far corner. His grimace only returned each time she touched or made some amused reference to his staff of acacia wood.

Jazirah smiled at Jyoti and Dhanu as they brought a tray of stuffed dates to the bridal couple. Muhammad took one and plopped it in Jazirah's mouth. She sighed at the taste of rosewater on her tongue.

Then she asked Jyoti, "Has the kitchen staff given you any difficulties as the new cook?"

"No, my Sultana, they are as biddable as may be. I would not allow anyone else to make or serve the stuffed dates you enjoy."

Jazirah and Muhammad fed each other and their children, each of whom joined them at intervals as the evening wore on. Hafsa brought Nasr from his wet nurse's side and his father took him, tickling Nasr's belly, and eliciting soft chortles.

When Jazirah would have put her daughter and sons to bed, Butayna laughed at her. "Do you truly believe my grandchildren shall sleep with all this activity? You still have so much to learn as a mother of four."

Jazirah nodded. "You are right. I am still learning from you."

Butayna smiled. "I shall always be here for you."

She kissed Jazirah's cheek and then Muhammad's own before she took Nasr in her arms and rose. "Come, my fine grandchildren, to my quarters. I want to show you a marvel your grandfather once introduced to me. It's called an astrolabe."

Leila asked, "Can we bring all the cats with us, Grandmother?"

With a grin, Butayna kissed Nasr's head. "If you can catch and hold them."

Muhammad rose and held his hand out to Jazirah. She gazed at him before placing her fingertips within his grasp. When she stood, he turned to their guests. At the opposite end of the courtyard, Ibn al-Khatib, Muhammad's secretary Ibn Kumasha, the doctor Ibn Khatima and the minister Ibn Zamrak paused in their lively discussion and bowed. Pero and Zabala raised glasses of *sekanjabin*. Muhammad led the way into his chamber and Jazirah closed the door behind them.

Within the room where lights glowed behind iron sconces, Suna, Bahar, and Qamar waited, but Muhammad waved them away. "Sultana Jazirah and I shall attend each other tonight without help."

The trio bowed and offered blessings. Before they left, Jazirah thanked them. "I would never have reunited with my husband except for your courage."

Bahar winked at her. "It takes little courage to distract a man with pleasures." She led her counterparts away.

Alone, Jazirah and Muhammad undressed each other. Neither of them hurried, for they anticipated a lifetime of love. Their brocaded state robes, her *khil'a* in gold and green, his matching garment in red and gold came first, followed by white cotton robes. Long tunics, sandals, and gossamer trousers came next. Muhammad's touch was gentle as he removed the pins affixing Jazirah's golden veil. He took her to the bed, a new one after she had insisted he must burn the previous mattress. They reclined side by side, his arm around her waist, her leg draped over his.

She stroked his lower lip with her thumb before pressing a kiss to his brow. "Nothing and no one shall ever part us again."

He repeated, "Nothing and no one."

***

The Mawlid al-Nabi
Sultan Muhammad V

Gharnatah, Al-Andalus or Granada, Andalusia
Rabi al-Awwal 764 AH or December A.D. 1362 or Tebeth 5123

On the day after his mother greeted her confessor for the feast of Christmas and the celebration of mass at a small church in Gharnatah, Muhammad welcomed his own important visitor within the garden courtyard of the harem.

He embraced and kissed both of Ibn Khaldun's bronzed cheeks. "Welcome home."

"My blessed Sultan, you honor me." Ibn Khaldun drew back and looked around him. "Never had I seen such opulence in any palace."

"Given the number you have viewed, I find such a claim hard to believe, but your admiration honors me," Muhammad said. He clapped Ibn Khaldun's shoulder and escorted him from beneath the pavilion outside his chamber into the center of the garden, where a fountain spilled water into the basin below and its four connecting channels. "Ibn al-Khatib has ordered the preparation of a magnificent feast at his house in tribute to you. I shall join you there. Tell me of your family. Are they well?"

"They are indeed. I hope you shall permit them to join me in Al-Andalus?"

"As soon as may be, but I would ask you to first complete the mission to King Pedro, which I mentioned in my last correspondence. His anger with me grows daily. He says I have tricked him. My promise of Andalusi cities never materialized. As if I could have forced my loyal governors to accept Christian rule over mine."

Ibn Khaldun chuckled. "I say Muslim lands for Muslims."

"Hmmm. Tell me of the Marinid court. Is Abu Zayyan still the sovereign or has Umar selected another brother of Abu Salim as his puppet?"

"Abu Zayyan still sits upon the throne, my Sultan. Umar is getting older and Abu Zayyan is less willing to defer to him. One of many reasons I thought it best to leave Fés el-Jedid at this time. Too much intrigue."

"I'm afraid you shall find such an element in every court, least of all mine or King Pedro's at Sevilla. Here Ibn al-Khatib has clashed tirelessly with the new head of the judiciary, Al-Nubahi."

"My poor friend Ibn al-Khatib. The experience seems no different than his quarrels with Al-Sabti."

"Indeed. I shall miss Al-Sabti's clarity of purpose most of all as chief judge. With his predecessor's passing, Al-Nubahi is too focused on rooting out Sufi heretics."

Ibn Khaldun nibbled at his fleshy lower lip. "Is my friend in danger?"

Muhammad shook his head, unsurprised at Ibn Khaldun's intimate knowledge of Ibn al-Khatib's personal pursuits. In fact, Muhammad suspected Ibn al-Khatib's interest in Sufism coincided with the comradeship he shared with Ibn Khaldun.

Muhammad answered, "Not if he remains cautious. I have told him, I will neither support his interests nor revile them. Ibn al-Khatib must find his path to the future."

"As we all must. Tell me of your family."

Muhammad smiled. "Sultana Butayna is well. My mother has been eager for your arrival for some time. In one of your last letters, you mentioned a term she is most keen to discuss. *'Asabiyah*, the solidarity between all of us as members of families, clans, and believers. The principle has directed my mother's actions throughout her lifetime. Although she is not a Muslim, she is a woman of strong faith."

"I would welcome an opportunity to converse with your honored mother, assuming the proper etiquette shall govern our interaction."

"Indeed. Her guards shall escort you to an agreed upon place where she may sit behind a screen with you in their presence and speak at her leisure."

"You always mention her with such admiration in your voice. Sultana Butayna must be an extraordinary woman to have so earned your admiration."

"My mother is the most remarkable woman I have ever known, except for my wife, Sultana Jazirah. She is above stairs with our daughter and sons. She teaches them to read *Al-Qur'an*. Although my children have excellent tutors in Ibn al-Khatib and Ibn Zamrak, their mother is devoted to their education. In the spring, we anticipate the birth of another child. A prince, as my wife swears she shall never give me daughters, just sons."

Ibn Khaldun intoned, "*Insha'Allah.*"

"Indeed, if Allah wills it." Muhammad gripped the forearm of his guest. "May I show you the newest addition to the palace? My poets have celebrated it as the Great *Qubba* of the Garden of Happiness, although I think of it as another hall among many. I had this antechamber beneath the quarters designated for the use by the Sultan's mother redone in celebration of my return to Gharnatah."

Muhammad led Ibn Khaldun up a few short steps. They passed through opened wooden doors across a marble floor with a water canal connected to the garden fountain. The men stopped in the shade of two semicircular arches, which featured niches inscribed with poems. Between the arches, a guardsman stood on duty, preventing access to the family rooms above.

Ibn Khaldun began by reading, "'These arches resembling the stars are the work of he who makes kings noble.'" He smiled at Muhammad. "Not Ibn al-Khatib's usual florid style. Who wrote this poetry?"

"These verses are the work of the minister Ibn Zamrak. Ibn al-Khatib admires and encourages him. Ibn Zamrak serves my personal secretary, Ibn Kumasha, whom you shall also meet later tonight."

Then they stood beneath a magnificent cupola of eight interlocked star shapes, the plasterwork painted with gold and silver. Pairs of eight lateral windows allowed light in, which set the cupola aglow. At the recesses of the hall, alcoves with windows featured a spectacular view of the neighborhood across the *Hadarro* River, Al-Bayazin.

"Magnificent," Ibn Khaldun proclaimed.

"The beauty of Fés el-Jedid's *madrasas* can compare. My time in Al-Maghrib al-Aksa proved beneficial in many ways. My sister writes to me of her husband. Umar has encouraged Abd al-Aziz's interest in expansion of the gardens, mosques, and *madrasas* of the city. Aisha's husband has great plans for new structures, I'm told."

"Prince Abd al-Aziz is a fine individual, my Sultan, but such great men oft run afoul of Umar. The prince should be cautious."

"I do not doubt he is. Abd al-Aziz has not survived these last years of one coup after another without vigilance. I expect much from Abd al-Aziz."

***

Three nights later, the court celebrated the birthday of the Prophet and Muhammad again granted access to the harem's courtyard to all male courtiers. The women kept above stairs. The *mawlid* festival, one of three official periods of celebration recognized by the Nasrid government, had become popular in the reign of Muhammad's great-great grandfather, Muhammad *al-Fakih*. While the chief judge Al-Nubahi frowned upon the gathering, believing only the festivities at the end of Ramadan's fast and the start of the Islamic New Year were valid, his opinion did not prevent the attendance of his fellow judges or the *imam* of Gharnatah.

Several hundred courtiers had crowded together for observance of the evening prayer, *Salat al-Maghrib*, at the great mosque. Afterward, Muhammad's guards ushered them within the harem's confines on the first floor. High-ranking guests sat beneath the cupola of the Great *Qubba*, including the *sharifs* who claimed descent directly from the Prophet and the *ulamas* absent Al-Nubahi. Muhammad suspected the chief judge also disdained attendance because Muhammad had invited the masters of Sufi orders. While he still held some concern about their practices, he could not condemn them without investigating their nature himself. No one else in attendance showed any outward aversion to the presence of the masters, not the *sharifs*, the governors of the provinces, or any among Muhammad's ministers, who by their considerable number spilled out into the adjacent garden courtyard. All admired the fine silk tablecloths shot through with gold thread, illuminated by torches and beeswax candles.

From the dais set in the alcove where Muhammad sat atop the throne, he caught the gaze of Ibn al-Khatib. Both men shared a nod of approval, before the chief minister settled on the plush rug and leaned on a pillow to speak with Ibn Khaldun. Slaves entered and navigated the teeming assembly, bearing gold trays of roasted lamb on wooden skewers, but also pots of lamb tagine, which Muhammad had enjoyed in Al-Maghrib al-Aksa. A *zirbiya* of hens sent the sweet fragrance of almonds, rosewater, and sugar wafting through the harem. There were also doves sprinkled with saffron and stuffed with dried grapes, cherries, and crushed walnuts and almonds. As custom required, the slaves served Muhammad first followed by his most important guests, before dispersing through the courtyard.

During the meal, the *imam* of Gharnatah arose to recite verses from *Al-Qur'an*. At the end of the first hour, Ibn al-Khatib performed poetry, which the guests received well, as evidenced by their applause. The masters of the Sufi orders spoke next, and Muhammad allowed their discourses, although his smile remained tight-lipped. The night prayer occurred within the harem, rather than the mosque again. The event proceeded with several poetic recitations from various ministers, but Ibn al-Khatib gave twelve. More food courses followed as well, included dried figs, pomegranates and apples drizzled in honey, a sesame and anise cake, and *dafair* bread. Twelve hours after its commencement, the final course of fried bread dusted with cinnamon, and pastries filled with cheese and honey preceded the dawn prayer.

Although exhausted, Muhammad made his farewells to each guest. All complemented him on the organization of the feast and the entertainment, the praise for which he deferred to Ibn al-Khatib. The ministers were the last to withdraw from the harem before the royal guard closed the doors.

With his hands clasped behind him, Muhammad strolled through the garden littered with the remnants of the evening. Slaves had fanned out and begun cleaning, but they stopped in their activities and bowed as Muhammad approached.

He shook his head. "Please, all of you continue as you were."

He strolled beneath the southern pavilion and pushed open the doors of the hall across from the Great *Qubba*. Workmen would return in the morning to resume the application of plaster and new tiles. Muhammad planned the complete alteration of the palace of his father and grandfather, a grand design evoking the beauty of the architectural styles he had encountered in Al-Maghrib al-Aksa. The restoration of his reign marked a time for celebration and renewal, expressed in the building projects he would undertake.

He took the narrow marble stairs two at a time and ambled down the corridor. Wisps of smoke trailed from burnt-out candles along the wall. When he reached Jazirah's door, Zabala's head lolled against the wood. He had been on duty along with his fellow captains all night below stairs, so Muhammad admired his intent to resume protection of Jazirah. However, the man's red-rimmed gaze and his drooping chin suggested his exhaustion.

Muhammad patted his shoulder. "Go to your rest and sleep the night's excesses away. My wife shall be safe with me."

Zabala could barely manage a nod before he shuffled away.

Muhammad opened the door and closed it quietly behind him. He crept across the carpet of the antechamber and into the bedroom. Jazirah rested on her side, one hand pillowed under her head, while the other palpated her rounded stomach beneath the sleeping tunic. He paused beside the doorway. The rise and fall of her form, the appearance of her black lashes like soot against her skin, and her deep, even breathing stirred more than love in his heart. How had he been so fortunate to have such a woman by his side? Not only did she love him, she also adored his children equally, whether she had birthed them or not. Once he had not cared whether she might have been a part of his life, in the early days before he knew of her pride, her beauty, and her devotion to family. Now, he could not imagine a life without her.

He crossed the room and knelt at her side. He trailed a hand along the contours of her abdomen. Their child twisted in response. He pressed a kiss there.

She murmured, "Muhammad?"

"I'm here, my love."

Her eyelashes fluttered. "Is the celebration over?"

"It is, my love."

She reached for him, her fingers curling at his nape. "Then come to bed."

He stretched out beside her and she cuddled against him, taking his fingers to kiss them before she rested them on her belly. The babe within her still turned.

He said, "Our child stirs."

"He is a Nasrid prince. He rises to greet the dawn."

He chuckled at her insistence upon knowing she carried another son for him. "I have been considering names for a boy or a girl."

She sighed. "Tell me."

"Fatima for one."

Her groan filled the room. "My love, there have been so many Nasrid princesses named Fatima in recent generations since our great-grandmother. Even my own sister was Fatima. Please, if we should have a daughter, don't give her the same name."

"What of Aisha for my sister?"

She nodded and snuggled closer to him. "I like it, although you will have wasted your time in such consideration. I shall bear you another son."

"Leila would like a sister."

"You shall have to wed another to sire more girls."

He laughed again, while she prodded him. "What names for a son?"

"My first choice would be Ismail."

When she made no comment, he nuzzled her ear. "To honor your father and the sacrifice he made at the end of his life for Gharnatah and for me."

"While I'm delighted you would consider it, please, not Ismail either. We could say you chose the name for my father or our grandfather, but some would say it evokes memories of your brother. I wish to keep the past at bay."

"All the names I have considered are from our past."

"Then name our child for his beloved father, whom I cherish."

As Muhammad closed his eyes, a sense of peace and comfort overcame him. By the side of his beloved Jazirah, at last he could truly claim to be at home.

Chapter 28

The Gift

Sultan Muhammad V

Gharnatah, Al-Andalus or Granada, Andalusia
Sha`ban 768 AH or April 1367 A.D. or Iyar 5127

Muhammad sat alone just after dawn in the recesses of the throne room. In all the nine official years of his reign, the first four following his father's demise and the five since his return to Gharnatah, he could not recall moments where he had been alone. Except for one instance where he had pondered the presence of his stepmother and her children in the harem while locked away in his quarters, other people had always surrounded him. He relished the brief opportunity now to sit cross-legged upon his throne, its familiar comfort cushioning him while he rubbed at his temple and considered the future of Al-Andalus.

Jaén preoccupied his thoughts. Once the ancestral home of the Nasrids and the birthplace of the first Muhammad of Gharnatah, Jaén now belonged to the kingdom of Aragón in the continued disputes between two determined rulers. Muhammad's plan would surprise King Pedro of Castilla-León, a bold course of action against their mutual enemy in Aragón. If Muhammad won, Pedro expected the territory would belong to Castilla-León. Muhammad did not arrive at such a conclusion. Did he dare tempt Pedro's wrath?

As the boom sounded at the entranceway to the chamber, Muhammad recalled his purpose. He had not left the comfort of Jazirah's bed and her long limbs for consideration of Jaén. He smoothed the folds of his *jubba* and called, "Enter!"

Ali ibn Musa bowed as soon as he stepped across the threshold. The double doors closed behind him. He repeated his obeisance as he drew nearer to Muhammad, who gestured for him to take a seat on the carpet and pillows arranged just below the dais. A plate of dates, a pitcher of ice-cold water, and a cup awaited Ali. Muhammad gestured for his guest to take refreshment. In the meantime, he ran his forefingers over the gilded throne's wooden frame, made of sandalwood and inlaid with ivory.

When Ali had finished his meal, Muhammad said, "*Al-salam 'alayka*, Ali ibn Musa."

"*Wa-'alayka*, mighty Sultan," Ali answered. "I was... uncertain whether you would welcome me in peace."

Muhammad nodded. "I was unsure whether I should greet you at all." He reached beneath him and withdrew a creased sheet of parchment. "I received this letter from my brother by marriage, Sultan Abd al-Aziz. He writes of his concerns regarding you. He says you are a traitor, an upstart of the Rahhu clan who would steal the Marinid throne. You must understand if, in a period where no less than five Sultans have reigned over Al-Maghrib al-Aksa since I first ascended to the rule of Gharnatah, Abd al-Aziz is justifiably concerned for the security and future of his kingdom."

"I am no threat to the Sultan of Al-Maghrib al-Aksa."

"Not even over my sister's heart? She informed me of your letter to her."

"I wrote once in these years since her marriage, three months after her husband became the sovereign. I wished to know whether she and her children had survived the struggle between the minister Umar and Abd al-Aziz. Only after I sent the missive I learned Abd al-Aziz had murdered the vizier. A just action since Umar had caused the deaths of so many monarchs."

"Indeed. Even Ibn al-Khatib did not mourn his downfall." Muhammad leaned forward. "Abd al-Aziz knew you would seek asylum in Al-Andalus. He begs me for the sake of our friendship, and the bond we share as brothers by marriage, to return you to his... care. Should I do so?"

"Will you?"

Muhammad smiled. He had always appreciated Ali's willingness to pierce the heart of a matter with the precision of one of his arrows.

"I believe it would be prudent for you to remain in Gharnatah as my guest. Abd al-Aziz would understand hospitality to a... guest. No harm shall come to you. With ease and freedom, you may move about *Al-Qal'at al-Hamra*. A detachment of my royal guard shall... protect you, lest any Marinid agents attempt to kill you on Abd al-Aziz's orders. You shall live in the citadel's great tower. It features an open-air patio on the sixth floor, which I'm told my ancestor the first Muhammad enjoyed when he chose to reside in the tower just after he took this palatine city."

"And what shall you tell Abd al-Aziz of my... residence in your tower?"

Muhammad countered with another question. "What do you believe I should say?"

Ali chuckled, a hollow laugh. "I believe you remain a practical man."

"You would be right. In my twenty-nine years, I have learned the lessons of action without caution and consideration. Now please, finish your repast."

When Ali had done so, he and Muhammad stood. Muhammad came down from the dais and clapped Ali's shoulder. "You were wiser to come here than anywhere else."

Ali nodded. "Do you receive many letters from Sultana Aisha?"

While the pair strolled to the door, Muhammad answered, "At least four a year. My honored mother receives more."

"Is Sultana Aisha happy with Abd al-Aziz?"

"She has learned... contentment. A hard lesson for many to master, but then my sister is a Nasrid. Difficult circumstances bring out the best in us."

"How many children has she given her husband?"

"Four daughters, by the grace of God. She is with child again. The court astrologer in Fés el-Jedid has predicted this will be the male heir Abd al-Aziz needs for the future of his kingdom."

"As he prophesied with the last two births?"

Muhammad grinned. "How long had you been lurking in Fés el-Jedid stirring up dissent against its ruler?"

"Upon the conclusion of the campaign in Marrakech just after our arrival, I returned to my birthplace."

"Then you were in the city when Abu Salim's reign ended and Aisha's first daughter Butayna came into the world?"

"I was." Ali wiped a hand over his glistening brow. "I should not have sent the missive, but I had to know of her well-being. I shall always love her."

"As much as you desire the throne of Al-Maghrib al-Aksa?"

Ali halted in the shadow of the arched entry. "More."

"If you knew she lived in happiness with her husband...?"

"I would never trouble her again."

Muhammad nodded. "I understand the first flush of love. It lingers within the heart, despite time and distance. I still recall with fondness my first love, Haziyya al-Riyad, but now there is only my wife Jazirah to hold my heart in her keeping."

"Your happiness gives me joy and hope."

"Hope?"

"Indeed. For I know Aisha still loves me. She sent a reply, warning me to refrain from further letters and to leave Al-Maghrib al-Aksa before her husband discovered I had written. Would a woman who did not love me do so?"

Muhammad pondered the question and arrived at the same conclusion Ali had, before shaking his head and patted Ali's arm. Together they stepped out into the pink light of dawn as it glittered over Gharnatah. Pero and his men bowed.

With a wave, Muhammad said to Ali, "Go with these men to the great tower. They shall ensure your protection and comfort. Come to me on the morrow. Let us hunt together."

Ali bowed. "I would enjoy the opportunity. Thank you, mighty Sultan."

"Don't thank me yet. Survive, Ali, survive the reign of Abd al-Aziz. After such a time, anything may be possible."

Ali rose and nodded. "Indeed." He saluted Muhammad again before Pero's men surrounded him and led him away.

Pero alone walked beside Muhammad on his return to the harem. Outside of its doors, the small deputation he had anticipated now awaited him, both men in black robes with yellow stars sewn to the left sleeve. Instead of going directly to them, Muhammad plucked an orange blossom from a tree and sniffed its aromatic odor.

The chief gardener directed his men and all fell into bows.

"*Al-salam 'alayka*. Rise, please. You are all well, I trust?" Muhammad addressed the workers, who raised their heads. With mystified expressions, they nodded. Muhammad chuckled at their puzzlement, for he had never inquired before. At the direction of his wife, he had learned to accept the love and loyalty his people demonstrated in the wake of his return. It could never hurt to display gratitude for their allegiances. He could not live in fear forever of a knife plunged into his back. He was not his father.

"The blossoms are beautiful this spring," he observed.

His chief gardener answered, "They always are, great Sultan. My family has tended your family's gardens for three generations from the time of your grandfather Sultan Ismail, may Allah preserve his memory."

"Do you have sons to carry on your line?"

The gardener waved to eight others behind him. "These are my sons, great Sultan."

Muhammad nodded. "Then I do not doubt my gardens are left in capable hands. The peace of God be with you and yours until the end of time."

"You also, great Sultan. May Allah, the Compassionate, the Merciful, bless you and yours forever."

Muhammad left them, the orange blossom in his grip. He would place it beside Jazirah's pillow before she awoke. The rabbi from Gharnatah's Jewish quarter awaited him, accompanied by a man with a familiar, if only timeworn face.

Muhammad exclaimed, "Doctor ben Zarzar! Do you intend to live forever?"

Pharez thumped his walking stick on the cobblestones. "*Shalom*, and joy to your house. Ah, my Sultan, I would live longer if only I did not have to clamber atop a horse up the Sabika hill."

Muhammad grinned. "That hill is difficult for me to climb, although I do not yet possess your years. Come, come, you must both see the fountain in the Garden of Happiness. Workmen have finished the installation this month."

He led them with Pero into the heart of the harem, where they stood beneath its eastern pavilion. At the center of the garden, four water channels intersected in the shade of orange trees. Twelve lions carved of pristine marble supported a large bowl of the same rock. A poem of twelve verses, composed by Ibn Zamrak, engraved the bowl's edge. Water flowed from the mouth of one statue at hourly intervals.

Pharez sighed. "Hmmm, spectacular. If Samuel ben Nagrela were alive today, he would have marveled as I do. Not only at the sight of the lions of his house within your beautiful palace, but at all you have done for the Jews of Gharnatah." He turned to Muhammad. "My people's gift of the twelve lions represents more than the tribes of Israel. For us, the Jews whom you have welcomed into your city, it is a sign of your generosity, which we shall never forget."

Muhammad placed his hand over his heart. "You honor me, ben Zarzar. When few would support me, the Jews of Al-Maghrib al-Aksa provided me with the means to live. When my family was in peril, the Jews of Gharnatah helped them return to our homeland. I have repaid monetary debts, but not the debt of gratitude owed to your people. From this day forth, let the lion fountain symbolize newfound relations between the Muslim and Jewish peoples of my kingdom."

***

The Lions of Gharnatah
Sultana Jazirah

Safar 769 AH or October 1367 A.D. or Marcheshvan 5128

The pair of massive lions, sculpted from gray marble, perched at the edge of the shimmery pool situated amid a patio. Seated on their hindquarters, thick manes covered most of the statues' bodies. Their opened mouths revealed large canines. At a signal from Muhammad, the superintendent of the *maristan* permitted the flow of water from the spout encased in marble within each lion's mouth. Leila shrieked, whether in fright or surprise, Jazirah did not know. She cradled the nine-year-old's head against her hip.

Muhammad flicked a worried glance in her direction while he spoke to the assembly of palace ministers and ordinary citizens, who had arrived to witness the opening of Gharnatah's new hospital completed during the past summer. Jazirah shook her head to reassure her husband all remained well.

She bent and whispered to Leila, "There's no cause for fear of the lions. They're only statues, not real lions like the one your father and I saw in Al-Maghrib al-Aksa. Besides, look to your brothers. They are not afraid."

Her voice muffled against Jazirah's silken robe, Leila replied, "Princes are never frightened of anything, *Ummi*."

Jazirah patted her daughter's thick braids hanging loose down her back. "You are a Sultana of Gharnatah. You can be just as brave as any prince may be. You'll see. When your father's speech is finished, we shall go to one of the lions and you can put your hand into its mouth."

As she spoke, she recalled life at Shalabuniya and a vision her father relayed of children at her side, in particular one daughter amid sons. She smiled and ducked her head. Her father had been right.

To her left, her lions of Gharnatah stood, each a proud prince in the image of his father. At ten years old, Yusuf almost reached Muhammad's shoulders. Butayna had long believed her eldest grandson would inherit the height of his mother. Two years younger than Yusuf, Saad had the fighting spirit of his ancestors, which ensured Yusuf would never browbeat him. At six years old, Nasr competed with his older brothers in archery contests and races. Jazirah feared so much for him, but he oft shrugged aside her concern and demanded she stop treating him like a baby. At least her youngest son, little Muhammad, still allowed her to coddle him. Given his age of four, his father believed it high time for the last of his brood to take up the bow and sword, but Jazirah wished the boy might remain ignorant of warfare for many years.

In a loud voice his father decreed, "The *maristan* of Gharnatah is open to all people of all faiths!"

As his ministers crowded and congratulated Muhammad, Butayna and the priest beside her in Christian robes with a crucifix around his neck moved through the patients who had arrived at the hospital on the right bank of the *Hadarro* River. The cleric spoke to those who called to him, identifying themselves as his coreligionists, while Butayna knelt alone by the side of Juan Manuel Gomero, attended by his faithful servant Binta. The glint of unshed tears and her downturned mouth softened Binta's grim visage.

Jazirah's sons begged to accompany their father as he led the tour of the hospital through its four wings. Their mother permitted them to follow, shooting a brief glance at Zabala and Kissenga. The guard and eunuch accompanied the princes.

Anyone within Kissenga's vicinity kept a good distance from the reach of his staff.

Leila remained with Jazirah. Together they approached Butayna.

Muhammad's mother touched the reddened forehead of the old slave merchant at her feet and he moaned in his stupor. "Esperanza."

A little sob filled her throat, but she patted him. "I'm here, Juan Manuel. You shall be well again in this place. God protect you always, my kinsman."

She looked up at Jazirah. "He burns. A fever of several days. The doctors of the *maristan* will care for him."

"We shall, my Sultana," said Ibn Khatima as he stopped beside the pallet and opened his medicine chest.

Juan Manuel's head lolled and he cried out. "The gifts! The gifts!"

Butayna stood and looked at Binta. "What does he mean?"

Binta reached into the satchel draped over her shoulder. "He did not want me to leave them at the House of Myrtles. He insisted they should go to you now." She withdrew two pieces of folded cotton from the bag. She unwrapped the first cloth and revealed a fine dagger, the hilt encrusted in brilliant gemstones. A cluster of sapphires, opals, emeralds, and amber gleamed in sunlight.

A warm glow suffused Butayna's face as she reached for the weapon. She caressed the handle and brought it to her lips before she turned to Jazirah. "This is a relic of my past, my father's blade. It belongs to Muhammad from this day forth. I shall give it to him when we return to the palace."

Jazirah patted Butayna's shoulder as she wrapped up the steel again. Binta revealed the contents of the other cloth. Within its crinkles, a gold brooch inlaid with reddish-brown stones. A brilliant piece, though not as extravagant as the dagger's ornamentation.

Butayna turned to Jazirah. "This was mine, from another life when I was a young girl who did not understand the path before me. Juan Manuel once said I belonged to the harem and I had a purpose there, which God would reveal. I have found a measure of it at the side of my children and grandchildren. Take this as a token of my love for you, daughter. May you find your own purpose."

Jazirah nodded. "I think I have. I know I have. I accept your gift and your love."

They embraced before Butayna took the brooch and pinned it to the neckline of Jazirah's *jubba*. Butayna stepped back, an admiring glance in her eyes before she nodded. "Yes, it is right for it to belong to you now." Then she took the satchel from Binta.

Jazirah asked, "Is Pharez ben Zarzar here? Have you seen him, Ibn Khatima?"

The doctor lifted his gaze and shook his head. "My Sultana, I am sorry to inform you, but the elder Doctor ben Zarzar died three days ago."

She swallowed. "Oh, I had not known. Will Abraham ben Zarzar return from Sevilla to honor his father? Muhammad saw the son at Sevilla some years past, but he would not speak to my husband for some unknown reason."

Butayna replied, "Abraham is dependent on the patronage of King Pedro now. Abraham likely did not wish any member of the Castillan court to associate him with Muhammad, when there are the king's councilors who resent their losses of Andalusi territories, which would not submit to Christian rule."

Leila asked, "*Ummi.* May I touch the inside of the lion's mouth now?"

"You may."

"Will you come with me?"

"I will."

She took her daughter to the pool while Muhammad led his ministers and other men via one of two wooden staircases up to the second level of the *maristan.* Later when Jazirah and Leila rejoined Butayna, she introduced her confessor, Fray Antonio Navas y Montilla.

With a kindly air about him, he bowed before Jazirah and Leila. "*Alteza, mi princesa.*"

Butayna said, "For years, Fray Antonio has ransomed Christian captives back to their homeland through my auspices." While Jazirah stared at her, she continued, "Each quarter of the year, I have visited the House of Myrtles to review the captives Juan Manuel held and ransomed as many as I could. If he does not recover from his illness, I shall free the remainder of those held as slaves in his household. His last will and testament grants me the authority to do so."

Jazirah asked, "Do you intend to reveal the truth to Muhammad? He cannot know for he would have spoken of it to me."

"He does not know, but he shall hear of it. I accepted this life. I chose. Others are not so fortunate as to receive a choice."

"Will you stop interfering in the slave trade of Gharnatah if your son asks?"

"I will not. You know enough of me, Jazirah, to understand why I cannot."

They fell silent as Muhammad rejoined them with his four sons, the royal guards, and Kissenga. "The princes are hungry and so am I. We should return to *Al-Qal'at al-Hamra*. There is little more we may do here. The work of the doctors begins."

They left the complex behind and headed south. Just outside the gate of the *maristan*, Jazirah stopped and read the words of the foundation stone to Leila who lingered beside her. "Praise be to Allah. He, who ordered the construction of this *maristan* as proof of his great mercy for the weakest and sickliest of Muslims and to bring him closer – if Allah chooses – to the lord of all worlds, who perpetuates his good deeds, who speaks in elegant language and who has carried out his duty to charity for the passing of time and the succession of years, until Allah inherits the Earth and leaves it to those who populate it. For he is the greatest of heirs, the lord, the *imam*, the Sultan, the hero, the great, the illustrious, the pure, the victorious, the happiest in his kingdom, the first to have taken the path of Allah, the keeper of victories. He, who has carried out the wishes of God, the magnanimous, he, who has received the help of angels, defender of tradition, refuge of religion, the prince of the Muslims *Al-Ghani bi-llah* Abu Abdallah Muhammad."

Jazirah looked to her husband, who led their family and retainers along the slopes above the river to the bridge, which would take them to the palace. He had selected the *laqab,* or regal title, of *Al-Ghani bi-llah,* meaning 'He who is content with the help of Allah,' after his recent victory at Jaén against the Aragónese.

"This monument speaks of your father's reign, Leila. Remember this day and his gift to the people of Gharnatah always."

"I will, *Ummi.*"

As they resumed walking, Muhammad awaited them. Leila skipped to join her grandmother, who chided the princes for running along the slippery bank.

"What would I say to your mother and father if you slipped into the river, my fine princes? *Madre de Dios!* Leila, don't join them! Sultanas aren't supposed to run!"

Jazirah and Muhammad laughed at his mother. Then he held out his hand. She took it and raised his fingertips to her lips.

"What was that for, my love?"

"Do I need a reason to show you how much I adore you, husband? Your generosity always astounds me, but no more so than when you spoke today."

"I meant my words. The *maristan* shall always be open to everyone, regardless of their religious beliefs." He held her hand and squeezed it. "Home?"

She gazed into his eyes and saw herself reflected there. "Home."

THE END

Author's Note

The Moors

The Moors were Islamic people of Arabian and Negro descent, who invaded the Iberian Peninsula, which encompasses modern-day Portugal and Spain, beginning in the Christian eighth century. They called the conquered land *Al-Jazirat al-Andalus*, but in later years, the term referred to the south of Spain and became Andalusia in modern times.

The Moors penetrated the interior and brought three-fifths of the peninsula under their control. They gave their unique culture, rich language, and the religion of Islam to a land that welcomed them at first, for the valuable riches and social order they brought. Where superstition and ignorance once pervaded all elements of life, the Moors brought intellectual pursuit and reasoning. Their blood mingled with that of the Visigoths and produced a mixed race of individuals.

By Islamic law, Muslim men could marry or have sexual relations with non-Muslim women. Periods of zealous anti-Christian and anti-Jewish views occurred and resulted in forced conversion, but mostly, Christians and Jews enjoyed religious tolerance under Moorish rule. Some families chose to convert willingly, for all the requisite benefits including the avoidance of certain taxes and the gains of political and social advancement, while others practiced their former religion in secret.

Spurred on by religious fanaticism, bigotry, and jealousy of the Moorish achievements, the people of the northern half of the peninsula began the *Reconquista*, a determined struggle against the Moors. Beginning in the Christian tenth century, the rebellion spread slowly southward, until one Moorish kingdom remained, Granada, nestled within the Sierra Nevada Mountains.

All the historical dates mentioned in this novel rely on calendar conversions obtained via http://www.fourmilab.ch/documents/calendar/. The Julian calendar was in force in this period, rather than the Gregorian calendar in use after A.D. 1582. Any errors in the relevant dates of the Hijri calendar are based on the Julian dates. The sighting of the crescent moon determines dates in the Hijri calendar. The term AH refers to events occurring in numbered periods after the year of the *Hijra* or the emigration of the Prophet Muhammad from Mecca to Medina in September A.D. 622. References to phases of the moon during the fourteenth century came from http://eclipse.gsfc.nasa.gov/phase/phases1301.html, again relying on the Julian calendar.

For More Information

The final age of the Nasrid Dynasty and the descendants of Muhammad V is the focus of the last two novels in this series, *Sultana: The Pomegranate Tree* and *Sultana: The White Mountains*. Thank you for purchasing and reading this book. Please consider leaving feedback where you bought this book. Your opinion is helpful, both to me and to other potential readers.

I hope you found the period and characters fascinating. For further information on the historical events and figures in this novel and details about the *Sultana* series, visit my website and the section entitled 'The *Sultana* Series – Learn More' where I provide information about the period and the historical figures that could not make it into this novel. Discover the truth behind scenes depicted in the book. I'll update the section whenever I discover interesting information about the Nasrids. If you would like to learn more about Alhambra Palace and Moorish Spain during the Nasrid period, visit Alhambra.org or Patronato de la Alhambra y Generalife.

You may always email me at lisa@lisajyarde.com or join my mailing list for information on upcoming releases at https://goo.gl/VLXHQK. I love to hear from readers.

Islamic Regions and Modern Equivalents

*Includes date of capture from the Moors by united Spain or Portugal (if applicable)

Moors under the governance of the Nasrid Dynasty divided the Andalusian territory into administrative provinces, such as Granada, Almería, and Malaga. Governors controlled the provinces. Within each province, there were subdivisions of districts under the control of governors, too; at least 33 official districts within Granada. These districts might be a city or town, e.g. Almería, a hamlet, e.g. Pechina, or later during the *Reconquista* period, a geographic region, e.g. Las Alpujarras. Nasrid princes, trusted officers of the military, judges, and other esteemed men controlled each area after an official appointment by the Nasrid ruler to whom they had offered an oath of loyalty.

Al-Andalus or Al-Jazirat al-Andalus: the Iberian Peninsula or southern Spain during periods of Moorish rule
Al-Bayazin: Albaicin neighborhood, Granada, Spain
Al-Hamma: Alhama de Granada, Spain
Al-Jazirah al-Khadra: Algeciras, Spain
Al-Mariyah: Almería, Spain
Gharnatah: Granada, Spain
*Ishbiliya: Sevilla, Spain (A.D. 1248)
*Jayyan: Jaén, Spain (A.D. 1246)
Lawsa: Loja, Spain
Madinah Antaqirah: Antequera, Spain
Malaka: Malaga, Spain
Marballa: Marbella, Spain
Naricha: Nerja, Spain
Qumarich: Comares, Spain
Runda: Ronda, Spain
Shalabuniya: Salobreña, Spain
Wadi-Ash: Guadix, Spain

Al-Arif Mountains: Rif Mountains, Morocco
Al-Maghrib al-Aksa: Morocco
Chella: Salé, Morocco
Fés el-Bali: old city of Fez, Morocco
Fés el-Jedid: new city of Fez, Morocco

Glossary

Adar: the twelfth Jewish month, which during leap years has 30 days, rather than 29 days

Addahbia: bridal trousseau in the Arabic language

Al-Bayazin: in the Arabic language, the Albaicin neighborhood north of Alhambra Palace

Al-bayt al-barid: the cool room in a Moorish bath in the Arabic language

Al-bayt al-maslakh: changing room in a Moorish bath in the Arabic language

Al-Fakih: in the Arabic language, the Lawgiver

Al-Ghani bi-llah: He who is content with the help of Allah in the Arabic language

Al-Jabbar: the Orion constellation of stars in the Arabic language

Allah: God in the Arabic language

Al-Qal'at al-Hamra: in the Arabic language, Alhambra Palace, a complex of fortresses, towers, houses, shops, mosques, etc. that served as the royal residence in Granada. Begun in A.D. 1237 under Sultan Muhammad I, each of his successors made improvements, especially Muhammad III, Ismail I, Yusuf I, Muhammad V, and Yusuf III

Al-Qasr Xenil: in the Arabic language, a Moorish palace built near the Genil River before the founding of the Nasrid Dynasty. It served as the residence of foreign rulers and dignitaries, but after the reign of Sultan Ismail I, the palace primarily became the residence of discarded harem women from Alhambra Palace

Al-Qaysariyya: in the Arabic language, the central marketplace in Granada, where the modern-day Alcaiceria stands

Al-Quasaba: in the Arabic language, in the Arabic language, the citadel within the royal residence in Granada

Al-Qur'an / El Corán: in the Arabic language, Muslim holy book

Al-salam 'alayka: in the Arabic language, the traditional Muslim greeting, 'may peace be upon you'

Al-Shaykh al-Ghuzat: in the Arabic language, commander of the Volunteers of the Faith

Alteza: Your highness in Spanish

Amanar: in the Arabic language, warrior in the desert

Amir al-Muminin: commander of the believers in the Arabic language

Amir al-Muslimin: prince of the faithful in the Arabic language

'Asabiyah: solidarity between tribes and clans in the Arabic language

Av: the fifth Jewish month

Bab al-Maqabir: in the Arabic language, the medieval entry gate for the Spanish city of Ronda

Bab al-Sharia: in the Arabic language, modern-day Puerta de la Justicia, the Gate of the Esplanade (incorrectly called the Gate of Justice) on the southwestern side of the Sabika Hill, built by Sultan Yusuf I and commemorated in June A.D. 1348. Today, it serves as the main entrance for visitors to Alhambra Palace

Bab Fayy al-Lawsa: in the Arabic language, Puerta de Fajalauza, the city gate north of the Albaicin neighborhood in the Arabic language

Beghah / Vega: the fertile lands of southern Spain

Bint: in the Arabic language, daughter of

Caballero(s): Christian knight(s)

Camisa (Spanish) / *Qamis* (Arabic): long shirt of white cotton or linen, worn as an undergarment by both sexes, in all social classes

Cendal: a type of silk

Conde: a Spanish nobleman of the rank of count

Corrals: slave pens

Dafair: in the Arabic language, loaves of bread, made from white flour, leavening, salt, eggs, and saffron, shaped like braids, browned in a frying pan with oil, and sprinkled with honey spiced with pepper, Chinese cinnamon, and lavender

Dhimmi: in the Arabic language, a non-Muslim living in a Muslim territory, allowed to keep his or her religion

Dhu al-Hijja: in the Arabic language, the twelfth Islamic month, a period of pilgrimage to Saudi Arabia

Dhu al-Qa`da: in the Arabic language, the eleventh Islamic month

Dinar: plural *dinars,* in the Arabic language, Islamic coin bearing a religious verse, commonly made of gold or silver, or rarely, copper. They were minted in Granada with the Sultans' motto, "none victorious but God" and could be round or square-shaped. Gold *dinars* weighed 2 grams, contained 22 carats of gold, and were widely used for internal and external trade. Their value fluctuated over the centuries. Silver *dinars* were square and had a fixed value. Copper *dinars* were used for internal trade in the Sultanate and had a fixed value. When the Sultans of Granada paid tribute to Castile, the amounts ranged between 10,000 and 40,000 *dinars*

Dirham: plural *dirhams,* in the Arabic language, Islamic coin bearing a religious verse, commonly made of silver or other base metal. In Granada, they were minted with the Sultans' motto, "none victorious but God" and weighed 2-3 grams

Diwan al-Insha: in the Arabic language, the Sultan's chancery of state
Djinn: in the Arabic language, a spirit able to assume other forms and inhabit human bodies

El Bermejo: the red in Spanish
El Dio: God in Ladino
Elul: the sixth Jewish month

Fanak: in the Arabic language, a sand-colored desert fox of Morocco
Faskh: in the Arabic language, a judicial decree of divorce

Ghaliya: in the Arabic language, a perfume of musk, camphor, oil from the moringa tree and ambergris
Ghusl: in the Arabic language, the full ablution
Ghuzat: in the Arabic language, the Volunteers of the Faith, the Moroccan soldiers billeted in Granada

Hadarro: in the Arabic language, modern-day river Darro that flows through Granada. The name originates with Granadine attempts to pan for gold along the river, which also supplied water to Alhambra Palace
Hadith: in the Arabic language, a collection of Prophet Muhammad's traditional sayings
Hajib: Prime Minister in the Arabic language
Halal: in the Arabic language, permissible food for a Muslim
Hammam: bathhouse in the Arabic language
Hashish: cannabis in the Arabic language
Henna: in the Arabic language, dye or paste prepared from a plant and applied to various parts of the body
Hijab: a veil in the Arabic language

Ibn: in the Arabic language, son of
Iftar: in the Arabic language, the evening meal taken by Muslims upon breaking each day's fasting Ramadan
Imam: in the Arabic language, the male prayer leader in a mosque
Infanta / Infante: a royal child in Spanish, plural *infantes*
Insha'Allah: God willing in the Arabic language
Iyar: the second Jewish month

Jannat al-'Arif: in the Arabic language, modern-day Generalife, the royal summer residence of Alhambra Palace, constructed during the reign of Sultan Muhammad II and enlarged mainly by his grandson Sultan Ismail I
Jarya: in the Arabic language, concubine, plural *jawari*

Jihad: in the Arabic language, the struggle; to personally maintain the Islamic faith, to improve Islamic society and to defend Islam and an Islamic way of life against its enemies
Jubba: in the Arabic language, floor-length robe with wide sleeves, opening at the neck, worn by both sexes of the nobility
Jumada al-Thani: in the Arabic language, the sixth Islamic month
Jumada al-Ula: in the Arabic language, the fifth Islamic month

Kadin: in the Arabic language, favored Moorish concubine, who has also had children for her master
Katib: in the Arabic language, secretary
Katib sirri-hi: in the Arabic language, the Sultan's personal secretary
Khamsa: in the Arabic language, the Hand of Fatima, an amulet in the shape of a hand, meant to convey patience, abundance, and faithfulness to the wearer, attributed to the daughter of Prophet Muhammad
Khanjar: Moorish dagger in the Arabic language
Khassa: collective Moorish nobility in the Arabic language
Khil'a: in the Arabic language, ceremonial floor-length robe with wide sleeves, opening at the neck, decorated with *tiraz* bands, worn by courtiers on special occasions
Kislev: the ninth Jewish month
Kohl: in the Arabic language, black eyeliner
Kufta: in the Arabic language, minced or ground meat formed into a shape, usually rounded

La: No in the Arabic language
Laqab: in the Arabic language, an honorific title in the Arabic language used instead of a personal name

Madina: a city in the Arabic language
Madira: in the Arabic language, meat cooked in mint, lemon, and yogurt
Madrasa: in the Arabic language, religious school of higher education, e.g. the Madrasa Yusufiyya built by the Granadan Sultan Yusuf in A.D. 1349
Madre de Dios: Mother of God in Spanish
Maravedies: Formerly Spanish gold coinage, singular *maravedi*, originating with the Islamic conquest; it was considered equivalent to a half-dinar. When the Spanish incorporated the coinage in their use, it eventually fell in value from silver to copper coinage. The Spanish government stopped issuing *maravedies* in the 1850's when the Spanish currency changed to the decimal system
Marcheshvan: the eighth Jewish month

Marinids: rulers of modern-day Morocco A.D. 1248-1465
Maristan: Persian for hospital, Sultan Muhammad V ordered the construction of an asylum for mental patients in October A.D. 1365. The four-winged structure had a pool at its center. The foundation slab reveals work ended in June A.D. 1367
Mashwar: in the Arabic language, the council chambers within Granada's Alhambra Palace where the ministers met
Masjid: in the Arabic language, mosque
Mawlid al-nabi: the celebration of Prophet Muhammad's birthday in the Arabic language
Msemen: fried, square-shaped dough in Morocco
Msemen: in the Arabic language, fried, square-shaped dough in Morocco
Muadhdhin: in the Arabic language, the official who summons Muslims to prayer from the minaret of a mosque
Muharram: in the Arabic language, the first Islamic month
Murabit: in 12th century Moorish nations in North Africa, a member of a Muslim religious community living in a fortified monastery. In the 14th century, the term referred to any religious teacher with a group of disciples, particularly among those who practiced Sufism. Today, it also refers to the domed tomb of a pious man's burial place in the Arabic language

Nakhwa: in the Arabic language, aromatic seeds crushed with a mortar pestle and brewed into a hot drink
Nam: in the Arabic language, Yes
Naskhi: a cursive form of Arabic writing
Nasrids: rulers of Granada A.D. 1232-1492
Nisbah: in the Arabic language, a name that indicates a person's origin, tribal affiliation, or ancestry
Nissan: the first Jewish month

Oud: in the Arabic language, a pear-shaped musical instrument similar to the lute

Pellote: a Spanish surcoat

Qadi: chief judge in the Arabic language
Qiblah: in the Arabic language, the wall of a mosque facing the city of Mecca, Saudi Arabia
Qubba: an Islamic building with a dome in the Arabic language

Rabi al-Awwal: in the Arabic language, the third Islamic month
Rabi al-Thani: in the Arabic language, the fourth Islamic month
Raïs: in the Arabic language, a provincial governor
Rajab: in the Arabic language, the seventh Islamic month

Ramadan: in the Arabic language, the ninth Islamic month, a venerated period of abstinence and fasting from sunrise to sunset
Rawda: cemetery in the Arabic language
Reconquista: the struggle to remove the Moors from Spain
Reina: queen in Spanish
Rey de mi reino: king of my kingdom in Spanish
Riad: in the Arabic language, a traditional Moroccan house with an indoor courtyard or garden
Rida: a Moorish housecoat for women in the Arabic language

Sabika: in the Arabic language, the hill where Alhambra Palace stands
Safar: in the Arabic language, the second Islamic month
Salat al-Asr: in the Arabic language, third Muslim prayer time, obligatory at afternoon (about four hours after *Salat al-Zahr*)
Salat al-Fajr: in the Arabic language, first prayer time, obligatory at sunrise
Salat al-Isha: in the Arabic language, fifth Muslim prayer time, obligatory at nighttime (about an hour after *Salat al-Maghrib*)
Salat al-Maghrib: in the Arabic language, fourth Muslim prayer time, obligatory after sunset (about three to four hours after *Salat al-Asr*)
Salat al-Zahr: in the Arabic language, second Muslim prayer time, obligatory at noon
Sarawil: Moorish trousers in the Arabic language
Sekanjabin: a sweet and sour Moorish drink of Persian origins, made of vinegar and honey
Sha`ban: in the Arabic language, the eighth Islamic month
Shabbat: the Jewish day of rest
Shalom: a greeting of peace among Jewish people
Sharbah: sherbet in the Arabic language
Sharia: in the Arabic language, the religious law of Islam
Sharifs: in the Arabic language, direct descendants of the Prophet Muhammad
Shashiya: skullcap in the Arabic language
Shawwal: in the Arabic language, the tenth Islamic month
Shevat: the eleventh Jewish month
Shimasas: in the Arabic language, the latticework screen over a window in the harem
Siwan: the third Jewish month
Skibaj: a sweet-sour stew served cold, from the Persian *sikbaj* made with saffron, vegetables, vinegar and honey or sugar, which became an Andalusian dish of fish or vegetables doused in vinegar
Sufism: in the Arabic language, the mystical element of Islam. In the 14th century, some adherents believed the roots of true

practice as Muslims dwelled in Sufism, but others deemed Sufism as heresy. Practitioners are known today as Sufis and they live in orders headed by a Sufi master
Suras: in the Arabic language, verses of the *Qur'an*

Talib: apprentice or student in the Arabic language
Tammuz: the fourth Jewish month
Tawhid: in the Arabic language, basic Muslim belief in the oneness of God, as opposed to the Trinity of Christianity
'Tharid: in the Arabic language, Moorish dish of crumbled pieces of bread served in a meat or vegetable broth
Thuya: in the Arabic language, aromatic, citron wood native to northwestern Africa
Tishrei: the seventh Jewish month

Ulama: plural *ulamas*, Muslim legal scholars who act as arbiters of Islamic law in the Arabic language,
Umm al-Walad: in the Arabic language, mother of a child
Ummi: my mother in the Arabic language

Wa-'alayka: in the Arabic language, traditional response to the greeting of *Al-salam 'alayka*
Wa-la ghaliba illa Allah: in the Arabic language, the motto of the Nasrid Sultans, meaning 'There is no conqueror but God'
Walima: Muslim wedding feast in the Arabic language
Wazir: in the Arabic language, Moorish minister
Wudu: in the Arabic language, partial ablution

Xenil: modern-day Genil River in the Arabic language

Zellij: in the Arabic language, Moroccan tiles
Zirbiya: in the Arabic language, a Moorish dish of hens, doves, pigeons, or lamb, cooked with salt, pepper, coriander, cinnamon, vinegar and saffron, boiled down in a sweet, thick paste of mashed almonds and sugar soaked in rosewater

About the Author

Lisa J. Yarde writes fiction inspired by the Middle Ages in Europe.

She is the author of a six-part series set in Moorish Spain, *Sultana, Sultana's Legacy, Sultana: Two Sisters, Sultana: The Bride Price, Sultana: The Pomegranate Tree*, and *Sultana: The White Mountains*, where rivalries and ambitions threaten the fragile bonds between members of the last Muslim dynasty to rule in Europe. The first title in the series is available in different languages.

Lisa has also published two historical novels set in medieval England and Normandy, *On Falcon's Wings*, featuring a star-crossed romance between Norman and Saxon lovers before the Battle of Hastings in 1066 and *The Burning Candle*, based on the life of the first Countess of Leicester and Surrey, Isabel de Vermandois, progenitor of royal and non-noble lines still living today. Lisa's short story, *The Legend Rises*, chronicles the Welsh princess Gwenllian of Gwynedd's valiant fight against twelfth-century English invaders and is also available now.

Born in Barbados, Lisa lives in New York City. She is a member of the Historical Novel Society, has been a presenter at its 2015 Denver conference and served as the co-chair of the Historical Novel Society – New York City chapter (2015-2017). An avid techie, she is a social media manager of the chapter and has presented before varied audiences on the topics of historical fiction, self-publishing, and website and social media management. Lisa is also an enthusiastic blogger and has moderated and contributed to Unusual Historicals, Great Historicals and History & Women. Her personal blog is The Brooklyn Scribbler.

Learn more about Lisa and her writing at the website www.lisajyarde.com. Follow her on Twitter or become a Facebook fan. For information on upcoming releases, discounts, and exclusive freebies from Lisa, join her mailing list at https://goo.gl/VLXHQK.

1. What did you like best about this novel?

2. What did you like least about this novel?

3. Which characters in the novel did you like best?

4. Which characters did you like least?

5. Have you ever read any other novels by the author or would you read more novels by the author? Why or why not?

6. If you got the chance to ask the author of this book one question, what would it be?

7. Share a favorite quote from the novel. Why did this quote stand out?

8. What feelings did this novel evoke for you?

9. Did this novel seem realistic? Why or why not?

10. If you have visited the primary setting of this novel, Granada's Alhambra, what memories did the reading evoke for you?

Your Notes on Sultana: Two Sisters

www.ingramcontent.com/pod-product-compliance
Lightning Source LLC
Chambersburg PA
CBHW051000180726
48291CB00006B/1912